WHAT'S THE GIRL WORTH?

Also by Christina Fitzpatrick

Where We Lived

WHAT'S THE GIRL WORTH?

A NOVEL

CHRISTINA FITZPATRICK

HarperCollins*Publishers*

HarperCollins books may be purchased for educational, business, or sales promotional use. For information, please write: Special Markets Department, HarperCollins Publishers Inc., 10 East 53rd Street, New York, NY 10022.

FIRST EDITION

Designed by Sarah Maya Gubkin

Printed on acid-free paper

Library of Congress Cataloging-in-Publication Data is available upon request.

ISBN 0-06-019910-5

02 03 04 05 06 WB/RRD 10 9 8 7 6 5 4 3 2 1

This book is for my father;
the character Harlan *is for Matt*

*"The world only concerns me in so far as I feel a certain debt
and duty towards it
and out of gratitude
want to leave some souvenir in the shape of drawings
or pictures, —not made to please a certain tendency . . . but to express
sincere human feeling."*

—Vincent Van Gogh

*I have a dream
A song to sing
To help me cope
With anything*

—Abba

CONTENTS

WHAT'S THE GIRL WORTH?

SHOOTERS

Two of the girls I worked with were dancing in their underwear on a pool table, hands moving above their heads, their armpits looking slightly gray, unshaven. Both of their faces were splotchy and drunken, their eyes filled with a certain energy, a shine. The skinnier one had short black hair that fell neatly around her face, a Kewpie-doll face with freckles and pink lips that looked drawn on. She was wearing a bra that didn't match her black underwear—it was pink cotton, adolescent, a leafed rose in the center. Her hips swished, they swayed, and the owner of our bar, along with our manager, Rick, stood in front of her laughing, cue sticks in their hands, their eyes level with the crotch of her panties.

The other girl dancing had red hair, a darker tone, one you couldn't have naturally. She was kicking the pool balls with her bare feet. Against the green felt, her feet looked childish and small, a smudge of black shoe dye across her toes. She kept kicking the stripes into the corner pockets. She said, "See how good a pool player I am," but you couldn't hear her over the music, over the techno beat of some disco-y song. The words went "Baby, work it," and the owner and Rick and the two girls dancing mouthed those lyrics looking at one another.

I watched all of this, sitting in one of the high lifeguardlike seats that were next to each pool table, all fifty-two of them. Our bar was a pool hall called Shooters—it had once been a roller-skating rink, the brass ring around the rink still there, but now it was filled with pool tables, a limitless warehouse of them. Usually the bar was bright, a dizzying number of swaying brass lamps hung from the distantly high ceiling, but now, at four in the morning, it was dark and empty, just the smell of cigarette smoke, of wheaty stale draft beer, of grease, of lost French fries that had fallen under the tables or into butt-filled ashtrays.

One of the other cocktail waitresses, Robby, came over to me. She had bleached-blond hair, heavy makeup around the eyes, a tough, street-girl accent. She said, "Have another shot; have one." She held a mini-plastic cup in front of me filled with something light green. A Kamikaze. After I drank it, I put the empty cup down next to my beer, next to my cake. The other cocktail waitresses had bought me a going-away cake—I was leaving Boston for the summer, going to Madrid. The white-frosted cake sat next to me, barely eaten, a red galloping bull across it along with the words: Hasta la Vista, Baby!

There were four other girls across the room at the bar making shots. With the music so loud, the room so large, they seemed far and distant. Everything separated us: fake ferns, deep green wallpaper, brass fixtures, black-and-white pictures of old 1920s movie stars shooting a pool shot, drinking a drink, laughing into their flapper pearls.

Robby dipped her finger in the frosting of my cake and sucked off the sweetness, looking over at Rick and the owner. She sat down next to me, an Amstel Light in her hand. She drank her beer fast, taking moments in between swigs only to breathe, to look at where the beer line rested in the bottle—it was as if she was racing toward something, running. When the bottle was finished, she said to me, motioning at the pool table, "These girls are so fucked up. Who let them get this fucked up?"

I said, "I dunno." I was slurring.

The redhead was now dancing directly in front of the owner. She was bigger than any of us, meatier. She had big breasts and a round belly to match, thighs that were smooth and tan, jiggly. Her bra was black, her panties yellow. I felt bad for her—for this mismatch of intimate apparel. The skinny one, I

thought, danced so well, looked so taut, that it didn't matter that her under-
wear was completely different, but with the redhead you noticed; it drew
attention to other imperfections: faint stretch marks across her hips, a bruise
near her left butt cheek, curly hairs outside of her yellow lace.

Robby turned to me and made a sour face—she saw what I saw. She
pulled her hair, which was long and thick, up behind her head, tying it, and
said, "These guys are such pigs." She was referring more to the owner than
to Rick—the owner was older, forty-ish, with a receding hairline; veiny
temples; thin, overly red lips. He was touching the redhead's belly with the
tip of his cue stick, a blue smudge of chalk etched across her waist. He
laughed and said, "The equator"—which somehow meant that she was fat,
that she was not the sleek sexy thing she imagined herself to be, dancing
and prancing under the dim red lights.

Watching all of this, I can't say what I felt. At least not genuinely. I was
drunk, and I felt separate from those dancing girls. You couldn't have gotten
me, not with a million shots, to dance in my own mismatched underwear.

Of course, I didn't interfere, I didn't save them. I didn't walk over to the
table, didn't touch their ankles, didn't say, "Come on down now, come on."
But I knew it was wrong—I knew they'd wake up sick in their own bunk
beds, not sure why they did any of this, not sure how they got sucked into this
behavior that was not their own; this night would become in their minds
dreamy and false, a mean story someone made up about them. The next
night at work, they might even wait on this same pool table, number five, and
stand there, a wet tray in their hands, their black uniform dresses itchy
against their chests, thinking, Was that really me last night? Was it?

I knew all of this because I was older than them, not smarter. These two
girls were only eighteen, fresh and new, while I was a tired, more cautious
version: twenty. Those two small years were not the only thing that divided
me from them though—there were years and years of other moments, an
entire collection of feeling, that had filled me with the experience of what
most men were, how little you could trust them.

The owner was touching the redhead, his hands in between her thighs. She
was sucking on her finger, as if she could feel through her drunkenness his
touch, his my-wife-will-never-know desire.

Rick looked over at Robby and me, grinned at us. He was tall with slicked-back brown hair, sharp green eyes, a rhythm to his walk. He came over to us, said something in Robby's ear. They had slept together before—I didn't know for sure, but I knew. She laughed, her hair loosened, and then he put his tongue against her neck. She let him touch her, lick her, and then she said, tossing her hair back, "Cut it out, you fuck. Cut it out."

Meanwhile I sat there looking down at my hands, at my fingernails— why weren't they even? Everything related to beauty in my mind. The skinny girl was pretty, so was the redhead, but not so much so. I was pretty, too, but I ranked somewhere in between them. If my nails were even, I'd be prettier. If Rick suddenly fell in love with me, stopped eyeing everyone else, I would be pretty, beautiful, a pool-hall goddess. But for now, I was just leaving. I did not want Rick; I wanted something else. Something unidentifiable that went beyond anything I learned waitressing or anything that was dully written out for me on a college blackboard. I wanted to feel as if I had something that went beyond my body, my face.

Robby said in my ear, "Are you glad you're leaving?"

I raised my eyebrows, said with certainty, "Yeah."

The owner was now touching the redhead beneath her underwear. His face against her leg. She was not dancing anymore, her legs were still. But the skinny one kept swaying, pelvis forward, in front of Rick.

"But still, you must be scared?" Robby asked me.

I shook my head no.

The owner had just pulled the redhead's yellow underwear down. Her buttocks were clearly visible, the faded tan lines, the vulnerable texture of her skin. I watched his big chubby hand on the back of her left butt cheek, a squeeze. I took a sip of beer.

I

MY OWN ARRIVAL

My first day in Madrid was on a Sunday. No one was waiting for me at the airport. It was just me and my luggage and the tasteless gum I kept chewing and chewing. Still . . . I was all dressed up. I was wearing a sleeveless dress that was long and pink, along with a black sweater. The sweater was tied around my waist, and every so often I tied it tighter, as if I were afraid it might fall right off me, unravel at my feet. I wore my hair different, too—it was parted in the middle and blown straight. I suppose I thought I was going to be someone new now, someone who wore matching underwear and had manicured hands, someone who was capable of doing anything well, including living here.

In the taxicab leaving the airport, I sat with my back stiff, leaning forward. The cab itself was a small white car similar to my mother's Toyota. A red stripe ran diagonally across the passenger door, and a cardboard sign that hung in the window read in green letters: *libre*, or in my case, *ocupado*. Unlike the cabs back in Boston, there was no divider, no plastic panel that sealed the driver off from me. I could see his bottle of Fanta Limón lying on the floor, the lint on the bucket seats, and even his tiger-striped lighter that sat on the dashboard in an open box of Marlboro Reds.

My driver was one of the most dressed-up cabdrivers I had ever seen. He was wearing a button-down shirt—stiff-looking and starched—and his black pants were pleated and cuffed. When he spoke to me, asked me where I wanted to go, his lips moved quickly, pulling all the words together into one garbled sound, and his accent contained that heavy girlish lisp that I had always known existed in Spain, although I had heard it only in classrooms on audiocassette.

From the airport, we drove down the highway with all of the windows an inch or two open. The wind felt like nothing, sounded like nothing—my ears hadn't completely adjusted to landing yet. My driver turned the radio up loud, something he wouldn't have done if I were older, not so sweet-faced. The singer's voice on the radio was sorrowful and male.

On the highway we passed a giant white Coca-Cola warehouse that was situated among stretches of roadside grass and shrubs—a few apartment buildings with bright pastel awnings were far in the distance. A Coca-Cola sign hung above the warehouse, like a cross above a steeple, and lines and lines of white trucks with the soda's red-and-white emblems sat parked out front—the words read *"Disfruta* Coca-Cola," instead of "Enjoy Coca-Cola." It was surreal to see something so American amongst the Spanish guitar music and the green Telefónica billboards and the wind that smelled different to me, sweeter.

But that mix of the familiar along with the unfamiliar only continued as we got off the highway, landed on a big wide street with tall buildings on each side and rows and rows of nontropical trees on their sidewalks. Despite what I had learned in school, despite what I saw in the *La Vida Española* section of my Spanish textbooks, I somehow imagined Madrid to be a European version of Mexico, with palm trees, small yellow buildings, and a few giant statues—all of Ferdinand and Isabella. After such a long eight-hour flight, it actually felt very uncomfortable to adjust to this new version of Madrid—a city full of banks and gleaming glass windows and parked cars and streets.

My cabdriver drove on and on for at least forty minutes, through intersections and rotaries, past towering buildings with giant signs on top: Panasonic, TDK, Heineken; there was another Telefónica billboard, one with a woman talking to her mother on a telephone, a cartoon caption above her head. I saw pharmacies, I saw shoe stores, I saw a shop that had an array of multicolored sausages arranged in its windows, wine bottles wedged in between, cans of olives shaped in a giant pyramid. At one intersection, a cross peeked over windows and buildings, and as we got closer that cross seemed to move higher, to reach up and twinkle, reflecting an uncomfortable amount of sunlight. But down below, the streets themselves were empty for a city, even if it was early Sunday morning—it seemed as if everyone had suddenly evacuated, as if I were the only stupid one to show up.

It was only after a few more unnecessary turns, a few more streets, that my cab driver finally decided to bring me to the address I had requested: la calle Arriaza, Número 23. He charged me 7,000 pesetas, about $50, and I tipped him another 1,500. Before I gave him the money, I had to go through it very carefully, making sure each number was what I thought it was. Only 1,000-peseta bills were green, the others were beige or pink or light blue. They didn't put presidents on their bills either; the names I recognized were all discoverers: Hernán Cortés, Pizarro, Christopher Columbus.

Once I was out of the cab, I stood in the street, on the pink cement in front of the entrance of my apartment building. I could see the gold cross on top of Palacio Real, the royal palace, which didn't mean that I was living in a swanky neighborhood. It wasn't even a particularly residential neighborhood. There were lots of bars, as there were on every street in Madrid, but also a video store, a butcher shop *(una carnicería)*, a giant movie theater (Teatro Princesa), with Mel Gibson's picture in the window. An ice cream parlor called Tutti Frutti was right next door, a bank with a green bear for an emblem across from it—and farther down the street, around the block, there were a succession of government buildings with scads of stairs and black-spear-tipped fences, statues of men with guns out front.

Before going into my new apartment, I sat on the steps with my suitcases. The front door was open—I didn't even have to buzz, but I didn't
feel like going up to my new home on the fourth floor yet. I just wanted
to rest for a moment, stay with myself.

I didn't know the two girls I was going to live with—hadn't written
to them or spoken to them on the phone. I knew they were sisters,
roughly my age, college students. Carlos, the man I was going to work
for, had found the apartment for me through a friend of his. Carlos was
a graduate of my college, Boston University, and one of my professors
had called him and gotten me an internship with his public relations
firm. It did not pay, but I had already saved up enough money to live off
of for the next three months. The point of the internship wasn't money
anyway; it was to get away, to take a rest from Shooters. To live a little.
My mother was always telling me that: Honey, why do you work so
hard? Why won't you let yourself live?

I stayed on the stairs for about ten minutes—until a man came over
to me. He came from across the street, and he was waving at me. He had
a tiny mustache, one that looked almost drawn on. It was early, around
nine, and the sun was not yet strong—I looked at him without wincing.
His face was round, and he had thick eyebrows and hair that was flecked
with gray. The shirt he had on was bright red, untucked, and he swung
his arms as he walked toward me—his gold watch reflecting a quick
flash of sunlight.

When he got close enough, he said, *"¿Estás bien?"*

I said *sí*.

He said, *"¿Sabes dónde estás?"* Do you know where you are?

I said *sí*.

He kept standing in front of me. I noticed he was looking at my
shoes—I was wearing black sandals with big block heels. They were
impractical shoes, shoes I looked good in. He said, *"¿Eres de Boston?"*

Now I suppose he glanced down at the tags on my luggage, but at the
time I was feeling a little dazed and the small possibility that he was psy-
chic lurked behind his big red shirt. I said, *"Sí*. How do you know that?"

"I know everything," he said, and then he added, as if it was proof that he knew everything, "I am from Valencia." I didn't know where Valencia was, couldn't have found it on a map with much ease. I just knew it had oranges. "I own that store," he said, pointing across the street at what looked like a much smaller, almost closet-size version of a convenience store—I imagined the inside to be full of brown burlap bags of oranges, all leaning against one another.

He asked me my name, I told him Catherine, and then he gave me his: Raúl.

There was a pause after that. Someone opened the window above us, the metal screeching. He continued staring at me, smiling in this long, deliberate way that reminded me of certain customers at Shooters, the lonely ones, the men who seemed to drunkenly think that if they gave you a long, knowing stare, you might put down your tray, might press your face into their neck.

"Would you like a Mars Bar from my store, Catherine?" he asked, his eyes purposely intense. He raised his eyebrows. *"Es el sabor más dulce en España."* It's the sweetest taste in Spain.

I shook my head, got up off the stairs—I had to get away from this guy. He was weird. As I bent down to pick up my suitcases, Raúl said, "If you change your mind, I'll be right across the street." He pointed. *"Ahí."* I looked over in the direction of his store, La Tienda Real, and nodded as if it were a place I actually might visit.

The girl who answered the apartment door had a peeled orange in her hand. She was wearing a pink cotton nightgown that was childish and ruffled. She said, *"¿Eres Catherine?"*

I nodded, suddenly unable even to pronounce the word *sí.*

We stood there for a moment—she was staring at me, and I was doing nothing, just balancing myself. Struggling with my suitcase in all the heat had made me dizzy, and I could hear the lulling echo of distant footsteps; someone was coming down the stairs, from way up high.

"Soy Celia, encantada," my new roommate said to me. She kissed me on each cheek, and I kissed her back.

She motioned for me to come in and reached down for one of my suitcases. I followed her and we stood for a moment in the hallway, and then the other one came out, Isabel. She was in her nightgown; it was lacy with spaghetti straps—she was the older one, I could tell. They both had dark blond hair—hair I didn't know Spanish woman could naturally have—and brown eyes that were the same size and shape. But Isabel was prettier somehow, her face more angular, lips fuller.

Isabel said, "Catherine?" as if she wasn't sure if I was the person they were expecting or someone else.

This time I ventured, *"Sí."*

Isabel kissed me on each cheek, and then Celia pulled one of my suitcases toward a door that was to the right. *"Tu dormitorio,"* she said, opening the door.

My room was big with one giant window that looked out to the street—a big piece of woven brown cloth that could be rolled up or down blocked the sun out, kept the room calm. I went over toward the window as if I planned on looking outside, but then I didn't. I already knew without looking that the view looked out to the front of the building, to Raúl's store. Beneath the window there was a long low bureau that matched the nightstand; they were both a pretty pale yellow, wooden, with a pink marble finish on top.

Celia was watching me observe the room, still eating her orange. She opened the closet behind her—there were clothes already inside. I was replacing the girl who usually lived with them; she had gone away for the summer. Celia pushed all the hangers to one side, "You can still use this closet. There's space."

Isabel was in the doorway. "You can even wear Aná's clothes if you want." Then she added, "But she's a little bit bigger than you."

I nodded. I looked at the pink bedspread, the soft eyelet pillows. I wanted to sleep. I wanted to dream myself far, far away, a calm place, one where my ears and stomach didn't hurt. I wanted to dream of Harlan. Harlan was my roommate in Boston, my best friend, and somehow—standing in that room full of strangeness, full of Aná's winter wool dresses, her family's photographs taped all around the mirror on the wall, an alarm clock shaped like a monkey's head—it seemed that if I could just think of Harlan long enough, I would feel some distant sense of comfort.

Strangely, Harlan would have been shocked to know that I was actually thinking about him; he often called himself the "Man of the Hour" because he thought people were always forgetting about him, losing sight of him, once he was physically not in their presence. This was particularly true of the men he dated, who often loved him and left him. I always imagined that Harlan scared these guys, frightened them—he was too eager to please while at the same time too shy about himself. And too beautiful. He was tall with shoulders that were broad but hunched, and he was girlish. Girlish in the sense that his lips were full, his eyes blue, his clear complexion constantly powdered with a Maybelline Ivory. Whether he looked into a compact or leaned against my bedroom wall, he pursed his lips in a permanent pout, one that deepened the slight two-inch scar across his forehead.

The afternoon before I left for Madrid I had found Harlan in the kitchen, crying into a rolled-up paper towel. He was still in his pajamas, and the windowless kitchen was dark, just the fake fluorescent light above the sink flickering.

I saw him out of the corner of my eye as I walked out of the bathroom wrapped in a big blue towel of his. I said, "What happened? What's wrong?"

He shook his head and looked down at the floor. "I killed a mouse."

It had been a baby mouse. One that came scurrying out of nowhere when he was standing in front of the open refrigerator. He stepped on it, smashed it with the bottom of his terry-cloth slipper.

"I didn't know what the fuck it was," Harlan said, his long ringlet curls dangled all around his face. "I thought it was like a giant . . . darting . . . bug." He smoothed his paper towel out on the countertop. He kept folding it and unfolding it.

I unraveled the towel around my head and stared at him a moment. I said, "Harlan, are you sure you're going to be all right while I'm gone?"

He put one hand behind his neck, the other across his chest. "I'm fuckin' fine," he said defensively. "It's just that mouse. I had to wipe him up. I threw his limp . . . scrunched body out my bedroom window." He tied his hair behind his head in a knot and stared off for a moment. "I can never wear those damn slippers again. If I had been barefoot, I wouldn't have been able to kill him . . . that little . . . baby thing."

I was combing my wet hair with my fingers. I said, "It's not your fault. You didn't mean it."

"I'll never kill another mouse again," he said, folding his arms. "I'm going to spend my life, the rest of my life, celebrating mice, loving them."

I laughed at him, and he got annoyed. "I'm serious, OK?"

I nodded, waited, and then smiled back at him and his bare feet and his pin-striped pajama top that was buttoned wrong—and it was then that I realized with a sudden uncomfortable surge how much I adored Harlan. He was the type of person I couldn't help but love completely and entirely, without reservation—he was so self-critical and neurotic, so obsessed with his jawline, that it couldn't be avoided. He existed in my mind in a special place outside of the world of men—he wasn't a man, he wasn't a woman, he was a generous emotional mix. And standing in the middle of Spain, in my new bedroom, with my new roommates, I felt a slight pang for Harlan. I missed him already.

Isabel and Celia gave me a tour of our apartment. It was much larger than the one I shared with Harlan. Past the entrance and my bedroom, there was a hallway that led to the living room and the dining room— they were the same room divided by different colored rugs and a small stretch of hardwood floor. They kept the refrigerator in the dining room because the kitchen was too small; there was just enough room to stand in front of the stove and sink. Everything in the kitchen was bright yellow: the stove, the plates, the floor, the walls, the dishtowels, the tip of the spatula. A red cloth bag hung from the wall, a baguette of bread hanging out, and then there was a plastic bag full of what looked like miniature corn muffins, *magdelenas*, leaning against a bag of salt.

There was also a window in the kitchen where we could hang clothes out to dry; each apartment had its own clothesline and it stretched across to another window of the apartment. The bottom of this large hollow sunlit place was white, a few potted plants could be seen beneath the cloud of hanging sheets and pillowcases. In Boston such a space would be covered in dead leaves, beer cans, twigs, and loose bricks, but in Madrid it was so clean you could almost picture the person who came every morning to hose it down.

Celia and Isabel's bedrooms were both a little bit smaller than mine. When they showed me them, I stood in the doorway of each, feeling as if I would be intruding if I walked in, if I looked at the Q-Tips and barrettes and candy wrappers that sat on their nightstands.

In the same hallway as their bedrooms, there were three bathrooms, but one didn't have a tub, so they used it as a closet. They kept old shoes and books in there, all propped along the wall in rows. A big bag of potatoes sat on the pink toilet seat, and there were tins of what looked like sardines stacked on the back of the toilet next to a bottle of vinegar. "You can keep your luggage in here, anything you want," Celia said. "Don't worry, nothing will get wet."

I said, "Oh," and then we wandered back down the hallway to the living room where Isabel had set up three lime green coffee mugs on a flowered metal tray. They sat on the couch, and I sat across from them in a chair that was covered in a stiff piece of yellow fabric. There was a painting over the television of an old woman playing chess in a café, her opponent wasn't in the picture, just a pale white hand on the table.

Celia noticed me looking at it. She said, "My mother's a painter."

Isabel said something else, something I didn't quite understand, but I somehow knew that she was making a joke about how creepy the painting was. I smiled.

They told me their father was a lawyer—that was why they were in Madrid, they were both studying to become lawyers, too. They were from Gijón, which is in northern Spain. They had a poster on the refrigerator that read "Asturias"—the name of the province in which Gijón is located. On the poster, there was a cluster of green trees, a waterfall, a sky streaked with thin clouds—it seemed a place that was dramatically different from Madrid, even more so than Boston.

"I go home every weekend to get away from here," Celia said, and pointed at the window to draw my attention to the noise outside. There was music from a passing car; beneath the sound of tambourines a girl was laughing.

Isabel said, "You go home for Francisco. No other reason."

"No, I don't."

"Yes, you do."

"No, I don't."

Isabel picked up a box of Fortuna cigarettes off the table. She offered me one, and I said, *"No, no fumo."* Isabel motioned at Celia, and said to me, "She's in love with this boy, Francisco. She'll tell you all about it. It's so boring."

Celia's lip curled up as she watched her sister light her cigarette.

Isabel looked over at me, exhaled some smoke. She said, "But tell us about you."

They asked me about Boston. I told them that I went to BU and cocktail waitressed at night. I didn't know how to say pool hall so I said bar. Isabel smiled at this. She said, "You must meet so many people."

I shrugged my shoulders. I said *sí.*

"Do you live with your parents?" Celia asked me.

I laughed, perhaps a little awkwardly, and then I told them I lived with Harlan. Isabel glanced at Celia as if it were something risqué. She said, "But do your parents know that you live with your boyfriend?"

"I don't live with my boyfriend. He's just a friend." I took a sip of coffee and then said for clarification, "He has his own room." I left out that Harlan was gay. "We are very good friends. He tells me everything, and I tell him everything. He's like my brother."

Celia smiled at me. "You speak Spanish well for an American."

That made me happy. I talked more. I told them that Harlan and I lived in a much smaller apartment. I said, "It's on the first floor, and we don't get much light. But Harlan likes it that way. He's studying film, so he watches movies all the time. He can't stand watching movies when it's bright in the room. It bothers him."

Celia asked, "What about your father and mother, where do they live?"

"They're divorced," I said, and the two of them looked at me in a way that most Americans never would—as if it made me different, sad.

I could have told them that my mother had a live-in boyfriend, but I didn't go into that—it seemed too complicated. Besides, the man my mother lived with seemed to be more of a roommate to her than Harlan was to me. His name was Gerry, and he had a certain thick-waisted warehouse-worker look to him, yet he wore brainy-looking glasses—thick brown-framed ones—and he had a white Santa Claus mustache that turned up on the ends. Around my mother, he was usually very smiley and jovial, but no matter what—whether she was in our presence or not—he was always distant toward me, as if I were something extra and unexpected, something he didn't quite know what to do with.

He was the type that, in his very stance, in the proximity in which he stood next to my mother, you could see he lived to love her—despite the fact that he knew she didn't love him the same way. She was still so pathetically caught up in the memory of my father that in her makeup bag—twelve years after their divorce—she still carried a wallet-size picture of him that was tinted pink from loose face powder.

"What does your father do?" Celia asked.

"My father works for Coca-Cola." I thought of the warehouse I passed on the way from the airport as I said this, knew they would both know what it was.

"Coca-Cola," Celia said, as if it were some exciting thing, and then she and Isabel looked at each other. They seemed to think my father actually owned Coca-Cola—which was a completely ridiculous thing to imagine; he was lucky if he still owned a driver's license, never mind a billion-dollar empire. He worked in sales and distribution. As a kid, I was driven around in his company car, which was full of papers, the cursive Coca-Cola words embossed across the top of each. He kept boxes lined up across the backseat, order forms and pens thrown haphazardly in each. There was always a stapler in his glove compartment, along with a pint of whiskey.

Celia said, "How old were you when your parents divorced?"

"Eight."

"You must have missed him so much," Celia said, and Isabel looked at her as if to say mind your own business.

I knew I was supposed to say, "Yes, yes I did." Then the topic would end. But I couldn't say that; I refused to. So instead I lied; I said, "We are actually very close."

I took a nap for about four hours and then Celia came into my room to ask me if I wanted to go out with them. *"¿Quieres salir o estás cansada todavía?"*

She insisted that I sleep if I wanted to, but I decided to get up. It seemed rude not to. This was their apartment, their world, and they were letting me in.

We went to a bar up the street; it was called El Oso Encantado. The Enchanted Bear. It was like any bar—long and thin, a cluster of wooden tables along a wall, a television going in the corner. Behind the bar they didn't have the same number of bottles as we did back at Shooters. They didn't have the long spectacular row of vodkas, only one, Absolut, and then two gins, and the rest appeared to be whiskey, scotches mostly. There were no straws or cocktail napkins, no soda guns.

I observed all of this with great interest as if the arena of bars was a specialty of mine, my own personal course of study. The beer bottles I did not recognize: Cruzcampo, San Miguel, and another familiar-looking beer, Aguila, which was apparently the Spanish version of Amstel. There was also food that they kept under glass cases at the bar—sandwiches, *bocadillos,* with thick, hard-looking ham; round *tortillas* that looked like pie-shaped omelets; glossy-looking croissants; and then very thin, very pink pieces of salmon, set on oval slices of baguette. Behind the bar there was also a piece of meat on the counter; it was a pig's entire leg, the hoof still intact. It seemed bizarre, out of this world, to order a drink at a bar that had an animal's severed leg sitting right before you, but that's what we did.

After our first drink, Isabel put her Fortuna cigarettes down on a big table in the corner. *"Para reservar la mesa,"* she said. A bunch of their friends were meeting us—a few of them had apparently been by the apartment while I was asleep. Celia said, "We told them all about you." She smiled. "They like you already."

Their friends all came within a half hour. I was introduced to each of them, kissed each stranger awkwardly on the cheek. One of them, a girl named Monica, had studied for two years in Connecticut at some school I had never heard of. After she shook my hand, she said in English, "This fuckin' place is too smoky, isn't it?"

I said *sí.*

"Abra la puerta," she yelled at the bartender, but he ignored her. She said it again, and I winced. She was very loud, and it wasn't just the quality of her voice that made her that way; it was also the abrupt gestures she made with her hands and the way she opened her glossy mouth so wide, so animated when she spoke. She seemed to think everyone should be listening to her; her eyes were never completely directed at anyone. Her gaze moved behind me, alongside me, toward the ceiling, everywhere. She made me nervous.

To make polite conversation, I asked her about Connecticut, why she went there.

"Because my father sent me there." She took a drag of her cigarette and added, "It's farther away than London." She smiled a smile that was not bitter, but jokey. "Another continent *is* another continent."

I should've just shut up right then or switched the subject, but instead I asked her how old she was when she lived in Connecticut, and she told me twelve. "My mother died when I was eleven, and then he sent me there when I was twelve." She delivered this with a certain nonchalance, as if it revealed nothing about her, as if we were talking about another person standing across the room in the corner.

Harlan had once told me that people who give too much personal information right away—and act as if it is nothing—are people to be afraid of, wary of, as they will soon expect the same from you. I stood next to Monica thinking of that, imagining her pointing at me with her wide-open eyes, asking probing questions about my own mother or father—suddenly I wanted to get away from her.

"Sit down with me," she insisted, touching my arm, and then she walked over to the table where Celia was already sitting. I followed and sat down next to Celia, not Monica. Whether it was in that very action that she decided she didn't like me, or perhaps earlier, I don't know; but from then on, I occasionally caught her staring at me, smiling a smile that was both hesitant and false.

Everyone who sat with us was talking about the World Cup. It was coming on the television in a few minutes—that was why we were there, to watch the game. Spain against Korea. That year the games were held in the United States, and people talked to me about that, about how weird it would be for me to see my home through a televised soccer field. I nodded, asked if Spain would be playing in Foxborough Stadium, but no one knew what that was, so I got quiet—I was still tired, still spacey from the flight.

"So Catherine, tell me," Monica said, during a lull in conversation, "I hear you're a cocktail waitress, the richest cocktail waitress in the world." She smiled at me as she said this, her cigarette angled attractively near her face. I couldn't entirely determine whether or not she was purposely being obnoxious. Either Celia or Isabel had told her about me, which was fine—I knew with a strange confidence that neither of them were catty about what they told her. But, nevertheless, Monica had this way of looking at me once she mentioned my job, as if she thought I was something small and amusing, and I didn't know how to react to that. I was too unsure of myself right then, so I tried to ignore it.

"I have a friend," Monica continued, "who actually *loves* cocktail waitresses."

"Oh, yeah?"

"Esteban," she said, and exhaled cigarette smoke. "He's a bit older than us, but fun, so fun." She shrugged. "I'll invite you to one of his parties. I'll *have* to."

I nodded, and then her attention fell away from me—the waiter had come and our drinks arrived. Everyone else had ordered whiskey and Coke, so I did too—even though I never liked whiskey, and I hadn't drunk Coke since I was a kid. The drinks came with just the whiskey on the rocks in a tall glass, a miniature bottle of Coke on the side. Celia picked up her Coca-Cola bottle and pointed at it, smiled at me. Earlier, on the way to the bar, we had passed Raúl's store, and there was a red-and-white Coca-Cola sign in the window. Celia had pointed at it out for me, as if it were in fact a picture of my father looming grandly in front of us. But the truth was that if indeed there had been a picture of him in front of me, I might not have recognized him. He was shadowy, a blur of black hair and thick eyebrows. Legs with wool pants. After he and my mother divorced, he had slowly but surely fallen out of my life, leaving only a trail of generic birthday cards that had balloons on them, a crisp twenty-dollar bill enclosed.

One of the boys next to Celia was arranging all the half-empty Coca-Cola bottles in a row in the middle of the table—he did it casually, slowly, each label facing him, the bottles each an inch apart. Staring at those bottle all lined up, it seemed impossible, unavoidable, not to think of my own father right then—and so that was what I did as I nodded at Celia, who was telling all of us a story.

Strangely, my earliest memories of my father, of when he lived with us, had become in my mind a vast dreamland full of blurred dinners, TV shows, car rides, Christmas trees, Easter baskets with green plastic grass. The times I remembered with a certain strange precision were the moments I felt most close to him: in the Blue Lagoon. The Blue Lagoon was a bar three blocks up the street from our house, a safe drunk drive. It was also one of the few bars that would let me inside— I was seven years old when he started taking me with him. Despite the name, it was not very tropical in there. It was dark, and there was a neon sign of a yellow starfish and two aquariums full of multicolored pebbles and slow-moving goldfish. It was your usual bar setup, the same as El Oso Encantado—booths on your left along the wall and a long bar to the right. A television with no sound in the far right-hand corner.

Renee was the name of the bartender, and I can still remember her face, the shade of eyeshadow she wore. It was teal, and it made her blue eyes look strange, moist. If I saw her today, I'd recognize her instantly, and she might even recognize me. She seemed to always be watching me, wondering.

I used to sit right next to my father, kneeling on the barstool so that I could see over the bar. We played a game called What's the Girl Worth? It was a make-believe game show—my father was the host, and I was the troubled contestant. He would use his drink as a microphone and ask me incredibly difficult questions. "In a glance, Squeaky," that was my nickname, "how many cocktail napkins are in that stack?" Or "How many ice cubes are in that man's glass?" "How many pink pebbles in this here fish tank?" The questions seemed to always involve counting. Sometimes I would try to come up with serious numbers: 27, 55, 7. But other times I got the hang of it, the humor: 3,541, 3.2 million, 6 zillion.

The more ridiculous my response, the more points I earned, and, as a consequence, I was worth more. Some days I was worth more than $5 million; other days, when I was feeling unimaginative and lazy, $10,000.

We also played a game where we drew pictures of other people in the bar on cocktail napkins and then drew horns coming out of their heads, extra eyes, tails—anything that could make us laugh. "Don't point," my father would say when I'd point at the person we were drawing—usually some forlorn-looking man holding a beer bottle, his eyes cast toward the soundless television high on the wall. "You should never point," he'd say, which made me point even more obviously until he pushed my hand down at my side, and then I'd wait, giggling, until he let go.

Despite the frequency of these games and barroom visits, my mother had no idea that my father and I went to the Blue Lagoon. She worked until six, didn't get home until seven, and my father was the one who worked from seven to two. Three o'clock to six o'clock were our bar hours. I can remember watching the hands on the clock go around and around and not wanting to leave. I could have lived in that bar. Slept there.

"Squeaks, you're not going to squeak, are you?" my father would ask me in the car. He meant tell my mother on him.

"No," I always said, and then I smiled as if to suggest I might or I might not. But of course I never planned to. There was something great about having a secret place, as well as a scheduled time, that was ours and ours alone.

But it all ended one evening. Summer. My mother and I were in the backyard—she was hanging clothes on the line, and I was sitting in the grass watching. It was eight o'clock, the part of a hot day that turns cooler and at the same time uplifting somehow. The sky was soft pink, comfortable to gaze at.

"Where did you get this money?" my mother asked me, holding a wad of one-dollar bills in her hand—she had just taken them out of my wet shorts. She stared at me appraisingly and then said, "You didn't take this from somewhere, did you?"

She thought I had stolen the money, and even at the age of eight, I had this certain sense of nobility, of what people could accuse me of and what they couldn't. I said, irritated, "No. I *made* that money."

She put the shorts back down in the basket of wet laundry. "What do you mean?"

"I made it. At the bar Daddy takes me to." I looked right at her. I thought I was proving her wrong—showing her she shouldn't think bad things of me. "I order drinks for people to the bartender, and then they tip her one dollar and then me one dollar."

It's strange how when you are so young, you often think when you say things that you are making yourself look smart, or perhaps you think you're being entertaining—you never realize that those things are the very same things that can upset adults, make them want to slap you.

"I only play the game with the regulars," I said. "No one I don't know well." Usually they told me their drink, I memorized the specifics: rocks, twist, cherry, dry—and then I ordered their next drink when they were nearly done. That way they never actually had to speak. They could just sit there, stare at their hands, twist their wedding bands, rub their lips. But, of course, it was all a memorization game to me. One with cash bonuses.

My mother picked up a T-shirt out of the basket. I watched her place clothespins on each shoulder. She said, "And what bar is this?"

I said, "The Blue Lagoon," and then, sensing some change in her face, in the way she stared down at the yellow nightgown she was now holding, I added, "It's a short drive. Nothing bad happens. One time he hit a dog, but the dog was OK. It walked away."

My mother nodded but didn't look at me. She had always known that my father drank all day, and she may have even known on some level that he brought me on his escapades. But it had never been made so clear. The Blue Lagoon had never been mentioned. The vision of my hopping from barstool to barstool, sitting up on my knees, ordering a drink, and then stashing a dollar in my jeans pocket, was not one she had ever had before. And it was perhaps then, standing in front of that clothesline, that she finally realized that his drunkenness was something she could ignore, he could ignore, but I was the one who watched it with great interest, great awe. With the exception of our zigzagging car rides, I had never realized that my father's drinking was bad. It seemed nor-mal—he was always doing it. In front of everyone. He drank cans of beer as if they were cans of soda: walking to the mailbox, sitting in a parking lot, lying on his back at the beach. I, of course, saw that there was a difference in him, the slow, dulled way that he buttered his bread, the way he sat in our La-Z-Boy chair, but I often saw him drunk, to the point that, in the morning, when I saw him sober, it seemed that it was then when he was under the influence of something—he looked a shade whiter, and his hands were shaky. He often dropped things.

My mother, of course, was present for all of this, too. She appeared to accept it the same way I did. It was a part of him.

So it seemed like no big deal when I mentioned my father and me at the Blue Lagoon. It was the same as if we had both spent hours at the ice cream parlor sitting at the counter drinking milk shake after milk shake.

Whenever my father told me not to squeak, not to tell on him, I didn't think it was because of the alcohol; I thought it was because we hadn't done anything important with our afternoon—no books, no geographical discussions, not a single heart-to-heart. We just played games and laughed at people, taunted them, and that I knew would be unacceptable to my mother, unfatherly. But I hadn't told her about any of that.

Shortly afterward, when my father came home, my mother and I were still in the backyard. What happened after that is "no longer on the screen," as Harlan would've put it. I remember my father's voice, my mother's voice. She said something about his being a drunk, "a filthy fucked-up drunk."

In the neighbor's yard, the sprinkler was on. It was lime green, and it sprayed out in a giant fan, like the lines on a seashell. The water was hitting the hood and window of the neighbor's car, and if you were to be sitting in the backseat of that car, your knees hugged up against your chest, you might hear only the rumble of the water, like rain. That's what I heard looking at the sprinkler, what I imagined.

I did not hear my father yell back at my mother; I did not see him hit her with the brick.

The brick was one we had on the top of the picnic table—it was originally there to keep the legs even, but it didn't really work, so that brick had sat on top of the table for months, through a snowy winter and a rainy spring. It sat there, patient and still, waiting to be used, waiting for the moment when it could become a permanent part of my blackened memory.

My mother was knocked unconscious.

My father emptied the backseat of his car, Coca-Cola papers spilled all over the lawn. The streetlight above our driveway was on; it was getting dark. He put my mother in the backseat, and then he told me to get in the front. We were going to the hospital. I don't remember if I was scared of him, but I don't think I was. I sat in the front seat and opened the glove compartment. I could hear my mother breathing behind me—in my mind her injury may have turned into something else. A headache or a bee sting.

Throughout our drive, I played with a stapler. At one point my father said, "Put that away."

I didn't. I kept pressing down on the stapler over and over. Loose staples fell all over the seat; some stuck to my legs.

At a red light, my father looked at me and said, "Please, just don't staple your goddamn fingers."

I shook my head, looking out the window. "I'm not stupid," I said, and then I sat there quietly, having no idea that that moment in the car, with my soundless mother and my father—whom I could not look directly at— was a moment that would stay with me so clearly yet distantly.

I suppose for most people such memories circulate somewhere—a continuous flow somewhere in one's mind, or perhaps in a hidden sector of the heart. But for me, I rarely thought of that summer night, hardly ever, and so when I did, the moment became all the more uncomfortable, particularly the older I got. It seemed a pain that should no longer be so tender; it should've been outgrown.

"*¿Te sientes bien?*" Celia asked me, squeezing my arm.

I said *Sí* and smiled. I took a sip of my drink. It tasted too sweet, like something that might make me fat. The game was on the television now, and the bar was crowded. I could see the green playing field, the close-up of a boy with a shaved head in a striped uniform drinking water.

Monica leaned over toward me. She said, "I heard your father is a bigwig at Coca-Cola."

I just stared at her—I suppose that was what she thought I was lying about. Cocktail waitresses generally do not have rich fathers. I said, "My father *works* for Coca-Cola," and shifted in my seat. Monica stared at me, nodded, and then I sat there feeling strange—as if everything I had been thinking about my father had some deep dark connection to things that were later said to me. I suppose it was then that I should've known with all of this continuous emphasis on my father that something was about to happen between him and me, right there in Madrid. It's strange the way you can look back on things and see a foreshadowing; it makes the world seem creepy and ominous, alive with its own force.

PART ONE

— ❀ —

BEFORE MY FATHER ARRIVED

$$\overline{2}$$

Work and the Party

The lighting in the office I worked in was fluorescent. If I looked up at the ceiling for a second too long, I'd end up seeing spots. Spots on the computer screen. Spots on my hands. Spots on my boss, Carlos. I shouldn't call Carlos my boss though—he was really just the person who gave me little tasks to do. He was twenty-four, with spiky hair and a nervous way of touching his lips all the time. I was taller than him, and that seemed to bother him—he often talked to me from a few feet away.

When I first met him, it was not in the main body of the office but in the reception area. Sitting in a brown wicker chair, I had to wait for him a few minutes. On the wall in blue lettering the agency's name, S.A.E. de Relaciones Públicas, was written high on a white sign. The agency was part of a bigger international PR firm, an American company, called Shandwick, and there was even an American *Inside PR* magazine on the coffee table, along with two Spanish newspapers, *ABC* and *El Mundo*.

Once Carlos came out to greet me, he was smiley and jubilant, as if something fantastic had just happened to him—perhaps a wedding proposal, a winning lottery ticket. His happiness, his chattiness, initially set

me more at ease. He asked me personal questions about my new roommates, my new neighborhood, the mutual people we knew at BU. He
even told me his favorite restaurant in Boston, La Trattoria. Then after
a pause, he asked, *"¿Y por qué estudias relaciones públicas? ¿En particular
qué te gusta?"* And why do you study public relations? What do you like
about it?

To all the previous personal questions he asked, I had answered in
Spanish, but right then I nervously swerved into the comfortable world
of English. What exactly I said, I don't entirely remember; I actually
had no real interest in public relations, which was what made the question so challenging. I had simply fallen into that major in the same way
most college students fall into undesirable majors. I had an advisor who
knew me for about three days. He talked to me, looked at my records,
assessed my skills. He felt I was creative, yet craved something "orderly."
He also concluded from my entrance essay that I liked people—which
somehow led to PR.

I think that's actually what I told Carlos, that I liked people and
thought public relations was a way of helping people.

"Sí," he said and smiled. *"Somos como La Cruz Roja."* We are like the
Red Cross. *"¿Y España?"* he asked, *"¿Por qué España?"*

This question I answered more honestly; I said I came to Spain
because my professor, the one we mutually knew, demanded it of me.
This teacher was always in my business, giving me a hard time, asking if
I had slept all right. She claimed that despite my grades, I seemed disinterested in class, "aloof." According to her, the world of PR was vast,
omnipresent, a gorgeous field of choices. I just had to find my personal
niche, she claimed, one that I "as an individual" cared about. And somehow within this conversation—while walking outside on an icy sidewalk—we landed on the idea of an internship that would be far, far
away in a culture and world that would *have* to interest me.

Spain we picked because I spoke Spanish. Carlos we picked because
he was once my professor's favorite pal and pet.

I told Carlos the abridged version of this, one in which I simply val-
ued my professor's opinion. From there we went into his office, and he

told me about the various accounts they had, pointed at decals and posters on the walls. He talked about Europcar, a car rental agency, and their desire to beat out Avis. He told me about a laundry detergent called Skip Poder that was in trouble because certain studies showed it burned holes through clothes. He pointed at a small Johnny Walker Black bottle he had on his desk, told me how it was not as popular here as it was in the United States. "We're going to change that though," he said, touching the bottle, and I nodded, as if that pleased me.

Of the three accounts, if I had been able to pick, I would've chosen Johnny Walker Black, as it seemed somehow closer to what I knew. Instead, I got stuck with another product: Lysol.

"Es un proyecto emocionante," it's an exciting project, Carlos told me as he gave me a tour through the agency. The entire office didn't even look like an office but instead a glamorous apartment. It had chandeliers and hard, shoe-smacking wood floors, bathrooms with showers. It had two floors, and the main entrance was a big mahogany door with a doorknob that did not turn, you just had to push it.

Earlier that morning as I had ridden the old rickety elevator, watched the floors pass by through the metal gates, I felt so hungover and tired; that dull queasiness didn't go away even hours later, though in the afternoon I read a whole stack of folders that were all about Lysol. Lysol's company history. Lysol's growth. Lysol's expansion. Lysol against the world of germs. I tried to read it all with zest, but it was quite impossible. At one point while I was reading, the secretary came in and said, *"Te apetece una Coca-Cola Light?"*

I said *sí.*

She brought me a can of Coca-Cola Light with a mug full of ice— that Coke tasted better than any other Coke I had ever had before. It tasted sweet and fizzy and cold. It tasted like home.

My second assignment, which started on Wednesday, my third day, was to call ten microbiologists who were all in the United States. Lysol was about to be introduced to Spain in October, and they were having this panel of microbiologists come to Madrid and educate the public on microbes, on germs, on staphylococcus. My job was to call the panelists, chat them up. I called all of them within a half hour, left messages on voice mail. I came back to Carlos's desk looking for something else to do. He stared at me; he was chewing on a pencil. He said, "You don't have to stay today. You can go. You should walk around. See Madrid."

I shrugged my shoulders. I said hesitantly, *"Vale,"* OK, and ended up walking aimlessly all day, eating ice cream cones when it got too hot, buying sandals when I got too bored. I was so unaccustomed to having free time that I felt guilty for it, as if I were being wasteful or irresponsible. The day before was the first day that, if I were home, I would've been scheduled to work at Shooters, and the whole day I thought about that, felt mildly worried, as if I believed that somehow I still belonged there, still needed to make the cash. This sort of thinking was probably just a masked form of homesickness, but in any case, I was beginning to worry about being in Madrid. My internship—and all its supposed importance—was my crutch; it was what gave me the guts to come. In my mind, I couldn't just go somewhere to go somewhere. I had to have a rationale, a higher purpose, and as I walked alone through those Madrilenian streets, getting bumped into a lot, blind people on corners shouting about lottery tickets, and the sun so hot, so strong above me, I wondered if I should've chosen someplace else. What if Carlos never gave me any work? What if it was all a big waste?

The following day Carlos gave me only one single assignment, one that seemed a means of keeping me out of the way. He gave me a stack of microbial studies on household germs that were all written in English. He wanted me to read them, "and translate them into simple English so that we," he pointed around the room, "can understand them." He smiled. "It's too complicated for us."

I translated all of twelve of them in three hours. I went back to his desk. He was not there; his chewed-up pencil was.

I went back into my room full of fluorescent light. It was the ugliest room of the office. There were no chandeliers, no wallpaper, not a painting. Just three giant posters of Johnny Walker Black, the bottles on the wall the size of human bodies. I waited for Carlos to come back as I twiddled my thumbs and stared at the desk. After about an hour, I began computing how much money I was losing by not working at Shooters over the summer. Summer was a good season; Fenway Park was nearby. We made money like mad on game nights.

On a piece of graph paper, I made a chart of how many days I could have worked per week: five or six, at least four being game nights. I multiplied that by twelve weeks. It came to $10,260, give or take. Then I added on the plane ticket, the cost of my Madrid rent. I was losing a minimum of $11,450 just sitting there in that office doing nothing. This was, of course, an exaggeration—I would never have earned that much money, and if I had, I would've blown at least half of it. But still, it was money I wasn't going to make.

I scattered the charts I had drawn all over my desk. Stared at them. There was one for each month: June, July, August. I often did this sort of thing, made these money charts. Harlan always found them scattered on the kitchen table, jam smudged on each page. He'd write different notes across the top—ones like: *If you just worked every day, twelve hours a day, for the next seven years, you'd have $1,356,808 in cash!!! (Your youth and beauty would be gone, but really, what's that?)*

I often get hostile over this—what Harlan didn't have to worry about, what I did, was everything. I paid for my tuition, my rent, my food, my toothbrush. All of it. My mother didn't have any money— except for Gerry's, and that wasn't that much—and my father, if he did have money, never offered. So I worked and worked and put together desperate charts in the middle of the night. I took into consideration the maximum I could earn, the minimum. I estimated costs for each month: rent and electricity and the phone and hair care and taxicabs and printer cartridges and books. One thousand dollars a month went to school, $500 into my savings. In my charts I forecasted things that might interfere with my moneymaking schedule: colds and snowstorms, holidays and exams. With each chart I made, I tried to predict all the things I could—I had to prepare for them, control them, make my life work.

All of this, this urgency to build myself up, to make the money—and security—I needed, was bottled up inside of me as I sat idly at my desk waiting for Carlos to come back. And when he finally arrived, smiling, *"Hola, Catherine,"* I felt a little out of control, as if I might start screaming at any moment. I wasn't going to get anything out of being here—all of the things he had already given me to do hadn't been real work. Just mindlessness to keep me out of the way. If he didn't have anything for me to do, I thought, then he shouldn't have agreed to have me come. I spent a lot of money coming, a lot of time.

Carlos had only stuck his head in the doorway when he said hello, and now he was at his own desk. I got up and walked down the hallway. With each step I took I felt the anger level and then finally, once I reached his office, subside. Within the long tunnel walls of that hallway, I slowly came to terms with my frustration, my edginess, and Carlos clearly wasn't the culprit. I was simply suffering from a pathetic bout of homesickness—one that I felt hit me in the stomach once I stood in front of Carlos's desk and noticed an American quarter sitting among a bunch of paper clips.

Carlos looked at me out of the corner of his eye—he was flipping idly through some papers stacked on his desk. "You know, I've been thinking," he said in English. "You don't have to work here every day. You should work just Tuesday, Wednesday, Thursday." He swiveled in his chair a little. "So you don't have to come in tomorrow. Tomorrow is"—he paused as if he had to think about it—"tomorrow is Friday."

I just stared at him.

"You can see Spain this way," he said. "You can have a long weekend and perhaps travel with Celia and Isabel, go to Gijón or Barcelona or—" He stopped himself. "Why do you look so serious?" He was smiling.

I smiled back awkwardly—I had to.

He picked up a picture that was on his desk and wiped the brass frame with his fingertip. His girlfriend was in the picture—she was leaning against a palm tree, smiling, her hands behind her back. There was a vibrancy to her, a certain presence that came out of the photograph and overlooked Carlos's computer keyboard. Still holding her picture, Carlos said, "You are going to like it here in Spain, Catherine. It's different from anywhere else."

I nodded—I didn't know how else to respond. I said *sí*.

That same day when I got out of work, I tried to call my mother to tell her my internship was a bust. I was at a pay phone outside of the metro station, Banco de España, which was few blocks from the office. The traffic was so loud that I couldn't hear the splash of the fountain that was in the center of the swirling rotary. I stood in front of a kiosk that had an *El País* banner across the top. While I waited for her to answer, I memorized the names of magazines as if that might improve my Spanish: *La Guía del Ocio, Hola, Fotogramas, El Mundo, Quo, Entrevista*.

My mother wasn't home. I had called collect, and the operator let the phone ring and ring twenty times before she told me no one was answering. The international operator's voice, British and proper, was strangely polite, as if she somehow sensed that I was desperate to talk to someone, anyone.

I thought about calling Harlan, but I didn't know if he'd be at Godiva—that was where he worked, at a chocolate store. I had already gotten a postcard from him the day before. It had a picture of Speedy Gonzalez on the front, and the back said, "Kitten of my heart, I miss you already, but don't worry about me. Not at all, chiquitita." Then he wrote in parenthesis: "Have you met anyone good yet?"

I had the postcard in my bag, and I stared at it while I decided whether or not to try to call him. There was a heart drawn around Speedy's face, and Harlan had written in the corner: "For the rest of my life, I celebrate mice, I love them."

I smiled a little, putting the postcard back in my bag, and then I walked past the metro station. I decided I shouldn't call—it might make me feel worse.

Instead I walked and walked in the heat, kept passing construction sites where the sidewalk was partially taken apart, loose sand every-where, the constant thudding of a jackhammer. All of Madrid seemed to be under construction that week. Even when I woke up in the morning I heard through my open window the distant shouting of men and then the crash of lumber or cobblestones or bricks being moved from one metal bin to another.

Right then it was midafternoon, and the construction workers were all shirtless, their round stomachs bulging in a froglike fashion, sand like a light brown haze all over their backs. They catcalled as I passed, not every block, but still . . . every few minutes: *Tesoro, bombón, muñeca, chhhhhhh.*

The street itself, Gran Vía, was filled with people, and it was a frustrat-ing walk; the Spanish were not ones to speed along a sidewalk, instead they always seemed to be in sociable packs, talking and gesturing and pointing. Even if they were alone, they had a tendency to stop abruptly without caring who was behind them, make you knock right into them.

"*¡Cuidado, eh!*" this one older man shouted after I bumped him hard. It was late afternoon, still hot, yet he had his suit jacket slung over his shoulders like a cape. When I bumped him, his jacket fell off one shoul-der, and after he yelled, he stared at me as if he was trying to figure out where my rushed rudeness was from.

After that, I went into a store called Zara. I walked through the store—past the racks and racks of matching suits, of dress jackets that all looked the same except they were different colors, some with zippers, some with buttons. I pulled on the arms of the jackets, zipped the zip-pers up and down, but I didn't look at the price tags. Salesclerks always seemed to notice when you did that. It meant you could buy anything; you didn't care. A saleswoman came over and started talking to me. I had been so lost inside of myself, thinking purely in English, that when she began talking to me in Spanish, it seemed like an invasion. I didn't make eye contact with her at first, but it didn't really faze her. She picked different dresses out for me, then a scarf and a strappy tank top. It was as if she had some innate ability to see through me, to see my need to buy.

It was only later when I stood barefoot in the dressing room, ten dresses I could not afford splayed all over the floor, that I realized how much I was like my mother. I was in my underwear, staring in the mirror and sucking in my stomach, making that pouty face she often made when she looked at herself, the one that was supposed to be seductive. The one that used to seduce her into buying all the dresses she ever wanted—she deserved it; the dresses made her feel beautiful, as if she could do anything, be anything. Live.

In the two years before my mother found Gerry, she spent most of her yearly salary, $20,000, on clothes. I was ten and eleven at the time, and together we organized our weekly schedule around shopping. We went to the malls on Tuesdays and Thursdays, and on weekends we went to the more obscure shops, the ones on side streets, the ones with construction paper signs in their windows. Sales were what got us—savings, savings, savings! We went mad for "buy one, get-one-free," "three for $19." "$7 rebate," and even these mystery discounts that you got when you scratched a ticket at the register. We fell for anything that saved us a dollar or two, and then we bought more and more, leaving with bags of things we would probably never wear: six sets of dangling beaded earrings, sweaters with white piping that matched lacy camisoles, dresses with flashy zippers, silver handbags, roles and roles of useless velvet ribbon. We were thrilled with anything we could get our hands on, anything that came in a set or looked good according to the salesclerk. "My God, your eyes just light up in that," they'd tell us or, even better, "You look great. So great. Beautiful." And we'd believe it because we needed to believe it. We had to.

"¡Qué vestido tan mono! ¡Eres tan linda como un ángel!" the Spanish salesclerk told me when I came out of the dressing room. I smiled at her, then looked in the mirror at my side profile, pulling one leg up a little, toes pointed. I did look all right.

I bought six of the dresses and a silk scarf. All on my credit card.

Outside in the street I snapped the price tag off the scarf and started to wrap it around my neck. I was in front of a café called Café y Té and a man who had been sitting at a table by himself came over and offered to help me put it on. I told him no, but then he stood there so close to me that I could smell coffee on his breath. Once I tied the scarf, I walked

away from him, annoyed, my shopping bag swinging next to me. For
blocks, I passed movie theaters that had giant, glittering chandeliers in
their foyers, the words *La Peste, The Plague,* written above one; I passed
a bookstore that had a display of old dictionaries, passed a fabric store
that had carpet-size rolls of floral cloth. As I walked by, I occasionally
glanced at my reflection, adjusted my new scarf. I was forever strange
that way: I always wanted to look good no matter how much trouble and
irritation it brought.

When I got home, the apartment was empty. Celia had left the day
before to go to Gijón, and Isabel, I knew, was leaving, too. They were
both taking the same summer class at the university on Tuesday and
Thursday nights—but on the weekends, they told me, they would definitely be gone. Originally I was happy about this; I looked forward
being alone—but then after a while, I wasn't so sure. I felt a little nervous. What would I do with myself?

Isabel was going to either Alicante or Barcelona. When I was in the
bathroom putting on mascara that morning, she was siding with
Barcelona. She stood in the hallway watching me through the doorway.
She was wearing a blue nightgown with blue slippers. She had slippers
that matched each of her nightgowns—all of them pastel, all of them
terry cloth like Harlan's slippers.

"Barcelona's better," she had told me. "There's more to do."

I looked at her in the mirror. "Do you have a boy there?"

"No," she said, "I'm not like Celia. I fall in love with no one." She
shrugged her shoulders. "Except myself."

I laughed. I wanted to say, "That's the only way to be," but I didn't
know how to manage it in Spanish. Instead I said *sí.*

Isabel left me a note on the kitchen table that said that Monica was
going to call me and take me to party that night. Isabel wrote, "*¡No pude
dejarte sola! Una Americana guapa sola, ¡Imposible!*" Translation: I
couldn't leave you alone. A pretty American girl alone, impossible!

I smiled, folding the note. I liked Isabel, and I liked Celia, too. They were being good to me. Over the past few days since I had arrived, I had spent more time with Celia though, rather than with Isabel. Isabel was always off somewhere—always dressed up, always in a tight dress with long beads that she looped over and over around her neck. After work, just looking at her, at her energy, made me tired. In her high heels, with her hair brushed straight and sleek to the middle of her back, she always looked very pretty, so incredibly so that it made me not want to pass a mirror or look down at my waist.

I did, of course, like Isabel very much, but in Celia's company I found more comfort—and, as a consequence, I felt closer to her. On both Tuesday and Wednesday of my first week in Madrid, Celia had taken me with her shopping for shoes and a new dress—she was going that weekend to see Francisco. She talked about Francisco incessantly. He was in the military for a year. His father was a baker and his mother a seamstress. When he was a child, someone in a schoolyard hit him with a rock, and to that day, Celia claimed, he jumped a little when he heard the sound of someone kicking a rock. He was also afraid of monkeys.

I listened to everything Celia said about Francisco, nodding my head, a dull smile on my face. It wasn't that I wasn't interested, I was— it was endearing to hear her speak with such unblanketed excitement. Around her sister, she was always a little standoffish about Francisco, as if he were a person she occasionally spoke to and not the love of her life. It embarrassed her, I suppose, to be so translucent—you could look at her sitting on a bench thinking about him, and you could see her fever for him in the slight twitch of her lips, in the way her hands tapped on her knees. That love-struck giddiness of hers often made me feel a little strange—it reminded me of what I didn't have. I felt almost incapable of such devotion.

"You could fall in love tonight," Monica told me when she called me Thursday. She said this somewhat sarcastically, as if she herself did not believe in such things, and then she went on to tell me about the two guys, Dan and Paco, whom we were going out with that night. One of them was named Dan, and he was from Colorado and in Madrid only a few days—he apparently knew this Spanish friend of Monica's, Paco, and so she had spent the past two days showing Dan around, taking him to bars and clubs, staying up with him all night.

The fact that the two of us were going out with the two of them didn't necessarily imply a double date though, as it was somewhat customary in Spain that if you went out in a boy-girl group, there had to be exactly one boy for each girl; it was the perfect social ratio. But I didn't entirely understand this at first, and I was a little annoyed—no matter where I went, it seemed, everyone was always trying to fix me up with someone.

At home, Harlan couldn't sit in a restaurant without zeroing in on somebody at another table—he was never casual about it either. He was always somewhat obnoxious, staring at the guy, waving, demanding that I blow a kiss. And the guy was always somebody older, in his late twenties, wearing khakis. "That guy right there, that guy, he"—Harlan would pause dramatically—"he would actually be good to you."

Even Celia had already started looking for me. She had this boy lined up for me in Gijón, a cousin of Francisco's. His name was Felipe.

"He's perfect for you. Perfect," Celia explained to me one afternoon while we walked through the city's biggest park, El Parque Retiro, which was the equivalent to The Commons in Boston, but it was about ten times larger. "Felipe is his name," she said as we passed through a section of the park where there were a lot of Latin Americans, all families, all sitting in giant groups. "He speaks a little English," she told me. "No, a lot of English, and he is tall and he has brown hair and pretty eyes and a face . . ." She made her own face very animated as if to show what his might be like. *"Parece como él,"* he looks like him, she said, pointing at a little boy who was getting his hair cut by his mom, a white sheet with pale pink stripes draped over him. As we watched his black hair fall in snippets all over the sheet, all over the grass, Celia decided I should come to Gijón with her in late July. The twenty-second. "By then," she said, "you'll be already used to it here. You'll be able to speak Spanish perfectly then."

I said OK, but without much enthusiasm, which she seemed to interpret as shyness. I didn't mind the idea of going somewhere else with her, of seeing another section of Spain, but the boy I had no interest in. In the same way that I later had no interest in meeting Monica's friend, Dan. If anything, these boys made me tense. They made me feel as if I had to be charming and dressed right, as if my nails had to shine and my hair had to be blown straight. I was going to have to smile. All of this annoyed me. They were all tests I could usually pass, but in the end I didn't feel any sense of accomplishment, any sense of goodness—instead I felt a little bit awful, I felt like a piece of ass.

"We're meeting Dan and Paco at eleven at Bar Cock," Monica explained to me on the phone, "and then we'll go to a party, Esteban's party." She hung up shortly after that—and then I stared at the phone afterward as if her abruptness marked something, as if it spelled out the fact that she was taking me out, not for Celia or Isabel's sake, but to fulfill her own boy-girl needs. But I went along with it anyway, went along wearing a beige knit dress and high-heel sandals that gave me giant crippling blisters.

"You look like a million pesetas," Monica told me when she first saw me outside my apartment, and then she said it a second time while we were driving. Her car, a black sports car that was a brand we didn't have in the States, had a perfume smell to it, like mint leaves and vanilla. We parked somewhere off a street called Fuencarral, and then we walked and walked down narrow streets where there was little light and big construction site holes in the sidewalks, loose rubble everywhere.

Bar Cock itself was not as I had imagined—for one, it did not have stuffed red roosters on the walls, and secondly, it didn't look anything like the first Spanish bar I had been in. It was instead extra swank, with intricate multicolored tiles on the floor, deep mahogany wood walls, and maroon leather booths with brassy buttonlike upholstery pins. The tables themselves were mirrored so that you could obsessively look at yourself or at whatever might be lurking up your nose. The lighting was soft, the floor marble; they had more bottles of vodka, more bottles of gin, and metal shakers—like a symbol of fanciness—set on the bar.

Dan, the American we were meeting, was a snotty ass. He was good-looking in that boring symmetrical way, and he was tall and blond and freckled. He stood against the wall, dressed in a tight white T-shirt and black pleated pants. When we first walked over toward him and his friend, there was a pause and then he said, looking at Monica, "This is Catherine?"

Paco smiled at me in a way that suggested he was somewhat embarrassed.

Dan stared at me, up then down. "She told me you looked like Rachel Hunter." He crossed his arms, a beer in his hand. "You don't look anything like her."

I looked at him, my eyes purposely calm, indifferent. "I know that."

"But she does," Monica insisted. "Her hair, her height, her lips."

"I'm only five seven," I said.

Monica looked at me. "So?"

"She doesn't look the way you said." Dan took a sip of beer. He appeared angry all of a sudden. Originally it seemed this might be a not-so-amusing joke, but it became more somehow—it was as if he had just bitterly realized how much time he had spent combing his hair and staring at himself sideways. The tightness of his shirt, the shininess of his shoes, the gum he was chewing all seemed part of that anger—he had apparently prepared for much more.

Monica said to me, "Do you want a drink?"

"Yeah." I nodded. "A whiskey and Coke is fine."

She looked at Dan. "Do you want to come with me?"

"I don't know," he said. "Can I trust you?"

She laughed, and then the two of them walked to the bar, leaving me alone with Paco. We stood there awkwardly, looking around as if we were scanning the area for a particular person, or thing, or perhaps a special color. After a minute or two, Paco explained in Spanish—without looking directly at me—that Dan had only come to meet Monica because she had promised to bring the most beautiful American girl he would ever see. "She keeps hitting on him," he said in English. "Over and over." He knocked on the mahogany wall to show me the "hitting."

"*¿Pero no le gusta?*"—but he doesn't like her—I asked.

"No." He smiled. "And so . . . she likes him more."

I nodded at that, as if I understood that logic perfectly.

Meanwhile Monica was looking at us from the bar, smiling, a bit of lipstick on her teeth. She was wearing all red: a red dress, red shoes, red dangling earrings. She was a pretty girl, but she wore so much makeup, so much color, that it turned her features against her—made her look somewhat harsh, mean. Once she returned from the bar, Dan stood on the other side of her, a distance away from me. Monica handed me my drink. She said, "I was just telling Dan that you're a cocktail waitress." Dan smiled as she said this and added, "I've been to Boston. Maybe you've waited on me before." He was kidding, it was a light easy joke, and I smiled halfheartedly, but inside of myself I felt something unpleasant, a burn, one that I tried to ignore as I gazed off at a woman who was cooling herself with a bright pink fan.

We went to Esteban's party an hour later, after we finished two drinks, after we listened to Dan explain why he would kiss the ground—or, rather, the actual pavement of the airport parking lot—once he arrived back home. Despite his rudeness, Monica kept smiling, kept insisting that he would love the party we were going to. From her enthusiasm, I had pictured Esteban's party to be one filled with outrageous people all dressed in white, an occasional person jumping off the diving board of the pool, martini glass in hand. But when we got there, it wasn't like that at all. There was a pool, kidney-shaped and blue, light gleaming on the surrounding clean white cement. But there were only about forty people, and they were all rather sedate, older in appearance—people who had conversations in hushed voices as though they possessed a wisdom not all of us should hear. Away from the pool, there was a patio attached to the house, sets of chairs were placed next to small bistro-style tables. Each table, all of which were currently empty, had a small flickering candle and a bowl of nuts. A kid, about sixteen, came around and periodically checked the bowls.

"I want a drink," Dan said within a few minutes of our arrival. He gestured toward the bar and walked away. The bar was in actuality not a bar. It was a long glass table with bottles of liquor lined up on top, mostly scotches. A big bucket of ice was next to the bottles—it had a glass lid and there were silver tongs nearby placed neatly on a white napkin. A Count Dracula–looking butler in a black jacket and bow tie stood in front of the table, his chest out, posture stiff. I watched Dan ask for his drink, saw the butler place each piece of ice in the glass. He picked up the Johnny Walker bottle and tilted it; the pour was slow, elegant. All of the butler's moves were deliberate and careful.

"Let's get a drink," Monica said to me. Paco was adrift looking at all the other people. There were many beautiful women, but they were regal somehow, older than us. Not thirty or forty, twenty-seven perhaps. Women young enough to still have long hair and soft, makeup-less faces, but at the same time, they were more complicated. Their posture, the way they nodded at a comment, the steadiness of their gaze, even the way they held their drinks away from their bodies instead of so close to their chest suggested that a man couldn't just walk up to them—not unless he had something worthwhile to say.

"Do you want whiskey straight?" Monica asked me.

"No, with Coke."

"Come on," she said, "be a man."

I thought of my father momentarily, of how he drank whiskey as if it were nothing—it seemed to be the true mark of an alcoholic, drinking liquor straight. I said, "No, I want mine with Coke."

We went over to the butler, and Monica ordered for us. She got Four Roses, straight, no ice. I watched her take a sip and wince. She said, looking not quite at me but out in front of her, "Isn't Paco cute?"

I took a sip of my own drink and swallowed. I wasn't going to answer her. The question somehow implied some sort of plan she had for me, which, of course, I didn't like. Besides, I didn't think Paco was cute, and I was sure she didn't either. He was a little chubby, particularly in the waist and face, and his hair was very coarse-looking, all tied back in a red elastic, just a sprout of hair against his forehead.

I had driven over to the party with Paco, not Monica—she drove with Dan. In the car, I had initially gotten along fine with Paco. There wasn't much awkwardness; he was rather sociable, polite. He asked me about my new neighborhood, and I told him about Raúl, the store owner. Every morning as I walked past his store on my way to the metro, Raúl knocked on the glass. Thursday, he even followed me for a block. I told Paco, "He keeps insisting I have a Mars Bar. But I really don't like them."

He laughed, and then shortly afterward a silence fell between us. We were on the highway—the party was in Moreleja, a suburb of Madrid—and there was just the lulling movement of the car along with the comfortable darkness of night. I could have stayed in that car for hours and never reached the party, never spoken to anyone, and I would've been fine.

But then Paco said abruptly, "You have wonderful legs," and that freedom, that comfort, fell away, and an edginess replaced it. I was aware of my posture, of my hands and how they were set on my lap; I was even aware of the car seat—how low to the ground I was. I said without looking at him, "Thanks."

I didn't say much to him the rest of the ride. He seemed to note that though, think I was strange.

But Monica, of course, didn't know about any of this, and even if she did, she wouldn't have cared. "Do you think these women are pretty?" she asked me.

I looked around as if hadn't already noticed them. There was a woman across from us who had her hair in cornrows, no eye makeup— just flesh-colored lipstick and an off-white linen dress that had beaded spaghetti straps. I said, "Yeah, I think all of them are very pretty." Then I waited a moment, as if I thought I had to pretend to ponder. "I think Spanish women are very elegant."

"These women *aren't* Spanish," Monica said, as if the idea was some-how insulting. "Just about all of them are from somewhere else:

Venezuela, Brazil, Argentina, that one's from Cuba, the other one"—
she pointed at a blond woman who had a very angular, delicate face and
shoulder-length hair that grazed her collarbone—"I think she's Russian. You can always tell a Russian woman; their teeth are disgusting."

I didn't say anything.

"They're from everywhere; the women here—they work. Cocktail
waitresses from all over." I glanced at her, quick and sharp, and she
laughed. "Well, you can't live so far away and not work."

"Unless you have Daddy," she added, in a softer voice, after she finished the last of her drink. She went to the bar right after that, brought
me a new drink, then she stood close to me, her shoulder grazing mine.
She said, "I think Dan wants me."

"Yeah?" I said, my voice purposely disinterested. I was reaching a
point with her where I couldn't be altogether nice. She was Celia and
Isabel's friend, and that was what kept me in check all along, even the first
night I met her. But now with each drink I finished, I felt more and more
as if I might say something, anything, just to show her momentarily that I
did not like her. She walked away from me shortly after that; I watched her
red dress, its A-line shape, move through the slight crowd toward Dan.

"Catherine," Paco shouted from a table. He was sitting by himself,
and he seemed to see me, just standing there, entranced by nothing. I
went over and sat across from him. He reached across the table and
pulled a strand of hair off my face.

"Where's Dan?" I asked, trying to ignore the fact that he had just
touched me.

He pointed and I nodded, looking past Paco at the people who were
standing near the pool and at the bar. It seemed as if there were more
people there now, but I realized it was just the music; it had gotten louder.

Paco was staring at me, and I was trying to act as if I didn't know,
but then I had to look at him, meet his eyes. He leaned over and said,
"You know what?" He touched me again, grazed his fingers over my
hand. "I think you are even more beautiful than Rachel Hunter." He
made circles with his fingers over my hand, my wrist, part of my arm.

I just stared at him—I thought I was going to throw up. He was so full of it, and the fact that he was looking at me with these wide-open, wistful eyes made it even worse. I took my hand away from him, rubbed my arms as if there were a sudden chill in the air. Then Monica came over. Her eyes were full of a gleam of her own, a drunken one. "Do you want to go with me to the bathroom?" she asked. She was leaning on a nearby chair as she spoke. I had been away from her for only five minutes, but she seemed incredibly drunk all of a sudden, as if she had done a series of shots by herself in the corner.

I said with great enthusiasm, "I'd love to go to the bathroom," and then I added, under my breath so that Monica could hear, "I want to get away from him."

As we walked into the house, I said, "Why aren't you talking to Dan?"

She said, "What do you mean? We're going to the bathroom. Why would I talk to Dan right now? I'm talking to you." Her tone was bitter, annoyed. She was letting loose, it appeared, and I followed her up the stairs, amused by that. It meant I could say whatever I wanted, too.

I followed her down a hallway and into a pink bedroom that had a small chandelier in it. I said, "Are we supposed to be up here?"

"It's a guest room; the bathroom is right here."

She opened a door and there it was: huge and two-roomed. The toilet was in one area and then around the corner, past a flowered beige rug, there was a sink along with a giant mirror. Monica went over to the mirror and began adjusting the lights so that it was dim.

"Where is this guy, Esteban?" I asked Monica from the toilet seat. She was around the corner doing her makeup. I could hear the clap of her compact open and shut.

"He went out. He throws parties and leaves, but then he comes back. He brings more people."

I said, "Oh."

After I flushed the toilet, I sat down in a wicker chair and watched Monica apply lip liner. It was dark red. I was tempted in my drunkenness to tell her a peachy color would be more flattering.

But then she turned to me, the lip liner still close to her face. "He wants to fuck you, you know?"

I wrinkled my forehead—I didn't like the word *fuck* when it referred to me. It was too harsh; it brought to mind the idea of someone knocking me out cold, dragging me somewhere. I said, "Who . . . wants to?"

She turned to me. "Who the hell do you think?" Her voice was getting nasty. It was a voice that seemed to have been waiting days, months, years to erupt, and now, here in this bathroom, it was bouncing off the cream-colored walls—and I got thrown by it somehow. I didn't know what to say to her. A part of me had been waiting to pick a fight with her, but now that it was actually happening I felt confused. I felt as if I had suddenly been dropped into this room, full of its coconut-scented soaps and softly lit mirrors. I could see my face in the mirror across from me—my eyes looked glassy and small, a smudge of brown eyeliner beneath them.

Still looking in the mirror, shaking my head, I said to Monica, "I don't know what you're talking about."

She stared at me a moment, arms folded, and then laughed a laugh that reminded me of this movie Harlan made me watch—one in which a crazy mom takes off all her clothes, laughs to herself on the couch, and then shoots everyone in the house with a white pistol. Monica picked up her eyeliner and made a mark, a line, on her palm. It was if she were suddenly alone in the room, without me.

While I was staring at her I came to believe, to falsely realize, that she was talking about Dan: Dan wanted me. Her anger made more sense to me that way. The fact that Dan didn't particularly like me made no difference to this assumption; in my mind, if he wanted me, that simply meant that he had decided I was the one to give him a quick jolt of fun-time feeling for the evening.

But then Monica screamed, "I'm talking about Paco! How can you act like you don't know! You know!"

Perhaps in retrospect she was not screaming, but because she had been so quiet, and the hum of the party had become so distant to us, her voice seemed loud and echoing.

I stood up from the wicker chair so that I was only a few feet from Monica, taller than her. I said defensively, "I don't like any of these fuckin' guys. None of them."

We started arguing more, but without really getting anywhere in terms of why we were both so angry. I told her she could have Paco if she wanted him, and she told me that wasn't it. She claimed it was the fact that I was acting as if I didn't know he wanted me. She was all fired up about how I was treating him "like some piece of shit."

She faced the mirror again and started putting her makeup back in her bag. When she was done, she said, "You won't fuck him, will you?"

"Of course not," I said hotly, and then stared at her, my mouth open.

She turned to me. "Why won't you fuck him? Why?"

It was then looking at her, at the coloring of her face, the severity to her eyes, that I realized what this argument was twistedly about. Dan would not sleep with *her*. He was ignoring *her*. And so instead of yelling at him, she was yelling at me, as if my rationale for not sleeping with Paco was Dan's rationale for not wanting her.

I said, "I don't just sleep with anyone."

"Why?" She shook her head the way you might when you are talking to someone who has done something very stupid. "It's not about falling in love," she said. "It's about feeling good. What's the matter, you won't let yourself feel good?"

Outside through the bathroom window, there was sudden sound of two or three people laughing so much they were coughing. Their amusement, their lightheartedness, bothered me right then—it seemed to accompany everything Monica was saying, making her momentarily right.

I knew, of course, that there was nothing wrong with not wanting Paco, but at the same time I knew that there was something inside of me, something different from other people, that kept me apart. Alone. Everyone else, it seemed, could run around and have sex with anyone, and it meant nothing—it never touched on any sense of intimacy or sensitivity, it was simply an action. But I was not like that. To me, sex was almost the very definition of intimacy—because, no matter how drunken or lackluster, you were still alone in a small room, in a small bed, in a small square of space, letting someone touch you and look at you in a deliberate way.

Perhaps that was one of the many problems with me: my mind was a part of my body, my body a part of my mind. I could not get them to disconnect.

"What happened? Did someone break your heart?" Monica asked. Her tone was spiteful, mocking, as that question so often has to be. She was standing near the window, a few feet from the mirror, her hand on the peach-colored curtain. She was looking straight at me, a slight bitter twist to her face, the lip liner evil against her pale uncolored lips. She said, "Did your Coca-Cola daddy not love you enough?"

There was a brief pause, and then I slapped her. It was quick, instinctive, like catching a ball that was hurled at me. Immediately afterward she turned from me, temporarily afraid of me, but I didn't feel any sense of regret. It was not my fault—it was her, it was the size of the room. If we had not been in a bathroom, if we had been in the living room, or outside, I was sure I would have contained myself.

She took two steps over to the sink, to the mirror. With her back to me, she picked up her makeup bag, zipped and unzipped it. She said sullenly, as if she felt regretful, "So someone did break your heart."

I didn't answer her. I didn't have to. I just stared back at her in the mirror, watching her rub the side of her face.

$$\overline{3}$$

SQUEAKY

At the hospital, after my father hit my mother with the brick, they separated me from him, told me I had to wait in another room that was special, only for children. It was a small white room with six upholstered chairs, a cutout of a Hispanic boy eating an apple on the wall. There were stacks of *Highlights* magazines on the floor, but they were all torn up and old, staple-less. I didn't read any of the magazines. Instead I put my legs up on a neighboring chair—I felt tired suddenly, as if I could fall asleep anywhere: on the carpet, on a bench outside, on the pavement in the parking lot.

A social worker came in to talk to me just as I was about to dream. She had glasses on, and there was a slight crack in the right lens. She asked me almost immediately after she told me her name—it was Donna—if my father ever hit me. Did he scare me? Did he ever do things that made me sad? Uncomfortable?

I said, "No."

"Do you like him when he drinks?"

I said, "Yes."

"You do?"

"Yes."

"Does he ever break things when he's drunk?"

I shook my head no. If I had been talking to someone else, someone I trusted, I might've told her that he did break things sometimes. Stupid things. Knickknacks, radios, cordless phones. He dropped them to the ground with a crash. Afterward, though, he came back to normal. He cleaned things up. In the case of the radio, he crawled under the kitchen table and picked up all the scattered AA batteries that were lying on the floor. He held them in his hand for hours, all six of them, as if they were a reminder that he needed to calm down.

The social worker asked me, "Are you afraid to tell me the truth, Catherine?"

I didn't answer.

She said, "If you want, you can just nod at my questions."

I stared at her for a moment, and then I said, with a forcefulness that seemed to disturb her, "I'm not afraid of anyone."

My mother did not divorce my father; he divorced her. The process took a while. First he moved out, into a motel across town called the Capri. There was a coconut on the sign, and long fernlike leaves that were supposed to look tropical. The sign always said vacancy and the "CO" in the amenity color TV was missing, scratched out.

My Auntie Joy, my father's sister, brought me to see my father at the Capri once. She didn't go in, she just dropped me off in front of the little aqua door that was marked number eight. She waited in her big red Chevrolet for my father to come to the door. When he opened the door, he was in just a towel. He waved at my Auntie Joy, and then I turned to see what she did back. She nodded; she had a very serious pink face. She waved.

On the car ride over, my aunt had told me that I should not be mad at my father.

"I don't know what you mean," I said, shaking my head. "I'm not."

She nodded. "Just checking."

My mother was not entirely angry with my father either. The first morning after the fight, she sat on the edge of my bed talking to me about it for over an hour. It was very early morning—the sky was gray, and my bedroom walls appeared a deeper, darker blue. When I first woke up, we just sat there quietly, as if neither one of us was in the room; then my mother said, her voice soft, careful, "I want you to know that it's OK to be upset with your father. I am, too."

I just blinked back at her. I was paying more attention to the bandage above her eye rather than what she was saying. It stretched across the left side of her forehead in a neat square. The only thing that made her look particularly strange was that some of the surgical tape cut across her left eyebrow, and it seemed to do something to her eye, make it twitch.

"It wasn't really him, you know, that acted like that," she said, and then cleared her throat—from her voice I could tell her nose was stuffed up. She was not crying though. "Your dad has a problem," she said, "something that makes him different from other people." She paused for a moment, touched the top of my pink bed frame, and then she stared at me as if she thought I might volunteer my own opinion on what his problem was, but I couldn't, I had no opinion. He was my father, and at the time that meant no matter what he did, it wasn't bad, it wasn't wrong—it was simply something that happened. Like a sudden thunderstorm or a long drizzling rain.

I said, "When is he coming back?"

My mother looked down at my blanket, traced the shape of a flower petal with her finger. She said, looking above me, at the wall, "As soon as we can get him to."

On that first day that I went to visit him at the Capri, my mother paid careful attention to how I looked. She blew-dry my hair herself, parting it perfectly in the middle, and then she sprayed my hair not just with hair spray, but also with a violet-scented perfume. She even let me wear a necklace of hers that I normally wasn't allowed ever to touch. My clothes, however, were casual, a T-shirt and a freshly ironed skirt. Everything that day—even what we had for breakfast, yogurt with cantaloupe—seemed to be about primping myself for him. It was as if my mother wanted my father to see all the beauty he had left behind—she wanted him to fall apart once he laid eyes upon me, right in the doorway of his motel room.

He didn't though. He just kissed me and then I followed him into the room. It had two double beds—both beds were unmade, newspaper sheets scattered all over one of them. Budweiser cans were on the nightstand, one of them dented and lying on its side. The room was the epitome of what I would later see on television as the destroyed man's hideaway: pizza boxes on the floor, a suitcase on the kitchenette table, socks and shirt sleeves hanging out of it, a pillowcase with a burn hole hanging over the lamp shade.

"Do you think I'm getting fat?" my father asked me. He was standing there in his towel, his bare chest barrel-like and hairy. My father was forever known for his vanity—he was particularly obsessed with his body hair. Every morning he used my mother's Maybelline mascara to cover a few premature gray hairs that had appeared in his sideburns. He never tweezed them—he was afraid they would come back longer, thicker, more noticeable. His chest hair was the worst though. When I was five or six I asked him how come he didn't have a hairless chest like the men in the TV commercials. He patted my head and said, "I think it's time you knew, Squeaky. I wasn't always a man. I was once a bear."

In his motel room, I played with his electric razor while I waited for him to get off the phone, someone from work called shortly after I arrived. I took the razor off the top of the TV and kept turning it on and off. He waved for me to turn it off, to put it down, but I ignored him. I shaved the bedspread, made little circles over its mustard colored flowers.

When he got off the phone, we went to the motel's bar—it was called the Leisure Lounge. It was a small square room that was very bright in comparison to the Blue Lagoon. The afternoon sun came through the pink curtains, hit the wooden tables, and made triangular shapes on the green carpet. There was no one there except a woman smoking cigarettes and doing a crossword puzzle, her face very close, very intent on the folded newspaper page.

My father said to me, getting off the barstool and putting his arms out, "Are you sure I'm not getting fat?"

I said, "I told you, you just look a little white is all."

He pulled up his shirt, started at his stomach. Black hair was all around his belly button. He said, "I think its the hair, it's adding weight to my body."

I shrugged. "That could be it."

The bartender looked up at us, smiled. He asked me if I wanted another cherry in my Rob Roy, and I said no. It was really a Roy Rogers, Coca-Cola with grenadine, but he must have heard my father refer to it as my Rob Roy (a Manhattan with scotch). "Are you enjoying your Rob Roy? Is it strong enough?"

Once in the Blue Lagoon, the bartender, Renee, had even served my "Rob Roy" in a martini glass, but she did it only once. She refused to after that. She said it looked weird.

My father said, "What do you mean weird?"

She shook her head, her long, beaded earrings slapping the sides of her face. "It's not right."

My father laughed. "She likes it. Come on, don't be a jerk."

Renee just walked away. She said over her shoulder, "You're so fucked up, James." That was my father's name, James.

"Fine," my father said, looking over at me—I was in front of the aquarium, tracing the fish with my finger against the glass. "Maybe we'll have to start going somewhere else," he said. "To another lagoon, one where a seven-year-old lady can drink her martini in peace."

Compared to our afternoons at the Blue Lagoon, my father wasn't as boisterous at the Leisure Lounge, and neither was I. We didn't bother the bartender or play any games or try to talk to the lady doing the crossword puzzle. We didn't talk at all really. There was no discussion of why he hit my mother, or why Auntie Joy moved in and he moved out. He didn't ask me why I squeaked on him, and I didn't tell him about the money my mother found in my shorts. We were silent, and I couldn't help but feel sitting in that empty bar full of its loud brightness that that silence meant something. My father didn't want to be my father anymore. I could feel it.

He told me he was leaving two weeks later in IHOP. I don't remember exactly how he worded it, but I do remember listening, taking a sip of warm orange juice, and then breaking my burnt bacon into little pieces with my fork. He said he was going to take another job for Coca-Cola in Maine. He told me the apartment he had picked out was small, but it was on the water and it was cheap in the winter.

"You remember Rye Beach," he said. "We've been there before."

I said no, I didn't remember—although I did have a very clear memory of lying on a plaid blanket with him, a sunburn on the back of my knees. My mother wore a pink bikini—she was the type of mother who could wear a bikini—and I remembered that when she was asleep, her face against the blanket, my father kept rubbing lotion on her back, meticulously, slowly, in a way that was calming to watch.

"What do you mean you don't remember Rye Beach?" my father said, his voice a little bit loud, a little bit accusing, as if he believed that place evoked one of the most beautiful memories of our lives.

"I remember the sand," I said, and frowned. The sand had been the kind that was painful to walk on, little sharp-edged shells everywhere. "I hated the sand."

He wiped his mouth with his napkin and said, annoyed, "You're just like your mother. You don't know how to remember things."

After that we were quiet. Talking about Rye Beach was the closest we came to an argument, to a moment of tension. In our silence, we looked around the restaurant awkwardly, the way that strangers do on a date. I kept glancing at an elderly couple that was sitting across from us; the woman was counting change for the check out of a beaded wallet. In my head, I counted the quarters and nickels with her.

"I'll send money though," my father told me later when we were in the car, leaving IHOP. He was lying. "I'll send money for you and your mom," he said. "Nothing will be different; you'll live the same."

I nodded without looking at him.

In the passenger seat of the car, there were still loose staples all over the place from our car ride to the emergency room a few weeks before. I picked the staples up one by one and bent them so that they were straight. I had a pile of them on my lap, and I kept doing this, a little feverishly, as we drove toward my house. It was as if I believed that if I got enough of the staples undone, the whole experience would come undone: My father would move back in, Auntie Joy would move out, and my mother would come out of her bedroom sharply dressed and smiling.

When we pulled into the driveway of our house, I handed him all of the staples I had made as straight as pins, and he stared at them quizzically. Then he reached down beneath the seat and said, "And I have something for you." He handed me a piece of paper that was a ripped section of a paper tablecloth that we had taken from an Italian restaurant about six months before. On it, in crayon and in his handwriting it said:

Squeaky is:

Spider-loving
Queenish in appearance
Unbearably swank
Evil when she is hungry and tired and in the car too long
Antler-free
Kooky
Y-shaped (when sleeping)

I took the list, stared at it. Then I put my hand on the door, opened it a crack, and waited for him to do something, to say something important, something that I could think about all day. Instead he kissed me on the cheek and said in my ear, a little too softly, "Love ya, darlin'."

At first, he did not completely disappear. There were trips to Maine promised. Isolated phone calls in which my mother spoke to him for only a minute and then she stared at me as I spoke to him—a certain intensity in her eyes, as if she was trying to send some sort of energy through me to him. There were four of those phone calls. All of them happened in the late evening, I was in pajamas, sometimes already in bed, my mother was watching television, a glass of red wine in her hand.

Later in my life when he no longer called, those phone calls became evil, strange, unwarranted. Birthday cards were still sent, but as I got older, fifteen, sixteen, I expected the cards to stop coming, and when that white envelope with his thin sloped penmanship did come, it made me feel worse—in my mind, if he had the capacity to send these cards, he also, if he wanted, could make other efforts, but he didn't.

If I had been more mild tempered, I suppose I would have made extra efforts of my own to reach him, to call him. I had his telephone number and his birthday cards had a PO box return address, but I never bothered. I did call his house on occasion and hang up. His voice, the sound of his cool ease as he said leave a message, angered me. It made me sharply aware that he was fully conscious, moving around and living, yet he felt nothing for me—I was unimportant, forgettable.

One month my mother noticed on the phone bill that I had called his number a few times. She could tell from the time durations listed that I had hung up. She said, "Honey, you can leave a message if you want. You can say hi."

I was nine at the time, and I was embarrassed that I had been caught. At first, I didn't answer her, I pretended to be watching TV, but then the thought came over me that she was telling me to leave a message because she was afraid to leave one herself. She wanted me to be the one whom he never called back, the one who got ignored. I said hotly, "If you want to call him, call him yourself."

My mother didn't say anything. She was sitting across from me in the living-room chair, looking down at the phone bill on her lap.

I said louder, "Why don't you leave a message?"

"All right, stop it," she said, and looked at me sharply, her eyes glassy.

I shrugged my shoulders and said under my breath, "No, *you* stop it."

Often I caught my mother dreaming of him. Once I saw her in her bedroom sitting on the edge of her bed in a pink cotton nightgown, gazing into the mirror above her bureau. She had in her hands a hat of my father's; it was plaid, a golfer's cap. She put it on and stared at herself for so long that it made me uncomfortable to watch. I was standing in the hallway peering in, staring at her and all her frail paleness. Her wavy brown hair looked a little disheveled, as if she had tried to sleep and then woken up, and her nightgown was unbuttoned, the slight curve of her breasts visible. And then she had that hat on her head. A hat I guessed from the distance smelled like him, like a mix of the hair spray he used, Aqua Net, and his cologne, a sandalwood musk. I stood there watching her watch herself: She let out not a single blink in the mirror. There was just the faint pinkish light that her night lamp emitted, and then what seemed like a drumming waiting before she took the hat off, put it in a drawer that was already open. There was no crying, no dramatic gesture made—she was quiet, still.

I dreamed about him, too, but I can't even describe those dreams because they went on for so many years in so many places that I can't quite say what exactly they were about. The only aspect that united those fantasies was that he showed up, he came to relieve me. He'd sit on the edge of my bed and tell me concretely why he left. He was always drunk in these dreams, and he was almost always on the edge of my bed. Sometimes he sat on the floor, his chin resting on the mattress; other times he was right there, sitting upright, a pint of Jameson's next to him. In the darkness, I could hear the swish of the whiskey as he put to his lips, as he said, "I didn't really leave you. I could never . . ."

This went on for years, a jagged, heated need. I wanted to give him a good reason for leaving, a why. My mother had explained to me long ago that he left us because he loved us—she believed this. She said that he was afraid of himself and his drinking and the anger, which his drinking brought on. But this rationale was something I never quite understood, seeing that my father had rarely ever been the type of drunk who got angry. He certainly never hit me, never hit my mother (with the exception of that one summer night). He did throw things, he broke an occasional knickknack, but then he made a joke out of it. He'd laugh. Once when he broke a ceramic Easter bunny, he kept saying over and over, "I broke the bunny, honey. Can you believe I broke the bunny?"

I leaned over the side of the couch, stared at him. I wasn't afraid of him. These broken knickknacks weren't ever experienced as violence— they were unpleasant noises, irritations.

"The bunny can be fixed though," he told me, standing above the ceramic mess, a beer in his hand. "He'll have a few fissures in his skull." My father enjoyed using words I didn't know. "But every good skull, every good bunny, has a few fissures."

I nodded, acted as if I knew what he was talking about. Then I got up to help him clean up the bunny. I'd even told him, "I never liked that bunny anyway."

Yet such episodes my mother insisted, in retrospect, were snippets of the volatility that lurked inside of my father. Beneath all the jokes and fun, she claimed, there was something uncontrollable and dark, some-thing someone else instilled inside of him.

A few months after my father moved to Maine, my mother tried to explain all of this to me. We were driving late at night, coming home from a Christmas party. There was no snow outside, but against the headlights the road's black pavement looked wet. We had the heater on too high, to the point that it nauseated me. My mother probably would've noticed the uncomfortable heat, but she was lost on a plane of thought where she could make the car take its necessary turns and stops; yet she herself was far, far away.

Once we stopped at a red light, once her foot hit the brake, she looked at me sideways and said, "Your father left his house when he was only sixteen. Did he ever tell you that?"

I said no.

"Yeah," she said softly. "He didn't get along with his father." She paused, took a right-hand turn. A soda can beneath the seat rolled out against my foot. "Your dad's dad used to hit him," my mother said. "He used to pick your father right off the ground by his hair." She glanced at me. "He used to make jokes about it all the time, your father. He'd say that that was why he was so hairy. Because his father pulled every hair in his head out and so it grew in even thicker and stronger everywhere else."

My mother went on to describe other things my father's father did to him: He threw food at him at the table—once a steaming piece of broccoli burnt his chin; he purposely pulled my father's finger out of its socket; he dumped a beer over my father's head in a restaurant.

Yet as I listened to these stories over and over, my mother always emphasized that my father was not the only one in his family to be hit. My grandfather beat my grandmother on a regular basis, sometimes monthly, sometimes weekly, but in any case he always "aimed for the eyes." As a consequence, my grandmother often wore big round Jackie-O sunglasses wherever she went, even to do simple tasks like go to the mailbox or pay the paperboy.

"And she wore these blue and green floral scarves," my mother told me in the car that night. "She tied the scarves around her head or neck depending on where there were . . ." My mother paused, frowned, "depending on where the marks were."

Originally when my mother first told me all of this, I tried to understand what she wanted it to mean, but it was hard. I had never met my grandparents; they died before I was born, and so I couldn't picture them. I also had difficulty thinking of my six-foot father as someone whom another person could pick up by his hair. The only detail that rang inside of me, made me make a rather adult-minded connection, was the flowered scarves. Once when I had slept at my Auntie Joy's, she let me put a pale shade of purple lipstick on and then she gave me a lilac scarf of hers to tie around my neck. When my father came to pick me up, when I got in the car, he said sharply, "What is that around your neck?"

I said, "Auntie Joy gave it to me. Isn't it pretty?"

He put his hand behind my headrest, backed the car in reverse out of the driveway, and then he said without any humorous lilt to his voice, "Take that thing off." I stared him. "Just take it off."

He waited, wouldn't start driving until I had unraveled it from around my neck. I folded it in a perfect square and put it in my coat pocket. Then I had stared out the window, away from him—uncertain as to why I felt so sick inside.

I thought of all of this that night in the car as I sat silently next to my mother, listening to her talk and talk about my father. The whole time I didn't say a word; I just nodded, let her know in my own distant, tired way that I was trying to pay attention. In front of us there was a car that swerved a little; it kept speeding up, then slowing down. My mother was getting aggravated. She beeped at the car, and then she said, her voice hostile, "Speaking of your father."

I sat up, in my childish sleepiness I misunderstood; I thought she meant that he was in the car in front of us, but then when we took a left down our street, the swerving car kept going, moving farther and farther away.

When we finally got to our house, pulled into the driveway, my mother waited a minute before pulling her keys out of the ignition. Everything we did at that point seemed to be in slow motion. She looked over me appraisingly—I hadn't opened the car door yet, I was just sitting there, looking blankly in front of me and blinking.

"Wherever he is, he misses us," my mother said. She put her hands through the top of my hair, which was snarled and tangled from the day. "He misses us just as hard as you miss him." She smiled at me weakly. "You have to try and remember that."

$$4$$

MEET ESTEBAN

After I slapped Monica in the face, I walked out of the bathroom while she was still in front of the mirror staring at her cheek. When I got downstairs, I stood by myself in the empty living room. It was a big airy white room with high ceilings and a fireplace that did not appear to work as there was a mirror set inside of it. In the corner, there was a hookah pipe—big and brass with mauve tubes—and above that on a shelf sat a set of different-shaped teapots that were all Arabic-looking, made from a coppery metal. The entire room had that coldness, that modern whiteness, with only a few hints of color, all some sort of brass or gold-colored metal. Even the rug on the floor was this fluffy mass of white that I didn't dare step on—it looked as if it was made out of real rabbit hair.

While I was standing there staring at everything, a woman in a backless sundress came into the room, heading toward another part of the house. She smiled at me, and I turned and looked at the bookshelf, pretending to read the many book titles on the shelves in front of me. I didn't want to be around anyone else yet; I wanted my adrenaline to settle down. I couldn't seem to calm myself though—I was still thinking of Monica and how quick I was to dislike her. It seemed to me at that moment that I lived my life always being quick about how I felt about things, and then I took it to the extreme. I either immediately loved you with a sudden violence or I despised you—all within a few moments after I met you. I evaluated people constantly, mechanically, and my feelers, the way in which I weighed things, was always governed by emotions and sensitivities as well as any random thing that initially struck me.

"Are you the American? *¿La americana perfecta? ¿La americana guapisima?*" this man called out to me—he was standing in the doorway between the patio, where everyone else was, and the living room. He was wearing these loose-fitting black pants, which were wide at the bottom like pajamas, and flip-flops. He was about forty; his nose was hooked from the side, birdlike, and his skin was slightly unshaven above his lip. He was leaning one hand against the wall—in the other hand he held a drink. His arms were hairy.

He said something else to me, but it was in Spanish and the music playing outside had gotten louder, speedier, and I couldn't hear him. With my forehead wrinkled, I just stared at him. He smiled and started to come closer, and as I waited for his approach, I noticed that the shirt he was wearing was buttoned one button too high—as if to hide what he did not want to show: more black hair.

"I have been looking for you everywhere," he said in English as he took my hand, kissed it. His accent was British, but not quite British, Irish almost, yet it still maintained a lilt of Spanish to it—he pronounced "looking" strangely.

Because I was drunk, and feeling a bit emotional, I said in a not-so-friendly way, "*¿Quién eres?*" Who are you?

He smiled at me. He had dimples. He said, "Esteban," and then waved his hand in the air dramatically. "Your host."

It was then, in that one gesture, that there was something so clearly identifiable, something coupled with the elegant way he moved his shoulders when he walked, which told me exactly what I needed to know: Esteban was gay.

"Monica told me she would bring you." He smiled, wide and happy, revealing one tooth that was a bit shorter than the other, as if it had once been broken or cracked. "Actually," he said, still grinning, "I demanded she bring you."

"Why?"

"Because you are lovely, just lovely."

He was like Harlan all of a sudden—saying things for the grandeur of their meaning, for its sheer entertainment, as opposed to actually answering the question.

"Why don't we sit out on the patio?" he said, motioning toward the sliding glass doors. "And I'll get you another drink."

I nodded, and we went outside to one of the tables. He pulled my chair out for me—it made a scratching sound against the cement. He was tall and thin, and the very act of picking up the heavy wrought-iron chair with his drinkless hand seemed to take a quite a bit of force.

After I sat down, he said, "What do you want to take?"

I told him a whiskey and Coke, but he ended up bringing me back a whiskey and soda. I didn't say anything.

As he sat down, he said, "You're from Boston; you were born there?"

I told him I grew up in Palmer, a town about an hour away from Boston. He asked me about its size, about what it was like there, how many McDonald's did it have?

"Sounds like a flashy place," he said, and I nodded, said, "*Sí, sí.*"

As we continued talking, I looked behind Esteban for Monica. I could not find her. I couldn't see Dan or Paco either. It was only then, sitting there, listening to a song that was slower than the others, calming, that I realized that she had probably left me there at that party. And who could blame her? I had slapped her—I didn't even know her, and I slapped her. I was in a foreign country, I knew no one, and I was walking around getting mad at people. And with Monica, it was over what?

Over my father, over something so small and distant, something I should've gotten over a long time ago.

Esteban was staring at me; he seemed to see that I was drifting off somewhere. He said with the intention of amusing me, or at least distracting me, "But you were the prettiest girl in Palmer?"

"No."

"No? You mean there were other pretty girls in McDonald's?"

"Many."

"Ones who look like Rachel Hunter?"

"She told *you* that, too."

He laughed a little, and said, "You don't look anything like Rachel Hunter—she's a bumpkin."

I shook my head, smiling. "I don't think you know what bumpkin really means."

"Actually," he paused, "I don't. I just like the way it sounds." He was also smiling. He had two kinds of smiles: one that was a full lip-curling one and another in which his lips were straight, but his face, his eyes, had a certain warmth—it was like when you look at a cat and you can tell without hearing his purr that he is content.

"OK," he said, "so *dime*. What is a bumpkin?"

I paused—there is nothing worse than not knowing what a word means in your own language. I said, "It's like . . . I don't know, a person who doesn't know how to act right, a person from the country."

He took a sip of his drink, swallowed. "Then would being from Palmer make you a bumpkin?" He was not being an ass, he was making a joke, and there was something about his banter, his wit, that set me at ease, made me like him.

I said, "Yeah, I think so."

He nodded, pleased with that, and then he said, "I like the word 'pumpkin,' too."

Shortly afterward, the music went off. Esteban turned in his seat, looked over at the butler behind the bar. The sixteen-year-old boy who seemed to be the butler's helper was in the process of picking up dirty glasses on a nearby table. Once the butler looked at the boy, and the boy looked at Esteban, he put the glasses down all in a rush and went into the house. Within a minute or two, another song came on. It was loud and full of guitars.

"What do you do?" I asked Esteban. I wanted to know how he got the big house and the butler and the boy. How people got rich always fascinated me—and not because I necessarily wanted to get rich. I was actually one of the few people in this world who was a little afraid of it. In my mind, too much wealth meant having a damaging amount of idle time. It meant a life free of work, free of distraction, a life where you just had to sit there and deal with yourself and all the selfish things you still pined for, still dreamed of.

"I have a house in Venezuela, in Caracas. I own a newspaper out there, but I do business here, too."

He went on to tell me that he lived half the year in Caracas, half in Madrid. He had studied English in Donington and London, and had lived for a few years in Miami—hence the perfect grammar and the weird accent. I nodded. I wanted him just to keep talking and talking, otherwise I would realize what a strange, uncomfortable position I was in. I was alone, stranded at this party.

A few minutes later, though, I saw Monica; she was still there, and she was coming over toward us. Once I caught a glimpse of her approaching, I looked down at the table, at the candle flickering in front of me. She leaned against the back of Esteban's chair and he reached back behind him, touched her hand—as if that was all he needed to identify a person, a hand.

She said to me, "We're going to Arci soon."

"Arci is a club," Esteban said, as if he had read the slight questioning arch of my eyebrow.

"It will be fun," Monica said, and smiled at me as if nothing had happened between us, as if all of that could be forgotten. We just had to pretend. We just had to smile. Drink some more, perhaps.

"I'll drive with Dan, you with Paco."

I looked behind her, as if I planned on seeing the two of them waiting, their arms crossed. But they weren't there.

"They're at the cars," she said.

I nodded but made no effort to get up. I was all of a sudden upset that Monica hadn't, in fact, left me. This night seemed to have gone on and on, and I wanted it to end.

Esteban said, "If you don't want to go to Arci—if you're tired, I can give you a ride home."

Monica just stared at me, one hand still holding Esteban's hand. I couldn't entirely tell what she wanted me to do, but it seemed in that moment, behind her still face, that she fully expected to leave me with Esteban. So I nodded at that, as if I was relieving her, and yawned. I said, not looking at either of them, "I think I just want to go home."

Esteban's car was a red Porsche. The interior was black leather, and if I put my hand on anything it left a sweaty imprint. We drove with the top down, with the warm wind in our faces. We both had a drink, half full so that it wouldn't spill. "For conversational purposes," Esteban had said when he first handed me the drink on his front steps where I had been waiting for him for more than twenty minutes. He was supposed to have been looking for his keys, but I think he was just talking to people—I could hear his voice even from the front of the house, loud and animated. I sat down on the steps, beneath the double-diamond windows of his house, staring at the azaleas and the blue violets of his garden, at the mosquitoes in the lamp light, and then over at the race-car Porsche and I wondered how the hell had I gotten myself here, how was I going to get home?

When Esteban came back though, he was normal and composed, sober in appearance. Once I got in the car, however, and noticed how close my face was to the windshield, I said, "You better not crash."

He waved his finger at me, in a "tsk tsk" manner, and said, "I never crash, Catherine. Never."

I put on my seat belt anyway, and he fiddled with his drink. First he put it between his legs, then he put on the console. Once he started the car, he looked back at the drink, took a sip, and put it between his legs again.

Watching him, I said, "I hope it wasn't too annoying to have to leave your own party."

"I always leave my parties," he said, and smiled. "I have to."

We pulled out of the driveway and then passed a number of darkened yards that were fenced in by high leafy green shrubs. There were only lights, lamps in the driveways, which made it clear that one yard had ended and another begun. Esteban stopped in the middle of the street, adjusted the radio, and then he said, "Sometimes I think I throw parties just to remind myself why I live alone."

Even though he was just kidding, I nodded back at him, my face serious. I was very tired all of a sudden. I turned my face away from Esteban and let my eyes close just a little, just for a minute.

"You don't like Monica, do you?" he said after waiting a few minutes, perhaps giving me time to rest.

I opened my eyes. "Why do you say that?"

"I don't know," he said, shrugging his shoulders. He was shouting a little. We had just turned onto the highway, passing a single car here or there. Above us the white signs with blue trim read: ZARAGOZA, BURGOS, CALLE CORAZÓN DE MARIA.

"So aren't you going to tell me why you don't like Monica?" He asked, pressing a button as he said this so the windows would roll up and we could hear each other better. He turned the radio down, too.

I said, "I got upset with her earlier. That's all." I shrugged my shoulders and then looked over at him, at his side profile. He had his mouth slightly open, which gave him the look that he was concentrating very hard. It occurred to me then that he was definitely too drunk to be driving. But he was staying in the lines of the road, and if he was speeding, it didn't seem so.

After a few minutes I said, "Do you know Monica well?"

He nodded. He said he had known her for years, met her at a party, and now she came over a lot to his house, used his pool. "She has her own pool at her own house," he explained, "but she uses mine."

"Why?" I said. "Is your pool better than hers?"

"Yes." He sipped his drink. "My pool usually has people in it."

I watched him take another sip of his drink, spilling some of it on himself. He wiped at his shirt—it was gray silk with little square mother of pearl buttons on it. A shirt he told me he wore often. It was his lucky shirt. His *camisa fabulosa.*

"Monica has a lot of trouble," Esteban continued again, as if he had momentarily forgotten what he had been talking about. "People don't ever like her and"—he shrugged his shoulders—"I don't think it's her fault."

"Why's that?"

"Well . . . her mother died; she was very sick for a long time; and her father—he isn't the best person. He isn't the nicest."

I shook my head. "I don't believe in that. I don't believe that just because bad things have happened to you, you have the right to walk around and be awful."

"I didn't say she has the right. I'm just telling you who she is."

"Still," I said, "she doesn't *have* to be such an ass."

"No, but she certainly has had help." In his tone, I realized we were arguing. I suppose I was the one who started it, who got all fiery. But I wasn't really arguing with him so much about Monica as I was about myself. It was one of my greatest peeves: That stupid belief that your parents, and what happened to you as a kid, controlled who you were. It was as if you yourself had no choice, no say, in what you became. The world just made you into whatever it wanted. And I hated that idea because I wanted a say, I wanted choice. I wanted to be responsible for everything I did, even the bad things, even losing my temper, or yelling at someone, or hurting them. It was me. Not anyone else.

I looked out the window. We were passing La Puerta de Alcalá, the entrance to Madrid—it was a giant set of columns with three archways in the middle and two smaller rectangular openings, one on each end. Limestone angels sat perched on the top of the columns like birds. I stared at the angels, counted them.

For the rest of the ride through the brightly lit streets called Alcalá and Gran Vía and San Vincente, we discussed nothing else, I just told him what street I lived on, what number. When we got to my building, I didn't even know we were there, not until I saw Raúl's store, a neon Coca-Cola sign in the window.

"I hope you're not mad at me," Esteban said once he stopped the car.

I shrugged. "I'm not. Are you mad at me?"

"Of course not." As he said this, he leaned over and opened the glove compartment, handed me a card. It had his name on it in gray italics along with two addresses, one in Moreleja and another in Madrid. The Madrid address appeared to be an office, it had a fax number and three phone lines. There was no business name though, no professional title.

He said, "Call me," as I stared at the card.

I nodded. I said, "OK." I opened the car door, emptied my untouched drink on the pavement, and then put the glass under the seat where it wouldn't break. As I did this, Esteban just stared at me in this strange way, as if he thought I was doing something sad.

In this voice that was a bit soft, a bit serious, he said, "All I was trying to tell you about Monica was one thing: She's lonely."

I didn't know what he wanted me to say to that. I nodded, got out of the car.

He took the last sip of his drink, looked down into the glass, and then up at me. "And you should always be nice to the lonely."

I had my hand still on the car door. I said, "Why is that?"

He shrugged his shoulders, smiled. "Because, my dear . . . they are just like you."

5

TRICYCLICLY SPEAKING

My mother was an expert in the field of magazine article psychology. She read *Self* and *Woman's Day* and *Cosmopolitan* and *Redbook*. She scanned through Dear Abbie and Dear Meg as well as any sections entitled "What Do I Do with Myself?" or, better yet, "Agony Column." Through her readings, my mother could pinpoint in any conversation I had with her exactly what was wrong with me. It was easy though, seeing that all of my troubles, according to her, were rooted to one particular thing: my abandonment complex.

She claimed I had a fear that I would maintain for the rest of my life, of being left behind, ignored. That's why I couldn't hold down a real relationship with a boy—because I was afraid. And through this wonderful never-ending stream of fearfulness and fright, I unconsciously picked men who I knew would never ever stay with me long term; that way I wouldn't get hurt. "Well," my mother added, "not as deeply as if you had a *real* relationship with a man."

By the same token, she claimed I also was madly attracted to the type of man who would abandon me. I adored them more than any other kind because once they left me, I could ruminate about them, dream and dream, the way I had as a child about my father—I'd give them reasons for leaving me, create a perfect romantic picture of why they really loved me, why they tragically felt they could not stay. "In this state, you're the most comfortable," my mother told me. "It's home to you; it's how you grew up."

When she said these things, usually on the phone, I'd move the phone away from my ear. I'd read my mail. I'd clean out the refrigerator. I'd mouth to Harlan, "My mother's crazy."

He'd mouth back, "So are you," sitting at the kitchen table smoking a cigarette, smiling. "It's inescapable," he'd say, and I'd smirk back at him as my mother's voice kept going and going, tracking not only my interpersonal problems but my behavioral problems. She'd explain why I worked so hard, why I pushed myself, why everything in my life had this desperate urgency.

"Because you're angry at him, vengeful," my mother had told me once. "It's like all you want to do is show your father that he had no right to ignore you, to leave you like that." This was one of the few times that I stopped what I was doing and listened. I was not in the kitchen that time; I was in my bed, lying on my back, an open book on my chest.

"You want to prove to your father," my mother said, "to all of the men who think they can just leave you that you aren't some worthless thing." I stared up at the ceiling as she said this, at the yellow, discolored stain near the brick wall. My curtain, which was thin and beige, like a veil, blew up out of the window.

My mother kept talking. She said, "Everything you do—all that working, all that worrying—is all in an effort to make them know, make them see, that you are so much more than what they ever thought. More than they ever dreamed."

The first guy I ever slept with was Rick, my manager at Shooters. He was thirty. He was tall and thin with eyes that seemed brown from a distance, but were green up close. He hired me once he met me, without looking at my application—he just folded it in half and asked me how many days I could work.

"Five or six," I said.

"Don't you go to school?"

I nodded. "But I have to work. As much as I can."

That was my freshman year at BU, and my mother had paid for the first semester, tuition as well as room and board, but she had already told me that she didn't know what would happen after that. She said she would try to work it out, try to "borrow" some money from Gerry—but I heard in her voice the same uncertainty that I often heard when I was a kid living alone with her, waiting for the phone to be turned back on or for the cable box to be returned. Yet my mother gave me all that she could that semester, as if it were nothing, as if it were money she never wanted to see again; but, of course, I understood that she had some secret hope that a miracle would come about once I got to Boston, once I landed in that great city of intelligence.

Perhaps when I first met Rick that's what he saw in my face—that urgency not to disappoint anyone, that edgy need to make the money my mother had invested in me worthwhile. I stood before him in a grown-up maroon blazer, high heels, and a black skirt—all of which I hoped would convey that I was hardworking and responsible, the type of person who would do anything, work any night, no matter what.

I started work the day after my interview. Rick gave me a tour of Shooters before my shift. He showed me the kitchen window where I would pick up my orders. He introduced me to the Haitian cook. The kitchen window was in the game room, a narrow green-carpeted area with pinball machines and video games lined against the walls. Rick brought me through the main floor, walked with me between aisles and aisles of pool tables. He showed me the two dark wooden bars with their shiny brass light fixtures, each on opposite sides of the room. Next to the bigger bar, "the main bar," I watched him open a green marbled cabinet that held trays and check pads and credit card slips. Rick showed me each of these items and then explained how the sections were divided amongst the waitresses—with a pencil he made a chart. Throughout all of this, I did not make much eye contact with him. He was wearing a suit and a tie. The tie had red and white stripes like a candy cane—something that would've looked awful on anyone else, but not on him.

As I walked through Shooters following Rick from place to place, he made me more and more nervous—and it was not because he was older, or because he was my new boss. It was something else, something about the way he jiggled his keys in his pocket and put his hands through his hair and walked. It was in the way he waited for me to nod when he showed me something and then smiled, not looking directly at me but at something else far away, distant. This nervousness I felt was not necessarily one of discomfort either; it was somewhat giddy, the fluttering feeling of desire.

He told me I did not have to keep my coat in the room where the other girls kept their things. He hung my coat up in his office. The others threw their things in a big bathroom that had a shower in it—book bags were flung in the tub, coats on hangers hung on the curtain rod. "You don't want to put your things in there," he told me my first day, "you want everything to be safe."

One night during my second week, Rick and I stayed late after work; the money in my cash out wasn't right. He found it though, the error—circled the number with a fancy gold pen. Then he said, "Do you want a drink?"

I had a class the following morning at eight. I said, "Uh . . . yeah."

He walked behind the bar. "What do you want?"

I didn't know what to ask for—I felt a little panicked. When I was in high school I drank vodka and orange juice, but I had drunk too much once and gotten very sick. I couldn't even take the taste of orange juice by itself ever since. "Make me whatever you want," I said.

He gave me an amaretto sour, which tasted nice, sweet.

He started asking me about my family, about my mother in particular. I told him that she was a secretary at a fire insurance company, which

I knew was rather bland. I wished suddenly that she was a famous ballet dancer or a cop.

I did end up telling him, by the end of my drink, that my mother was a shopaholic. This piqued his interest, I could tell—perhaps because I made it out to be funny, just a quirky side to my mother's personality, as opposed to what it really was: an emptiness, a sadness, a never-ending need.

I told Rick the story of how a bill collector called from Chase Visa and screamed at me once when I was eleven. The woman had asked to talk to my mother, and when I went to get her, I realized she was taking a shower. I told the woman that, and then she said, "Don't you lie to me. I know she's there, goddamn it. Put her on the phone. Don't you try to trick me, young man."

"She thought I was a little boy!" I said, laughing. "So she kept yelling at me, and I got all shook up about it and I had to get my mother out of the shower, dripping wet."

I told him how my mother went into a rage. She took the phone and started screaming at the woman, told her she would fly all the way to Dallas and beat the crap out of her if she ever, ever talked to her daughter like that again. Then she hung up and laughed a little. But I failed to explain to Rick that it was not a happy laugh, but a bitter one. A laugh you laugh only when you are angry and on the verge of tears.

I told Rick, "My mom's a little fiery sometimes."

He nodded, took a sip of his vodka tonic. "I like that," he said. "I like that a lot."

The story I gave him ended there. I didn't tell him how later, after my mother got off the phone, she started crying. I didn't tell him that she stood there, her wavy hair dripping cold rivulets of water down her freckled back as she shivered, barefoot, in front of the kitchen phone. I didn't tell him that for at least an hour we sat together, her in her towel, me with my head not quite on her shoulder, but near it. We sat there silently on the blue flowered couch we had recently ordered at Sears.

"I don't know what we're going to do," my mother had said. She rubbed her stuffy nose and looked at me. "How are we ever going to make it? How are we ever going to pay?"

That section of the story was not for the sharing. That helplessness that I felt on that couch was a hidden feeling—one I never wanted to revisit, one I was sure I never would have to as long as I worked and worked.

Rick ended up asking me other things—how many boyfriends did I have? I told him none. When he asked about high school, I told him I went to the prom by myself and he stared at me, he had his mouth open. He said, "You?"

I laughed; I kept talking to him in a chattery voice, smiling with purposeful dimples. I was so unaccustomed to men being interested in who I actually was, in where I came from, that it thrilled me a little. That always seemed to be one of the great tricks of older men—they knew that young men didn't take such a careful interest in you, in what you knew and where you'd been, and it was endearing somehow, when they sat right next to you and listened to every word you said without interrupting or adding their own scenario. They just sat there quietly. And their eyes and their expression took you outside of yourself, made you realize that you were indeed somewhat different, potentially interesting.

At some point while I was talking, Rick had moved his hand onto my leg, moving up and down across my black nylons. It was gentle though, light. I kept chattering, acting as if I didn't feel his fingertips. I felt so lucky that I was with him on that barstool that it was pathetic—and that luck I felt didn't have to do with the fact that he was beautiful, or desirable; it was that he was all grown up. He wasn't just some boy—he was a full-fledged man, one who picked out only certain women. He'd never touch just anyone.

I watched his hands. I watched the one that edged along the hem of my dress and then at the one that was still on the bar fingering the dark brown wood. His thumb moved in light circles. Circles that entranced me. Circles that indicated through the words and the drip of the brass tap in front of us that there was so much else here if I wanted it, and I did want it. Badly.

When he finally kissed me, it was of no shock; there was no sudden awkwardness. My legs were already open, and I pulled him closer, feeling the sharpness of his stubble against my face, my lips.

We took a cab to his apartment. The elevator in his building wasn't working—we had to walk up seven flights of stairs. Stairs that careened and twisted all the way up. In front of his apartment while he fiddled with the key, I leaned against the door frame, out of breath. He kissed me on the nose. Then we went in, straight into his bedroom. He had a blue bedspread, light blue pillowcases, an alarm clock on the headboard that kept blinking 12:00.

In the morning, he walked me to the elevator, which still didn't work. In front of the stairs, he said good-bye, but he didn't kiss me, and I suppose that should've served as some sort of a hint. But I was completely unaccustomed to any of this—I had never slept in another man's apartment. I had never slept with anyone. I suppose it seems strange that I would've so quickly gone home with Rick—but it didn't to me. I was actually attracted to him, something I rarely felt, something I found impossible to ignore. In the past with most boys, the ones in high school, I felt oddly disinterested in them—I never knew what to do with the notes they crammed in the slots of my gray locker; their hallway grunts and shouts annoyed me, and if they came up to me, even in a stammering state, I felt this sudden urgency to get away from them, to run.

Rick was completely different from those boys though; he had something that reeled me in—it was like a heat, a nagging, one that stretched across my mind, my vision. During that first week at work, even the lighting in the employee bathroom mirror seemed awkwardly bright—I could see tiny bumps on my face, splotch marks on my neck, mascara that was too clumpy, not perfect enough. I wanted more from myself; I wanted a chiseled, startling beauty—the kind you can't ignore, the kind that incites trembling and nervousness and worry. And if that need and all its internal demands were to present themselves physically, they would've rested somewhere on my forehead, particularly as I walked out of Rick's apartment building, the sun too bright above me, my fore-head thumping.

The next night I worked, I didn't see Rick for a few hours and I was glad for that. I felt nervous and embarrassed. I didn't know how I was sup-posed to act around him, and I had this paranoia that the other girls I worked with, in just looking at me, would know that I had slept with him. Ever since I had started, all the other cocktail waitresses were a bit guarded around me. They talked to me, but it was always in such a way that I knew that once I walked away, took my tray away from the bar, they'd eye one another and smile—a slight bitter twist to their school-girl faces.

I was also worried about my underwear—I had left them in Rick's bedroom, on the floor somewhere. They were my favorite pair: silk with lace trim, a tiny pink tulip embroidered on the front. My mother bought them for me during one of her mad shopping sprees—they were French, and she had paid forty dollars for them. I worried that I wouldn't get the underwear back, something would happen to them. I suppose that was my own innocent way of worrying about what had actually happened. It was as if I innately knew, without reason, to distrust.

At work that night, Rick did not even make eye contact with me. When he came to the bar to give one of the bartenders more ones, or to void something, he didn't look at me and I didn't look at him. I just lined the drinks up on my tray, putting the heavy drinks in the middle, rocks glasses on the outside. I concentrated on the overall presentation of my tray, its balance.

At the end of the night, he finally spoke to me. He was behind the bar counting ones, and I came to the bar with a tray full of dirty glasses. The other girls were sitting at barstools, smoking cigarettes, counting their own money. Rick said to me, "Did you have the front section tonight, Catherine?"

"You mean one through twelve?"

"That would be the front section, wouldn't it?"

I didn't say anything. I was stacking ashtrays on the bar, but in my heart I felt that burn which is on the cusp of regret. I knew right then and there that he was going to act awfully, and I couldn't decide what I felt worse about: the fact that I had slept with him, or the fact that I had in my own roundabout way told him something intimate, something personal about my mother. I felt that telling him that credit card story had been like giving him a little piece of myself, but now he was flicking it away, ignoring it. Which was the biggest betrayal to me—I actually wanted to believe back then in some silent human promise, one that said: If I let you know me, you must adore me.

"Did you clean any of your tables all night long?" Rick asked me. His voice was harsh, a voice he had never used with me. "There was shit all over the place over there."

Lou, the owner, was somewhere nearby talking to someone at a table, but that wasn't why Rick was talking to me like that. It wasn't because he was doing his job. I knew that. I suppose the girls who sat there counting their money knew that, too, but they kept their faces blank, expressionless—as if they had not seen my coat, which was now next to theirs in the bathtub upstairs.

I said meekly, "I was really busy tonight." He stared at me. "I was."

"That's doesn't fuckin' matter, Catherine. You've got to keep up, and if you can't . . ." He was putting money in a bag, concentrating on stacking it right. "If you can't," he began again, "I'll have to put you on the slower nights, in the slower sections, and then . . . you won't make as much."

I nodded.

He turned the key in the register, and a long stream of register paper came out, rolled onto the floor. I stared at it, standing in the very same spot in which I had sat the night before. I said, "I'm sorry."

He didn't say anything, didn't look at me. In his side profile, I saw something in his face tense, then let go. He said, irritated, "You don't have to say you're sorry."

Later that night when I got back to my dorm, I sat down on the floor of the elevator in my minidress and Doc Martens. The fluorescent lightbulbs above me were big and bright. When the doors opened at the sixth floor, I didn't get out. I watched them close, and then the old elevator creaked a little but still hovered there. It was past three, and very few people in my dorm were up. My roommate certainly wasn't—she was asleep in our bunk bed in her PJs and socks, the teddy bear her boyfriend gave her squished under her face.

At that moment, that elevator seemed my only private place. I stayed there playing with my shoelaces, tying them and then untying them, threading them through the loops and then taking them out. I thought about Rick, but I didn't cry over him. I wasn't even sure what I felt—how could I, when I hadn't known in the first place what to expect? Whatever humiliation I should've felt I couldn't quite reach either; I couldn't tap into it. Instead I worried about my job. I thought about my bank account. I computed on the back of a check slip how much money I needed to make; then I drew asterisks all over the paper like snowflakes coming down on the thousand-dollar amounts. After sitting there awhile, staring, feeling nothing, I got out of the elevator and went to my room. In the hallway, I passed a boy sitting by himself on the floor. He said, "Hey," but I said nothing back. I would forever be reminded of this moment—that boy was Harlan.

One night Harlan and I, somehow by awkward chance, ended up exchanging virginity stories. When I told him mine, he said, "That's fuckin' awful. And you still work for him?"

I shrugged my shoulders. "Yeah."

At the time we had known each other for only a month or so—Harlan was my neighbor in my dorm, and I had come to know him simply because he was the only one up when I came home late at night. I often found him stoned, sitting in the hallway, eating ice cream with a pink spoon. When I first started seeing him, I often ignored him, too shy. But once I got in my room, I couldn't ever sleep right away, and my roommate would always get mad at me if I turned on any kind of light, even if I lit a candle.

The first time I came out to join Harlan, he said, "Your roommate gets mad at you?" He shook his head. "She has no business getting mad at you. She's a dirty whore."

It was right then that I knew Harlan was a keeper, and it wasn't because my roommate was anything like a dirty whore—it was simply because he had delivered that comment so sternly, so bitterly, and then after a pause, he laughed hysterically into his sleeve.

Shortly after that we started meeting late at night in the floor lounge, an unfurnished, blue-carpeted room with white walls, bay windows, and no lightbulbs. In our plaid robes we sat across from each other in the darkness, a flickering street lamp our only light, and we talked and talked, until a gray light came in, until it was time to sleep.

On the night when we were talking about losing our virginity, I told him my story and then he told me his. I can't share, and I won't share, what happened to him. I promised never to repeat it, and when I made that promise I didn't do it with my voice, I did it with one very small, hesitant gesture, my hand on his arm. It was the type of story that, when you hear it, you feel as if you somehow forced the person to tell you what he was not ready to tell. It was a story that made me feel petty and small for all the miniature tragedies I ruminated about. He had a real one, a live one, and he sat there in his plaid pajamas talking about it with all the humor and verve that one of the girls at work might've used after getting a bad tip.

Once he finished telling me all about it, we reverted to talking about my story—it was the safer, the easier of the two. He asked me, "Doesn't it bother you that you still work for that guy?" He shook his head. "That guy used you."

Above us on the roof there were pigeons, and when we were silent, we could hear their coos, spooky and whimpering. I waited a minute, listening, and said, "It would've been worse if I quit."

He said, "What do you mean?"

"If I quit, then I wouldn't see him anymore, and if I don't see him anymore, then he becomes something else, someone else." Harlan just stared at me. I talked louder, defensive. "I'd make him better than who he is. I'd make him a star."

Harlan laughed at the word *star*, and said, "How do you even know you'd do this when you've never had a boyfriend before?"

"Because," I said, "I do it all the time. I do it with strangers. I see a cute boy on the bus, I make him into all that and more. But if he comes over—it's like dealing with Rick—then I see him and hear him. And he's not anything like what I made him into."

He smiled. "Have you ever considered tricyclics?"

"Shut up," I said.

His favorite word in the world was *tricyclics*. Whenever he could, he began sentences with the phrase "tricyclicly speaking"—which was supposed to mean "psychologically speaking."

"Everybody does that though," Harlan said. "Everyone imagines things about other people. Tricyclically speaking," he smiled for emphasis, "it's very normal. Very OK."

"Yeah, but I do it different. I do it worse," I said, feeling annoyed a little. He didn't seem to understand the severity of it. "I go deeper," I touched my forehead. "I imagine everything about them."

Harlan nodded as if he understood. He said, "But working for them, working for that asshole you work for, cures this?"

I nodded. I said with certainty, "Yes."

Harlan paused, scratched a stain on the carpet we were sitting on, and then he said, "I still think you should quit." He shook his head. "That place is going to fuck you up." He pointed at his head when he said this, and I nodded back.

Harlan often considered himself an expert on what "fucked people up," and how he got that expertise had to do with a number of things, but most importantly with a certain period of time during his senior year in high school when he had been "away"—in a mental hospital. It had been for only a short time, two months, but the experience seemed to make him think he had some sort of strange wisdom, one that gave him the ability to look at you and know not just what was wrong with you, but also what was inevitably going to hurt you.

Harlan said, "You'll never make it out of that bar normal."

I laughed. "You really think that?"

He nodded matter-of-factly, exhaling smoke, and I stared at him, thinking, What did he know? He was no such thing, normal. It seemed no one I ever cared about could be. I was forever in pursuit of the broken, the distanced, people who were comfortably out of reach.

6

THE REST OF JUNE

My first full weekend in Madrid, I spent with Esteban. I called him two days after Monica brought me to his party. It was a Saturday afternoon, and I had spent all day alone on Friday—Celia was in Gijón, Isabel was in Barcelona, and Monica, I was certain, I couldn't ever see again.

When I first called, I got his answering machine, so I hung up. Then later, after a minute or two, I called back, left a message. His voice on the machine was very businesslike, orderly, which was strange to me—I thought he would say something snazzy and upbeat. Perhaps I got that impression from Harlan; he seemed to think answering machines were an art form, a reflection of who you were. He changed ours every few days. If he was happy, he played ABBA in the background. If he was in love or lust, he played this '70s song, "You Can Ring My Bell." When he was hostile, his announcement was very simple, terse, and then he would add something onto it, usually directed at a particular person. "And if this is Billy, you're nothing but a small, useless fuck with a frog belly. Don't think I don't know about that ponytailed Hispano in the red shirt. I saw you two last night. I hope you had lots of frog-bellied fun together. Don't call me anymore. Ever."

I suppose you could know too much about Harlan through his answering machine messages; perhaps it was better to leave one like Esteban's: so general, so distant, not a hint about who he actually was.

Esteban called me back, peppy and loud, only about twenty minutes after I left my message. We agreed to meet after siesta in Puerta del Sol, which was the first place any foreigner in Madrid knew because it was in the center of the city, a whole series of wide streets led right into it. Puerta del Sol was an oval-shaped plaza with buildings that were yellow or a whitish gray all facing one another, overlooking a gray and pink cobblestoned area with kiosks on the corner, people carrying shopping bags and stopping in windows, a giant Tío Pepe sign lurking above. It was where the department store El Cortes Inglés was; it was a place filled with many smaller shops; it was where I had first gone shopping with Celia. In the windows of every other shop there were big green signs that said, *rebajas,* or *liquidaciones,* which meant sales. While I waited for Esteban to meet me, standing in front of a statue of a bear on its hind legs in front of a tree, I stared at those liquidation signs and thought of my mother. I wondered what it would be like if she were there. I thought of her standing next to me looking at one particular dress in the window that was incredibly swank; it was black with a wide belt at the waist, cream-colored stitching on the cuffs and hem, a tiny button like a pearl at the neck. I could see my mother in that dress actually—but at the same time I could also picture my mother simply staring at it in the window, her face in the reflection, the unreachable dress beneath it.

Esteban arrived forty-five minutes late and didn't say he was sorry. He just kissed me on the cheek and said, "Let's go to my car. I don't like it here. Too many people." He smiled. "Too many bumpkins to bump into."

In his Porsche we drove down la calle Alcalá, a wide street that led through a number of plazas, ones that turned the straight road into a curving rotary. Esteban was driving fast again, the music loud. Whitney Houston was playing: "I Wanna Dance with Somebody." He pushed the volume up higher, and I looked at him, made a face. He mouthed the words of the song back at me. "Don't you wanna dance, say you wanna dance, don't you wanna dance." He was wearing sunglasses—ones that were shaded darker at the bottom than at the top, and they had gold rims.

I said, "Those glasses remind me of the kind old men wear to racetracks."

"Stylish men wear to racetracks."

"No, old men."

"Stylish," he said and pointed at his outfit with one giant elegant sweep. He was wearing all blue with a black-and-white-striped belt. The blue he was wearing wasn't a regular blue, it wasn't navy or pale, it was a brilliant blue, one that almost matched his sandals. His toenails, I noticed, had a certain gleam to them too—they had obviously been painted with clear nail polish and perfectly clipped. I imagined a woman tending to his toenails while he sat by his pool, Monica in the background fanning herself, the butler behind them holding a silver tray.

As Esteban slowed down for an approaching traffic light, I felt my weight go forward. I held on to the seat. I had my seat belt on, but it seemed not to be working all that well—perhaps because Esteban had come to a slow stop, not a sudden deathly one.

At the light, I could see out my window a man sitting on an olive green towel right in front of some black wrought-iron bars. He had his head down, his forehead pressed against the towel. In front of him, there was a piece of cardboard that was jagged on the ends, as if it had been hurriedly torn off a box. The sign said: ESTOY MUY ENFERMA, AYUDÉME, TENGO SIDA. Translation: I am very sick, help me, I have AIDS.

The word for sick ended with an "a," which meant that this person I believed was a man was actually a woman. In English I wouldn't have known the difference. I thought about that for a moment, as if it had some deep dark significance; the whole time I had my eyes fixed on the woman on the towel. She did not move.

"I want to drink some champagne outside if that's OK," Esteban said. The streetlight turned green, and we started curling around a rotary into another street.

I nodded. I said, *"Sí, sí."*

After Esteban parked the car, we walked from a side street to el paseo Castellana and then we sat at an outdoor café that was situated in the middle of the street on a long cement island. Two lanes of traffic passed on each side of us. We sat in honey-colored wicker chairs under a yellow Bacardi umbrella and drank Spanish champagne, *cava*.

Esteban was telling me about a few trips he had recently taken. His stories were not boring as traveling stories often can be; they were instead interesting, full of embarrassing moments. He told me how he went through a metal detector with a gift his friend had bought him, a vibrator. Apparently it was wrapped up, hidden away in a rectangular cardboard box, but the X-ray vision that his bag passed through detected it as something more, something potentially explosive.

He said, "Never bring a vibrator to Egypt."

I smiled and said, "I'll try not to."

Esteban went on to tell me about other places, particularly ones in Spain. He said I had to see Barcelona and Toledo and Granada and Sevilla. If I was going to go outside of Spain, I had to go to the French Riviera, to St. Tropez.

"Where have you gone before?" he asked me.

"I haven't been anywhere," I said, and then I smiled, embarrassed by that.

I didn't come from a family who traveled. My mother and father had never been out of the country, and my grandparents, when they were alive, hadn't either. Often at BU I ran into other kids my age who had been all over the world: to Hong Kong and Cairo and Paris, to Montevideo and Sydney and Japan—meanwhile I hadn't even been to L.A. In all of my classes, it seemed those same kids who had traveled were the ones who were always raising their hands, interrupting the class, telling random stories about their experiences.

In my high school Spanish class, there had been this one guy who was always blurting out annoying details about the summer trip he took with his parents to Spain. Once he told us how in Sevilla it was so hot that the bottoms of his sneakers started to melt; then when he went into his hotel, lint from the lobby's red carpet got stuck in the grooves of his shoes. He pointed at his shoes as he said this, and I remember sitting diagonally behind him and staring at the black scuffed shoes he was currently wearing.

Prior to that, the teacher hadn't been talking about Sevilla or heat or the melting possibilities in Spain. But this guy had still insisted on telling us all about his little experience, quite proudly, and it seemed to me at the time that he had done so only to prove to the rest of us that he was different: He had actually been to the places that people like me, people like my mother and father, would never see. Places that he didn't have to trust some flat rolled-up map to know they actually existed—he had been there, stood there, felt its sun on his face and feet.

"You're young," Esteban said. "You should go everywhere." He was holding his champagne glass with his pinky up, and he was looking at the waiter behind me.

I said, "It's not that I don't want to go. It's not that I'm too lazy." I sat up; I felt as if I had been slouching. "It's that I can't."

Esteban just stared at me as if he were trying to guess why. "I don't understand."

"I'm not rich," I said, "I can't just travel around anywhere I want."

Whether it was then or much later that the chip on my shoulder started to take shape for Esteban, started to glow with its neon color, I don't know. He said, "Your parents must try to—"

"My parents pay for nothing," I said, irritated. "I am on my own." This idea, I knew, was something that most people had difficulty believing. Particularly in Madrid. It seemed a given that if you were young, if you were abroad, your parents paid for everything—that's the way the Spanish did it, and so they assumed that that's the way the rest of us did it, too. Isabel and Celia had never even had a job. They looked upon the notion as some exciting upcoming event. Isabel often talked about the clothes she would wear: the pinstripe suits and the pumps and the tiny

lacy handkerchiefs in her lapel pocket; while Celia constantly eyed brief-
cases in the department stores, put them over her shoulder, turned to the
side—"Which one looks best?" she'd ask. *"¿Cuál es mejor?"* They were
like children dreaming of becoming firemen or doctors or cops: It was
all about the look of things, the outfit.

"If you're on your own," Esteban asked, eyebrows raised, "how did
you come here?"

"I saved my money."

"Cocktail waitressing?"

Without saying Monica's name, I said, annoyed, "She told you that,
too, did she?"

"Well, of course. The cocktail waitress who looks like Rachel
Hunter is an exciting mix." He laughed, but I didn't. "Working in bars,"
he said after a pause, "you must meet a lot of wonderful boys."

I shrugged my shoulders, as if that was uninteresting, and looked
around us, noticed that there were more people in the café—initially we
were the only ones. There was an old woman in a pink-and-white-
striped dress sitting next to us with her husband, her lipstick was very
dark, a bit of it on her teeth. Past her, cars were going by, all very
quickly—highway speed—but the motors of the cars seemed so soft,
not a single horn beeped. I looked beyond the street up at the pale peach
buildings and then at the sky, which was hazy and bright. I felt a sudden
appreciation for Madrid right then; perhaps that is the only thing you
can have when you are sitting outside, drinking and drinking, pausing
only to see everything, hear everything. Even the sudden clink of a
spoon falling from a nearby table sounded strangely melodic, elegant,
like the tinkering of a glass bell.

"I could live here," I said to Esteban.

"Why don't you?" he asked, his eyebrows raised. He reached over,
put his hand on the edge of champagne bucket, dipped his fingers in the
ice water. Originally I thought he was going to take out a piece of ice—
perhaps do something embarrassing like put it against his forehead.
Instead he just left his hand there, beneath the pink linen napkin draped

over the champagne. After a long pause, he said, "I think you should live here. It would benefit you."

I felt the breeze; loose leaves rustled on the pavement. There were trees all around us, short trees with thin spindly trunks.

He said, "I could get you work."

"Doing?"

With his free hand, the one that wasn't in the ice, he took what looked like a miniature breadstick from the basket between us, bit into it. "What would you like to do?"

"I don't know."

He was still chewing and seemed to continue chewing for such a long time that I thought he was stalling for time. Finally he swallowed, took a sip of champagne, then he held the glass under his nose as if he were enjoying the slight spark of the champagne bubbles rising against his nostrils. He said, "There must be something you could do. Something you could love."

I thought about that, shook my head. "I doubt it."

"Yes," he said, amused. "We'll have to fix that."

I spent the rest of the day and night with Esteban. Sunday, too. He seemed to know that I would be alone otherwise—which made me a feel a little pathetic at first, but he made it all out to be a game. He was training me, he said, training me to become a true *gato*, a cat. According to Esteban, Madrileños (people who lived in Madrid) were called *gatos* because they stayed out all night, prowled the streets. I had to learn how to prowl, too. "You're too accustomed to being locked up all night . . . working." He made a disapproving face. "But that's all over now." He pouted glamorously. "It's all over."

"*Qué suerte,*" I said. What luck.

Both nights we went to dinner, we ate from ten to practically midnight—the first night in a *terraza* in an old cobblestoned section called Opera, across from Palacio Real, the second night at a dark candlelit restaurant that looked like an old theater with dizzyingly high ceilings and gauzy white curtains that hung limply like ghosts above us. We ate in courses, slow, long, lazy courses, and we shared everything that landed on our table.

After the restaurants, we never ever stayed in one place—according to Esteban that was a waste of time, "a waste of night." I went out with him later in the week after that weekend also—and in total, we went to so many places it was often confusing for me to later explain to Celia and Isabel where I had gone in their absence, what I had seen. On the first night I went out with him, a Saturday, I know we went to a night-club fashion show that had dizzying blinking lights, and then the rest of that night and all the other nights is a mix of bars that were *muy típico*— typically Spanish—bars that had blue-tiled walls and plain wooden chairs, bright lights, olive pits, and cigarette butts all over the floor. There were dark cavernous bars, too, one in particular where messy-haired poets hung out; one where we drank *caipirinhas*, got sugar all over our lips. We drank scotch, Chivas, or red wine, served in little miniature rocks glasses, or *ginebra*, gin, with Fanta naranja.

Esteban introduced me to people, more gay ones than straight. At the party at his house there had been more women than men, but now it was the opposite: I met men named Carlos and Lorenzo and Ángel who looked only minutely gay from a distance, dressed in checkered shirts and pressed pants, hair greased to a Ken doll perfection—and then I met others who would've amused Harlan to pieces, men who wore no shirts and leopard cowboy hats, ones who had dangling earrings shaped like moons, ones who used the word *fantastico* over and over, with great wide-eyed drama.

Amongst his friends, we spoke in Spanish; alone, in English. *"Tienes que practicar"*—you have to practice—he'd tell me, as if he thought I had walked around the whole day speaking a certain brand of obnoxious loud-mouthed English, the type I heard occasionally on the metro or on some tourist-filled street. "That Raúl is the only one you talk to in Span-ish," he'd say, and then his friends would ask who Raúl was, rolling and purring the R in his name with teasing zest. *¿Quién es Raúl? ¿Quién?*

After I told them, they'd ask me about his Mars Bar. How long was it? Did it taste *rico*—delicious?

His friends were always nice to me, always told me I spoke well—they'd say it with great mystified wonder, even asked if my parents were half Spanish—but it was really my accent that got me through. I could lisp quite nicely and handle my r's in a softer way than most Americans could. *Hablas casi perfecto*, you speak almost perfect, Esteban would forever say to me whenever we had our short-lived moments of Spanish, and I'd smile, not entirely believing him, but still satisfied; there was a certain pleasure—and power—in being able to say what I felt, what I knew, all in Spanish. The language wasn't my mother's, wasn't my father's. I found it and I learned it. It was just like this entire country, my own separate thing.

"Do you ever get tired though?" Esteban asked me while we were walking toward his car late at night.

At first I thought he meant about going out so much, and then I thought he meant the language, "With Spanish?"

"Yes, maybe," he said. "But do you . . . ever get tired doing everything"—he paused—"on your own."

I shook my head. "It's the only way."

I was walking arm in arm with him as I said this, walking through el barrio Salamanca, the fancy section of town. It was my fifth or sixth night out with him, and I was used to Esteban, so used to him that when he put my arm in his, I noted with a smile how slowly he had done it—as if he thought he needed to show me how—and then he pulled on my arm a little, so that I had to lean into him, press my shoulder into his. And in the warmth of the night air mixed with the fuzziness of my gin-induced buzz, I felt happy next to him—in the way I did with Harlan, although Harlan's companionship was never so touchy, never his warm fingertips on my arm.

"Those shoes are breathtaking," Esteban said, pointing at some cork-heeled sandals he caught me glancing at in a shop window.

I smiled. I said, a little sarcastic, "They're beyond belief."

At the next shop, there was a faceless, see-through mannequin in a black lacy nightgown that was tight and fitted with high, high slits. The store was called La Perla, and I looked up at its sign for a moment or two, as if I had to memorize it.

"You like *things*," Esteban said. "Don't you, Catherine?"

I nodded. "Of course."

"Well, I think," he said, using the tone of someone who had come up with a new and exciting idea, "I think you deserve nice things." I nodded, as if I didn't care one way or the other. "We'll have to come up with a plan to get you nice things," he continued. "Maybe . . . rob a bank."

"Only if we wear masks," I said—I was more than a little drunk. "I won't do it without a mask."

"Well then, I'll get you one."

"A Spanish mask," I added. "Not a Marsian mask."

"One with feathers," he said, and I nodded, a little sleepily—never understanding until weeks later what that conversation really meant.

————

During those first four weeks, the month of June, time seemed to move differently than anywhere else I had ever been, it crept along, slower— it was as if Madrid had its own special time zone, one that was ruled by a melted, misshapen clock—a clock that needed more time for its hands to move from number to number. The sun in the summer didn't set until ten o'clock, and those sunlit days, particularly if you were wide-eyed and foreign, could go on forever and ever. For this reason, it sometimes seems in my memory as though certain events happened either all in one day, or weeks and weeks apart.

There was a definite two weeks, midmonth, that Celia and Isabel stayed in Madrid and I saw Esteban a little bit less. They both knew about Esteban, took a certain silent relief in the fact that I had another friend to take me out. But they were a little wary when I told them how old he was—until I explained that he was gay, *una mariposa*—which in slang meant fag, or, literally, a butterfly.

As for Monica, they never asked me about her, which I found odd, nerve-wracking, as I was never sure if they knew about our little tiff in the bathroom or not. My constant fear when I went out with them was that I would run into her, but then we didn't end up ever seeing her, and so I rationalized that they must've not liked her too much themselves.

During this same period, Celia and Isabel had a test in their law class, a midterm of some kind, and they attempted to study for it an hour or two every night. Usually what they really did was flip through their notes, all neatly written in a notebook full of graph paper, certain lines illuminated with a fluorescent green marker. They had a thick black law book, too, one that they said cost the equivalent of one month's rent. Usually it sat, unopened, at the dining room table. Sometimes we put stuff on top of it: napkins, envelopes, pens. Once I opened it and tried to read it, and I couldn't, which depressed me a little—I so desperately wanted to be extra smart.

With both Isabel and Celia around, I worked less, as Carlos wanted, only Tuesday, Wednesday, Thursday—and I made all of those days half days: I didn't even make it to siesta; I left around twelve o'clock. When I got home, one of them was always waiting for me; they switched off, took turns dealing with me. It was weird—showing me Madrid was like a job to them. Isabel liked the museums more than Celia, so she was the one who took me to El Prado, to Reina Sofía, to El Museo Thyssen-Bornemisza. We stood in front of paintings for hours, spending long deliberate moments in front of the ones we saw first, and then by the end of our tours, we breezed through rooms and rooms of art, catching glimpses and then nodding at one another, ready to leave. There were always foreigners in the museums, always Americans in beige shorts. Usually the Americans were the loudest, the ones who had to be told not to put their faces so close to the paintings, the ones who felt important enough to make long-winded artsy commentaries. When we were at El Prado in front of Velazquez's *Las Meninas*, an American boy in a J. Geil's Band T-shirt explained to his mother that with the very size of the painting—which was grandiose, awe-inspiring—the painter was "validating" his power, "wielding" it. I looked at Isabel, who probably hadn't understood anything the boy had just said, and made the gesture of putting my finger down my throat. I said in Spanish, "That boy is an obnoxious toad." Well . . . actually, with my limited vocabulary, what I really said was, "That boy is a horrible frog."

Isabel understood though. She said, "Yes, I don't like him either."

In the museums, men were always staring at Isabel. She often wore very tight, very long dresses, with no bra on underneath. She was particularly thin, reasonably curvy, and when she walked she made a certain noise with her shoes, which made people turn around and stare. Once I asked her how she learned to walk like that, and she answered, smiling, "I imagine myself on stage."

Usually Celia met us after the museums. She'd have a coffee with us under an umbrelled table; then we'd walk down the long curving streets of the old section of Madrid called La Latina. There you could find the Madrid that everyone who was foreign dreamed about. There were curving streets with very few passing cars, apartment buildings with open windows, accordion music flowing down, down, down, onto the cobblestone, onto the narrow walkway.

We often sat in the Plaza Humildero during siesta—and Celia and Isabel would talk while I all too often stared off. I liked to look at the colors of the buildings, the way some were made of miniature-size maroon bricks while others were made of bigger-size cement blocks. The pale yellow buildings were made of the calmest-looking bricks, the kind I decided were the prettiest. There was a church nearby, too, one that loomed high in front of us, and it had hexagon-shaped lamps that hung off the sides, as well as statues of men in robes on each of its rooftop corners.

Often it seemed to me, sitting amongst all of this, that there was too much to take in, too much to like. On our very table there were always these toothpick holders that had pink hand-painted rosebuds or purple wide-petaled petunias with blue vines that curled and unfurled like the wrought-iron balconies on the building above us. Everything was ornate, everything beautiful—and there was something about looking at it all that made me feel in a way I knew I'd never be able to describe accurately. It wasn't just pretty, it wasn't just calming, it was in some strange way luxurious—luxurious just to sit there, just to be there, just to know.

"Maybe you should stay here," Celia said to me once, catching me staring up at the church, at the headless statue that loomed over a doorway.

"You could come and study with us," Isabel added.

"Oh, like you ever fuckin' study," I would've joked if they spoke English. Instead, I made a quizzical face and said in Spanish, "You study?" as if I were suddenly confused.

They laughed at that. Isabel said, "Sometimes yes, sometimes no," then she took a sip of her drink, vermouth on the rocks. "Other times," she said, folding her hands, "we just sit."

Harlan wrote me two postcards during my second week, one with Mighty Mouse, the other with Mickey Mouse in a space suit, and then my third week he sent me a long letter. All three were addressed to "Chiquitita Kelly"—*Chiquitita* means little girl in Spanish, but I don't think Harlan was aware of that; he was instead referring to this ABBA song that he sometimes sang to me with irritating melodramatic gestures.

The letter he wrote me was written in a more frantic slant of penmanship than his postcards—he seemed very upset all of a sudden, angry. If he was in a bad mood over a boy, which almost always was the case, he didn't say. Instead, he kept talking about Esteban. I had told him all about my adventures with Esteban in a letter I had written him at work—I had used fancy company letterhead that had a globe on it and signed it "Chiquitita in chief."

Across the top of Harlan's letter to me, it said: 40-YEAR-OLD FAGGOT + PORSCHE = YOUR DESTRUCTION.

He was being a little dramatic. He claimed that it didn't make sense to him why some old guy would want to hang around with me. "He must want something," he wrote, "he must have some secret plan for you." Through paragraph after paragraph—about three pages, front and back—Harlan established his case that Esteban was in fact a drug dealer. He claimed all the obvious clues were there: Esteban's work in Venezuela, his sports car, his house with a pool.

He warned me not to take any trips with Esteban and not to carry any suitcases for him. "You should just ease yourself away from this Porsche person," he said, and then he explained how I should go about it: Stop going out with him, stop calling him, stop answering the phone, ignore him little by little. "Or maybe," he said, "maybe you should just come home, get the hell out of that mess!"

I smiled when I read that line and then frowned. He had written such a frantic note not because he was concerned about me, but because he missed me and he was just dysfunctional enough not to say so. I thought of calling him, thought of hearing his voice, but as I stared at his flowery slanted scrawl, I knew better. He was very fragile sometimes, to the point that he really needed me, and I knew if he were in such a mood—he would try to make me feel guilty, try to make me come home. The two of us were very selfish in this way. We depended on each other, we adored each other, we made irrational demands.

In his letter, in the corner, close to the last line, Harlan had put a little sticker of a mouse holding a feather. It took me about twenty minutes to figure out that it was the mouse from *Dumbo,* the one who sat on the elephant's head and helped him fly.

Harlan had written beneath the mouse: Don't get in the Porsche.

Despite Harlan's warning, I got in the Porsche quite frequently. Esteban took me out about three or four times a week. During the period when Celia and Isabel were back, I knew I was expected to go out with them, too, and so I did, but usually I preferred to go out with Esteban. Often after a whole day of speaking Spanish and hearing Spanish and trying to memorize Spanish, I just felt like talking without thinking, and I could do that with him. In English, I could talk and talk, and everything I said he claimed was witty, and I told him he was witty, and so together we sat around and felt witty—all of which was a nice reprieve from my full day of jumbling around words and conjugating verbs and then making weird sounds and gestures whenever I was at a loss for vocabulary. Besides, with Isabel and Celia we always went out in a big group of twelve or fifteen, and within their circle of friends everyone spoke fast, using swears and slang. Some of their male friends would look at me, and I'd feel in their gaze that they liked me—maybe it was just because I was foreign or my hair was light or my dress was tight—but then after talking with me a while, they would lose patience, get bored. I wasn't like the other girls; I couldn't crack jokes, which the Spanish were big on, and I certainly couldn't understand the complicated jokes they told me. In many ways it was very lonely on those nights in those noisy bars listening to all that Spanish talk—without my humor, without my own language, I had very little to offer.

With Esteban though, it was just so easy, so comfortable. Everything I told him about myself amused him. I told him about school and work and "my little boy"—Esteban's nickname for Harlan, but he seemed to like my bar stories the best, and the racier—the grittier—the better. His favorite person was Rick, although he purposely called him Vick— "Vick's such a ladies man, I *love* a ladies man," he'd say. He especially liked to hear about the late-night parties we had after work—the ones with the stripteases on pool tables. He was a pleased, laughing audience who liked to know specifics. "All right, so how many shots did this girl have before she stuffed her panties in the corner pocket?" Or "Did Vick ever give you cash bonuses for his fun? Or a new necklace perhaps? A Budweiser key chain?"

All of it, because I was so distant from it, seemed jokey and ridiculous, and together we laughed and laughed until our eyes watered.

Throughout all of this, Esteban continued to play the game in which I was in training, training for my new permanent life in Madrid. It was always delivered as a joke though: "If you get homesick on Thanksgiving we'll take you here"—he pointed out the car window at a red-and-white Kentucky Fried Chicken sign. More than once he also brought up a New Year's Eve party he was throwing. "You'll have to wear silver to the party," he kept saying, "all the women, I've decided, are wearing silver."

Although his comments were not necessarily serious, on some level they still got me thinking about the life I had here and the life I had at home.

One night in particular I contemplated all of this as we drove by a palatial-looking building near Banco de España, near my work—it was a building I hadn't noticed before at night. During the day it looked just as giant and white, but I had previously thought it was another bank, one with a little more wealth than the others, a little more size. But seeing it at night with all the soft pink light surrounding it, a clock illuminated in the center, it looked like something you might see on a Disneyland postcard.

"That," Esteban said, seeing me look up at it, "is the post office."

"The post office?" I said, not believing him, thinking he was just playing a boring joke, but then I realized with the way he didn't glance at me, the way he nodded, that he was telling the truth. He was smiling though, and I could see in his big cat smile that he was actually pleased with my awe at that building's beauty, as if that post office somehow represented himself.

"But when you live here," he said, "will you still look at things like that?"

I nodded. "I think I might."

Then I sat there silently, contemplating what indeed it would be like to live so far away from where I was born. I imagined the apartment I might have, the way the wine bottles would be stacked on the kitchen floor. I saw a orange-tiled terrace that was small and square shaped, with a wrought-iron balcony, two chairs, and a miniature round table with three thin legs. I would light candles on the terrace, and from it I'd see the pink pleasing light of the post office.

I thought about all of this as we zoomed far away from the post office through a rotary, around which the car careened so quickly that I had to hold on to the door. Headlights kept flashing by. We were on Gran Vía, passing a building that had a bronze man with wings perched on the roof, the word *Metropolis* beneath it. When we stopped at a red streetlight, the jumpy techno song on the stereo changed, and there was a brief silence, just the lulling hiss of a running fountain nearby. Then the light turned green, the music came back, and the car started to go. The wind lifted my hair off my face. Esteban looked at me, saw I was smiling. He said, "Don't you love your life here? Isn't it the best?"

Work, however, was another, less exciting issue. Since I had to work only three times a week, during those four weeks, the month of June, I had to been in the office only twelve days, and during the weeks that Isabel took me to the museums, I had shown up for only half days. No one ever checked on me in the little mint green corner where I worked. I could've been playing solitaire, or painting my toenails, or curled up under the desk like a cat. But despite such freedom, those days, those hours at work, seemed long, never-ending.

My only enthusiasm, my single highlight in the workplace, was a certain American microbiologist that I nicknamed in my head, as a light form of entertainment, Kansas Katy. She lived in Lawrence, Kansas, worked at K-State, and she was one of the selected microbiologists that Carlos wanted on the panel to endorse Lysol. The panel wasn't needed until October, and so I had the whole summer to badger Kansas Katy, convince her that Spain was a wonderful place to visit.

Her real name was Dr. Katherine Funke, and once I told her my name was also Catherine, she became very excited about this, as if we were cosmically connected. I had to explain to her though that my name was spelled with a *C*, and then we talked about that, why certain names were spelled with a *C* or a *K*. We both got really involved in the conversation, as if our very identities were somehow deeply tied to the letter our names began with, as if it somehow made us predestined toward opposite things.

"Don't talk to her about Lysol," Carlos had instructed me before I called her. "Talk to her about you, how much you like it here, tell her about Madrid, about the food, the music, the nightlife." He shook his head. "She won't just come for Lysol—you need to make her want something else." I took that to mean that Lysol was not going to pay her much. "She's single, and she's older," Carlos added with a grin, "make her think she could fall in love, find a Spanish prince."

The first thing I decided to tell her about was the palace, Palacio Real—it seemed a place that might lure her, might give her a place to house her Spaniard dreams. But prior to that, I did have to discuss a few other things: Did men wear deodorant? I said yes, that I hadn't actually seen them put it on firsthand, but yes they did. Then there was the issue of Mexico, she kept confusing Mexico with Spain. I had to explain to her that in Madrid, there were no ponchos, no mules, no cacti.

"Any nice beaches?" she asked, and I told her no, Madrid was land-locked—which I think embarrassed her. I went on to explain that it was a city that was dry in the summer and "extra hot," but at night, it cooled down, became romantic and breezy. That's when I got to Palacio Real.

I told her there was a cross on the top of the palace, and because of the way certain neighborhoods were more elevated than others, I could see its brassy cross from distant places like the 7-Eleven or the metro station or even my bedroom window.

"Is it a real 7-Eleven?" she asked, interrupting me.

I said, "Yes, it's exactly the same, except they have a bakery." She paused after that, as if the 7-Eleven in her imagination offered more than the palace, as if the small narrow aisles, the rows and rows of American soft drinks, the smell of damp newspapers—mixed with chocolate and croissants, perhaps even cookies shaped like bulls, was exciting to her.

We talked about 7-Eleven for ten more minutes.

In our next conversation, I told her about the *gitanas*, gypsies. She had rented *For Whom the Bell Tolls* over the weekend, and she wanted to know if there were gypsies still in Spain and could they *actually* tell your fortune. I told her as much—and as little—as I knew about them: how they dressed in long skirts and button-down shirts that were mis-matched and billowy, how they stood on street corners nudging you, grabbing you, *por favor*, asking for money or trying to sell you sage or a newspaper or your fortune. On certain streets in touristy areas, there were so many of them that they were like an obstacle course, annoying and touchy and whiny, and if you made the mistake of looking at them, of allowing your eyes to meet theirs, you felt a certain urgency in their soft faces and in the shiny heat of their cheeks. Esteban claimed that they had powers, that they knew things—I told Kansas Katy that, and she said in a happy voice, "Oh, no!"

"But they don't hang out at the 7-Eleven," I told her, and then she laughed, pleased with that.

After the first two calls, she started getting more personal with her questions. She asked me once, "But don't your parents worry about you? Being so far away?"

"My mother calls," I said—this was my way of dealing with the word parents, I just didn't mention my father, I canceled him out. Such a thing was harder to get away with when talking to anyone Spanish, but with Kansas Katy, with anybody back home, you could get away with it—the conversation would just swerve naturally around it.

"Still you must miss home?"

"Not really," I said, "only my best friend."

By that point, I had gotten a postcard from Harlan that balanced out his other previous unhappy ones. The postcard had a picture of a mouse crawling along a dirt-filled path. It was a real mouse, a real photograph, like something he might have taken in his mother's backyard. There was a flower drawn in pen on the mouse's head, and the postcard read, "You can ring my bell," which was the secret code for the fact that he had suddenly fallen in love. He fell in love frequently, about once a month.

"You don't have a boyfriend in Boston?" Kansas Katy asked.

"No."

"A girl like you?" she said incredulously. She seemed to think I was very worldly. "You must be dating someone there though." I didn't say anything. "Are you?"

If Carlos had been present and eavesdropping, it would've been my cue to describe some glamorous guy or at least some glamorous event. But the only thing I really had to tell her about, to describe, was a note that Celia had given me from her boyfriend's cousin, Felipe. The note itself sat under my pillow—Celia had placed it there—folded in a small tiny box, like the kind I used to write my friends in junior high. On the top it said, Catherine, and then in different-color ink, a brighter blue, my name was underlined twice. In careful clear print, it said in English:

Dear Catherine,

    Celia has told me about you. She says I will like you. She says I will bite my fingernails over you (I do that). She says that you are funny. She says that when you don't know a word in Spanish, you make sounds to show what it is. She showed Francisco and me your mouse sound and your hair-dryer sound. We liked it.

    When I see you, I will talk to you as good as I can in English and you will talk in Spanish. And with sounds! But if I bite my nails, don't worry—I always bite my nails when I talk in English. It makes me nervous and timid.

Until then,
Felipe

I wasn't sure if this note would be exciting enough for Kansas Katy, but I told her about it anyway. She seemed pleased though, almost giddy. She even made me make my hair-dryer sound for her, and as I did so, Carlos came into the room, glanced at me casually, as if he thought I were merely pronouncing a long unrecognizable English word, and then left.

Later in the conversation Kansas Katy asked me if it would be OK, if it would be all right, if I would bring to work any further notes I got, read them to her. I laughed, liked her very much all of a sudden, but at the same time felt sad—as there was something about her voice, about her shyness, which made me picture her office, her walls, her dress, the very phone she spoke into, even her face, to be gray—as if she were lost somewhere on a distant black-and-white screen.

"I want you to find that Felipe," she said to me a few minutes later after a pause. "I live through you and with you in that country. And I *want* a summer fling."

I laughed a little and said, "I'll try to work that out." But afterward, after I got off the phone with her, I felt fidgety and strange. For a whole hour I sat at my desk staring at the wall, transfixed. But I wasn't thinking about Felipe—I was thinking of a certain other person, someone whose voice, whose name, I could so easily feel creeping up on me as I sat in my office staring at the Johnny Walker poster on the wall. His name wasn't Johnny, but at that moment it seemed strangely close: It was Lenny.

$$\overline{7}$$

LENNY

Lenny, I met at Shooters. He was a doorman at a nightclub down the street, and he came in every Tuesday and Thursday for a cappuccino before work. He had dark brown hair that was straight—it fell in his face at the corners of his mouth, but the rest of his hair was short. He had a farm boy look, although his features were sharp: sharp nose, sharp chin, sharp, worried lines across his forehead. He was older than me, twenty-two.

He started coming in two months after I began working at Shooters. At the time I was still nervous around Rick, unable to look him directly in the eye. He had become chatty again with me, but it was a casual, guarded chatty, one that revolved around difficult customers and other humorous events.

By that point, I had already been watching other new waitresses come and go, all following after him. He had something in him that seemed to enamor them, and it went beyond his slicked-back hair and his shiny shoes. I suppose it was power, a limited junior-achiever amount of power, but it still had its luster. Nevertheless, I was on the other side now, with all the other waitresses who had been conquered, yet stayed, and as a consequence, I was part of an entire alliance, it seemed, a group of girls who would do anything for you, no matter what, as long as you realized you weren't any better than them.

Robby was the one closest to me, the one who told me that "this guy named Lenny" was after me. She sat on the corner of the tub in the changing room, smoking a cigarette, and told me matter-of-factly, "He's obsessed with you. It's obvious."

She claimed that he had somehow figured out how our sections were divided, how they rotated each week. He always landed in my section, sitting there, reading a book, waiting for me. On the days when I had only pool tables for my section, he rented a table but never played. He just sat there in a nearby wooden chair until I came, and then he ordered his cappuccino. Again and again, he did this for weeks.

"He can't really be obsessed with me," I said, and then smiled. I was enthralled. It made me feel in my dull world of PR case studies and trays full of beer that I was a starlet. I was picked out. I was seen.

Often it seemed to me that the only thing that got my mother through her own dull life was Gerry—not her love for him, but her ability to assess that he was so incredibly in love with her, so devoted. That's what life was supposed to be about in my mind: being worshiped by someone. And it seemed to me that because I got cheated out of having a father who adored me, I deserved, more so than any other girl, to have a man who adored me. One who could not get to sleep at night over me. One who called my house, listened to my voice in a weak effort to subside the edginess, the burn, but still that tortured feeling would go on and on, ruining every free minute he had as he walked down sidewalks, sat on subway cars, showered.

I wanted that power, deserved it, and here it was.

A week after Robby alerted me to Lenny's obsession, I made her go with me after work to the nightclub he worked in, the Cavern Club. She and I had shots before we left, Absolut with a drop of Chambord. Those were our favorite shots: They were sweet, they were strong, they hit us fast.

The nightclub was only one block away from Shooters, and we

walked quickly, our faces in our scarves, laughing a little. Lenny was standing in the doorway, which was illuminated with red Christmas lights. There was a long line of people, but we pushed through them, not aggressively but sweetly. *Excuse me, excuse me.*

Once we got to the door, I waited for Lenny to see me—I was only a foot away from him. At first he glanced at me and looked away. Then he looked back, as if he had made a mistake, as if he wasn't sure what he actually saw.

I said, "Hey," in this extra-happy voice, and then, after a moment, he answered, "Hi, Catherine." He said my name loud, like an announcement, as if he were trying to get the other doorman next to him to pay attention, to recognize my name. But other guy couldn't have heard him; the music inside of the club echoed outside. It was techno, the kind that makes your heart beat faster, your adrenaline rise higher— or perhaps it was just the shots that made me feel that way. I could still taste the vodka—it burned and burned at the back of my throat, giving me a feeling, a fire. I could say anything.

"What are you doing later?" I asked him. He was snapping a fluorescent orange wristband on someone's wrist. Robby stood behind me like a prop, making sure I didn't look too forward, too weird.

"What am I doing?" Lenny said, stammering a little. He looked own at the wristbands he had in his hands, fiddled with them, dropped a few in the dirty snow. Then he smiled shyly. "We could do something," he said, but he posed as if it were question, as if he were afraid I was just asking to ask, not because I had any interest in him.

I waited for Lenny to get out of work and then we went to his apartment. We could've taken a cab, we could've gotten a ride from one of his friends. Instead, we walked. It was snowing outside, but the flakes were light, and the wind was barely present. At first, I felt awkward— the alcohol had worn off, leaving me feeling tired-looking and slow. When Lenny said something, I didn't look directly at him, at his face; I kept my eyes on his shoulder. He was wearing a long wool coat that made his shoulders look broader than usual—snowflakes landed on the wool, got caught it in somehow, but they didn't melt.

We were walking through Kenmore Square, and, despite the fact that it was Wednesday and three o'clock in the morning, everything was still reasonably lit—Pizza Pad's sign still flashed red and white, and the Store 24 looked, from the outside, miserably bright. There was a steady stream of cars, of headlights, mostly from taxis passing by us, the sound of their wheels splish-splashing on the wet street.

All I was thinking about as I walked alongside of Lenny was not where we were going, what we would do when we got there—instead I was considering the fact that I had potentially made a big mistake in having sought him out like this. I became suddenly scared of him—and I couldn't tell if this was because I was afraid that he would ignore me the way that Rick had, or because he might go the other way, might cling to me forever and ever.

Throughout those months that Lenny was showing up at Shooters, even before Robby had said anything to me, I had secretly developed some sort of fantasy in which he was, in fact, interested in me, and I played the scenarios of what we would do, where we would go, in my mind over and over again. Such thinking got me through shifts. If it was midnight and I was tired, too tired to stand buzzing around a room full of fifty pool tables, I'd imagine him there. Lenny.

I'd imagine that at two-thirty, after closing, he'd come. I'd be wiping off the tables and putting down the clean ashtrays, and he'd come up alongside of me. He might stammer. He might stare. But he'd be there in that giant darkened room with its gleaming brass lamps and pine green wallpaper, and there would be a feeling in his presence—a feeling I could not find in Rick's, not in anyone else's. It was perfection, an ease.

Often just imagining Lenny gave me a special sizzling excitement that got me through my night's work. It made me smile, made me laugh. It earned me extra money. Thinking about him was like a lucky charm, a magic wand; it made me into something else.

But when Robby told me that she thought he was obsessed with me, it was like all those things that I had been imagining were being transformed into reality. Which scared me as much as it thrilled me. As a child I developed this strange belief that if you wanted something too much, with all your being, you wouldn't get it—but if you acted as if you had only a slight interest in whatever that thing was, it would come to you. You could have it.

All of this reeled around inside of me as I walked side by side with Lenny toward his apartment. At some point in my thoughtful silence, Lenny gave me his hat to wear. It was too big and fell over my eyebrows. Looking at my reflection in a CVS window we were passing, I said, "I don't know if I can wear this. It makes me look stupid."

He shook his head. "No it doesn't."

I said, "Yes, it does," and smiled at him, felt something cold land on my cheek. "You want me to look stupid," I joked.

He pulled me by my hand toward him, squeezed me a little. "No, I want you to be warm." I could feel his breath on my ear.

I said, "I do feel warm. Very."

Later, when we got to his apartment, when we sat side by side on his couch, Lenny revealed something to me, something wonderful and tragic. When he first told me what it was, I sipped a watery cocoa. I nodded. I listened to every word he said and felt with certainty that his obsession with me, and mine with him, was no mistake. It was a connection we made across a crowded pool-tabled room, across smoke and pool-ball-clatter, across a world of people who I thought were so particularly unlike us. His tragedy: His mother had left him.

She left him when he was eleven. He told me that she put all of her things together while he was at school, and when he came home he knew there was something wrong from the way the house smelled. He said it smelled like the perfume his mother wore, like roses.

"It was like she had run from room to room," he said, "or at least that's how I pictured it, her running around the house hysterically spraying her perfume and then finally spilling it in places, on the carpet, on the curtains, on our bathroom towels, all so that she wouldn't have to feel bad for leaving us. Leaving the perfume, the smell of her, was . . ."

He shrugged. "It was like leaving a piece of herself behind. A useless piece of herself."

His mother left him a note, too—one he told me his father read to him. It said: I'm not a mother, I'm a singer.

I suppose the note may have expressed other things—perhaps it contained a more sympathetic explanation, or at least a more rhythmic heartfelt feeling, but that was not how Lenny described it to me, looking away from me into his cocoa mug. I stared at his fingers while he did this—I noticed how tightly they held the mug. I could've kissed them.

He told me how when she still lived with him, he spent a number of nights as a kid, sitting in a lounge that was connected to a Chinese restaurant, drinking virgin daiquiris and watching his mother sing to five or six tables full of people who looked up at her occasionally, but mostly talked among themselves. She always wore velvet dresses, he said, blue ones or red ones, and long dangling pearls.

"You never saw her again? After she left?" I asked, and he said, "Nah," as if it didn't matter anymore, as if it were nothing. Then he paused, there was the sound of the kitchen sink, the plink of water. He said, "I called her once though."

I waited. I thought he was going to tell me about it, but he didn't. He just sat there quietly, and then he started unlacing his boots.

I slept with Lenny that night, but we didn't have sex. Instead we lay side by side in his bed, him in boxer shorts, me in one of his white T-shirts. We talked. The gray light from outside came through the window, got brighter and brighter, until finally Lenny got up and pulled the shade. I watched him at the window, saw how skinny he was, vulnerable. His chest was particularly pale, smooth and hairless. I said something about it when he got into bed, and he said, "I'm still waiting for puberty. I swear it's gonna come."

I laughed, put my face against his neck.

We did not sleep. We just kept talking and talking. Occasionally I crawled on top of him while he was saying something, kissed him hard, pressed myself against him. Then I'd lie back down alongside of him— wait for him to compose himself and start talking again. We stayed like this until morning, then he fell asleep—his hand loosely around my waist, his face in my hair.

Throughout the three months that I went out with Lenny, I didn't ever tell him about my father—something I would later bitterly thank myself for. I didn't like telling anyone about my father. I didn't tell any of the girls at work. I didn't tell Rick. I did tell Harlan, but even after years of knowing him, he knew only pieces that he strung together in his own intuitive way. I, of course, knew that it was no big deal, not that unique of a case, that I had a father who had left me, who was an alcoholic, who had once hit my mother in the face. What made me swerve away from any conversation was that I knew that in talking about him, they would see, they would sense, how much I still thought about him. I was forever in fear that they'd see the fantasy life that existed inside of me: the glittering array of moments I concocted when he showed up in the back row of my debate class, on the street standing next to me in a jogging suit, in a van in front of my apartment listening to the radio, and also the richest one, the most prevalent: He showed up at Shooters.

Often it seemed to me that if anyone were ever to come looking for me, it would be at work. I was so accessible there, so alone.

I had many possibilities when imagining him at Shooters: He could be playing pool (although I usually didn't go for that), he could be drinking at the bar (again, too obvious), or he could just sneak up on me somewhere (much better). Preferably, my tray would be full and I would have the dramatic option of dropping the tray or telling him that he was going to have to wait if he wanted to talk to me as I had work to do.

In all scenarios, he was drunk and literally he smelled bad, like whiskey and Aqua Net hairspray. His face was shiny and red—although even with the photographs that lurked around my mother's house, I could never clearly say what his face looked like. But it didn't matter, it was a face and it was his. He was never taller than me either. In all of my fantasies I just happened to be wearing the highest of heels. I was five-seven and he was six feet, so those heels would have had to be clownish in size, but that didn't matter; the idea was that we were eye to eye, there was no daddy-looking-down-on-daughter stance.

We didn't always have to be in Shooters either—he could come after work, too. For instance, one time I purposely thought of him, imagined him, as I walked home from Shooters at three in the morning. Normally I took a cab home, but it was an especially bad night, one in which I made only seventy bucks—an intense psychological misery for me—and then to top things off, I spent an hour after closing in the bathroom baby-sitting a thirty-eight-year-old customer who told me as she threw up into the sink that men were incapable of loving a woman who had marbles. She pronounced the word *marbles* in that special Bostonian way, losing the "r," mah-bles.

"You got mah-bles, I got mah-bles, they don't give a fuck," she kept telling me. "If they gave a fuck, they would let us keep our mah-bles. Don't you want your mah-bles?" I nodded, I thought she was funny at first, but then when I stood behind her while she got sick and listened to the stricken sound of her heaving, I felt as if I might get sick myself. I noticed how she held her shiny purse, kept the thin black strap on her shoulder while she got sick, and then I stared at the perfect blond shape of her French twist, and I thought of how she had left the house, so pretty and polished, never knowing she would end the night sick in a rest room with a strip of toilet paper around her neck, while an eighteen-year-old girl in a minidress stood behind her, waiting to help her into a cab.

The vision of that woman and her hot pink pants, the brassy gold rings on her fingers, stayed with me for a while, even after she left, even when Rick offered me a drink as I was leaving. I told him no, and he said, "What's the matter? The girl who's in love can't have a drink?"

He was talking about Lenny. He had seen him a number of times by that point—usually waiting for me after work. Half the time he was mean to Lenny and told him he couldn't wait for me inside of the bar, that he had to stand out in the cold. I would stare out the window at him, watch him under the lamplight in his big wool coat.

"The girl who's in love can't have a drink?" Rick said to me again. I was putting on my jacket, and I didn't answer him. "Hello . . . I'm asking you a question." He was standing behind the bar, his hands flat on the counter. "Are you in love with your farm boy?" That's what he called Lenny: farm boy.

I put my bag over my shoulder, looked past Rick at four of the other cocktail waitresses who were playing pool nearby, drinking beers. The one who was shooting had a cigarette in her mouth, and she hadn't changed out of her uniform. I watched her shoot as if I could see the balls and how they were laid out on the table.

"There's nothing to be embarrassed about," Rick said, speaking a bit softer than necessary, as if he didn't want the other girls to hear. He stirred his drink, stared down at it. The brass lamps above the bar dangled only an inch or two from his forehead—I could see the pores in his cheeks, the soft lines around his eyes. "I hope he loves you back," he said. "I want him to actually." He smiled as he said this, a wry smile, and then there was the distant click of pool balls hitting one another.

I walked out shortly afterward, but I took Rick's comment with me, took it past Fenway Park, through Kenmore Square, beneath an underpass. I walked in the opposite direction of my dorm. It was January, and the wind was mild that night; it almost seemed warm. I didn't have my gloves on, and the snow was melted, so I didn't have to stumble around too much. Cabs came by, slowed down for me as if I might want to get inside. I didn't.

I started thinking about my father. I started imagining him there with me, coming around a corner on Mass Ave. where the Starbucks was and the BayBank. I didn't have a tray to ignore him with—I had just a scarf, which I pulled tighter and tighter around the lower section of my face, against my lips. It smelled like cigarette smoke, like Shooters.

My father didn't say anything. He was just there.

I let myself imagine the sound of his footsteps next to mine on the wet cement. I let him have breath that condensed and took shape in the cold. We walked past Hynes Convention T stop together, past Au Bon Pain, past Tower Records. He was not taller than me, he was not close to me. But he walked with me for a while. I went around the block between Beacon and Marlborough an extra time, looked at the doorways and gates of the brownstones.

He did not make any comments, didn't ask about my mother. He was just moving alongside of me—and as I played this game with myself, it occurred to me what I was actually doing when I dreamed of my father. I wasn't asking to talk to him, to touch him; I just wanted his presence. I just wanted what very few other people could give: comfort.

"Does your mother ever send you stuff?" I asked Lenny once when we were sitting on his couch in our underwear, eating blueberry muffins. It was hot in the apartment, the radiator hissing and clanging. Lenny had just opened the window a crack, and small wisps of cold air came in, made the hair on my arms stand on end. I rubbed my arms a little and said, "Like cards, do you get cards from your mom?"

"Once she sent me a gift," he said, looking up at me. He had his head in my lap—he was lying down and I was sitting up on the couch. I thought about what he had just said, a gift—I never got a gift from my father, only those birthday cards, which I was still getting at the time; but they didn't come to my address in Boston. They went to my mom's house.

Tracing a line with my finger across Lenny's forehead, I said, "What was it? The gift she sent you?"

He got up, and I watched him on his hands and knees, in his Skivvies and socks, go through a series of wooden drawers beneath his empty bookshelf. After rummaging through scraps of papers and envelopes and matchbooks, he handed me a set of playing cards. The cards had the same picture of a woman holding a microphone on the front of each. I knew without asking that the woman was his mother. The picture was

taken from a distance; you couldn't really make out her face. She was
not that thin, not that pretty, but her pose was sexy. One long leg was
visible through her dress's revealing slit.

The cards were not worn, were not used. They were in a small box
that was red with a black stripe across it. A box that Lenny must have
carried with him from Honeyeye Falls, New York, where he came from,
to Providence, where he once lived, and now here. I imagined that box
going with him everywhere, sitting in hidden places: in a drawer full of
silverware or socks, under his bathroom sink, in between towels in the
linen closet, in a giant department store bag stashed under his bed.

After a minute or so of looking at the cards, Lenny took them out of
my hands, put them back in the drawer in which he found them. For a
moment he stared at a sheet of blue paper, a flyer of some kind, which
was also in the drawer, then he came back to the couch, continued eating
the blueberry muffin he had been eating before. The muffin's wrapper
was near my leg. He kept touching my ankle as he stared at the television—a cheesy rerun of *Love Boat* was on, and we had been making fun
of it before I so abruptly asked if his mother sent him cards.

I had asked him that question because I was thinking of my father,
but not in terms of where he had gone, or what he was doing—I was
thinking about him in terms of me. I was thinking the way my mother
did, about what it meant for me to be there right next to Lenny in my
pink cotton underwear, sitting so still, so intimate, and feeling so
strange about it. I had developed this awkward discomfort in how close
I was becoming to Lenny—which was something I sensed that normal
girls with normal fathers did not feel. Yet I couldn't stop myself,
couldn't help it. Even that first night when I slept in Lenny's bedroom,
I stayed up, blinked and blinked, wondering how long I would actually
stay with him, how long would he last?

Lenny ended up dumping me in a very slow, invisible, tedious way: He
ignored me. I had midterms at the time, and initially I fooled myself into
believing that he was giving me some space. The last time I saw him I

sat at his kitchen table counting the things I had to do: I had to write two twenty-page papers, study for three tests, prepare for a thirty-minute debate—and I was working at Shooters, six to two, four nights that same week. "Do you think I'll make it," I said to Lenny, sitting with my feet on the chair, my chin on my knees. "Or do you think I'll just die?"

He didn't say anything, he just nodded—he was buttering my bagel for me. He always did this sort of thing: He put my milk and sugar in my tea; he took my shoes off, even my socks; he combed my hair when it was wet. All of these things I never expected him to do—I was completely unaccustomed to such behavior—and so when it happened, I just stared at him.

That morning we had gotten up early; he said he had something important to do at the club. When we parted outside of his apartment, he did not kiss me good-bye. He hugged me for a long time, so long that I stared and stared at the apartment building across the way: at the inscribed street address in the cement archway, 126 Burbank, and then at the two cracked flower pots on the steps and the gray cat that sat in a window, still and silent, lifeless.

It was springtime, still cold, and I stood in Lenny's arms, ready to shiver, until he let go of me. Then he said good-bye to me, but he didn't really say it, he whispered it—and I knew right then that there was something wrong, but with an equal amount of certainty I felt I couldn't say anything, couldn't ask. I didn't even give Lenny a questioning expression. I just smiled and walked away.

After ten days of not hearing from Lenny, I made the first call, left him a message, acting as if nothing were wrong—I was hyper almost, incredibly upbeat. "Hey, it's Catherine—the fabulous, most wondrous debate speaker-slash-test taker in the world. Call me or I'll crush your head in." It was a joke, all laughs. The next message was simpler, although it was painful for me to leave—it infringed on my pride. But I had made up a few potential excuses for Lenny: His father had died; his phone didn't work; he was in the hospital.

The hospital excuse I liked the best. It was the richest and most well seen in my mind. I imagined that he had gotten in a fight at work. The last day I had seen him was a Sunday, and Sunday nights at the Cavern Club were reggae nights—despite the calm, supposed happiness of reggae music, it brought on the most violent of crowds. Lenny often told me long-winded, detailed stories about reggae night, about people found in the bathroom stalls beaten and unconscious. He claimed that everyone who came in had a gun or a knife on them and if they weren't already in a fight, they were constantly looking for one.

So initially I imagined that Lenny had gotten shot at work, but then that was too dramatic; so instead he got stabbed. Somewhere on his side, I decided, in a clean easy swipe that left only a line of blood like a cat scratch.

Of course, if he had been stabbed, I suppose he could've still used the phone, particularly a few days later, but I chose to live in this fantasy just for the slim amount of satisfaction it gave: He was wounded, he could not call—it served as my rationale for calling him that second time. I said, "Hi, this is Catherine. Call me if you can."

He never called me back though. So I was left as I always was: imagining.

$$8$$

MY MOTHER'S CALL

My mother called me in Madrid, made a certain unforgettable request regarding my father, during the first week of July. It was on a Wednesday, it was around midnight, I was sitting on the couch on the middle cushion. I had on a shirt that was Celia's—it was yellow, and it tied on the bottom with two suede strings. In front of me, I remember, the television was on, and the red light above the power knob kept getting dull, as if it might burn out, but then it turned bright again.

All of that I can recall with clarity, but what happened directly before—at work, for instance, I don't really remember.

It always seems to me that I had a certain important conversation with Esteban exactly the night before, but I can't entirely trust that—as it may have been a few weeks before, on some evening amongst the listless heat of June. Nevertheless, days and moments, how they are remembered, are often shaped by their significance—and although this particular conversation was only momentarily about my father, it was one I would always think of—it made me feel a certain closeness to Esteban.

We were at his house at the time, eating dinner on the patio by the pool. The back of his white house against the nine o'clock in the evening sunlight looked smaller than it had on the night of his party. Without all those people around the pool, without the butler and the music, it was a cozier world with pink-flowered bushes, fernlike plants, dangling clovers, pretty blue pots with nothing in them.

For dinner we had a white gazpacho soup, a *tortilla española* that did not taste as salty or dry as the kind in cafés, and then *ternera*, veal, that was cooked in olive oil, capers, and lemon. Esteban hadn't made the food himself; he had bought it at Majorca, a gourmet food shop—he admitted that only after we had finished eating, after the first bottle of wine was finished and we were about to have coffee. I told him he was a liar, a fake, and he shook his head, smiling, and said, "You're not a liar if you plan on telling the truth in the end."

"Then you're just a fake," I said.

He shrugged, took a sip of wine, as if the comment actually bothered him. I gazed behind him inside the house; I could see his living-room wall. The only picture he had up was a framed print of the Spanish poet García Lorca, but it was a very sad, sullen-looking picture, one in which you could almost see, in the tight set of his lips, that he knew what would later happen to him.

Harlan had a thing for García Lorca, and I told Esteban that, but I failed to mention that Harlan's interest had nothing to do with Lorca's actual work—it was based on the fact that he was gay and an artist and had died tragically, shot to death by a firing squad. Harlan was still in the age range where horrible fates were not just fascinating but glamorous.

"You think about him a lot, don't you?" Esteban asked.

"Harlan?"

He nodded. He was smoking a cigarette, inhaling.

I shrugged. "Well, I usually live with him. And I don't live with him now, so . . . yeah, I think about him."

"You sound like,"—he paused, put his cigarette in the ashtray, put his hands behind his head—"you sound like you don't just think about him . . . you worry?"

"No," I said flatly.

"No?"

"He's fine."

Esteban stared at me for a minute. "There's something weird about you two." He was rubbing his thumb and pinky together as he thought about this, eyeing me.

I stared down at the coffee in front of us on the wrought-iron table, its circular tray. For a while we were quiet, and then he sat up abruptly and poured us each a cup, his cigarette in the corner of his mouth. I watched him put a small metal strainer over each cup, separating the skin from the hot milk.

We didn't talk as we sipped our coffee, we didn't look at each other—the sun had fallen by this point; and his neighborhood, with its weeping willow trees and star-filled sky, had no noise, no car doors slamming, no dogs barking, no voices of any kind. Just an occasional car passing, but you didn't hear the motor, just the sound of loose gravel against the tires, a subtle, soft, popping sound.

"So what does you mother look like?" Esteban asked me, rather abruptly.

"Whah?" I said, disoriented by the question—I was still thinking about Harlan. Esteban repeated himself, and I sat there thinking. "My mom's blond . . . she's thin . . . she has a mole above her lip."

He waited. "And your father?"

"I don't know what my father looks like. I haven't seen him in a while."

He didn't say anything. He seemed to be thinking about that, deciding what it meant.

"What about you? You've got no pictures," I said, motioning at the house. "Do you have a physical description for me?"

"I'll give you my boyfriend, Juan, in Venezuela." This was the first time I had ever heard of his boyfriend. "He lives with me in my house there—he is my own García Lorca–obsessed roommate." He paused, swallowed. "My house is pink, and the tiles on the roof are orange. Juan is twenty-two. He has black hair and very long thin legs. He has leukemia."

I waited a moment, shifted in my seat. "Is he OK?"

"No," he said flatly, "he has leukemia." Esteban leaned forward, scratched his ankle, as if a bug had just bitten him. "Juan's the reason I'm not in Venezuela right now. Usually I spend June there."

"I don't understand," I said. "If he's sick, why aren't you there?"

He shook his head, kept his gaze out at the pool, at its aqua-blue light. "Maybe you have never been around someone who is very sick, but it is one of the hardest things . . . to watch someone . . ." He shrugged. "To see someone . . ." He made the gesture of something falling apart, the palm of his hand upturned, fingers separated.

"But I am going back," he said, looking down at his shirt.

"When?"

"When I can," he said, his voice soft.

A breeze came after that. Not a strong one, one you could see only in the ripples of pool water, in the flap of a napkin. The trees' leaves made no whooshing noise; my hair moved only slightly, like a tickle, against my shoulders.

"Sometimes," Esteban said, and waited. "Sometimes when you feel guilty for leaving people, you think about them all the time." He looked at me sideways, but still right in the eyes. "You think if you think of them, if you love them from a distance, then it's OK. It's not bad. It's like you think they can feel it." He was talking about Juan, but he was talking about Harlan, too, somehow, from the way he was looking at me. But I didn't want to talk about Harlan, about what made me worry. So my mind purposely drifted somewhere else. "So does that mean," I asked, "if you had, say, a father, who left you long ago, that he would have to think about you sometimes?"

Esteban stared at me, nodded, and said with a sympathetic certainty, "Of course." He paused after that, touched the edge of the table with his pinky. "There is never any real escape," he added softly. "Not one that lasts."

When my mother called that following Wednesday, when the telephone rang, I just stared at it. I didn't think it was anyone for me, and I hated having to answer the phone. Talking and understanding Spanish demanded more on the phone than it did in person—it was like speaking a third language, a fast-talking, garbled one. Besides, Celia and Isabel were home. They had their big test the following morning, and they were sitting out on the candlelit terrace trying to study. Really all they were doing was sitting there with pens and notebooks, two lime-green coffee cups in front of them, staring off into space.

We had two phones: one was a big red phone with rotary dialing that looked as if it had once sat on a hospital desk in the 1950s—that was the one sitting in the living room with me—and then we had a cordless.

Isabel was the one who finally picked up, the one who listened to my mother ask for me in her usual fashion, a mix of the few Spanish words she knew along with the rusty French she learned back in high school. *Je suis la madre de Catherine. Elle está?"*

Isabel smiled, said, *"Sí, sí."* She came into the living room and handed me the phone. *"Una francesa para ti."*

The first thing I said to my mother was, "Why are you talking to them in French?"

"That's how they understand me."

"They don't speak French."

"They gave you the phone, didn't they?"

"Right, because you're the only person who calls and speaks in French."

"Well, then, it's working."

I was annoyed all of a sudden. It seemed as if she never ever listened to me. I said, "Mom, no French, OK!"

"*What* are you getting so hostile about?"

I leaned back in the chair I was sitting in, put my hand on the back of the headrest. "I'm *not* hostile."

There was a pause.

"So what have you been doing? Tell me about your Spanish life."

"It's all good."

She asked me if I had any health problems, any intestinal disturbances. I told her no. There was another pause that seemed to mean she

was about to say something, but then she didn't. Instead she started talking about Gerry. We never ever talked about Gerry. He was about as
interesting as talking about air. He never did anything different; it was
always the same. He worked at Milton Bradley assembling Monopoly
games or some such thing, and then he came home and worked in his garden. She was talking about his garden. She was telling me how ruby red
his tomatoes were. And giant, so big. She told me how she drew a face
with Magic Marker on one of them and put it on top of the refrigerator.

I said flatly, "That sounds great."

There was a pause.

My mother said, "I talked to someone the other day."

"The tomato with the face?"

"No," she said matter-of-factly. "I talked to your father."

In the other room, I could hear Celia and Isabel fighting over the big
black law book.

"Es capítilo doce."

"No, es capítilo trece."

"¡Venga, dámelo!"

"No."

"¡Dámelo Celia! Ahora mismo."

"I went to the hairdresser on Tuesday," my mother was saying, "to
get my roots done, and then when I got back, just as I was coming in the
door, the phone rang and it was him."

My father had never called my house since those few phone calls I
received when he first moved to Maine. My mother did keep a certain
secret correspondence with him through letters, but that was it. I saw the
letters she got from him when I went through her things once when I
was fifteen or so. I found them all in a box: perfect penmanship, blue
ink—all signed: "Yours, James."

None of his letters ever mentioned me. He talked about Coca-Cola,
about a problem he was having with a store that wouldn't let him put up
the proper displays; he talked about the apartment he lived in, a woman
who lived upstairs from him who sang with a very high-pitched voice—
he wrote: "Her name is DeDe, and DeDe, I believe, is psychotic."

"He still lives and works in the same place," my mother was saying.

"What does he want?"

"He was just talking, ya know, about things." She paused. "He was a little drunk, slurring a lot."

"What time was it, ten in the morning?"

"No, it was much later than that," she said calmly, as if what I just said was a real question, not an insult. "It took about two hours at the salon. I guess, maybe six-thirty."

I was somewhat surprised that my mother didn't know the exact time, hadn't written it down in some sort of log. She never changed our home phone number, even when Gerry moved in and asked her to switch to his number. We didn't though; we kept our own—something I knew, and I suppose he knew, was about my father and the slim fantasy that he might call. There were times when Gerry tried to get her to change the number—he claimed that someone kept calling and hanging up on him.

He told us this once, I remember, in the car. We were on the Mass Pike coming back from a shopping mall. "Someone called last night around four and later at six," he said, and then he turned his head for one quick moment to look at my mother. He had his index finger on his bottom lip. "But just before I could even say hello, the guy hung up."

I was sitting in the backseat, my mother's shopping bags stacked all around me, my head turned slightly, staring out at the peaks of the pine trees, at the triangular shapes they made against the sky—I was, of course, thinking, as I knew my mother was, that the person who was hanging up on Gerry was my father. It afforded such wonder, such possibility. He was in a bar somewhere, I imagined, and the windows were stained glass. The pay phone was on a wooden shelf. My father was wearing a black scarf around his neck even though he had been inside the bar for hours. He was standing in front of the phone thinking of us. He was sad.

"I told him you were in Madrid," my mother said. "He was shocked. He said he never imagined you so far away."

"Really."

"Yeah."

"I'm sure."

"He called for a reason though."

The possibility that he was dying occurred to me—I felt no sense of panic though. In that moment, in all of my hostility, it felt like any old thing that might come at me and happen.

My mother said, "He wants to see you. When you come back."

"What do mean *see* me?"

"You know, *see* you. Have dinner."

I said, "It's a little fuckin' late for that, don't you think?"

"I knew you were going to get like this," she said.

"Oh?"

She didn't answer me.

"Oh?" I said again.

"You haven't seen him for seven years—"

"I don't count the last time I saw him," I said, "I don't count that."

"Fine, you haven't seen him in twelve years then. Even better." She waited a moment and then said again, "He wants to see you."

"No, he's just *saying* that! He's just saying that because I'm far away and he knows he can say it and not do it."

"That's not true," she said, and then there was something in her voice that made me feel all of a sudden as if she were lying—as if he hadn't called her, but she called him. In my mother's mind, which was always wheeling and dealing with my father and me, it seemed very possible that she might've concocted some scheme, one in which she took advantage of the fact that my father and I were currently so far away physically from each other. She was using that distance—I imagined—using all that false safety, to get us to promise something we normally never would.

"Are you lying to me!" I yelled.

She said, "No, I'm not lying! What do you think I'm lying about?"

"Everything. I think you lie about everything, and he's full of shit, too."

"No, he isn't. He means it. He—"

"He just wants me to say I'll see him, and then he won't go. He just wants to know he still can." I stopped, took a breath. I felt as though I had suddenly stopped breathing right. "And when is he going to see me anyway?" I said, "Is he going to go to the airport and pick me up with you?"

"He'll do whatever you want. If you want that, he'll do it."

There was something so preposterous about her saying that he would do anything I wanted. She was trying to make him sound like some apologetic doe-eyed thing instead of what he really was in my mind: a drunken person who had suddenly gotten bored.

"If I want him to knock me unconscious," I said, "will he do that for me?"

"Catherine."

"What?"

"You don't have to like him," she said. "You don't have to kiss him and hug him, but you could see him."

"For what crappy purpose?"

"Because there'll be no more wondering. No more mystery. If you just see him, all of that thinking, that questioning, will stop." The phone creaked a little, as if she were holding it too hard. "Don't you want it to stop?"

I didn't answer; I just stared in front of me at the television that had no volume, the two voiceless people talking to each other in red chairs.

On the phone in the background, I could hear the shrill dinging of a ice cream cart going by my mother's house, the jack-in-the-box-type tune getting louder and louder. It was already midnight in Madrid, and it was strange to realize that where my mother was, it was still light out, still daytime. I pictured my mother's lawn, the chemically induced green coloring, the white truck slowly going by, and I felt deeply distanced, as if it would be years before I would ever see her again.

"I sometimes worry that you will never get over him," my mother said abruptly—her voice louder than the ringing of the ice cream cart.

I didn't answer. I looked out the living room window at the pinkish light that came from the street lamp; it was a soft light, an easy light, one that just barely illuminated the octagon-shaped designs on the sidewalk.

"I won't see him."

"Why don't you just think about it?" she said, "Just—"

"What did I just tell you?" I yelled back at her, "*What* did *I* just tell you?"

She paused a moment, and then her voice became calm and smooth. "You just told me you didn't want to see him. You said you were afraid."

"I have to go," I said.

"Do you?"

"Yes."

A pause.

"Will you call me? In a few days?"

"Maybe."

"S'il vous plaît?"

"Maybe."

There was another pause; then she told me she loved me. I said it back. Shortly after, we hung up.

———

The last time I saw my father was at my confirmation. It was just before my mother had decided to let Gerry move in—she had already been dating him for a while, and she had written a letter announcing this to my father. I suppose it was all part of a wishful plan to tell him that she was with someone and then offer him the opportunity to mysteriously pop up on the stairs of St. Patrick's Church, face-to-face with her.

For the entire ceremony, he stood at the back of the church. I knew he was there without even seeing him. I could feel it. My mother had said that he might show up, that she had given him the address, the time. But I felt it in the sweatiness of my palms, in my inability to hold on to the words and prayers around me, in the brightness of the candle, in the shrill sounds of the bells they rang before communion, in the sections of stained glass—particularly the amber ones that seemed to glow with an intensity that wasn't just sunlight—in all of this, I could tell that he was there. It was one of the few times in my life when I felt I had the power to distinguish between what I sensed was happening and what I desperately wanted to happen.

Sitting in my pew, I kept my posture straight and stiff, and I did not turn my face to the side at all. I didn't want him to catch a side profile of me. I feared he would see how much older I had gotten—I had acne, not a lot but just enough to make me stare in my bathroom mirror as I covered patches of my face with my fingers. My teeth had grown a little crooked, too, a small space between my two front teeth. When I was a little girl, when he had last seen me, I was more perfect then, angelic-looking. I had the face of girl who did not need too much, did not demand too much. A girl who could sit still.

Outside I saw him leaning against the railing that divided the wide cement stairs in front of the church. He was wearing a brown suit and a green tie. He often didn't match. Once in the Blue Lagoon, he had told me, "When you're a looker like me, you don't have to worry about all that matching stuff."

I would say what it felt like walking down those stairs toward him, what he looked like with all the other kids and their parents in the distance behind him, but it's hard to describe. All I remember was the cement—it was the newer white kind with all those specks of silver that glitter and glitter like magic.

He gave me as a gift a card that said congratulations. It was a card that wasn't necessarily a card for a confirmation—it could've been for a graduation, a marriage, a pregnancy. The envelope was white, and it had stray pen marks all over it, as if it had been in the bottom of a drawer packed with junk. My father looked sweaty, his face bigger than it had been before, rounder, and he didn't smell good. It was not the smell of alcohol; it was the smell of someone who did not entirely take care of himself.

He recognized me once he saw me. He said, "Hey, ya big Catholic." He did not, however, hug me or kiss me, and I stood in front of him fully aware of the fact that he could not bring himself to touch me.

I moved a few inches away from him, stood on another stair. I was afraid that if I stood too close it might make it harder to talk, to act normal. Besides, there was no point in standing closer; he would be leaving within a few minutes—I knew that with an unspoken certainty.

"How do you feel?" he asked with the enthusiasm you would use with a person who had just run a race.

I said, "Fine."

At the very bottom of the stairs, my mother stood with Gerry. The suit she was wearing was mint green with intricate stitching around the lapel, and it had a matching strapless bag. She held the bag with both hands, as if it were very heavy, filled with things no one knew about. Gerry stood close to her, but I could not read his face. He had sunglasses on. His mouth was moving and moving. My mother's face was tilted in his direction, but her eyes climbed up those hot white stairs to me, to my father.

After my father left, when we were in Gerry's car, I opened my card. There was a twenty-dollar bill inside. In black pen, it was signed: "Love, Dad."

I put the twenty back in the card and looked out the window. It was hot it the car, so hot it put a strange metallic taste in my mouth. I opened the window, laid my head down on the seat cushion. On the floor, on the black car mat, I saw a staple. I picked it up, held it, then threw it back down.

9

THE RESURFACING COMPLEX

The number one rule of men who leave you is that they will always resurface. The timetable on this varies—it is never as soon as you want it to be, it's certainly not when you are still ripe with hotheaded hallucinatory visions of what you will say to him, how you will strike out against him, looking not just gorgeous but doe-eyed and thin. The man who leaves you will instead appear weeks, months, most often years after the fact. They may pretend they don't remember you or they'll go the other way, act like they've had you on their minds forever like a constant nagging guilt.

In any case, your anger will have subsided by this point, and you'll be left bereft, disoriented—do I tell him to go screw? Or do I tell him he looks great, wonderful, better than ever?

My personal feeling was always to act as if you didn't care. Why remain loyal to your old feelings, your old self, when it would only make you look mental and, more importantly, still affected. Let him squirm. Let him go home and think more deeply, more darkly, about whatever crappy event made him look for you in the first place—and make no mistake, he was looking for you, he didn't just stumble upon you; he was searching and hopeful, desperate for someone to tell him: I missed you.

Lenny reappeared in Shooters eleven months after he dumped me. The whole time he worked right down the street; I could've run into him on purpose if I'd wanted. But I was too proud for that. I was not like the other girls I worked with, the ones who ran weeping after their ex-boyfriends. I wouldn't go to his work. I wouldn't get drunk there or dance there or cry there. I wouldn't walk past his apartment. I wouldn't call to him from a speeding car or a high window or a distant rooftop. I wouldn't talk to his friends. I wouldn't have my friends talk to his friends. In essence, I wouldn't do anything in any way that had an identifiable connection to him.

But in my mind, in that hideous thing known as my imagination, my every action twirled and twirled around him. I thought about him every single day, repeatedly. I had visions of his appearing in places where I had to go: the dentist's office, the grocery store, the cleaner's, my mother's house, even on the bus sitting next to me.

I also created bizarre fictitious connections between him and the people I knew—like I'd dream up that my professor who told me that I was "incredibly bright, incredibly gifted" had suddenly moved into Lenny's building. I established a relationship for them: They were happy, chatty neighbors who had conversations in front of the mailboxes in Lenny's foyer. I created various Catherine-obsessed episodes between them: Lenny happens to see my professor carrying a BU envelope in her hand and asks her if she knows me, and she says to him, "Oh, you mean Catherine Kelly. My God, she's a breathtaking girl. She's so bright, so gifted." And then my professor would sigh, walk away from Lenny, leave him standing there in his gray-walled hallway, miserable with himself. I could imagine all of this in such detail—Lenny's red-and-black-plaid shirt, his jeans with a stain on one leg, the blotchiness of his skin, the way he stood with one hand on his hip. Even my professor's key ring—which I had never seen—I could imagine as she stood there praising me: It was a little black terrier with a bone in its mouth.

There were even certain days when I'd get up and I'd think, Today is the day I'll see Lenny. Perhaps I thought I'd see him because of the imagined conversation he had with my professor; but, in any case, even if that was something I only dreamed, certain days I knew I would see him. I had to. And because my days went on so late, I continued to believe it as I walked between rows and rows of pool tables, glancing at my watch now and again, waiting, looking; but then he wouldn't show, and I'd sit there doing my paperwork, counting my cash, and I'd feel not just disappointed, but sick, disgusted with myself. As time went on, I felt as if this obsessive thinking was getting worse and worse instead of better, and what disturbed me wasn't how I felt for Lenny as much as it was my inability to control how much I thought about him, in what great detail. Often I found myself, without even knowing it, concocting dialogues between us—sometimes they were angry, other times friendly and fun. But they were always reeling in the back of my head, to the point that late at night I would squeeze my eyes shut and think as hard as I could, like a shout, Please make it go away. Make it stop.

But it wouldn't. It lived and breathed inside of me.

Lenny reappeared at Shooters on a Thursday. It was about eight o'clock, it was raining outside, all of the pool tables were full. Most people were still waiting to play—they sat at the tables near the bar, or they just stood around in my way.

One of the girls had called in sick, and so I had more tables than usual, eighteen of them. It was one of those nights when I was already frazzled, and we weren't even at our busiest hour. I had started forgetting to get things, something I didn't usually do—it was just that I couldn't actually fit everything I needed on my tray. I forgot Budweisers and cigarettes and plates of nachos and Purple Hooter shots. I told people I would bring waters and clean ashtrays and extra napkins, and then I didn't. They asked for checks, and I said, "Yeah, next time around, next time."

People were getting a little bit mad at me, a little bit mean.

"I asked you for French fries three times," one woman said to me. She held up three fingers as if didn't I know what the number three represented. "When are we going to get them?"

She was a preppy woman in her midthirties with a ponytail; her entire outfit was khaki. When she spoke to me, she had this way of looking at me in my minidress and boots, as if I were very stupid, as if she thought I had made several attempts to find the French fries and failed.

The guy with her, who was bent down, leaning across the pool table, immersed in his shot, said, "Why don't you leave her alone? She's busy."

I looked at the guy, felt some sort of warmth in the pink plaid shirt of his. "They'll be here in five minutes," I said. "I promise."

I passed Rick on the way to the kitchen and said as a joke, "These people are trying to destroy me."

He smirked. He shook his keys. He said, "No, no. They're just trying to hurt you." He pointed at the kitchen. "And you better watch out, your farm boy's here."

My farm boy was, of course, Lenny. He was standing at the kitchen window, with one hand on the marbled counter, the other holding a cappuccino in a flowered paper cup. He had a ridiculous-looking yellow bandanna wrapped around his head, and he was looking at a movie poster on the wall that had Tom Cruise holding a pool stick. He was standing just close enough to spot Rick and me in his peripheral vision.

Under my breath, I said to Rick, "Oh, fucking great," as if seeing Lenny was merely a light disturbance, instead of a mind-altering horror.

When I went over to kitchen window, I handed the cook my order and then looked at Lenny out of the corner of my eye. I said, "Hey."

"How are you?" he said in a very happy, animated way.

Mimicking his enthusiasm, I said, "Good."

"How's school?"

I said, "Good."

He waited a moment, as if he were trying to think of something very specific and thoughtful to ask. He said, "Is that teacher of yours still giving you a hard time?"

I felt like saying, "Oh, you mean your neighbor?" Instead I said, "No, we get along now. It's fine."

"Great," he said, moving his head up and down. "Great."

He asked me a few other things, and I answered, but I didn't ask him anything about his life, nothing at all. The cook came in the window, told me the French fries would be at least twenty minutes. I argued with him about it, told him I needed them now. Lenny just stood there watching us; I could see his hand out of the corner of my eye: His nails were all cut short, his knuckles appeared hairless. The cook gave Lenny a white to-go box, his dinner.

I said, "Those better not be French fries."

He laughed, said no they weren't. Then he backed away, took his hand off the counter. "It was good seeing you."

I nodded. "Yeah."

Then he left, and I went to the bar to pick up my drinks.

The French fry people never got their French fries. Table 12 never got their Black and Tans. Table 6 never got their Kamikazes. Table 8 walked out on me without paying their check. I moved as quickly as possible between the tables as I brought orders one by one. People flagged me down or whistled or just plain grabbed my shoulder. The French fry woman said, "What is going on here? Are you purposely not getting us what we asked for?"

My eyes were glassy—glassy from having already been yelled at three times, from being unable to think, from the frustration of knowing I had to get things that I couldn't seem to get to. I could do only a few things at a time—it was not that I was directly thinking of Lenny because I wasn't; I was just shaky, overwhelmed, unable to deal with the weird heated feeling in my chest coupled with these people, these strangers, talking to me, yelling at me, asking for things all at once.

I told the French fry woman, "I'm trying, but I just can't . . . I can't . . . get to it right now." As I said this I pointed all around the room, as if that might mean something to her. The guy with her, no longer patient, said to me, "How much is our check?" They had had two beers. I said, "Five," and then, as he flipped through his wallet, I stood there awkwardly, looking away from him. He looked up at me, about to give me a five, and then, whether it was the way I couldn't look at him, or the way my fingers shook just a little, he gave me two fives. He said, "Keep it."

He did not smile, he didn't say have a great night, but he didn't have to. The feeling that five-dollar tip inspired, I cannot fully explain to anyone who has never waited tables. That five dollars did not mean cab fare or a bag of chips and a Coke; it meant more: It was a small rectangular piece of human goodness.

That five-dollar bill buoyed me up a little for the next ten minutes or so—made me feel as if I could manage my tables, get myself in order. But then something happened. I brought a beer to a guy who was playing pool by himself—he was drunk, so drunk that his face was flushed a dark pink, and when he walked, he held on to the edge of the pool table, grazed the green felt with his fingertips. When he had first arrived, he had been wearing mirrored sunglasses, and when I looked at him, I could see my face, my tray, the paleness of my arms. Now he had the glasses off and had put them in the middle of all the pool balls, right next to the eight ball. As I stood there in front of him with his beer, he ignored me—he was planning a shot, or pretending to. He angled the stick across the table, then started to shoot, then didn't.

I said, "Two fifty, please," for the third time, and then he came over to me, walked around the table. He said, "I ordered this here beer a long time ago." He got closer, leaned in. I could feel his breath at my neck, not my ear. He said, "What's the matter, can't walk fast enough?" Then he backed away, looked right into my eyes. "Somebody fuck you too hard last night?"

All around us there was the heavy loud smack of pool balls hitting one another. The girl voice's on the loudspeaker said, "D12. D12, your pool table is now ready."

If I had had the strength, the capacity, I would've taken my tray and smashed that guy over the head. I could envision it—I'd hit him and hit him and hit him right in the face. I could even hear the hollow sound it would make, like slapping your open hand on a wall. But I couldn't quite get myself to physically do it. Instead, I lost my tray's balance and it fell onto his pool table: There was only one Amstel and plastic cup of Coke, along with some loose quarters, and a Blistex I kept in a plastic shot glass. The Amstel fell on its side, spilled all foamy on the green felt. The man didn't say anything. I was crying, but I didn't know it. I thought I was just standing there. But then I felt the heat on my face and an inability to control my breath—it kept coming in big, long sweeps, and then, lastly, I felt the tears, wet, rolling.

If people were staring at me, if the man said anything else to me, I didn't realize it. I just walked toward the entrance of Shooters. There were two flights of stairs before you got onto the street level. I ran down the stairs, past a few people were walking up. A doorman who I didn't really know was checking IDs at the front. He had shiny corn-silk blond hair, big wide lips, white teeth. He said, "Catherine?" and reached out his hand like he was going to touch me, pull me toward him.

I moved out of his reach, quick and desperate, as if his very touch might make me scream and scream. Once I got out the door, I stood out front hailing a cab. It was raining, not incredibly hard, but still it felt cold against my bare arms and shoulders. There was a taxicab garage across the street, but none of the taxis were stopping—their bright headlights just whooshed past me. I kept looking back at Shooters, afraid the doorman was going to come out, or Rick or someone else—I didn't want any of them near me; I wanted out.

I walked farther into the middle of the street, still waving at the cabs. I had my tip money in one hand—it was folded the long way, wrapped in between my fingers, the same way I held it under my tray. I waved with that hand, as if the sight of money might make someone stop faster. Finally a cab did stop, and then I sat in its backseat, shivering.

When I got to my apartment, I realized only once I stood at the front door that I didn't have my keys. I buzzed and buzzed my apartment, as if the more I did it, the faster Harlan would come.

"What?" he yelled through the intercom, annoyed.

"Come open the door."

He recognized my voice, could tell I was upset. He said, "One sec, OK. Just one sec."

Once he appeared at the hallway in his terry-cloth slippers and jeans, I pounded on the window of the door, as if someone were chasing behind me. Harlan ran down the hallway, opened the door, and then as soon as I got inside I immediately grabbed him, put my face against his neck. Normally Harlan and I didn't touch—it took him a few moments to put his arms around me, as if he needed time to get used to it.

He tried to get me to go into the apartment, but I didn't want to. I just wanted to stay in the hallway with the bright fluorescent lights and the white walls and the cheap gray carpeting. We sat down on the floor, but I kept my head on his chest.

"What happened?" he said.

I wouldn't tell him about Lenny; I couldn't stand to. Instead, I told him about everything else: about the French fry woman and the yelling and the whistling and the table that walked out. Then I told him about the drunk, how he asked me if I got fucked too hard.

After that we were both silent; there was just the sound of an alarm clock in a nearby apartment beeping and beeping. When the alarm finally was turned off, I said, my voice more calm than I felt, "You will never know what it's like, what it does to you, to have some guy come up to you and with one simple look or word or touch, degrade you, flatten you out, make you into shit." I shook my head, wiped my face with my hand. "You will never know what that's like."

Harlan didn't say anything at first. With his finger he was making a square shape on the carpet. I watched his finger go around and around the imaginary box, and then he said, "But Catherine, honey." I looked up at him—he never used the word *honey*. "You've to got remember something."

A tear dripped off my chin. "What?"

His voice was soft, but stern—he said, "You let them do it to you."

WHAT MEN CAN OFFER

I spent the next few days after my mother called about my father feeling emotional and freakish. I kept misplacing my keys—each time I tried to leave the apartment I spent a minimum of twenty minutes backtracking to where I might have put them. Sometimes I got so desperate I looked for the keys under the couch, in the refrigerator, under some towels in the bathroom. Throughout my search I'd whisper, *ay Dios mío*, oh my God, over and over. I'd get angry with myself, as well as with the keys themselves, as if they were hiding from me, giggling at me, thrilled with my discontent, until finally, glassy-eyed and shaky, I'd find them sitting somewhere, clear and obvious.

On Saturday, I lost my keys outside of my apartment, not inside, and I sat on one of the steps pulling everything out of my purse. Then Raúl appeared. His mustache looked even thinner than usual that day, the skin on his chin had a strange ruddy rash of some kind, as if he had just shaved minutes before.

"*¿Te gustaría un Mars Bar, Boston?*" he asked. Would you like a Mars Bar? He had the candy bar in his hand; I knew without even looking. I could hear the wrapper, its crinkling. I didn't answer him. I kept going through my things, which were scattered loose on the steps: my wallet; a lip gloss; a blush that had no cover; a pink fan that Isabel had given me which was tinted from the blush powder, streaked with an orangy brown. I opened the fan, stared at it as if within its wooden slats I might find my big silver keys.

"*¿Boston?*" Raúl said, and sat down next to me. He had taken to calling me Boston instead of Catherine, as if the place from which I came was more important to him, more memorable, than my name. I kept looking in my bag, ignoring him, not even smiling. "*Hola Boston,*" he said, What's going on—"*¿Qué tal?*"

My eyes, he noticed, were wet—I had already that day lost my new scarf on the metro, left my ATM card on the counter of a Caixa bank where two elderly women were staring at it when I returned, almost hesitant to give it back to me.

"*¿Qué te pasó hoy?*" Raúl was asking. What happened to you today?

"*Nada,*" I said, digging in my bag, feeling for my keys. I couldn't find them though, only loose change and what felt against my fingertips like granules of sugar.

"*¿Qué pasó?*" he said to me again. What happened? What's wrong? As he said this, he was smiling at me, smiling as if he already knew what was wrong with me and thought it was quite foolish, petty. I kept searching each zippered compartment of my bag for my keys, and then it occurred to me, as it always did when I couldn't find them, that I never would. I would be locked out—Celia and Isabel weren't home. "*Tienes que decirme. ¿Por qué no puedes decirme? Dime.*" He leaned in closer; I could smell the sweetness of his cologne mixed with sweat. "*Puedo entender todo, puedo ayudarte, puedo ser tu intimo amigo, tu chico favorito.*" He touched my arm.

"Don't fuckin' touch me!" I screamed in English. "Don't you fucking FUCKING touch me!"

There was the distant sound of someone hammering at something far down the street, and I listened to it momentarily, thinking Raúl would leave, but he kept staring at me with this dull uncomfortable softness to his eyes.

I swept everything off the steps back into my bag and half walked, half ran up the street. I crossed San Vicente to the gardens outside of Palacio Real. It was shady there, full of trees, a place to hide from the white heat that seemed to seep into you, moisten the backs of your knees, your palms, your hairline.

I sat there on a bench, went through my purse more calmly, as if I were looking for a spare pen, and I found my keys in a side compartment, zipped up and safe.

Things finally seemed better, I felt more in control, on Tuesday when I was again at work. They gave me a batch of about twenty letters written in English that I had to proofread. The letters were all boring, all in-house, written to the mother company, which was American; nevertheless, there was something all-engrossing about the actual labor of reading and fixing all those words, which made no sense, and hours and hours passed.

Kansas Katy called me at some point while I was correcting the sentence, "We have hoped you could understand the urgency." She sounded very upbeat and excited, as if she were very happy to be talking to me. I hadn't talked to her in a few days.

The first thing she said to me was "Happy Fourth of July!" even though it was the fifth of July. "Did you feel sad," she asked, "without any fireworks yesterday?"

I told her no—that I hadn't even remembered. A lie.

She paused for a minute, and then said, "Well, I've been thinking and thinking, and I've decided, *I've decided*, that I *know* I want to come . . . but I want to know, you can say no if you want to, but I want to know if I can . . . if I can . . . bring someone with me. A companion."

I didn't say anything.

"I'm not trying to be pushy or anything," she said quickly, "Really, I'm not, but I just think if I'm coming all that way, if I'm going to spend a whole week there, I should be able to have someone with me. Someone to share it with."

What she meant was she wanted Lysol to pay for her companion to come. I said, "OK, well, I have to ask Carlos . . ."

"Who's Carlos?" she said, sounding a little exasperated, as if the name Carlos brought to her mind something awful, perhaps a man in a long leather jacket with a pistol in his pocket.

"He's my boss," I said, "he's the guy who talked to you first. He wrote you that letter."

"Oh, yeah, yeah, and then they gave me you." She paused. "Do you think he'll say OK?"

"I don't know," I said without much concern. "But who are you going to bring?"

"Well, I'm not sure," she said. "A girl has to choose." Then she laughed and added, "I was actually thinking of bringing my dad."

I let go of my pen. "Why?"

"Because," she said, "I have a good time with him."

I already knew that she lived with her father, that he was sixty-six and he could run "like a race car." She attributed his fine health to the fact that he didn't smoke or drink or gamble. When she told me this, she had gone off on a tangent about gambling, said it was the worst of all afflictions, and I had drifted off, thinking of all the rinky-dink casinos they had in Madrid—how they would appall her with their smoke and blinking money signs and green barstools. There was also a government-run lottery, la ONCE, which was omnipresent in Madrid. Only blind people sold the tickets, either in cabinlike booths or while they were walking on the street, sheets of tickets attached to their shirts.

"My father likes the rodeo," Kansas Katy was telling me, "and I bet he'd like that whole bullfighting thing."

"They kill the bulls here though. They don't just chase them around."

"You've been to one?"

"No, I refuse to go to one." I only knew about them through Esteban. Celia and Isabel didn't like them either—they said they were boring.

"They throw a damn body part out into the crowd, don't they?"

"It's an ear, and I don't think they throw it."

"Are you sure it's not the testicles?" She was laughing.

"No, they leave those alone."

"Can you imagine," she said, "having a bull's balls land right on your lap?"

I picked up my pen, starting doodling again. I said, "I don't think I would like it."

"It would ruin your skirt for sure."

I said, "Yup," and then switched the subject back to Carlos. I said I would ask him about her companion and get back to her.

"Well, OK," she said. "But are you all right?"

I said, "yeah."

"Are you sure?"

"I'm sure," I said. "Why? Are you all right?"

"Of course," she said, and laughed. "I'm going to Spain with my father. I'm as happy as can be."

Shortly after Kansas Katy's phone call, I started to get emotional again. I was always weird like that, whatever upset me worked in spurts, and the longer I went being calm and collected, the bigger price I paid in the end. I had once read in a book that grief, or, as they put it, "cause-related sadness," was a never-ending experience, a constant battle—the idea was that things never healed; they just moved on and on inside of you, attaching themselves to, and continuously being expressed through, as the book put it, "later misfortunes." The book was, of course, Harlan's. After I read a page or two, I said to him, "Where did you get this shitty fuckin' book?"

He stared at it, winced as if he were trying to focus. He was in the middle of moving out of his dorm room at the time, and I was going through all the odd things he separated out on his bed.

"I hate that book, too," he said. "My mother gave it to me. Gimme it." He reached over, took it out of my hand, and threw it out the window. It landed five stories down on top of a NYNEX van; the book was red with black lettering, and it sat there almost perfectly centered in the middle of the rectangular white roof of the van. He and I stared at it for a while as if it might move, or perhaps someone might come out of the van and decide to read it.

"You could've hurt someone throwing that," I said.

He nodded indifferently and picked up his pot pipe, which had fluorescent alien heads all over it. He lit it and inhaled.

Tuesday night after work, I planned to stay in. Celia and Isabel weren't home; they had both gone back to Gijón and would not be back until Thursday—they had decided to skip Tuesday's class as compensation for undergoing such a rigorous test the week before.

I ate dinner by myself that night, a premade *tortilla española* that I bought in the supermarket and some leftover red wine that I poured into a white coffee cup. I sat in the living room; a nighttime Argentinean soap opera was on TV. In the scene that I was watching, a woman was lying in a hospital bed wearing mascara and fuchsia lipstick, her hair perfectly parted and glossy. Her doctor had apparently just told her she was going to die. There were some close-ups of her trembling lips; shortly after, her six-year-old daughter was let into the room. The woman began telling her little girl that something was going to happen to her soon, she wasn't going to be there all the time. The little girl kept asking why.

"I'm going somewhere else," her mother said.

"*¿Dónde?*"

"To a place where I can see you all the time, but you," she said, covering her little girls eyes, "won't be able to see me. But you'll know I'm there." The mother paused, swallowed. "When you get older, scary things might almost happen, like a car might almost hit you, or a dog might try to bite you, but then it won't. *Nunca lo pasará.*"

The mother was crying at this point, tears dripping off her chin. The little girl didn't seem affected by it, she just stared, blank-faced, pulling on the tips of her mother's hair.

"But this is the part you should always remember. Always," the mother said.

The little girl nodded.

"Whenever one of those bad things almost happened and didn't—it was because I was there and I pushed it out of the way. Someday you will get very mad at me. You will think I left you, but I didn't." She shook her head. "I just wanted to watch you from a better place."

"You will watch from someplace very high?" the little girl asked.

Her mother nodded.

"You will watch me from behind the sun?"

The mother started to say something, and then I grabbed the remote control, clicked the TV off. I was crying so hard that my nose was running. I had that tight feeling in the back of my throat, the one that feels as if your esophagus is surely shrinking. I tried to calm myself, tried to breathe in and out, but I was fooling myself somehow, all I really wanted do was sit there cry and cry over two people I didn't even know, two make-believe people in a TV show.

That's what I told myself I was getting upset about.

"You will watch me from behind the sun?" I remembered the little girl's voice saying. *¿Me mirarás de tras del sol?* I let it play over and over in my mind, and with those words, all the emotion, like a heaping pressure, sifted out of me, made my hands shake. Then the phone rang, the big red 1950s phone. I stared at it, had no intention of getting it, but it kept ringing and I knew it was Esteban.

I waited, wiped my face. Then I picked up the phone and said, *"¿Sí?"*

"Soy yo. What time do you want to go out tonight?"

"It's eleven already," I said. "I don't want to go out."

"What do you mean? What's wrong with you?"

I could not tell if he was asking that because I wouldn't go out or because I sounded upset.

I said, "I don't feel good today."

"Come out and have some champagne. You'll feel better if you have some champagne."

"I don't think so."

"A whiskey?" he asked. "Or how about a bottle of *Ribera*—I'll find something nice." I didn't say anything. "Somewhere quiet," he paused, "we'll go somewhere quiet."

Across from the couch that I was sitting on, I could see myself in the mirror on the wall, the mirror was tilted a little from hanging on two extra-long pegs, and it had a way of making me look wider than I really was, particularly my face. I was just sitting there, puffy-eyed, wearing a peach bathrobe, the red phone looking big and bulky in my hand. I kept staring at the mirror, but not at myself so much as at the other objects in the room: the lit lamp next to me, the sofa's straight wooden arm, the yellow curtains that shifted a little in the window.

Esteban seemed to be driving while he was talking to me because he didn't really notice that I hadn't answered him, or said anything at all, for an extra-long time. He said, "Come out, come out, will you come out?"

After a minute or two of watching the curtains move, I said, "OK, but we have to go somewhere quiet."

"I know the place," he said, "I know just the one."

Esteban brought me to Exposición, a cigar bar in el barrio Salamanca. Once we walked in, I told him we had to leave. It was very bright, full of big lamps with blue-and-white-striped lampshades, couches with tasseled pillows, and a white marble floor that reflected all the bright light. I couldn't stand it. I wanted to go somewhere on Castellana, to some *terraza*, where we could sit outside in the dark. Esteban insisted we stay, said we would have only one drink, but then after three drinks, we were still there, and I suddenly in my drunkenness got mad about it, that he had lied, that we were still somewhere I didn't want to be. We started bickering and then we left, walked down a block toward where I wanted to go.

After two minutes of silent walking, Esteban said, "You're being very unhappy tonight; what's wrong with you?"

"Nothing."

"Are you homesick?"

"No."

"It's OK to be homesick."

"I'm not homesick."

"I am," he said, "I'm going back to Venezuela on Thursday. For a week or so."

Esteban was from Spain, not Venezuela, so it was kind of a lie to say he was homesick, but I wasn't thinking of that. I was thinking why he might be going there: his boyfriend, Juan.

Since that one night at his house, Esteban never mentioned him again, but I was sure that despite his jokey ways he thought about Juan all the time. I saw it in the way he couldn't go through a long pause without saying something sarcastic, without smiling abruptly, without taking a sip of his drink. His continuously upbeat humor, like all humor to me, was not the symptom of a happy light-hearted person. If that was the case, drunks wouldn't be so funny, and crazy people wouldn't be laughing all the time. Humor was, and always would be, in my mind, the rejection of all you felt, of every dark thing that loomed over you—it was your own personal fight.

"Are you going to be unhappy without me here to entertain you?" Esteban asked.

I didn't answer—I was thinking about what it would be like without him around for a while. I made this little sound that came out of my throat, one of slight discomfort, and then I said, "No."

"I have a friend," he said, "a friend who wants to meet you."

We were approaching the corner; he stopped. "Where do you want to go, to ABC or Castellana?"

"ABC is bright."

He shrugged. "OK."

We walked in the direction of Castellana.

"Will you meet my friend?" he asked again, and there was something in his tone that I didn't like. It gave away somehow the fact that he had purposely waited a moment before he asked the question over again—it occurred to me then, in the persistence of his voice, that he was trying to set me up with someone.

"How *old* is your friend?"

"I don't know, forty-five maybe."

"Why would I want to hang out with a guy who's forty-five?"

"I'm forty-five, Catherine."

"I know, but that's different."

"How's it different?"

"It just is."

"He works in London. He's Spanish though."

I didn't say anything.

"You could just go out with him once, meet him, go to some places the way that we do. Have fun."

"I don't want to—it doesn't sound fun."

"Just once?"

He waited and said it again. "Just once?"

I wanted him to shut up about it. I said, "Maybe."

An ambulance was approaching, the sirens very loud—but the sirens were not like American sirens. They had a different beat, like the warning sound of a school bus when it's backing up. The sirens kept getting closer and closer, and then the ambulance turned down a side street away from us.

Esteban said, "So I'll book your flight for next weekend?"

For a drunken minute, I thought he was talking about my going to Venezuela. Then I thought he was still talking about Venezuela, but as a joke.

"What are you talking about?" I said. "What flight?"

"He lives in London, how else do you want to get there?"

"I thought he was here." I was starting to get mad. I said, "No, I'm not doing that. I'm not going to London!"

"He's a friend of mine, Catherine."

I said, "So what?"

We walked a little farther. We were on Ortega y Gasset, and there we were passing all the fancy shops: Gucci and Calvin Klein and Armani. There were pictures of people with very pouty lips in some of the windows, while others had white hairless mannequins, most of them wearing leather.

"My friend's got everything," Esteban said as he slowed down and stared in the bright white windows of one of the stores. "Really he does. He's got a house in just about every place you'd want to go: Venice and St. Tropez and Marbella."

I stopped walking—I could feel what he was saying before he fully said it. I stared at him with my arms wrapped tightly around myself, as if I were cold.

He took a step closer to me, and then made a gesture as if he were going to touch my arm, but he didn't. He said, "My friend would be good to you." His eyes were moving ever so slightly back and forth, as if he were trying to read something on my face. He added after a dramatic pause, "He would give you things."

"I am not a hooker!" I screamed at him. "Why do you think that? Why do you think that I would do that?"

He said, *"Baja tu voz"*—keep your voice down.

"Fuck you!" I screamed, and started to walk away from him, but I was wearing a long skirt with no slit, and it was hard to take big proud strides.

"I'm not saying you are a hooker," he said, walking behind me. "I'm not saying that."

I turned around. "Then what are you saying?"

"That you would make a nice companion . . . for someone."

I screamed, "I can't believe, I can't fuckin' believe you're saying this to me! You can't say this to me right now! You can't. If you wanna say this stuff tomorrow, go ahead, but today could you just stop, could just stop saying what you are *saying*!"

I started walking again, took a right. He walked behind me. There was a store on my left, The Taste of America. It had Paul Newman's salad dressing and Duncan Hines cake mix in the window. A Fourth of July banner was across the top of the window, in each corner were drawn-on fireworks in red, white, and blue. I walked by the store quickly, my heels clicking unsteadily against the cement.

"Tell me something," he called out from behind me. "Are you happy?"

I said, "Oh, shut up."

"How about if I answer that for you," he said, walking alongside of me. He pointed his index finger at me, touched my shoulder. "You are not happy, Catherine. And . . . I have the sense that you have not been happy for a long time. I don't imagine you as a very happy cocktail waitress, and I don't imagine you as being particularly happy studying whatever it is you study, which you cannot even afford and don't even like."

I took a left—the light in front of us was green. He said, "Where are you going?"

"I don't know. I'm just walking!"

Both of our shoes were loud against the cement, stomping almost. "That's exactly the problem," he said, pointing at me. "You don't ever think about where you're going." He shrugged and then turned to me, faced me. "What do you like to do, Catherine? Tell me what you like to do?"

"I know what I don't like, I don't like you."

"OK," he said, "you don't like me, but what *do* you like? Can you answer that? I bet you can't." He waited. "OK, so I'll answer for you, I'll tell you what you like." He started naming things on his fingers. "You like to go out, you like to drink, you like to go to *terrazas,* you like the dark . . .

"And what *would* you like to do? You'd like to travel, see places, but you can't, you say. You can't, you can't, you can't." He took a breath. "You said the other day that you like languages, you said you'd like to be like Monica and know French and Italian and Russian and Greek, but you can't, you say. You don't have time. And the most important, you don't have money. No one supports you—it's you, you, you, or you die.

"Oh, it's so sad being Catherine, isn't it?"

I said, *"Stop talking to me!"*

"Because you know it's not true." He pulled on my arm, made me

stop walking. "Because you do have time. And you do have money—
you have it all over you." He poked me in the forehead hard. "You have
it right there, and there are people in this world—or, I should say, there
are men who would gladly give you their money, and you don't have to
fuck them to get it. You just have to talk to them, amuse them, make
them happy. Do you think you could do that?"

If I hadn't been crying like mad earlier that day, I would've been
crying then, not out of sadness but out of frustration. I didn't know
where I was because I had taken too many turns, and I didn't know how
to get back home, and Esteban was not going to let go of me. He just
kept talking and talking and squeezing my arm, and I couldn't get away
from him because of the damn slitless dress I was wearing and the tee-
tering shoes. So he just kept going on and on, it felt, yelling at me outside on a dark corner that had a big round streetlight that glowed and
glowed full force, like a flashlight.

Finally, he ran out of the things he was saying, and he said, almost
breathlessly, "And you don't have to sleep with Borja."

There was a pause—and then I started to laugh, the kind of laugh
you laugh at a funeral or a wake, the kind that comes from any stupid
thing that someone says that takes on some giant comic force simply
because you are so tired, so sick, of feeling what you feel. I said, laughing, "Who the fuck is *Borja*? What kind of name is Borja?"

"That's his name, my friend."

"It's awful."

"But did you hear me? You don't have to sleep with him."

I said, slurring a little, "That's bullshit."

"It's not bullshit, it's the way it is. It's the way *he* is." He stared at
me, waited. "Couldn't you just meet him? Here in Madrid he could
come. You could just talk to him, just listen to him a minute or two." In
my drunkenness I associated his words with my mother's words about
my father: *You don't have to hug him or kiss him. You could just see him,
honey, can't you do that?*

I looked down at the sidewalk, grazed the heel of my shoe over the
polka-dot imprint on the pink cement. I felt tired, very tired, as if the

fight I was fighting was one I had always been fighting and it never did anything, never got me anywhere.

"I'm not leaving here," I said. "If he wants to come here, he can, but it doesn't mean anything. Doesn't mean I'll like him."

Esteban shook his head. "You don't have to like him."

I said softly, "Yeah."

We stood there on the corner for what felt like a half hour, and then he took my arm in his, the same way a father takes his daughter down a wedding aisle, and slowly we walked back to the Porsche.

We were silent the whole ride home, and I didn't look directly at him, and he didn't look at me. At a red light I noticed in my peripheral vision that he was turning and turning this ring that he always wore on his left hand. The ring was coppery-looking and cheap; it looked like something a child might find if he were digging in the dirt. I had decided from the moment I first noticed the ring that it was Juan's.

Over the past few days, I had come to attribute a number of positive things about Esteban to Juan, to his dying existence somewhere far off, and in that car, in that distrustful silence I now had with Esteban, I realized that I had probably made it all up. Or maybe he had, just to make me feel close to him.

His story about Juan wasn't even a story, but a small bit of information, yet it had made me feel the same sudden warmth that I had felt for Lenny when he told me about his mother, or for Harlan when he told me about losing his virginity. It was a feeling that I did not normally feel for just anyone; it was sudden and all consuming.

I thought about this as we moved through the streets toward my neighborhood and then—after I said good-bye to Esteban and he told me he would call me "about everything" —I took my distrust with me upstairs to the empty apartment. I sat on the couch where I had sat when Esteban originally called, and sipped the wine in the same white coffee cup. I poured myself more.

In my dull drunkenness, I connected in my head all the shady pieces of

Esteban. I remembered the party of his to which I had first gone, with all the pretty foreign women Monica had been so disdainful of, and it seemed to make perfect sense, right then, that those women might've all been a bunch of rentable "companions," too. In the newspaper I often saw ads in a section called "Relax" that was always offering escorts and companions, and the bigger selling point was that these women were young and foreign.

From the moment Esteban met me, he had already known that I was young, I was American, I was a cocktail waitress—Monica had already informed him of all of this.

I thought of the training he had put me through over the past few weeks, training to be *una Madrileña, un gato,* and I saw what the training was really for. I saw all the checks at all the bars and restaurants that he paid. I heard my voice say *"Gracias"* each time, saw him smile at me as if my discomfort for not having money was his pleasure. It seemed to me to make perfect sense that the whole time he was feeling me out, seeing just how rentable I was—and then I sat around, telling him all those stories about Shooters, about strip teases and screwed-up customers who inadvertently paid my rent.

All of these pieces to the puzzle formed a perfect plausible picture in my head. There were no loopholes, no other possibilities. My imagination had put everything together, and it felt a little painful, a little disgusting, to think of all the signs that were around me, yet I still had tried to believe, like some desperate idiot, that Esteban actually liked me, wanted to spend time with me.

It was just like when I was a kid and my father ran around breaking things and talking too loud and making people stare at him—he was clearly so violent; yet I had maintained in a section of my foolish mind, for years and years, that he was wonderful, sweet, charming. Even ever since he had left me, I wanted to believe that he was someone who missed me so much, loved me so, that it was destroying him. I needed that possibility, dreamed of it—to the point where I couldn't deal with whatever actually existed between us.

I kept drinking the wine, kept thinking about this. The big red hospital phone was next to me on the end table. I stared at it and thought about calling Harlan, about telling him everything that I had in my head right then. But I knew what he would say. He would tell me that he told me so about Esteban, and then about my father he'd say simply, as if it were nothing, see him.

He'd be like my mother: *Don't you want to know about him? Don't you want all that imagining and thinking to end?*

I thought about that for a while, watching the second hand go around the living room clock, listening to it tick. Then I picked up the big red phone, called my mother collect. When I got through, I said, "Mom?"

"Yeah?"

"Mom?"

"What?"

"Mom?"

"What's wrong?" she said.

"It's Catherine."

"The operator already told me that."

"Mom?"

She said, matter-of-factly, "You are very drunk."

"Maybe."

"You shouldn't be making phone calls when you are this drunk."

"Mom?"

"What?"

I could hear Gerry in the background murmuring something and then coughing. I said, "Tell that guy in the background to stop coughing."

"It's not some guy; it's Gerry."

"Tell him to shut up."

"Why are you calling this late? It's got to be four o'clock in the morning your time."

"Mom?"

"What?"

"I want you to call Dad."

"OK." Her voice was suddenly slow, calm, as if she thought raising her voice might make me change my mind.

"I wan' you to call that fuckin' idiot." I was slurring a little, so I paused. "Tell him, tell him . . ." Gerry was coughing in the background again. "Tell that guy to shut up."

"Who?"

"The cougher."

"What do you want me to tell . . . *your friend?*" She always spoke about my father in code around Gerry.

"Tell my friend, my pal, my amigo . . . if he wants to see me, Catherine Kelly . . ."

"What?" My mother said irritated. "If he wants to see you, what?"

"Tell him if he wants to see me so bad, then he has to come here. To Spain." She didn't say anything, so I said it again. "He has to come here."

"Catherine," my mother said, "Spain is very far away."

"That's right."

There was a pause, and then my mother said softly, "Maybe you should go to sleep now."

"Are you gonna tell him?"

"Yes," she said. "Now go to sleep."

"I'll go to sleep when I want to," I said. "Only when I'm ready will I go sleep. Only then." I said that like five more times, and then at some point I did fall asleep, still holding the phone. I didn't pass out—as I remember staring at the receiver—I just didn't feel like reaching over and hanging up the phone. I slept the whole night on the couch with my shoes still on, the phone in my lap, the uncomfortable slitless dress pulled up around my waist.

My mother later yelled at me for having made a collect phone call and then not hanging up—she actually wrote this in a letter, so I suppose it's a lie to say she yelled, but her use of exclamation points had a similar effect. The card she sent me was blank with a yellow flower on the front. Two days passed in between the phone call I made and the letter she sent. During that time, I tried to pretend I hadn't made the call. I pretended that what happened between me and Esteban hadn't happened either. Both were somewhat easy to do, seeing that no one came in contact with me those two days, not my mother, not Esteban. In my solitude, I watched television. I ate peaches. I felt calm. As long as no one bothered me, things could be good.

Then Celia and Isabel came home on Thursday and handed me a FedEx package. I stared at the thick cardboard envelope, at the big blue stripe across the front. I knew a reply to my phone call was in it. I turned the big envelope around and around, stared at my mother's printed return address on the top. An hour later, Celia asked me what was in it, and I still sat in front of the TV without having opened it. I had already decided what was in it—I was certain that my mother had written me a letter instead of calling me because she could not bear to tell me, to hear my voice, when she said he would not come.

"*¿Qué te mandó tu madre?*" Celia asked again, sitting down on the couch next to me, a half-eaten apple in her hand.

I started to open the envelope. Celia watched for a moment and then abruptly looked over at the TV, as if she suddenly sensed there was something wrong with me. Inside there was a soft yellow Hallmark card, and it said on the top line in my mother's very small, hard-to-read cursive:

> *"He will be coming on July 23rd at eight in the morning.*
> *He'll be staying at the Holiday Inn. He does not have a room*
> *number yet. You'll have to call."*

She wrote several other things about how proud she was of me, about how much she missed me, but I glanced over all of that to the very bottom, where she wrote in single sentences, which were all dramatically centered:

> *This isn't a lie, Catherine.*
> *He's coming for you.*
> *Your father is actually, honestly, coming.*
> *I hope you're ready for this.*

PART TWO

AFTER MY FATHER ARRIVED

TOGETHER AT THE HOLIDAY INN

My father came on a Saturday. There had been a thunderstorm but without rain the night before. There was just the boom of the thunder and the sky lit up on occasion, but I didn't look out at it. I had the straw shade in my bedroom pulled halfway down, my eyes cast on my wallpapered ceiling. Every wall in my room was wallpapered with a different pink floral print, except for the ceiling; it was a plain solid pink, one that looked shiny when a flash of lightning hit, but when the room was dark, it looked perfect and smooth, like something you might want to press your face against.

Every night since my mother's FedEx, I counted the days before my father would arrive. On the soft pink ceiling, I pictured the days I had to wait, a miniature calendar of two weeks, their numbers and square boxes of time I envisioned with the same clarity with which I normally created my money charts and tip forecasts. I gauged time using the time I had already experienced to distinguish how much more I had left.

Only two days after I found out my father was coming, a car bomb went off in the center of Madrid—it wasn't that serious, it killed only one person—but still it was all over the newspapers and on the television, yellow flyers against *terrorismo* strewn all over the sidewalks. One week after the bomb, I had only seven more days to wait for my father's arrival, and so I used that time period, how I experienced it, to measure my wait: That's how long it will take before he gets here, I'd think; that's how long.

Sometimes I thought about how mean I'd be to him once I finally saw him. My mind was full of these scenarios, and the Holiday Inn, with its imagined green décor, was all around us. I imagined that we would sit at a round table with a pine-green tablecloth, a round piece of glass on top. Our glasses would make a loud clink every time we set them back down. He would drink whiskey, and I would drink wine. His ice would melt very quickly.

He'd say: I'm here to give you whatever you need. (Awful and cheesy, I know, but that's how it would go. He would say the things that gave me pleasure, the things that I knew no one would ever really say to me.) I'd behave with indifference, easily absorbed in the faces of people passing by. If he kept talking, I'd tell him to shut up.

Of course, I didn't only think of these scenarios at night, lying awake under my shiny, wallpapered ceiling—I thought about him all day, too. Among the people on the metro who stood very close to me, their faces, their eyes only inches from mine, I thought and thought. At work on the creaking elevator, at home in the shower, on the street standing in front of a *zapatería* that had rows and rows of sandals all lined up, pink flowers dangling on plastic vines, I thought of him.

It was to the point at which I felt as if I were going crazy, and when I say crazy, I don't mean it in the loose sense of the word: I mean, literally, that I was unable to control my mind—it went places and saw things, all forecasting the future.

Where would we go? What would we do? How much could I stand it?

As part of my obsessing, I started dieting while I waited. I cut out anything I could think of that seemed bad: peaches, pasta, olive oil, *café con leche, tortilla española.* I tried to cut out wine, but it didn't work out well. So instead I concentrated on the food: Every night I ate salad without dressing, and a handful of raisins.

I finished obsessing about him only on that night before he arrived, the night of the storm. By then, I was too tired of it. I felt the same exhaustion I often feel after I have been grieving too much, after I have thought and thought about someone long gone. I concentrate on objects when I feel as tired as this. Or I listen to sounds. I listened to the storm. In between the roar of thunder, I counted the seconds in between to see if the storm was approaching or moving away. Then, without wanting to, I started imagining: I imagined the lightning and what it looked like over the palatial post office with all its pink light. I saw its Disneyland castle size, the yellow and red flag unfurled above, the rooms and rooms of letters sitting in bins—a flash of lightning illuminating those bins, making the cursive black writing on the envelopes momentarily visible. As I pictured all of this, I squeezed my eyes shut, squeezed and squeezed. If I wished for anything that night, it was sleep. I wished for a dreamless sleep. I wanted to be fully unconscious, unable to imagine things, unable to count things, unable to decipher the days to come.

Saturday morning my mother called to warn me that there were two Holiday Inns in Madrid, not one. She gave me the address and telephone number, said it four times—even though it was the same Holiday Inn I had planned on going to in the first place. For a little while after that, we talked stiffly about my work and my roommates, and then she asked me if I was all right. I said yes.

I ended up having some trouble actually finding the hotel; it was in a section of Madrid that I had never been to, near Plaza de Picasso. It was situated among a series of skyscrapers that I did not even know Madrid had; most of them were banks, and there was a *centro comercio*, a shopping mall, with the department store El Corte Inglés connected to it, as well as a cluster of restaurants that all had bright gaudy signs; one café had a twirling blue mug above its sign.

I thought that the Holiday Inn was going to be like any of the Holiday Inns in the States, with its big glass appearance and 1970s-looking balconies. I imagined the interior to be full of brass fixtures and green rugs, a little like Shooters. It wasn't though. The carpeting was blue, and the walls were white. When you first walked in there was a giant picture of a man on a gymnastic bar balancing on his hands.

At the reception desk, I had to ask for my father's room number. I gave them his last name, which the woman at the desk pronounced as if it were Russian. She told me he was in 603 and then pointed in the direction of the elevators. I stared at the elevator doors for a while, my elbow still on the marbled counter, before I walked over. There were six British flight attendants in front of the elevators, all in matching navy jackets, staring up at the changing digital numbers above the metal doors. I waited with them but got into an elevator by myself.

As always the elevator was cursed with a mirror, so I stared and stared, deconstructed myself as I stood there in a pink flowered dress with spaghetti straps and my highest heels. I was particularly unhappy with my face; it looked shiny, and all the makeup I had put on seemed to have slid off in the heat—there was only the mascara on my eyelashes, which was brown and slightly smudged.

The elevator opened onto a pink rug. The walls were a darker, maroonish pink, and the doors to the rooms were beige. When I got to 603, there was a note taped on the door: *I'm at the pool.* Below it in another color it said, in penmanship that looked a little rushed, as if he had suddenly remembered to add the detail: *The pool is on the roof.*

I took the note with me, as if I needed constant physical proof that he was actually there—or at least someone was. I had to get back on the elevator and go up to the health club floor, then find the white spiral staircase that led up to the roof. In all the moments I had spent imagining meeting my father, it would never have been this way. When I first got up to the roof, to the not-so-spacious square of bamboo tables and white plastic lounge chairs, I found the sun the most disturbing. It was so bright, particularly against the white cement rim of the pool, that I had to squint and stare down at my feet before getting used to it.

My father was on a chair. He had his back to me, and I could not see his face. I knew who he was from his voice, a voice that in his prolonged absence I could no longer conjure up on my own; but once I heard it, I knew it, as if it had been speaking to me every day of my life. He was talking to two topless British women who had slightly burnt pink skin. They were not the flight attendants I had seen minutes before; these women were older, not so fragile-faced. They had the type of face that belonged to women who worked in banks, women who normally wore full suits of beige tweed.

I heard my father say to one of them, "When did that happen?" and then she said, "Last August," and he said, "Oh, OK."

I didn't know whether or not to go up to them or just to wait, as if some slight prickly feeling might creep up on my father's neck and let him know I was behind him. I stood there silently. I didn't look at him or the women. I watched a boy with plastic floaters on his arms swim around in the pool's blue water. It seemed best to hang back like this. To wait. I needed to allot myself time to accept that everything I was seeing was real. I needed to gaze over at the Banco de Zaragoza sign and the big red satellite dish next to it. I needed the clouds.

Just a half hour before, I had stood on the metro watching the stops getting closer and closer to the Holiday Inn, to him, and I had felt very frightened of myself. It was like long ago when I was a kid, and my mother had primped me to visit him at his motel room. Back then, I had not seen my father for only a week and a half, but in childhood time that probably seemed equal to the seven years I had now gone without seeing him. I could remember driving with my aunt down the highway toward my father and seeing the Capri Motel sign approaching far off on the right-hand side—the whole time I had been thinking: It will never be the same; you will never be the same. I knew that at age eight. And standing there by that pool, I knew it again.

My father had a drink behind him underneath the lounge chair—when he turned to get it, he saw me. There was a pause. I was about ten feet away from him, and I knew if I wanted to behave normally it was time to move closer, act as if I originally hadn't spotted him.

He said, "Catherine?"

I said, "Yeah."

The British women were talking between themselves, but they were looking at me. One of them couldn't find her cigarettes, and she was searching beneath a towel.

I walked closer, feeling awkward standing in such high heels next to a rooftop pool. He stood up as if he planned on hugging me or something. To my dismay, he was taller than me.

He didn't look different; he didn't look the same. His face was the face I had always seen in photographs, the one I had seen on those church steps long ago, but it was lined deeply around his eyes, and his coloring seemed more flushed, as if he had already acquired a mild sunburn. He had the same big Irish ears, the same heavy bags under his eyes. Only his hair was dramatically different—it was still black, but it was stiff-looking and strangely shaped. In the sunlight, I could see from the way slight gray hairs appeared on the sides and not on the top that his hair was in fact a toupee.

Once I stood close enough to him, he hugged me. I very loosely touched his shoulders in return. He was not shirtless; he had on a dark green tank top, which was not the most flattering, and a pair of gray swim trunks. The British women watched us hug, and in their gaze I could tell that they sensed there was something weird going on. They still smiled though.

"This is your daughter who lives here in Madrid?" the one to the left asked, the one with the cigarette.

"Yes," he said.

I didn't look at him. I looked over at the boy who was still in the pool by himself. I suddenly wished I were a little kid so that I could be talked about by these two women and my father without actually entering the conversation myself. That way I could just stand there, stare off.

The woman who was smoking took a drag of her cigarette. I could see her out of my peripheral vision, and, more uncomfortably, I could feel her eyes moving up and down: from my face to my waist to my bony kneecaps. "What do you study?" she asked me, leaning forward.

"We asked your father," the other woman said, "and he couldn't tell us."

"Public relations."

"Oh, that's lovely," the smoker said. "What do you want to do in particular?"

"Yes, how does Spain fit in?" the other one asked.

I smiled as if I were about to say something intelligent, but then I didn't, I couldn't. It was too bright on the roof to be answering such questions.

"She wants to relate to the public," my father said, talking for me. "She loves the public." He seemed nervous; he kept rattling on. "Spanish public, American public, French public"—he pointed at them—"English public, she loves any kind of public she can find." He looked at me. "Right?"

I nodded. "Right."

The smoker smiled; the other didn't. The two of them at that moment were like a tag team of discomfort. Their intent gaze along with their amused expressions bothered me, and what made them even worse somehow was that they looked too much alike. They were both blond with thin, colorless lips and overplucked eyebrows. The only difference was that the smoker had better breasts—they were bigger and more pert—and she stood up straighter, her cigarette pointed perfectly vertical in the air.

"We were telling your father about the bullfights," the smoker said. "Have you been to one yet?"

"No."

"They're definitely an experience."

"Yeah?" I said. I was still standing awkwardly in front of the two women, and my father had just sat back down and taken a sip of his drink, which I knew even from a distance, from the way the sun illuminated the melting shape of a remaining ice cube, that it was whiskey. It was ten o'clock in the morning.

"I'd like to go to one," my father added. But he said it in the way that a child would say it—as if he knew whether or not we went wasn't up to him.

"I don't know if I'd be able to stand it," I said. "I don't like to see stuff like that." I was looking right at him as I spoke—it was the second time since I arrived that I had addressed him directly; it seemed impossible that we could spend a whole week like this—talking to each other, looking at each other.

"They are a little bloody," the smoker was saying about the bullfights, "but you get used to it."

"They have a bus from the hotel that takes you right there," the other one said. "On Saturdays and Sundays only."

"We're going tomorrow if you'd like to come."

"Maybe," I said.

My father looked at me. "I'd like to go."

"Maybe," I said again.

He nodded and drank the last bit of his whiskey, which was in a plastic hotel cup, the kind they give you for water in your room. He put his empty cup under his chair, and it tipped over, rolled slowly against the pavement. "If you want," he said to the women, "you can give us your room number, and we can call or leave a message telling you if we're going."

The two women looked at each other in a way that did not just suggest unease, but also a mutual wariness. The nonsmoker said, "We'll be there at five o'clock out front. That's what time they meet. You can meet us there."

They so clearly did not want him to have their room number, and I thought about that as I watched them get up from their lounge chairs and excuse themselves. I had a father to whom two grown women were afraid to give their room number. That made me a little angry all of a sudden—not with them though, with him.

After they left, I sat down where they had been sitting. I took off my shoes, taking great care with the straps. It gave me something to do. Without those women there, we had to talk now, and I needed time to stall.

"Did you talk to your mother today?" he asked.

"Yeah." I leaned back in the chair, looking directly forward. Against the sky, I could see the backside of the giant H in the cursive Holiday Inn sign.

"Do you want a towel?" he asked, pointing at my chair. "I can get you a towel; there's towels over there."

I said, "No."

"Your mother called me about an hour ago." He shrugged his shoulders. "And she called me yesterday three times and the week before that like seven times."

I nodded. It occurred to me then, as I stared off, that I should ask if she was the one who called him and asked him to see me, or if indeed he was the one who called her. I didn't feel like asking though. I already knew anyway. I knew in the way he just sat there, his bare feet rubbing against each other, that he hadn't done anything. I was certain of it. She was the one who made the reservations, probably bought the ticket with one of her credit cards, and then she must've called him all the time to make sure he was coming. She may have even picked him up herself and packed his suitcase for him while he lay on his bed rubbing his big toe against his little toe, staring at her.

"What airport did you fly out of?" I asked.

"Logan."

I watched a little Asian boy who had just arrived ease himself into the pool water. He kept making faces, squeezing his hands into fists, as if it were too cold to take.

"Did you already have a passport," I asked, still looking at the boy, "or did you have to get one just to come?"

"I already had one. I went to Aruba a few years ago."

"Aruba," I said, looking right at him. "Well, *that* must've been nice."

He nodded. "It was OK."

We sat by the pool for another hour. We didn't say much else.

My father couldn't last longer than an hour without a drink—I learned this within the first few hours of being with him. I had already imagined him this way, so it wasn't much of a shock. What annoyed me was that he never said he needed another drink. He always made up some other excuse.

To leave the pool, he said that he was hungry, so we went to the hotel restaurant, La Terraza. The first thing he ordered was a whiskey; he asked for it before they even had a chance to place the menus in front of us.

The menus were typical tourist menus, with everything written in Spanish and then in English, which was a relief—I did not want to fail so soon in front of my father, and with food, I often had difficulty translating. Without Esteban or Isabel or Celia around, I often ended up ordering things that weren't what I though they were: blood sausage instead of shrimp, codfish instead of mussels, fried meat instead of grilled meat.

When the waiter came, my father ordered in English, and I ordered in Spanish. He got a Spanish *tortilla* and another whiskey, and I got a salad and a sparkling water. We were like two opposite ends of the spectrum sitting at that table. I was worried about what I ate, and he was worried about what he drank. He seemed to want a constant supply of whiskeys, and I wanted a constant supply of water. The more we drank, the more he talked.

"So, do you like it here in Spain?"

"Yes."

"Yeah, it seems all right to me." He shrugged his shoulders. "It seems safe." He was looking around us as he said this, as if scanning the room for people with guns or grenades. His caution seemed to have more to do with being in a foreign place, in a foreign world, rather than any specific concerns about Spain. I knew he didn't know about the bomb—my mother didn't know about it (she never called, never demanded I come home, as I imagined she might); Harlan didn't either; and at work, Kansas Katy never asked me a single question about it. It seemed in the newspapers back home it wasn't even covered, or if it was, it was a small paragraph somewhere without a picture, the word *Madrid* written in parentheses on the top line.

"There was a bomb," I told my father, "two weeks ago."

"Oh, yeah?" He nodded and pointed at my salad. "Aren't you going to put any oil on that?"

"No." I cut a tomato in half on my plate. "I don't like oil."

He waited, took a sip of his drink. "What kind of a bomb was it?"

"A small one, a car bomb."

The waiter came over, asked if we were OK. I said *sí*. Then he went away and there was just the sound of soft guitar music mixed with muffled Spanish chatter. *"Qué maravilla,"* I heard someone say with great zest, which meant, literally, What a marvel.

"Did a lot of people get hurt?" my father asked abruptly. "In the bombing?"

I said, "Not a lot, but a few," and then I explained where it had gone off: in Puerta del Sol, the center of the city. With my fork on the tablecloth, I showed him how far it was in relation to where we were and where I lived. I told him what happened on the morning that it went off, how I had woken up abruptly and looked at my alarm clock—it had been exactly six o'clock, the same time the bomb exploded.

"You must've heard it," he said, and I shook my head, said no, that I didn't think so. The bomb wasn't that big of a bomb, and our apartment was not particularly close by.

"My roommates didn't wake up," I told him. "They slept right through." I shook my head. "I think I felt it; I think I have some sensitivity to that kind of stuff."

"To bombs?"

"Yeah," I said, "to bombs."

He was quiet for a minute after that. He had his hand on the white tablecloth near his drink, resting on a spoon. I stared at his fingers, at the square shape of his fingernails, how flat they were at the top, as if they had been filed, and then I made a mental note, I felt I had to: Those are your father's fingers, those are his.

My father started asking me about my internship after that. I told him all about Kansas Katy, how I didn't know if she was going to come. She kept saying she wanted to bring a companion, but then she'd constantly change her mind about who her companion should be: First it was her father, then it was her friend, and later it was a man she had just met at the supermarket. Every time she changed her mind, it seemed more and more as if she were redesigning her fantasy of Madrid as opposed to actually planning a real-life trip.

"It's kind of useless," I said, referring to the job itself, and my father nodded, asked me why I didn't just quit—he said so with the same care-free tone that Harlan often used when he told me to quit Shooters.

"I can't quit," I said, a bit irritated. "I can't just be here and not work. I need the experience."

He shook his head, moved his fork from his plate onto the doily placemat. "You can get experience anywhere. You don't have to do something you don't want to do." He took yet another sip of his drink—it was his third. "The world's full of experience."

My father was entering "philosopher stage"—that's what the girls at Shooters called it. It was our little label for the period in which the guy who's getting drunk starts to think he's really smart. This was when they usually started telling us what we needed to do with our lives: We needed to quit our jobs, dump our boyfriends, travel cross-country. We needed to open ourselves up, hitchhike, let ourselves become something new—like a Rockette, a stripper, a movie star.

Within the philosopher stage, the word *experience* was almost always a prerequisite—experience, experience, experience was said over and over. Perhaps it was because we were young, perhaps it was because they thought we were stupid. In any case, I never liked being talked down to, never liked being told what to do with myself.

I said to my father, "I know what I need to experience and what I don't."

He nodded. "Well, that's good." Then he waited a minute, as if he were holding the idea in his head, and frowned. "I guess."

The waiter came over and took our plates. My father ordered another drink.

I said, "Don't you want to get out of this hotel? Take a walk or something."

"I have to take a shower first, if that's OK."

I kept looking at him, and I think there was something in that stare that made him momentarily self-conscious. He canceled his drink.

Nevertheless, when we went upstairs to his room, the first thing he did was pour a whiskey for himself. There were three bottles of Jameson's on the dresser next to a little wooden bucket of melting ice. The whiskey bottles did not have the blue-and-white *España* seal on the top, so I knew he hadn't bought them in Madrid. He must've packed them in his suitcase the way that a normal person would bring along a toothbrush or shampoo.

Sitting on the corner of the bed, I waited while he showered. I was momentarily reminded of visiting him at Motel Capri when I was a kid. Although that connection made no real physical sense—this hotel room was not trashed like the one he once lived in, and the color scheme was much different; this one was a calm blend of blues instead of a '70ish mix of gold and brown. Even the carpet in this room was blue, and it smelled falsely of violets. Above the dresser across from me was a big mirror with an ornate gold frame; it was the type of object you would never ever find anywhere in my hometown, never mind associate with such a dumpy motel like the Capri. Yet this room did seem as dark as that room. The shades and heavy wool curtains were pulled over the windows; within that darkness, there was a feeling that accompanied the soft sound of the shower my father was taking—it made me feel antsy, as if I needed to listen to fast music or pace. Instead, I flipped through the pages of the brochures that were spread out in a fan on the table near the window. In the brochure I spotted an ad for a bar called Al Mon Te. That was the place I was going later that night. To meet Borja.

Esteban had come back from Venezuela a few days before and made all the arrangements. He had originally wanted me to see Borja on Friday night, but I refused—my father was arriving Saturday morning, and I had known that I could not take meeting Borja first and then my father. I had to allot myself time to deal with one thing, the bigger thing; I figured that afterward, after finally seeing my father face-to-face, I could successfully deal with anything, including a man who wanted to buy me.

I was meeting Borja at ten o'clock. The place we were meeting, according to the brochure, was a Sevillana bar that featured music and dance from Sevilla as well as a "pleasant décor with a green-and-white-striped ceiling, canopied bar, and sweet country-style chairs and tables that are red on the left side of the room, green on the right."

"What are ya reading?" my father asked, standing in the doorway of the bathroom. He had a towel wrapped around his head like a turban. When I was kid, he used to walk around in front of me, all hair and skin, one single towel tied around his waist, but now, here, as two adults, he had already put on a fresh pair of shorts, a T-shirt, and even some socks. The towel wrapped around his head seemed only to emphasize how uncomfortable he was around me—he was trying to hide the fact that he was partially bald.

"I'm reading these brochures they gave you," I said, answering his question after a long pause, after I started at him for a moment.

He went over to his suitcase, started fiddling around with zippers and compartments. He said, "It'll only take me, like, fifteen more minutes, and we can get out of here." He shook a can of deodorant and sprayed his armpits under his T-shirt. "I just have to wait for the bathroom to defog and then I can do my hair."

I nodded and watched him take into the bathroom a black pouch that matched his luggage. He shut the door. I heard the sound of caps being taken off, then some sort of foam or mousse being sprayed; he turned the hair dryer on low, then high; finally there was quiet. I decided that in the silence he was gently placing the toupee on his head. After a few minutes, I heard the sound of spraying; they were short sporadic spurts, and I sat there wishing with all my being that it was Aqua Net. Let it be Aqua Net. Please God, please.

He came out of the bathroom with the pouch in his hand and a small round brush. He stood in front of the fancy mirror above the dresser, and then he went back in the bathroom. I watched; I waited. And then it came: a purple can, extra hold.

It was Aqua Net.

I was elated by the sight of that can, by the cheap perfumy smell it brought, and I can't even say why. It was as if I knew things all of a sudden, I was really smart.

I watched him spray and spray, turn to the side and spray, and then he got really close to the mirror, his nose practically touching it, and stared at himself. I heard, somewhere in my head, the voice of Harlan as if he were sitting in the room with me—he said, "No wonder you like faggots so much."

"You ready," my father said, still looking at himself out of the corner of his eye.

"Yeah."

"You don't want to do anything first?" He pointed at the bathroom, the mirror.

I shook my head.

He paused, went into the bathroom again, flossed, brushed his teeth, sprayed something else onto himself, and then, finally, we left.

It was almost siesta by the time we got out of the hotel, and everything except the restaurants and bars were closed until four. I didn't really feel like taking him too far away from his hotel either—I knew I was going to have to escort him back. That was the strange thing about his being with me in Madrid: He was completely dependent on me. He couldn't speak much Spanish except for words like *hola* and *cómo está*, and he certainly didn't know his way around. If I left him alone, I realized, he would be completely vulnerable, lost.

I secretly enjoyed that idea.

We walked around for a while, my directing us in big sweeping circles, until we ended up in a bar that had blue-tiled walls out front, a barking rooster on its door. The bar was around the corner from VIPS, an American-type convenience store that I made a point of showing my father because it was close to the hotel and it sold liquor, lots of liquor, an entire shelved wall of whiskey—all of it set alongside another section that had canned octopus, Green Giant corn, giant jars full of black olives, and roasted red peppers. My father didn't buy any whiskey though. He just said he felt hungry again.

The bar we went to specialized in *bacalao,* cod, and its overwhelming aroma, garlic and fried fish, was a bit unpleasant at first, but the music and the noise in the room seemed to dilute its strength somehow—particularly after we sat down, after we were there a while. The room itself was typical of all Spanish bars: There were blue-and-white-tiled walls; hard, uncomfortable wooden chairs; a long bar full of people standing next to one another, the air full of a certain fog that can be created only by cigarette smoke. When we first walked in, as we walked past the bar to a clean table in the corner, people stared at us—not necessarily because we looked foreign, or because my father had a bad toupee, but more because that's what they did at the bar. They smoked, they stared, they sipped.

"Do they always hang legs over the bar?" my father asked after we first sat down. He was talking about the ham they hung on the wall next to the shelves of liquor.

"It's cured," I said, "It's ham that's cured."

"Does each person eat a whole leg like that?"

The hanging pieces of ham were three feet long and weighed about ten pounds. "No," I said, irritated. "They're not cavemen." Then I paused, realizing I was raising my voice a little. I was never all that good, never patient, when I had to explain things that seemed obvious to me. You'd think I would've behaved better after spending a whole month during which Celia and Isabel had to teach me the most remedial of skills: how to order fruit by the kilo at the *frutería,* how to bag my own groceries at the checkout, how to say *"hasta luego,"* see you later, over my shoulder as I left any place, including an elevator, a dressing room, a stranger's house.

I did try to explain things to my father though—as much as I could. About the ham, I said, "They slice it just like we do at home. In little pieces. They don't just bite into it like that."

"If you want we can order some," I added after a pause, but he wanted only a drink. When the waiter finally came over, I decided to let go of the calorie counting—I ordered a drink, too, a whiskey with Coke. After it was set in front of me, my father stared at the long tubular glass of whiskey with mild, shifty discomfort—but I couldn't tell if it was because it made him feel old to see me drink or just strange, out of place.

"You aren't old enough to drink at home," he said, and then added, with less certainty, his eyes squinting. "Are you?"

I don't know if he really didn't know my age, or if he was just pretending—perhaps he had only momentarily forgotten—but the very question created against the heat of the room, against the slight headache that pulsed in my head, a slight trickling burn that ran in a straight line through my chest: How the fuck could he not know how old I was?

Nevertheless, I said in a calm way, after a slow, steady blink. "I'm twenty. The drinking age is twenty-one."

"Here?"

"At home," I said. "Here you can drink when you're ten."

He looked around the room. "All these people have been drinking since they were ten?"

I didn't answer. I just looked around the room at the people who were standing at the bar. It was so hot; there wasn't air-conditioning. There were just wooden fans twirling overhead, the slight sound of something inside of them ticking.

"Ten years old," he said again, as if to fill the silence.

And then the idea of a ten-year-old temporarily made me think of the Blue Lagoon, of all the time I used to spend with my father as a kid seated at a bar. And now here we were in a foreign place, feeling hot and headachy, staring at each other. It seemed we had more to say when I was kid, more to offer each other. He was not fun for me anymore, he was not easy, and I had spent only about a few hours with him. We had a whole week.

As if reading my thoughts, or perhaps feeling them, my father said, about a half hour later, in a voice that didn't quite have the same spirit it once did, "In a glance, how many legs are hanging over the bar?" He was trying in a forced, deliberate way to play our old game, What's the Girl Worth?, the game in which he would ask me to count things and I was expected, if I wanted to win, to give very exact grandiose answers.

I looked at the wall, at all the cured ham legs, and counted. "There are twelve."

"No," he said in his game-show-host voice, "that is incorrect."

"There's twelve," I said again, and counted the legs out loud. As I did this, the waiter came over and brought us two more drinks—in the waiter's presence, I became a little self-conscious speaking in English, so I started counting out loud in Spanish. He was young, about seventeen, with a straight hair that fell in his eyes and a soft girlish face. When he poured me my drink, he gave me more whiskey than he gave my father, and then, instead of just setting the full bottle of Coca-Cola down next to the glass, he poured it very carefully with his lips slightly parted as if he were concentrating, making sure he didn't spill anything. When he was done, I looked up at him, said, *"gracias,"* and then looked sharply away—there was something in his smile, in his eye contact, that seemed sudden and strange. Too bright.

My father leaned forward. "OK, in a glance, how many waiters like you?"

"Perhaps one."

"No," he said shaking his head, "That is incorrect." He took a sip of his drink. "You aren't going to win anything if you keep that up."

I said, a little bitterly, "You mean I won't be worth anything?"

"No, you won't," he said in a flat even tone. A joke. "You won't be worth a dime."

With a little alcohol, I wasn't always one to become outrageously friendly and fun—I often spun the other way. It was as if a match had been lit, and if you tried to touch me or tell me I was "oh, so pretty" or put your finger against my neck, I'd practically spit fire in your face. Harlan often considered this one of my greatest talents: Alcohol couldn't soften me, couldn't make me suddenly adore things that I normally didn't. If anything, the blur of drinking, its accompanied fuzziness, often made me concentrate more, made me feel and see certain moments with—what I believed—was more clarity: I saw insults and lies; I saw tricks. I saw who you were.

So after three drinks, after what felt like a lifetime of sitting and stewing in smoke and long bouts of silence, my father and I left that bar, and, shortly after, I let him have it.

We were in Zara. The store was on the same block of the bar we had left, and when we passed its window, I saw this leopard-print dress in the window, and suddenly had the urge to go in there, to make my father stand around while I shopped. All of my life, I had seen girls with fathers in stores, and I suddenly felt this insistent need to know what it would be like to be in one with my own. I had somehow expected that he would be awkward, that he would stand with his arms crossed in the corner of the room; instead, he was looking at things, pulling on sleeves, unfolding tank tops and staring at them.

"Do you like this?" I asked him, holding the dress I had seen in the window against me, the metal hanger under my neck. It was a dress my mother wouldn't have liked. She would say it was cheap, "not even cute." It was short with black lace on the bottom and thin strappy straps; the material was the type that you couldn't wear underwear beneath.

"Do you think I should try it on?" I asked him.

He shrugged, he was holding a maroon leather bag in his hand. He zipped it open, zipped it closed.

I said, "You buy this for me, and I'll buy that for you."

He was looking at another bag that was hanging from a metal peg. "If you like that, buy it for yourself." He shook his head, smiled. "I already have *a number* of nice purses."

"I think you should buy it for me," I said, flipping absently through some more hangers. "A nice fatherly gift."

The salesclerk came over then; she was short with high heels and lots of bracelets. She paused when she got close enough to us, as if she were trying to gauge how to deal with us. I think she knew we were both drunk—when she came over she spoke to me very slowly, *"¿Quieres probar?"* and then she smiled with her lips together. Perhaps she really just recognized that we were foreign, that I might not understand her, but then my father knocked a few bags off one of the pegs, and it seemed she knew for certain. The bags fell onto the ground in a heap and neither of us helped him. We just watched him pick each one up, one at a time, and put it back. When he had this one small knit bag in his hand, the salesclerk said, "That purse is perfect for the dress." She took it out of his hand and put it against the dress. *"¿Perfecto, no?"*

My drunkenness became suddenly chipper. I said, *"Sí, sí, sí."* I took the bag and then I motioned in a happy sweep of my hand for the three of us to go over toward the cash register.

They rang up the dress, the bag, and then the salesclerk who worked the cash register, along with the other girl we had originally talked to, stared at my father. He was looking at rhinestone necklaces in a glass case, and they both watched him in their matching aqua shirts and black miniskirts—they had the same twinlike quality the women by the pool had earlier that morning, the same amused expressions on their faces.

"They're waiting for you to pay," I said.

He looked at me, and nothing in his eyes changed, but his voice came out different. "No, they're waiting for you to pay, Catherine." He pointed at me. "You pay."

I shook my head. "You."

"I am not paying for that. I am not buying you your tiger dress."

"It's leopard."

He shook his head, walked away from the counter.

I smiled, embarrassed, and glanced momentarily at the salesclerks, then looked farther behind them to the big mirrored wall behind the cash register. I could see in the reflection a stream of about five women standing behind me, all looking at the same table full of folded pastel pants. They all had on bracelets, and with each tag they touched, each color they smoothed their hands over, I could hear jingling and there seemed to be something about that jingling that affected me—or maybe it was the fact that they were standing behind me, talking and touching things, their faces so intent and serious.

Or it was exactly that: their faces. Their faces that were so round and pretty, full of mascara and lip liner and blush, yet they were worn-looking, older faces, fortyish faces, faces like my mother's.

My father the whole time was standing close by, but away from the counter, not looking at me.

I backed away from the register, from the salesclerks, and picked up a pair of baby blue pants that were folded on the table where the women behind me were. I unfolded them, held them over my head like a flag, and said, "OK, Dad. How about these? Will you buy me these?"

He turned only slightly and stared at me.

The women nearby stopped talking; the bracelets stopped jingling.

I picked up a purple hat, a fisherman's-type hat, and put it on. "What about this, Dad? What about this?" I was talking quick, manic. "Can I have this? Would this be OK? Or do you think no? Is that not possible? Too much?"

A slight flush came over his face, but the set of his expression, his lips, his eyes remained still. It was as if he were just standing there thinking, and no noise, no sound, was reaching him. Then he started walking toward the door, but the store was long and narrow, and he wasn't moving that fast.

"Hello?" I shouted, "Hello?"

He turned.

"It's only a thousand pesetas, seven bucks!"

"Catherine?" he said, loudly yet calm.

"What?"

"You are going . . ." He made a motion at his forehead. "You're gone."

If I had tilted my head away from his direction, the women staring at me would've been in my vision, or at least the image of me in the mirror across the way, standing there in a purple fisherman's hat and pink sundress, high heels, the coloring of my face uneven and splotchy. I would've seen what they saw, I would've seen myself in some sort of monstrous state which I couldn't quite trace how I got there. If I had been totally calm the whole day, then it would've made sense to me that I was being so screwed up now, but I had been siphoning off what it was that I felt for him, that fire, slowly as the day went on, and it seemed I shouldn't be like this now, shouldn't have a room full of women staring at me, looking at me, thinking that I actually had something of real merit moving through me. I could feel them staring at my father, more than me, as if he had hurt me, just slapped me dead in the face.

"I'm going to go outside," my father said to me in low voice that I could barely hear, "and when you're better, why don't you join me and tell me where my hotel is."

I bought the dress and the bag, not the hat or the pants. Then I walked my father back to the Holiday Inn silently, the big, navy blue Zara bag swinging slightly in my hand. When we got to the revolving doors to the entrance, he said, "You don't have to walk me in."

We stood there. It was still very hot, and the heat had a way of making me feel as if we might not remember anything that had happened all day, it might get erased if we just stood out there long enough. I kept looking down at the carpet, at the letter "i" in the word *Holiday,* which was small and in cursive, dotted daintily. I grazed the heel of my sandals back and forth over it, and then I said with my head down, "Everything's gonna be closed tomorrow. What do you wanna do?"

He shrugged, had his hands in his pockets. "I don't know. You're the one in charge." His voice had a lilt to it, as if he suddenly couldn't stand me.

I waited. "Do you want to go to that bullfight?"

He wrinkled his nose, then shook his head indifferently as if he didn't care, even though I knew he wanted to go. I had seen him glancing up at a bullfight that was on the TV in the bar we went to—although rather than the actual event, he seemed more fascinated by the audience, by the claps and grunts the people at the bar made. In reaction to each of the matador's turns, each of his ballerina footsteps, the bartender in particular had a comment, and my father kept asking me what he was saying. Half the time I didn't understand, but I was too proud to admit it, so I just made something up.

"We don't have to if you don't want to," my father was saying about the bullfight. His voice was very flat, lifeless.

"We'll go."

"We don't have to if you don't want to," he said again in the same tone.

"We'll go," I said more urgently.

We stood there a bit longer. A couple passed us—they were Spanish and arguing. The woman kept saying, *"No me importa,"* I don't care, and the man was saying something else that was too fast, too complicated, for me to figure out entirely. When their voices still weren't quite out of earshot, my father said, "And there's something else I want to do tomorrow."

Before I could ask him what, he added, "Church. I want to go to church."

I waited, hoping he would add once again: We don't have to go if you don't want to. But that apparently wasn't an option.

I said, "It's in Spanish though."

He shrugged as if that were irrelevant, a stupid comment.

I kept rubbing my heel over the letter "i" on the rug. "I'll have to find one," I said, my voice a little doubtful, as if the entire city weren't filled with churches. You couldn't stand on any street corner in any neighborhood and not see a cross rising up above orange-tiled rooftops and wrought-iron balconies—the sky, the clouds, were the only things higher, bigger.

"I can meet you at ten," I told him. "That way we can go to eleven o'clock Mass."

He nodded.

We stood awkwardly for a moment after, then he went through the revolving door into the hotel. He didn't wave, didn't say good-bye, and neither did I. I just watched him leave, and then I watched the spinning door continue to turn without him.

12

DOMINOES

When I was little, five and six, my father used to read the Bible every Sunday night. He'd lie on his bed with the lights dimmed so low that the white walls looked beige and the room itself seemed to have gotten smaller. The Bible he read was our family Bible, and it had gold-trimmed pages and a maroon leather cover that was bigger than the actual pages. He used to read it with the red ribbon down the center of the page, and when he turned a page, he carefully lifted the ribbon, held it with his two fingers with the same delicacy that someone might pick a dead mouse up by its tail.

I was so young I couldn't read yet, but I used to lie next to him on the bed, look over his shoulder. In certain sections, the words were written in black ink, while other sections were written in red. I used to stare at the three columns on the page, at the shapes the red paragraphs made. Sometimes they looked like two eyes, or a big splotch moving up and down; other times the red paragraphs had no pattern. They made no sense.

"Why do you keep reading that?" I asked him once.

He ignored me. He was in the middle of a page, I guessed, from how his head was cocked and his eyes moved ever so slightly.

"Why are you reading that?" I asked again.

"Because God wrote it."

"I know that," I said, "but why do you keep reading it? Haven't you already read it before?"

"It tells me stuff," he said, "about God. Why he does the things he does."

I waited a minute. "What does he do?"

"Who?"

"God."

"What *does* God do?"

I nodded.

"Many many things. *Sooo* many things," he said in this jokey voice, which I sensed meant he didn't entirely know the answer.

I said, "Like what? What does he do?"

My father touched the edge of the pillowcase—it was plaid, and it smelled, even from a distance, like my mother's hair, like vanilla-scented shampoo. He kept touching the pillow softly as if it were, in fact, a part of my mother, and then he said, shrugging his shoulders, "God . . . He, well ya know. He works. He . . . sits down sometimes, and He . . . plays games."

"What kind of games?"

"Dominoes," my father said quickly. "He plays dominoes."

"He does *not*."

"He plays dominoes."

I shook my head. "Liar."

"Why are you giving me trouble?" my father said, staring at me. "God *plays* dominoes. I know He does. There's even a picture in the back here,"—he pointed at the Bible—"it's got Him playing dominoes."

"Let me see it."

"No, you can't see it until you yourself know how to play dominoes."

"I know how to play," I said, my voice haughty. "You match the dots."

"But do you know how to play Fives?"

I didn't say anything.

"No, you don't because you don't know your times tables. You need to know your times tables to play Fives." He took a sip of the beer that was on the nightstand next to a pair of my mother's clip-on pearl earrings. He clipped one onto my ear with one hand—it took him a minute or two.

"When you know how to play Fives," he was telling me, "you can see God playing dominoes. But until then, you can't see it." He had his hand on the Bible to keep me from turning the page, from trying to look.

I took the clip-on earring off and stared at it. It was pearl with gold edges that were warped a little, silverish. "If He plays dominoes, where does He play dominoes?"

"In the forest."

"Which one?"

"He has access to all forests, Catherine. All of them."

I nodded. I got up from the edge of the bed and walked over to the doorway. From a healthy distance I said, "You know what? I think you lie."

He smiled, somehow amused. He said, "That's very sad. So sad."

I had my hands on my hips. "I don't believe you. Not at all."

He picked up his beer, finished it, then held the empty can over his head, as if he was going to throw it at me. There was nothing scary or threatening about it. My father was like a little boy to me, the kind I played with at the playground, the ones who pretended they would throw me down the slide or shove me off the monkey bars.

My father said, "You take that back."

"No."

"Take it back." He was moving the can back and forth, as if he were taking aim, ready to strike.

I ran from the doorway and shouted back, "God doesn't even like you!" Then I laughed and laughed, happy with how mean that sounded. The empty beer can plinked onto the tile floor a good thirty seconds after I was out of the doorway. I watched the can roll against the wall and under the lace curtains of our hallway window, and I put my arms up, elated by my escape. I shouted, "God can't stand you!"

"You shut your face, lady!" he shouted back.

"I don't have to shut my face," I said, "God likes *me*."

At some point we both started laughing, but we kept going on like that probably for a good half hour: him on his bed, me in the hallway, a wall between us. The two of us shouting and shouting—all in play— about God.

$$\underline{13}$$

THE VOICE OF HARLAN

After I left the Holiday Inn, I decided I needed Harlan. I didn't wait until I got home though, I called him from a pay phone in a corridor of the metro station across from a bar—there were bars in the metro stations in Madrid but only in the big stations, the ones that had lots of twisting corridors and escalators that climbed dizzying heights. The bars weren't real bars though—they were just wide openings with a short, skinny bar, no seats, no tables, no bathrooms or doors.

Before my phone call, I went over to the bar and ordered a *café con leche*. As I waited for my coffee, listened to the screech of the steaming milk, I stared at a Coca-Cola sign that was twirling on top of a metal bin filled with fried calamari. Music was playing low, from a boombox that had big red buttons—strangely, the song playing was the same one that the girls at Shooters had been dancing to at my going-away party. The bartender, who was skinny and baby-faced, mouthed the English words, "Work it, baby," as he poured the hot milk into my cup, and then the single customer standing at the bar shook his shoulders and raised his draft beer into the air above his head in little disco-y circles. He was about sixty years old, dressed in a pink oxford, and there was something about him that made me smile right at him, into his eyes, as if he were the most wonderful thing I had seen all day.

The bartender himself—perhaps because I was thinking of Harlan—reminded me of one of Harlan's ex-boyfriends. He had the same blond hair with black eyebrows, the same chiseled shape of scruff around his mouth. The bartender told me his name was Pepe, and in that moment I couldn't remember Harlan's ex's name—he was just, in my mind, the nameless star in one of Harlan's many confusing plotless films. He played The Assassin, a nameless Godiva Chocolatier salesclerk who systematically killed customers who were rude or bossy or indecisive. He didn't kill these people with poisoned chocolates, as one might guess; instead, he sprayed them with acid and then he disposed of their bodies by wrapping them in Godiva foil and leaving them in a Faneuil Hall Dumpster, a thick gold bow tied around each of their necks.

It was one of Harlan's best films.

If I remember correctly, it was actually called "The Assassin." Harlan had gone out with his blond starlet, the Pepe look-alike, for about two weeks, and then he had disappeared. Perhaps that was why I couldn't remember The Assassin's real name. I was not allowed to mention him—his name was forbidden.

Right after I paid Pepe, I called Harlan, took my coffee cup and saucer with me to the pay phone nearby, set it on top. It took nearly ten times of dialing to get the telephone number and the calling card right, and then I got the answering machine. The ever-so-familiar song "You Can Ring My Bell" was playing so loud that I had to pull the receiver away from my ear. Then it abruptly clicked over and I screamed, "Pick it up, pal! Pick it up!"

Harlan was obviously standing right over the phone, waiting to see who it was, because he picked up just as quickly as I spoke, and then there was that damn song again, playing in the background, and he started singing it loudly, "Ring it, ring it, ring it."

I said, "All right, stop that."

"Ring it."

"Cut it out."

He started laughing very high pitched, so high pitched that I knew it wasn't just that he was feeling love-struck or giddy—he was high. He smoked every morning and every night, and usually it affected him mildly, like a haze, but then every once in a while, he got something that hit him the way he wanted it to.

In all of his feel-good feeling, it apparently didn't even occur to him how odd it was that I was calling him from a million miles away. There was no concern, no worry. Instead, he just asked me about Felipe. "So how's the boy?" he asked. "Did you touch him yet?"

I had already written Harlan a letter trying to quell his distrust for Esteban by telling him that I was going to meet a nice Spanish boy soon, Felipe. Customarily, Harlan didn't want to hear about anything but boys. He had written me only the week before, "Please do not bore with your whiny rambling. Cut to the boys. Where are they? How many have you acquired?" Then, at the bottom of the postcard, it had said, "P.S. Murderous drug-dealing faggots don't count."

"Now don't be shy," Harlan was saying to me, "tell me what's going on with Bobo." That was Harlan's nickname for Felipe. "Is he silky?" He started laughing after that. When he was high, he thought he was so goddamn funny.

I said, "I haven't seen that guy yet."

"If Bobo can't be silky, forget about it. No silkiness. No Bobo."

"All right," I said, "Stop calling him Bobo." Harlan was always doing that, making these obnoxious names for the men I knew. For Lenny, it was Leminster, or simply, the Lemming. Rick from Shooters was Tricky Ricky, and the owner was, in Harlan's eyes, the Famous Mr. Sugar Cat.

I said, "I'm not calling you about *Bobo* anyway. I'm calling you about something. I'm not just calling to call."

"Did somebody die?" he asked, but he said it like a joke, like he knew whatever I called about wasn't as dramatic as I wanted it to be.

He didn't know that my father was coming—I hadn't written him about it. I kept it to myself, a secret. That way, if my father didn't really come, I wouldn't have to explain, wouldn't have to be plagued by questions and sympathetic moments.

"No," I said, "nobody died yet." I could hear crinkling; he was eating something, ever so softly. I said, irritated, "But when you're done eating the Peppermint Patty, I'll tell you what did happen."

He started snickering some more, told me it was a dark chocolate "medallion." Then he said, "But tell me anyway. What *happened*?"

I waited. "My father's here."

The candy crinkling stopped. "Your father lives in Madrid?"

I shook my head, annoyed. "Don't be a fuckin' moron, Harlan! He came here, he doesn't live here."

"But . . . did he *know* you were going to be there?"

"Yes!" I screamed. "He came to visit me. He came, I was already here, he knew!"

"Hey! Don't yell at me."

"Well, don't be stupid!"

"Listen, you don't have to go crazy, all right?" Then he said, in a singsongy voice, "You don't have to lose your marbles, babe."

I said, "Shut up."

"You don't have to lose your cool, you don't have to lose your spool. You don't have to do that, babe."

"Stop calling me babe. Where did you get that?"

"My new beau says it all the time." He paused, and then said dramatically, "Stevie." Then he started talking about Stevie, telling me how he met him at Ramrod, this gay biker bar, on Free Pizza night. In the middle of explaining something about how their forearms had casually rubbed against each other at the bar, I interrupted Harlan, screamed at him, "You know what, I can't actually hold on to this story right now, OK?"

"Relax," he said, "Relax. I was just trying to change the focus. Give you a breather." He paused. "So do you like him?"

"Stevie?"

"No, your father."

"What do you mean, do I like him? No." I shook my head. "He's a loser." As soon as I said that, I felt sharp pain go right through me, as if in having said such thing, my father would somehow hear it, somehow know.

"He came to visit you, though. That must count."

"No, I had to tell him to." I took a sip of my coffee—it tasted harsh, like sand. "I don't want to go into it. It's a long story."

"Well then . . . what exactly do you want to talk about?"

"I don't know," I said defensively, "I just want to talk to you."

He got quiet. I was quiet. Somewhere distant, in another part of the metro station, a person was playing the flute. I imagined it was high pitched up close, but from where I stood, from under the low disco music of the bar behind me, it sounded soft and fluttery, like something that could put you to sleep.

"I have an idea," Harlan said, "I'll ask you stupid questions about your father, and you can scream at me. How about that?"

I thought about it for a minute, listened to the flute. "OK."

So then he started asking me things: What color was my father wearing? Did he have on any jewelry? An anklet? Did he smell like toast? Did he kiss the tips of my fingers and tell me I was full of alarming beauty?

After a few questions it became hard to yell, to remain hostile; perhaps it was the the softness of the music drifting down the empty metro corridor. In any case, I answered most questions flatly, or I laughed, hesitantly though, as if I were being weak if I laughed full force.

After about twenty questions, I said, "All right, enough." I swallowed. "I think I should go."

"Will you call me when he leaves?"

"Yes."

He waited. "I miss you, kitten."

"Yeah," I said, moving closer to the phone, ready to hang up. There was suddenly a flood of people coming by, all of them loud and unruly. I said over their ruckus, my face inches from the telephone's number keys, "I think I might miss you, too."

14

BORJA

When I got home, I didn't get ready for my date with Borja right away. I just sat on the couch and watched the way my stomach moved when I breathed. I was much skinnier now, or at least I thought so. I had probably lost only five or six pounds, but seeing that I wasn't overweight in the first place, I felt ultrathin. The whole week, whenever I went into the bathroom, I pulled up my shirt, stood to the side, admired the shape of my rib cage and hipbones. Just looking at them made me feel more confident—it was as if I could do anything, everything.

Somehow I fell asleep while I was staring down at my stomach, which must've meant I had either drunk too much, or slept too little the night before. When I woke up, it was abrupt and sudden, as if someone had just shook me. I paced for a while, feeling headachy; then I ate a peach and put on my new dress. I suppose I should've taken a shower, should've paid more attention to my hair, which had developed a bit of curl in the heat of sleeping. But I couldn't bear standing around in the bathroom so much. There was no window in either of our bathrooms, no natural light. They were both small and pastel—the kind of rooms in which, if you thought too hard, you might upset yourself, might end up sitting on the tile with your arm resting against the cool white tub.

Instead, I stood in front of the hallway mirror, thinking and thinking, as I put on careful amounts of mascara and lip gloss and shimmering eye shadow—but what I thought about exactly is not something just anyone can understand. Putting on that makeup, putting on that dress, did not feel to me like a decision process; I certainly didn't feel active in what I was doing. It was as if I have being drawn somewhere, as if I had fallen into a situation that was always waiting for me, always mine, and somehow it felt that now was the time to experience it. Again that word, *experience*—the same word the philosophizing drunks loved to give me. You had to *experience*. Perhaps that was what Borja was to me, the way that meeting my father was an experience. A lesson. I didn't think either of the two meetings were going to be fun, redeeming, but at the same time, they felt like things I had to do, things I couldn't avoid. Of course, this bizarre certainty, this overwhelming pull, did not lessen the discomfort, just thinking about either one of them incited a sick tight feeling in my chest—it was like climbing and climbing a very tall, very frightening wall, one to which I saw no end.

When I first walked into Al Mon Te, I stood near the bar, although I knew Borja would be at a table. I wanted to get used to the place first, before I had to get used to him. The bar had a host who seated people when they walked in, and he kept coming over to me to ask me who I was meeting. I became paranoid that the bar was full of arranged meetings, so I told him that I would recognize who I was waiting for when I saw him, he was a good friend.

"*¿Seguro?*" he said—Are you sure? He pointed at a sheet of white paper that had names in pencil scribbled all over it. "*El puede estar arriba,* "—He could be upstairs. He pointed up. I nodded, told him I'd go up in a minute, and then he kept staring at me from the host's podium.

At the bar I tried to order a drink, but the bartender was mean. I was asking her for a glass of wine, and she kept pretending that she had no idea what I was saying. I was speaking perfectly, and the request was not that complicated, but she took some sort of strange bitter pleasure in making me repeat it over and over: *Un vino tinto, por favor. Un vino tinto.*

She kept shaking her head and smirking. Finally she gave me a pencil and paper and told me to write it down. I did, and then she nodded reluctantly, as if I had placed the wrong order, a bad one.

Once I got my wine, I stood there feeling incredibly foreign, misplaced. The music was Spanish, not one single English lyric—something I was unaccustomed to—and the dancing was hard to describe. All the men and women stood across from one another on a narrow strip of dance floor. When the music came on, they came at one another, arms over their heads. They kept their arms stiff-looking yet bent, as if they were about to caress one another, or strike one another, depending on the singer's pitch. There were, of course, some couples I saw who simply looked like demented birds, but then there were others who danced so wonderfully, so rigid, that within their mutual gaze there seemed to be a certain electricity, an enviable spark.

Just the women themselves were something to stare at. Most were older, in their late forties or fifties, but they didn't look anything like older American women. They had makeup on, complete with eyeliner and dark eye shadow and narrow patches of blush that you could see from across the room. They dressed in real dresses that were not matronly, not beige or gray; their dresses were black or pastel with high leggy slits and spaghetti straps. And these women carried themselves with a confident elegance. I had never, ever seen older women who looked like that. I sipped my wine and stared.

I was actually in the midst of staring at one woman, who was at least sixty and was wearing a backless black dress and high-heel sandals, when I felt someone's hand on my back and then I heard, "Catherine?" When I turned, he said, *"Soy yo, Borja."*

The first thing I noticed about him was his sideburns—they were long and thin, carefully crafted. He looked much better than I expected. He was not gray-haired; he was not overweight. There was nothing hideous or disfiguring about his face. He actually had a rather sweet face, the face of someone whom you can instantly imagine as a child running in circles with his arms stretched out. His nose was a little too small, a little pointy—"a rodential nose," Harlan called them. The rest of his features were also small, his eyes, his cheeks, his entire head. But I don't mean to say he was freakish-looking, or dwarfish—he just looked fragile, like someone you couldn't squeeze too hard if you hugged him.

We kissed each other hello on each cheek, and I asked him how he knew who I was. I asked him in Spanish though—I felt for some reason as if we had to speak in Spanish; I had to prove I was actually capable.

"I just knew it was you," he said; then he smiled. There was something in his smile I didn't believe. It made me feel as if he had seen me somewhere in the distance, perhaps at one of the many bars Esteban often insisted we go to. In all my newfound distrust for Esteban, I had been going over in my mind all the bars that we went to, all the places where we often stayed for what seemed, in retrospect, like a scheduled amount of time. Even at that cigar bar we had gone to the last night I went out with him, he had claimed we were meeting some of his friends. None of his friends ever came, yet we stayed and stayed. We sat in the middle of the room; we sat where everyone at the bar could see us. He had even told me that night, "Take your ponytail down for a minute, just a minute," and then later he asked me to get him some matches at the bar, even though he was perfectly capable of getting up himself. But I did, I got him his matches, and as I stood at the bar waiting for the bartender in my strappy dress and high heels, I felt people looking at me, but I kept my eyes averted, shy. There was always some part of me that was very afraid to make eye contact with anyone who looked at me too intently. That sort of gaze could make me drop things, make me stammer, make me trip on things that weren't there.

"Do you want to sit?" Borja asked me, and then without waiting for my response, he led me by the arm to a little red table that had two chairs that were very small and delicate-looking, with wooden backs that had flowers painted on them. I sat down very lightly, as if I were afraid I was going to break the chair, and then he sat down afterward—he actually waited for me to sit down first, a gesture that made me feel awkward, as if I should've stood momentarily next to him.

He ordered from the waiter two *finos*. He did not ask me first if I liked *fino*; it seemed not to matter, and I considered that as I sat there: Is this what happens when you meet someone like this? You drink what they drink. You sit where they sit. You do what they do. Such a situation, I knew, would not last long for me—which I found a relief. Once Borja made me uncomfortable enough, once he made it clear that this arrangement was not an arrangement I could ever stomach, I would just leave. I had decided that while I sat in the cab on the way over, while I walked through the green-and-white-tiled door of the bar. I was here to see what it was like, feel it, and then I would leave with it, carry it with me like a souvenir, back to Boston, back to Shooters, back to a place where I could walk down narrow strips of space between pool tables, tray in hand, and feel all right.

I so desperately wanted to feel all right.

"Do you like it here?" Borja asked me, leaning over, touching my hand. The gesture was only slightly hesitant, his fingertips a bit moist, clammy, and within his touch I felt an absence of something. I don't mean warmth; I don't mean affection. It felt like when a little boy touches you—there was nothing hidden beneath it, no energy, no spark. He was just touching me out of habit, the way he might touch anyone's hand that rested near him.

"I like this bar," I said in Spanish as I looked up at the green-and-white-striped ceiling and then at some writing on the wall that read, HERMANIDAD DE MADRID. Brotherhood of Madrid. "It's different in here," I said nodding, "pretty."

"If you don't like it," he said quickly, "if you think it's boring, we can go somewhere else." Then he added, looking away from me, "Anywhere you want."

With his fingertip he was tracing the ridge of the ashtray, ever so

lightly, and as I watched his finger go around and around, the nail perfectly square, perfectly polished, I considered the delicacy of his movements, the delicacy of his features, how neatly pressed his shirt was, and
I wanted to believe with all my might that Borja was gay.

There was nothing to prove that he was, though. He did not have
Esteban's flamboyant gestures; he did not have Harlan's overly obvious
pout. All he had was a weirdness, a strange feeling about him, one that
was not scary or nerve-wracking. It was one I was simply aware of
because I was so eager to figure him out, so in need.

"What do you do?" I asked. A question that I knew in Spanish culture was considered a bit rude, a bit much. It was like asking: How much
money do you have?

"I work in a bank," he said. "Deutsche Bank."

"Oh," I said and nodded, as if I had lots of familiarity with
Deutsche Bank.

"I work a lot. Quite a lot. Too much."

The waiter came over right then, put our glasses down, and then
filled them with *fino*. Then he whispered something in Borja's ear, and
Borja stood up, started talking to him, moving his hands a lot as he
spoke. He touched the cuff of the waiter's shirt, a tap; there was nothing
sexual about the gesture—the waiter was about sixty years old, balding,
with a big paunch of a belly, yet there was something about how close he
stood to the waiter, how much he smiled.

One of my strangest, yet most accurate ways of measuring how
much I liked a person was how good they were to the waiter. If you
could not say thank you and smile each time the waiter came, if you
couldn't be patient, if you couldn't acknowledge his presence when he
came to clear things, then I somehow presumed you couldn't be genuinely appreciative of anything—anything, that is, outside of yourself.

When Borja sat back down, he was still smiling, and he seemed to
be trying to backtrack to what we had been talking about. He said,
"Yes, I work at the bank." He took a sip of his drink. "And all I ever
seem to be able to talk about is the bank . . . but with you, you are foreign and young, and so I have much to talk to you about, to tell you."

I swallowed what I had just sipped and said in a tone that was not flirty, "You're going to be the teacher?"

He shook his head. "No, I would be a bad teacher. But I could teach you to dance." He pointed at the dance floor, which was only a few feet in front of us. "Or rather, I could pay someone to teach you to dance."

I didn't know what to do with that comment, so I just looked out at the people dancing, watched the turns they took, the way their feet were positioned and their wrists moved. Among the two lines of prancing people, I noticed a blond woman who looked familiar, but not very familiar, like someone I might've seen on the metro or eating in a café. I watched her spin, watched her hands above her head—they were not stiffly arched the way they were supposed to be. She laughed. I watched her mouth open wide, saw the shape of her teeth; they were very small, like children's teeth, but stained a bit, discolored.

Then I knew who she was: one of the Englishwomen from the pool this morning, the smoker. I hadn't recognized her at first because her hair was different—it was tied up in a bun, wet-looking. She had on a lot more makeup, too, a lot of eyeliner in particular, eyeliner that was heavy and smudged and looked incredibly stark against her fair face.

Whether or not she had seen me, I didn't know, but I desperately didn't want her to. She seemed nosy to me, the type who would come over, stare right into Borja and me. Perhaps that was the only way that she could lie on the deck of that rooftop pool, close her eyes against the brightness—only if she had strange people to think about, to dream about, stories to fill the heat, the boredom.

"Do you like to dance?" Borja asked.

"Only when I am very drunk." I was watching the Englishwoman while I spoke, she was heading upstairs. A man who had very puffy gray hair, an afro almost, was climbing the stairs alongside of her, his hand on her back.

Borja got the waiter's attention, ordered a bottle of *manzanilla*. He presumably wanted to get me drunk so I would dance, but I was not going to dance. That was the only way the Englishwoman would catch sight of me. Over the dance floor, the ceiling had a little rectangular

cutout so that the people upstairs could see the people downstairs dancing. At one point someone had thrown something from upstairs down
on the dancers—at first I thought it was confetti, but then I saw, as it
landed on the wooden floor, that it was flower petals, all white and tiny
like baby's breath.

Once the sherry bottle came, Borja and I drank faster—with a ready
supply, it was impossible just to sip. He started talking to me about his
work, what he did, why he lived in London for the time being. I couldn't
entirely understand though—all of it wasn't making sense to me. Perhaps it was the drinking that distorted my attention span, although it
really seemed to be that Englishwoman with her new vampirish appearance lurking around upstairs in her heels and white dress. I could feel
her presence above me, and the very sight of her had brought my father
back to me.

Borja stopped talking. "I'm being boring," he said. "I'm sorry I'm
being boring."

I said defensively, "No, no you're not." He apparently could tell I
wasn't listening to what he was saying, but I didn't know how to fix it.
The emotion of the day, along with the drinking and my father and that
woman upstairs, had instilled a mild spaciness in which Borja could talk
to me, his lips could move, in either English or Spanish, and I couldn't
hold on. I was slipping inside of myself: I was eight, I was ten, I was
twenty. I was talking to my father sitting on a barstool in front of a fish
tank that had white pebbles; I was sitting on a dressing-room floor while
my mother tried on a pink skirt that would not button; I was in Zara still
in that purple fisherman's hat, screaming.

"Esteban says you are not just a student, but a cocktail waitress,"
Borja was saying. He was reeling me back in—into the conversation,
into the bar, into the wooden seat in which I sat stiffly.

He filled my glass and stared into it, smiling.

I said, "Yeah, so what?" I did not like him looking bemused. He had
the same smirk that Esteban had when he originally mentioned waitressing, as if it made a great story, a fun joke.

"He says you work a lot. So much."

I nodded.

"You're like me," he said.

I didn't answer.

He leaned forward. "We have a saying that you've probably already heard: *Hay gente que viven para trabajar y hay gente que trabajan para vivir.*" There are people who live to work and people who work to live. "The Spanish work only to live, but other people, the Germans for example, live to work."

"Uh-huh?"

"You look a little German," he said, smiling a smile that came from only one side of his face.

"I'm not German."

"You could be German."

"I'm not."

"Are you sure?"

I decided to look away from him, act as if he were bothering me, but I did so with a smile so it wasn't too severe. Out of my peripheral vision, I could him see him rubbing the *manzanilla* bottle with his finger, tracing the edge of the label, which was square and off white. "I like the idea of rescuing you," he said absently, looking at the bottle, not at me.

I shrugged. "I don't need to be rescued." I was watching his finger on the bottle.

"But I want to."

"I don't need it."

He looked up at me. "Oh, no?"

I shook my head, said, "No," then I frowned—it seemed a very unhappy thing to suddenly realize.

About a half hour later, Borja decided we were leaving without asking me. He asked for the check without my even noticing. I noticed only when the waiter set it down on the table and Borja put down his

Deutsche Bank Visa. It seemed, actually, that at the exact moment the credit card was placed on top of the check, a woman's voice went off in my ear. "Hello, Kathleen!"

It was the Englishwoman, and she was drunk, very drunk. Her face was a certain shade of red that only the very fair skinned can achieve.

"Kathleen, what are you doing here? I though only I knew about this place."

I would've corrected her, told her my name was Catherine, but that seemed inappropriate, seeing that I didn't know her name at all. I said instead, "Is your friend here, too?"

"No, she's asleep," she said, in a tone that suggested that she was very annoyed with her friend.

I said, "Oh."

"Who's this?" she said, pointing at Borja. Then she turned a little so that she was facing me and not him. "It's not your father, obviously."

Borja had heard her, but he didn't say anything, he just looked at me. It was as if the very presence of this woman and her overwhelming energy were weakening him, making him into someone who could only sit there and stroke the edge of his shirt collar.

I said, "He's my uncle," and then smiled at Borja. I thought that might give him some spark, make him pipe up, at least in a joking way. But he just sat there, as if she had made him feel guilty, perverted, for being older than me.

"Your uncle? I bet he's your uncle." Then she said in my ear, all laughs, "Your uncle's kinda cute and everything, but I think's he's a little . . ." She made a gesture with her hand to suggest he was "funny."

"How can you not see it?" she said, laughing in a taunting way that seemed to put Borja on edge. He seemed to know what she was saying, and within the set of his face—which remained stiff, as if he were ignoring us, didn't even know us—there was no irritation, no slight facial flare-up of any kind. It was only in his hands, in the way that one hand kept rubbing the other wrist that you could find an inkling, a vague picture, as to who he was when alone: He was someone who had to touch himself, rub himself, to make things around him, the numerous voices, settle down and fade.

"*¿Estás listo?*" I asked him. Are you ready?

The Englishwoman was standing alongside of us, smiling, a glass containing only a soggy lemon in one hand.

"*Sí, estoy listo,*" Borja said slowly, as if we were speaking in code and not in another language.

The Englishwoman, apparently understanding Spanish, said, "Well, aren't you going to dance before you leave?" She looked at Borja. "I'm sure you're a *wonderful* dancer."

"We're leaving," I said.

She made a glamorous gesture with her hand. "Oh, what a pity. I—" If there was more coming from her sentence, it didn't come, as the gray-haired man with the pseudo-afro came over, touched her arm, and she waved good-bye to us with the same hand in which she held the glass, and then headed over to the bar.

In the cab, Borja didn't ask me where I wanted to go, what I wanted to do. He just gave the cabdriver an address, something on la calle Princesa, and that was the direction we went. We were silent, so silent that I felt awkward and weird, as if I were somehow responsible for the Englishwoman being rude to him. He didn't even ask how I had met her or what her name was, but then I didn't offer the information either. We just sat there riding down Gran Vía, down the same street I had driven with Esteban in his Porsche over and over again since the first night I met him. We stopped at a light in front of calle Montera, a street that was known for its shadiness—for its prostitutes and drug dealers and blinking sex-shop signs. There were no hookers out though, although usually during the day you could pass right by them while they stood there in mildly risqué outfits: a red leather tank top; a black shiny skirt; high boots that were too tight, too sweaty for summer; perhaps a different-colored bra strap, red, pink, or green, hanging loosely off one shoulder. They were women whose faces you did not look into when you passed; you didn't ask them the time, didn't ask them directions. You just saw them in the distance as you approached, and then your gaze turned elsewhere, anywhere.

But those women were not out that night, and even if they were, I don't think I would've felt any similarity between what they did and what I was doing sitting in a cab next a man who kept touching the stiff starched collar of his shirt as he stared out the window, looking strangely pensive and worried. About a block or two after calle Montera, at another light, he stopped touching his collar and touched my hand, and again his touch, its energy, felt odd, as if he weren't sure what he was doing, as if he were afraid I would yank my hand away. It did not feel like the hand of a pervert; it did not feel like the hand of a lover. It felt like someone touching me because he had to, he needed to, and so I let him.

What exactly I thought about at this point, what exactly I felt, is difficult to remember, difficult to understand. I'm not entirely sure how I lost that feistiness I normally had, that protective radar, that often led me to abruptly change seats on buses and subways if a man sat next to me and gave off a certain unpleasant feeling, a heat. It was a feistiness that I was very proud of, almost in love with, because it impassioned me, gave me the nerve to do things I normally couldn't do, like slap a customer in the face once, for putting my tip, a rolled-up one-dollar bill, down my dress. Perhaps I lost that anger, that fire, in Zara that day, or maybe I had put it away, was storing it up, for the next day, for when I saw my father, all dressed up and hungover, on the front steps of the Holiday Inn.

In any case, I kept my hand in Borja's, and when the cab stopped, we were in front of his hotel. I got out first, stared up at the lights that said PRINCESA in glowing pink letters on the top of a neighboring hotel. I heard the slam of the car door shutting, then the cab left us, and we were alone. Borja was on the other side of the curb, and in the distance that we stood apart from each other, he looked different to me, his sideburns longer—he was suddenly like a small-faced forty-five-year-old Elvis.

We stood there silently in front of the hotel's entrance for a few minutes. It was as if he knew I needed time, time to glance at the hotel's sliding glass doors and brass-trimmed windows and the empty white vase that sat in one of the windows. Then he came over to me; his footsteps against the cement were soft. He stood next to me, his face very close to mine, so close that I suppose it was more comfortable: He didn't have to look into my eyes, he could stare somewhere behind me as he said, "I just want you to sleep *next* to me, not with me." He said this in Spanish though, as if saying it in English were more uncomfortable.

"Do you understand what I mean?" he asked, and I nodded, I said, "Yes." Whether the yes was to the proposition or to the fact that I understood, I suppose did not matter, because then I went up with him through the brightly lit lobby full of chairs with flowered hassocks and looming chandeliers that had long pieces of pointed crystal.

In the elevator, I thought.

In the hallway, which was narrow and blue, I thought.

Everywhere I went that night, I thought, and I know that within all that thinking I did not in any way have any certain sense that Borja was gay—something that I would learn only in an argument with Esteban a few days later. I suppose I could lie, make myself sound more street smart, more wary, by saying I did have some secret extrasensory feeling that told me that Borja would not try anything raw or sexual; but it seems ridiculous even to try to say that because I felt a certain affection for Borja, whether he was gay or not—an affection for his soft sideburns and his small nose and his fingertips that could not stop feeling and feeling. I think in some secret part of myself I may have wanted— from the moment I saw him—to sleep next to him, to feel once again what I knew it felt like to have someone's hand on my waist, his weight pressed against me, his face, his soft sleeping breath, at the back of my neck.

It started off strange though, uncomfortable. His hotel room was actually two rooms, a sitting area and then a bedroom. We went directly into the bedroom, or rather he did and I followed. We stood on opposite sides of the bed and took off our shoes. He loosened his shirt, unbuttoned a few buttons, then fiddled with his watch, trying to take it off, but couldn't. I didn't offer to help—I just moved my shoes side by side against the wall under the window. Outside through the sheer curtains, I could see the square shape of a building, the words *agencia de viajes*, and a blinking red crosswalk light below. Meanwhile, Borja was pulling the lavender comforter back, pulling it neatly to the foot of the bed. I left the window, came over to the bed, touched the pillow as if I were going to fluff it or arrange it more attractively against the headboard. Instead I just grazed my hand over it, and he watched my hand, how it moved, how far my fingers were spread apart.

He said, *"Tienes manos bonitas."* You have pretty hands.

I nodded and smiled slightly.

He took off his shirt. He took off his pants. He took off each nylon sock. I watched, sitting on the edge of the bed. He was skinny, so skinny that I could see the outline of his ribs, and the slight shape of muscles that were once strong in his arms. He was wearing gray cotton briefs, the kind of underwear you don't expect a man in such a stiff buttoned-down shirt to wear. I expected boxers, silk and paisley.

He took his underwear off. He got under the sheets.

I just sat there on the edge of the bed. He touched my arm very softly; if I had been more relaxed, it would've tickled. It was time for me to take my dress off, get under the sheets, too, but I took my time, acted as if I had to think about it a lot—that way I thought he would know, he would see, that he had to be slow with me, gentle.

He touched my hair softly, smoothed it against my back, against my shoulders. Then I told him to turn the light off. He reached above the headboard and clicked the switch on the wall. In the darkness, I stood up, took my dress off with great care. First I let the spaghetti straps fall off my shoulder, then I pulled the dress down little by little so that it finally fell at my feet. I had no underwear on, no bra.

I stood there in the dark light of the window, folding my dress carefully instead of looking up at Borja. Part of the dress's sales tag, the clear plastic, was still attached—I tucked it inside and put the dress on the nightstand, as if I might reach for it later in the night, put it back on.

When I finally got into bed, I didn't face Borja. I put my back to him and then I pulled his arm around me, held his hand at my chest. He felt warm, so warm that any nervousness I had started to fade, and there was just him and the coolness of the humming air-conditioner and the soft, white sheets. After a few minutes, he moved so that my back was no longer to him and kissed me. It was at first just a gentle kiss on the lips, a childish kiss, but then it became more—but it wasn't really passionate; it was absent of something. It was like kissing just to kiss, to remember what it felt like. He kept one hand in my hair, near my ear, the other beneath his own pillow. Occasionally his hand moved down from my ear, to my collarbone, my arm, my waist, but no farther. It was too strange, I suppose, too forced. We kissed a bit more and then we leaned against each other. We slept. And amongst the vanilla scent of my hair, amongst the flowery scent of his cologne, amongst the world of noises that could not find us in that bed, we slept soundly—we slept pressed up against each other, spooned together; we slept as we never could alone.

$$\overline{15}$$

CHURCH AND AFTERWARD

I met my father the next morning at ten. He was not in his room, but standing outside of the Holiday Inn when I got there. He was wearing a white T-shirt and jeans and a pair of leather sandals with two wide straps—the sandals made him look somewhat European. In the cab we took to church, I stared down at his feet, noticed that his toenails were clipped short, yet on one of his big toes there was still one tiny, tiny clipping of nail still hanging on by the corner. I had the urge to reach down and pull it off, but instead I stared out the window, imagined him hurriedly clipping his nails on the edge of his hotel bed.

"How did you sleep?" I asked him.

He shrugged and said, "Fine." He was looking out the window, although there was nothing to look at as we were driving down Castellana, a very long, wide street where cars moved at highway speed, zooming past one another. "I met up with Doria last night though." He looked at me. "We had a drink."

"Doria?"

"The women who were on the roof at the pool. One of them's Doria."

"The one who was smoking?"

"That's Maureen." He paused. "Doria smokes, but I don't think she was smoking when you were there."

I nodded. I suppose I could've told him that I had run into the other one, acted like it was casual and minor, but I didn't want to talk about the night before, so I just stared out the window, my hands clasped together primly on my lap, while I envisioned the giant white church we were headed toward, Catedral de la Almudena. It was in my neighborhood next to Palacio Real. If I had been smart, I would've called my father in his hotel room and had him meet me there; it was only five minutes from my apartment—but I thought of my father alone in the midst of Madrid as being like a little boy who couldn't possibly navigate his way, even with the church's name on a piece of paper and a taxicab driver there to drive him. There was also the issue of the telephone—I didn't want to talk to my father on the phone. This may seem strange and illogical, since I had already spent the whole day before with him, but the phone brought forth—or really I was afraid it would bring forth—a certain all-consuming edginess. An edginess that stemmed from the fact that my father had always had a phone, in every place he had ever lived, and I had always had a phone, yet he had never ever bothered to dial those specific numbers that would've brought my voice to his. And if he wasn't going to call me, I had promised myself as a kid, I wouldn't call him either. Not ever.

So instead I had woken up early, got to my apartment as quickly as I could, did my hair and makeup, ironed a skirt and shirt, and then raced to the metro to get my father. Despite all the rushing around, we made it to church quite early. I led my father without touching his hand or his arm through a crowded sidewalk full of tourists and churchgoers and *gitanas*. We stood outside of the church in the hot morning sun looking over an embankment that had an entire citywide view of Madrid—there were distant buildings, balconies with flower pots, and then a vast, forestlike greenness farther away. My father stared and stared. All around us tourists were taking photographs. I stood there, not looking at the view, with both hands behind me. The cement wall was still a bit cool from the night before, and as I stood there, stiff and tired-eyed, I thought of Borja.

I had left him around eight. Earlier that morning, I had woken up, felt his fingertips moving softly on my bare shoulder, the warmth of his legs against mine, but I didn't let him know I was awake. I stayed as quiet as could be, kept my breath like sleeping breath, and watched the way that the gray light came through the beige curtains, leaving a growing shape on the carpet.

After about a half hour, his fingers finally stopped moving, he fell back asleep, and I watched in that stillness the light in the room get brighter and brighter. I heard the ticking of his watch, still on his wrist draped outside of the sheets on my hip. With each tick, I knew I soon had to go back to my father, but the feeling wasn't as dreadful as it had been the morning before. It was easier somehow, as if the worst of the worst had passed.

I didn't leave Borja a note or make any attempt to wake him. I put on my dress in the bathroom without turning on the light, and then I checked my face for smudged mascara in the darkened mirror. I left the hotel room, closing the door as gently as possible, and then I strolled casually down the hallway, which seemed brighter and longer than it had the night before.

I ended up walking back to my apartment from the hotel, it was very close, only a few blocks away. Amongst the cars and the beeping and the overpass I had to walk under, I kept my gaze down, on the sidewalk. The girls at Shooters used to call this walk—the walk from a man's house to your own so early in the morning—the Walk of Shame. They always said it sarcastically, a big joke, but I think they always sort of meant it, and even in my own case, walking from a hotel room where I hadn't done anything except let another human being lie against me, I felt it, too. I felt it in my stomach, I felt it in my face, I felt it in the way the sun didn't just hurt my eyes, it made my head pound. It was as if I were fully aware that I had just done something a bit risqué, a bit confusing, something that would stay with me forever and ever.

———

The inside of Catedral de la Almudena was not the prettiest. It was a bit dark, and to make up for this, it had too much color on the walls, too much gold. Because it was the only church my father had ever seen in Europe, he probably thought they were all like this. He stared at things, tilted his neck up. When he looked at the high, high ceiling, I noticed how irritated the whites of his eyes were, how red. It hadn't occurred to me that the two of us were equally hungover, equally tired, until I looked down at his hands on the pew in front of us and saw how they trembled.

The Mass itself was more than fifty minutes long. When we had to kneel, they didn't have the nice cushions that I was used to. It was just wood. They didn't have the little prayer books for following the readings either—and that seemed to make it even more difficult to pay attention. Even if it were in English, I would have been all over the place. My eyes traced the heavy, wide arabesque peaks, the gold-colored symbols in the ceilings, the stained-glass windows that seemed to have no light, no sun, coming through them, even though I knew the sun was out there, uncomfortable and bright, gleaming against the white fairy-tale walls of Palacio Real.

When Mass was over, I showed my father the cathedral's main altar, which you couldn't see from where we had been sitting—a giant dangling Crucifix had blocked our view. There was a set of stairs that led up to a giant gold box that looked like a miniature coffin. There were pictures above it everywhere, crucifixion stations, and during the day a person stood there at the altar with a handkerchief in his hand.

"They line up," I told my father, "and they kiss it."

"They kiss what?"

"The altar," I said, as if it were obvious. "They climb up those stairs and then they kiss the altar, and then this guy with a handkerchief wipes away where they kissed and somebody else kisses it. But they don't just kiss anywhere, they kiss the alter in this special spot." I looked at him, smiled. "A special kissing spot."

I was in an all-right mood all of a sudden. Originally that morning I had been feeling a little sick—partially from drinking, but more so from Borja. I had left him without saying a word, without giving him even a light kiss on the cheek. Once I slithered out of that bed, once I stood fiddling with my dress in his dark bathroom, the marble cold against my bare feet, I decided in all my haste and sneakiness that I would never see him again.

So I left him alone, only to wake up in that gloomy overly air-conditioned room with sun trapped in the curtains and not a single lip-sticked word left on the mirror for him. He had no way of contacting me either; Esteban had promised he would initially keep it that way, and I believed him—the main reason being that if Borja were able to reach me without Esteban, then Esteban wasn't guaranteed whatever reward he got for introducing us, or so I imagined.

I thought about all of this during Mass.

I thought about the fact that Borja was asleep right then. I pictured him in the tangle of white sheets, his brown hair ruffled, one of his hands under the pillow. As I sat in that pew, he was dreaming of me, I decided, and I didn't just feel bad, I felt sick, disgusted with myself. I knew from my own vision-filled mind that it was cruel to make someone think of you too much, to wish for you and want you. I imagined all the sherries he thought we would drink and all the dances he thought I would learn and all the houses and planes he envisioned us in. He probably already had a slew of imagined parties lined up for us, dresses I would wear, specific colors in mind, and the set of people's faces, other bankers perhaps, when they saw me leaning gingerly against him. From his reaction to the Englishwoman and her laughing nastiness, I knew he was used to being taunted a little bit, giggled at— or in other cases, just being treated as if he were odd, slow-minded— simply because of his daintiness, his girlishness, his nonmasculine elegance.

So I prayed for Borja in that church. I prayed and prayed. I prayed that people would be nice to him and laugh with him and like him. To make my prayer stronger, to make it mean more, I gave specifics: I wanted a woman, preferably elderly and ritzy-looking, to tell him in the elevator that he had gorgeous hands; I wanted the people at his work to throw him a party, a big party, a party at which he drank lots of sherry and danced with so many different women that he could not distinguish in his memory one face from the next—they'd just become one big welcoming entity; I also wanted him to be given a new suit, either at the party or somewhere else, but it had to be a suit that made him chipper and giddy when he looked at himself.

Praying for all of this as I squeezed my clasped hands extra tight made me feel somewhat better. That was one of the few things I liked about church: If you believed enough, it erased any wrongdoing—you could be good again.

When I was done with my prayer, I glanced sideways at my father. The lines in his forehead had deepened, and he seemed to me to be saying things very passionately in a silent, secret place in his head—and it occurred to me then that that same forgiveness, that same goodness I sought, was perhaps exactly the same reason my father was so set on going to church today, whether the Mass itself was held in Spanish, English, or Chinese. As long as he could stand there. As long as he could pray and hear himself saying soundless things, as long as he felt a certain sense of calm, he'd be OK.

He had been like this when I was a kid, too—forever thinking about God, forever adamant that we go to church every Sunday no matter how sick, no matter how tired; that ruling faded only after he left my mother and me. She never forced me to go; she let me sleep and sleep. It was as if for her, for me, my father's memory lurked like some bright, disheartening light among the church's stained glass and its organ music and all those murmuring, jumbled voices. He was everywhere. I could find him in the soft tinkle of coins in collection baskets, in the word *Amen*, in the specific nongarbled words from the Profession of Faith: *Light from Light, true God from true God*; even in the shuffling sound of dress shoes against stern white linoleum, he was there. And as I got older, I avoided church more and more—particularly after I was confirmed. It was my secret way of trying to forget my father, to ignore him.

I hadn't even stepped foot in a church for four years until right before my father arrived in Madrid. That week I went twice. But the first time I didn't pray or even sit down. I felt too proud—which sounds odd, I suppose, weird, but my father and God were closely related in my mind; they were both imaginary and shapeless at times, difficult to reach.

I did pray the second time I went, but I delivered my concerns as casual "if you have the time" requests—that way there could be no disappointment, no sudden fits of "Why?"

Those two times were the only times I had previously been in Catedral de la Almudena, walked past its big medieval doors. Without my father coming, I would never have bothered to peek at its high, high ceilings or its candlelit chapels, never would have stumbled upon the altar's big gold box, the one I told my father about, the one people lined up to kiss.

"But did you kiss it?" he asked me.

I said, "No, I'm not going to kiss some box." Which was a lie. I had actually gone up on the those stairs to see what they were all gawking at and then when I got close enough, it seemed I couldn't get back down without kissing it myself. Besides, I felt pressured by the handkerchief guy. And then there was something eerie about the way the rest of the church looked from that height on the stairs. If you looked down it was like you were in midair, over the pews, over the baskets with red flowers. Even the Crucifix in the middle of the church seemed from this view not to be suspended from anything; it was just up there, heavy and large.

So, of course, I kissed the box, I had to. And then I walked down those stairs, feeling weird and different. It was as if I halfheartedly wanted to believe that that kiss might do something, perhaps give me special powers.

After church, I had no idea what to do with my father. We had a whole five hours before the bullfight began, and most tourist attractions were soon closing—most museums were done at two, most restaurants and stores hadn't been open all day. According to Celia, Sundays were days reserved to spend with your family. You didn't have to go to church, and you didn't have to get up early, and you definitely shouldn't work. You were supposed to go for a walk, sit in Retiro, the city's park, or go down to La Latina, the older section, and sit for hours in a café and talk. The only major activity on Sunday afternoons was El Rastro, an outdoor market where you could buy used or, often, stolen things. But I didn't imagine my father had much interest in buying old picture frames or plate sets or touristy magnets, and besides, it required a lot of energy to walk through streets and streets of vendors, the sun so hot and the people so loud, so close, always bumping into you. I was also a little afraid to go shopping with my father again—who knew, I might flip out, might suddenly get mad that he wouldn't buy me a frying pan or a teapot or a lacy Spanish fan.

"I'm hungry," my father said while I contemplated where we should go as we stood on the front steps of the church. There were people taking pictures of one another in front of a fountain that had no water, and a few beggars were nearby; they waited for you to come out of church and then they held out a hat or a basket. One elderly woman just sat down on the hot, hot cement, a pink handkerchief laid out in front of her. Each coin someone dropped on the handkerchief she arranged in a neat pattern so that you could clearly see what she had, what she still needed.

There were *gitanas*, too, a whole squadron of them, and as my father and I started walking away from the church, one of them stopped me, tried to sell me some sage. She said it would keep the bad spirits away. She pointed at the cathedral as she said this, as if she knew that was the very reason the two of us had gone to Mass. The sage she had didn't look like sage though—it looked like the branch of a pine tree. She kept putting it in my hand. *"Un regalo,"* a gift, she kept saying. "Don't you want a gift?"

"What's she going on about?" my father asked.

"Nothing," I said, "nothing," and started digging around in my bag for loose change. I ended up giving the *gitana* 500 pesetas for the sage, and then she kept walking alongside of us—it was as if she could sense, could see, that I was a foolish buyer.

"*Guapa,*" she said over and over, which my father understood to be "Whopper."

"It means pretty," I told him, although in the sense she was using it, it was the equivalent of calling someone "honey" or "dear."

"*Tienes mucha suerte,*" she told me. You have a lot of luck. She claimed I had luck not just in a general way, but within the special arenas of *amor y dinero,* love and money. "*Dame la mano,*" she said. Give me your hand. "I can tell you exactly when you'll get the love, when you'll get the money." She pointed at a woman in beige shorts who was a bit farther away from us on the sidewalk having her palm read. The *gitana* reading her fortune did this weird tapping motion on the pads of the woman's palms, then on her wrist. Just the sight of it gave me a quick flash of the chills even though it was daylight, even though we were standing in front of a great white church.

"*Puedo decirte todo,*" the *gitana* was telling me—I can tell you every-thing—her voice was singsongy, and she kept repeating everything twice. She had her open palm on my arm. "*¿No quieres saber?*" she said. You don't want to know?

I shook my head, moved away from her, bumping clumsily into my father. "What's going on with her?" he asked, not looking concerned, just interested—as if he were watching something amusing from a dis-tance. "What's she telling you?"

"*Nada,*" I said with an American accent, "*nada,*" and then the *gitana* kept talking behind us. I heard her voice amongst a bunch of other garbled voices say: "*Mucho va a pasarte.*" A lot is going to happen to you.

My father and I spent the next hour and a half in a café, the *gitana*'s sage on the table between us. The café was on the other side of Palacio Real, where you could sit outside and see its big vast rectangular shape, the statues in the garden, the bushes shaped in perfectly round globes. It was the same café where I had eaten dinner with Esteban the second night I had gone out with him. The thought that I had been there only a few weeks ago and had no idea that I would later revisit the place with my father bothered me a little. It made feel as if I had no real sense of anything that would later happen to me, no intuition, no extrasensory feeling. I was perceptionless in that way, blind.

While my father and I waited for our breakfast we said very little. We were both hungover and tired, both stuck in a place where conversation seemed unnatural and forced. We watched people sit down near us, moved our chairs when waiters came by. The things that interested us were in the distance, away from the actual table where we were sitting.

"These people really know how to touch, don't they?" my father said only later, after our breakfast arrived, after he finished his third beer. He was referring to a man and woman who were sitting on a long red chair together, mauling each other. The guy had one leg draped over the woman and one arm around her, his finger making little special shapes on her shoulder. With his other free hand, he kept touching her lips, grazing them with his fingertips. At one point she even started sucking on his fingers, but that was only after they had kissed and kissed, making quivery sounds, full of tingling and breathing, which broadcasted across the room as if on speakers to the table where we sat.

In our awkwardness, we started joking about the couple, making fun of the sounds they made, coughing on purpose to cover them up—and then laughing. We behaved like goofy children for those few minutes—as if we had known each other all our lives, as if nothing had ever separated or changed us. My father had a laugh that I had forgotten—it was hard felt and deep, a choking sound that could almost be disturbing if you weren't looking at him, seeing the reddened happy-face smirk.

"In a glance, Squeaks," my father started to say, and then stopped himself—he saw the frown I made at the reference to my old nickname, Squeaky. For a moment, we had been all right, giggly with each another, but there was a line to be drawn, and Squeaky was a name that was too close to me, to who I was as a devoted child, for him ever to think of using again.

"Fine," he said. "In a glance, Catherine,"—he paused as if he were annoyed I wouldn't let him call me Squeaky, then he posed his question—"how many people in this place are making out?"

There was another couple going at it, sitting parallel to us one table away. They were not Spanish though; their language sounded like German, although it could've been Polish, but no matter what their nationality, they had apparently caught the "let's make out in public" bug that everyone else in Madrid had. They were sitting side by side, not across from each other, some sort of egg concoction on their plates, but they were just kissing, and at one point the woman pretended she was going to bite the guy on the neck, then she laughed, and I noticed she had very long eyeteeth.

"You didn't answer the question," my father said after a minute. "How many people?"

"Two very scary people are making out. Two Dracula people." I gestured over at the first couple. "And then some regular ones."

My father shook his head. "That is incorrect."

He apparently wanted a bigger number, an exaggerated one, but even if I had said a whole million were making out in Madrid right then, it could've been accurate. Celia had told me more than once, *"Somos muy cariñosos,"* which meant: We, as in all the entire Spanish population, are very affectionate. And this affection went beyond any affection I had seen before in the States, as it was not only for the young or the drunken. It was for everybody and anybody, whether you were an adolescent or sixty, and the more public the spectacle the more the gasping enjoyment. Wherever you looked, somebody was wrapped around somebody else: on park benches and escalators, in grocery stores and shoe stores and tobacco stores—in all stores at all times—there was this kissing giggliness that I couldn't entirely stand. It was particularly unavoidable on the subway, and no matter how many nuns or priests or pleading panhandlers came on the train, the couples kept going and going—and if there was a vigorous banjo player on board, the excitement heightened to the degree that neighboring couples leaned into you, pressed against you, as if you too were invited.

"How many people are making out?" my father asked again.

I shrugged as if I didn't know, as if I didn't care, as if the game were boring.

"You're no fun," he said, not looking directly at me. "No fun at all." And then we stopped playing the game, stopped talking, and we became awkward again. Silent.

We went to my apartment after the café. It seemed like something to do. It involved a short walk, a cool place to sit, and there was a picture on my nightstand that I wanted to show him. It was of my mother and me. Harlan had taken it out front of our apartment in Boston. It had the pink petunias that our landlord put in the heavy pots on the steps, and my mother and I sat amongst the flowers looking entirely healthy and attractive. She was wearing a white T-shirt with a pair of pants that were fitted and flattering, and I was wearing a navy sweater that made my eyes look not just blue, but very serene, as if I were looking into the ocean and not at Harlan, who was sitting on a car hood taking the photograph.

I wanted my father to see that picture, hold its framed beauty in his hands, touch the glass with his fingertips.

On the way to my apartment we passed Raúl's store, but he didn't come out. As I fiddled in my bag for the keys, it occurred to me that Raúl must've seen us. He hadn't approached me since the day I had yelled at him, but he still appeared in the doorway, in the window, waving like a shy child. But now he was nowhere, and all because of my father, I was sure. Otherwise he might have been right in front of me, the Mars Bar in his hand—his smile, his face, so close.

"Can't get away from Coca-Cola around here, can ya?" my father said, pointing at the sign in front of Raúl's store.

I shook my head, said, "No, no you can't." Then once we were inside the foyer, I asked him if he still worked for Coca-Cola.

He nodded, said, "Yeah, I never left." His voice was marked with a certain uncomfortable softness, one that echoed against the marble walls and followed us up the stairs.

When we got inside my apartment, Celia was home, which rattled me. I didn't really want to introduce her to my father, and that upset me, made me angry with myself. There was nothing to be embarrassed about, but I was embarrassed, or worried, I guess, that he might do something or say something inappropriate. Somehow in my mind I had attributed my father with very bad social skills, but that was not the case. Once he saw Celia in the living room, he said, *"Hola,"* and smiled at her. She was in the recliner with the TV on, volume down, and the stereo on high. She was painting her toenails pink. Once she saw my father, she quickly put the nail polish brush down, as if my father's presence commanded attention—then she tried to stand up, but it took a while because the cotton between her toes somehow imbalanced her, gave her the same unsteady movements a lumbering pregnant woman might have.

I kissed her hello first, and then my father, without one single pause, copied me, kissed her on each cheek quickly and deftly. I thought he would have just stood there awkwardly, as I originally did when I first arrived, but he seemed to have the hang of it—perhaps he had learned their customs just by watching people come in and out of the café we had just been in.

Celia smiled at him for a moment afterward—all three of us stood close together in an awkward triangle. Then, Celia explained why she was home early; she said she had an appointment the following morning with a teacher. Yet it seemed to me in her gaze—in the way she seemed to take note of my father's hair and face and sandals—that she might have come early out of curiosity, as if my father was some mysterious being she did not want to miss.

"Where have you taken him so far?" she asked, after a moment or two and I shrugged. I hadn't really taken him anywhere, and I knew that wouldn't be met with much approval. Celia and Isabel had already instructed me on the places to take my father. They were adamant that we take a day trip to El Escorial, an old monastery turned museum, and El Valle de los Caídos, Valley of the Fallen, a monument that was for those who had died in their civil war. Both places, they insisted, were beautiful and Spanish and important.

"My father was very tired yesterday," I told Celia. "So we didn't go anywhere. But today," I raised my voice, as if I were about to announce something exciting, "we went to church."

Celia smiled and nodded, as if the idea of us sitting together in a pew was very cute and attractive. Then she motioned for my father to sit down on the sofa, and he did with casual ease, placing one hand on each knee. Celia kept staring at him, smiling. She was wearing a light blue tank top and a pair of white shorts that made her look extra tan. She looked as if she belonged at the beach or in a café, not sitting in our sweltering apartment. It was very hot that day, about 95 degrees, and my father's cheeks were so red he looked as if he had just done a handstand. Whether that was from the heat of walking or the beer he had drunk or a combination, I could not tell, but I knew Celia couldn't tell he had been drinking. He held it rather well.

On the soundless television in front us, the news was on. They were showing the footage of people thrashing around and screaming in a fountain that was in front of the post office on the night that Spain won against Switzerland and made it to the World Cup semifinals. The people who jumped in the fountain went so berserk they broke the arm off a statue of a Roman goddess. As I watched, I remembered the night that it had happened—it had been a few days after my mother called to say my father wanted to see me. I didn't go out that night; it was a Saturday, the same day I had yelled at Raúl and almost lost my wallet. I had stayed in and watched television and flipped through my Spanish-English dictionary trying to memorize words. When they showed on the news what had happened to the statue, I had been sitting there in our hot apartment in a tank top and underwear and Isabel's slippers. I watched all those drunken men's faces, heard them shout *"Viva España,"* and I felt a slight emptiness, a loss.

But now as I watched all of this over again, my father sitting red-faced on the couch in front of me, I did not feel that loss as much. Celia mumbled, *"Idiotas,"* looking at the TV, and my father sat there silently with his hands clasped together like a child. He was staring up at the pictures on the wall that Celia's mother had painted. He pointed at one, the one with the deathly white hand playing chess with a forlorn woman, and nodded. He liked it apparently, but he didn't say so to me—in Celia's Spanish-speaking presence he had lost the ability to speak out loud, even to me. He was reduced to hand gestures and then sudden animated smiles that minutely reminded of Harlan.

"Tu padre es muy muy guapo," Celia told me.

I smiled, said, *"Gracias."* Then I translated for my father. "She thinks you're very handsome." This brought out a gleam in his eyes as if someone had just flashed a picture in his face. He said, *"Gracias,"* with a very American accent even though earlier in the afternoon I had given him a brief lesson on how to pronounce the Spanish lisp in *gracias.*

My father—in his new "you are so handsome" state—became suddenly suave, his gestures contained more of an elegant wave to them. I later caught him looking at himself in the mirror across from the couch; he looked at himself sideways debonairly, and I could've laughed. The very look he gave himself reminded me of 007, perhaps because my mother claimed that my father looked exactly like James Bond, but only when Sean Connery played the part. She insisted they had the same steely eyes, the same lips, the same way of raising their eyebrows when they said something funny or obnoxious. I myself did not see the connection, although there were pictures strewn along the wall in the hallway of our house that showed him as a twenty-year-old, and he did have the same widower's peak, the same Dracula look that Sean Connery occasionally adopted.

"Why don't you show your father around the apartment?" Celia said after we sat in a dull silence for too long, my father looking at himself in the mirror, me fiddling with a Spanish coin I had found on the floor next to my chair.

I got up and he followed me through the dining room and kitchen and three bathrooms. I skipped their bedrooms, as if I thought that it would be rude to show him their own private places, and then I brought him to my bedroom, showed him the picture of my mother and me. He stared for a long time. "Do you like her blond?" he asked, and I nodded.

Then Celia came into the room. She handed me a note, and I knew from the way it was folded that it was from Felipe. She stood in the doorway while I opened it, and my father had his back to us, he was looking out the window.

The note said one single line in fat block letters: *I think for you—* which, of course, meant: I am thinking of you.

It was that same weekend my father arrived that I was supposed to have met Felipe. Celia had told him that I couldn't make it the week before and he had sent me a note in the mail, folded in an envelope in the same schoolboyish way as the others. It said:

Querida Catherine,

I hope that you have very much fun showing your father Madrid. It must be so nice to show him a place so different, so strange, from where you live. He must be very proud of you. He must think you are a superstar.

But . . . if you still would see me, I can come to Madrid maybe. I like where Celia lives. I like Palacio Real at night on those benches where you can sit very silent and stare.

If you would see me, I would see you. Tell me what you want.

A strong hug,

Felipe

When I first got the note, I read it on the train to work and then at my desk at work and then over the phone to Kansas Katy. She was greatly pleased by it, as if within its words, its simplicity, she could envision his posture as he wrote the note, the pen grazing his lips during thoughtful English conjugations, his left hand touching the sheet of paper, bending its corner.

When I got off the phone with Kansas Katy, I doodled Felipe's name over and over. His address on the envelope had his last name, Guzmán. I wrote Catherine Guzmán, but only once and then I crossed it out, embarrassed by such pathetic behavior. Later that same day I wrote

Harlan a letter, telling him about Felipe again. I said as a joke that Felipe would be coming back with me, moving in. I told Harlan he would have to get rid of some of the stuffed animals in his room because "it wouldn't look right." In particular I wanted the pink elephant that he kept on his stereo destroyed. He sent me back a postcard with mouse cartoon on one side, a pencil drawing of my face with an elephant's footprint across it. The caption read: Girl Brutally Crushed.

That same postcard was taped on the wall above my father's head as he stood with his back to me while Celia watched me read the note. I handed it to her afterward. She smiled—she understood English, but she was very shy about it, as if knowing only a little was an embarrassment somehow, a failure. I tried to put the note back in my nightstand where I kept the other two, but Celia took it out of the drawer, put it under my pillow. She laughed as she did this, and then I tried to put it back in the drawer; then she slapped my hand and put the note again under the pillow. My father the whole time kept looking at us and then turning back around, as if he were uncomfortable, unsure. He glanced over when he heard us laughing, but he didn't say anything.

Before Celia left us alone, she asked me if I was going to sleep at my father's hotel again. That apparently was where she thought I was the night before. "I was a little worried about you," she said. "I didn't know where you were."

"*Estuve bien, muy bien,*" I said—I was fine, very fine—and then I glanced over at my father, who was still holding the picture of my mother and me, looking out the window. He thankfully had no idea what we were saying. He seemed suddenly absorbed in whatever he saw outside anyway. From the back I noticed that his white cotton shirt that was a little bit wrinkled at the bottom as if he had tucked it in his pants and then pulled it back out. I watched and watched him stand there, and then I wondered if it felt very disorienting for him to be staring out at Raúl's store sign, La Tienda Real, with the Madrid sun hot on his arms and forehead, while he held a picture of my mother in one hand and listened to me talk to my Spanish roommate in strange lisping sounds.

After a minute or two, he turned away from the window and stared up at the pink wall of my bedroom. I had Harlan's postcards taped on the wall close together like a collage. "What's with all the mice?" he asked.

"They're from my friend, the one I told you about." I had already mentioned Harlan in passing as my father and I had walked from the café to the apartment, and he had nodded at the name Harlan as if my mother had already briefed him on our friendship.

"You mean the gay guy?" my father said. That's what my father called Harlan, the gay guy, but he didn't say it necessarily rudely, or uncomfortably; he said it in the same calm, nonchalant tone that he would've used if he actually said Harlan's name. He was not acting like Gerry, my mother's boyfriend, who couldn't even stand to overhear me chat about Harlan without making a wincing face as if I were talking about something crass or disgusting.

I said, "Yeah, the gay guy sent those."

He stared at the images of Mickey and Minnie, of Mighty Mouse soaring through a planet of cheese, of a white albino mouse with red eyes that had a magazine picture of a giant joint pasted near its mouth.

"Why mice?" he asked.

"Why else?"

He stood there for a minute, as if he were trying to come up with a logical answer, and then I said, looking not at him but at the wall of postcards, "Because he loves them."

16

THE BULLFIGHT

The bullfight wasn't until six o'clock but Celia told us to get there early. We took the subway to the bullring, to Las Ventas, and bought our tickets right away. There were three sections to sit in: *sol, sombra,* and *sol y sombra,* which meant literally, sun, shade, or sun and shade. The section called sun and shade meant that you spent the first half of the bullfight, the first three rounds, more or less, in the sweltering heat, and then the late-afternoon sun would finally shift and there would be shade for the last hour. That afternoon was particularly unpleasant in terms of sweating and overall discomfort, so we bought tickets in the more expensive, shady section, *sombra.* There was a picture, a diagram of the ring above the *taquilla,* the ticket booth, and my father let me choose how close to the ring we sat. I picked seats that were close but not so close that we'd smell or hear anything that went on in the ring. I wanted to limit our experience to sight.

After we got our tickets, we still had a half hour to kill before the ring even opened, so we walked amongst the stands that were set up outside. They sold cheese puffs, peanuts, cashews, fluorescent pink candies, raisins, and sunflower seeds. All were packaged in plastic bags with twist ties, as if the vendors had made the items themselves in their own kitchens the night before. There were also touristy things, of course: red capes, *torero* hats; swords that were plastic but at the same time were long enough, fancy enough to thrill any little boy. My father got a beer at one of the stands, and then we stood far away from all of them, looking up at the giant walls of the *plaza de toros*. It was giant and circular and Moorish in design. There were keyhole-shaped openings every few feet, ones that, if you stared at them for long enough, you could almost imagine, almost see, what it would be like to look out the window from inside, see the scurry of people on that hot pavement, feel the scratchy cement against your fingertips, squint against the sun's close white presence.

Gitanas were also walking around, offering to read fortunes. As we walked toward the plaza, one called out to me, *"Guapa, guapa."* I ignored her, pretended to be staring off at some old bullfighting posters, and then I looked up above the main entrance, at the Star of David that hung high.

When we finally went in, we didn't rent cushions to sit on—because I didn't know better—so we ended up sitting on the bare cement. A man in a black biker hat, with many, many gold chains around his neck, led us to our designated seats and then we sat with all the other tourists in our overpriced section. There was very little room between rows, and if I so much as moved my knee slightly to the left the Japanese man in front of me could feel it on his back. There was an entire row of Japanese people in front of us and two of the women were giggling at each other as they practiced covering their eyes before the bullfight began. My father was clearly amused by them, and he started practicing himself; then he noticed two men with turbans, and said, "Look, two sheiks."

"Stop that," I said, "don't point."

Next to the men with turbans were two women with flowing maroon outfits. I stared at them a while and then listened to the people behind us—they were both talking in French, and it reminded me momentarily of my mother.

"Whiskey! Whiskey!" shouted a man who was holding a bottle of Cutty Sark over his head as he moved through the aisles. Another man behind him carried an egg crate full of Coke bottles and thin glasses filled with ice. Each of them were wearing white coats, lab coats practically, with the red cursive words *Coca-Cola* on the back. My father waved them down, and after they served two or three people, they came over. I ordered two whiskeys, one with Coke.

"I don't usually drink whiskey in the afternoon," my father said as I passed him his drink, "but a bullfight is a special occasion."

I nodded, sipped my own drink, and then we sat, shoulders touching, and waited. Even though it was late afternoon and we were sitting in the shade, it was still very hot. The sun seemed extra bright against the sandy ring with its light brown walls and giant white clock. I could feel sweat ever so slightly rolling down my back. Perhaps it was that intense sun, or the whiskey we were drinking, but a sudden strange tingling high came with the sweatiness on my back, the moisture at my temples. One that I don't think just I felt, but everyone, including my father, felt—it was the thrill of being in a place that wasn't just foreign, but entirely fantastic, a place you never knew you'd be.

The bullfight started with a band, a band full of trumpets and drumbeats, playing what sounded to me like parade music. Then the *banderilleros* came out, the four guys who tire the bull out before the matador even enters the ring—they all wore lavender tights with gold shiny material going down the outer sides of their legs and a funny-shaped black hat, which my father insisted was a musketeer hat. The *banderilleros* stood very erect, very still, in all different spots of the ring. Their capes were fuchsia, not red, and that detail, the difference in the capes' color, bothered me a little—it was as if all those Bugs Bunny skits I had watched as a kid were wrong, so wrong that maybe the bull didn't even charge the capes, maybe he just walked around lazily and got stabbed.

As the music played and the first squad of *banderilleros* posed, everyone stood up, and so we did, too, awkwardly though, as there wasn't much space to move. There was some random clapping and yelling, which I didn't entirely understand, although Esteban had told me that the whole fun of going to a bullfight was to heckle the matador or conversely applaud him, tell him he's the best ever, make him feel like God.

Once the first bull came out, running in circles like a cat after its tail, the applause started again, and when the bull ran through the disappointingly fuchsia capes, the crowd shouted *olé*. At the same time, three latecomers came and sat on the other side of my father. The first man who sat directly next to my father I can identify only as the Know-It-All. He walked like a Know-It-All, he stood like a Know-It-All, and he opened and closed his mouth with the certainty of a Know-It-All. You could see his expertise concerning bullfighting and fine wines and seventeenth-century art in the crispness of his white shirt and the tan color of his nose and even in the soft brown tint of his sunglasses. He was with a man and a woman, a couple, who were clearly American— only an American man would wear a Chicago Bulls T-shirt to a bull-fight, and only an American wife would let him.

The Know-It-All sounded English originally, but then he wasn't— he was just an American who softened his r's in the dream of looking fancy and smart. I looked at my father once they sat down and mouthed, "Don't talk."

"Whah?"

"Don't talk," I said in his ear. "Don't say a single word. Don't you even think of letting them know we're American." I had already scolded my father earlier, told him that once he heard an American speaking, he should go instantly mute. Otherwise they'd come over and try to bond with you, complain about the food or their hotel or the sun.

The American woman was saying distantly, she was on the far end, "I don't know if I'm going to be able to stand this."

"The key is not to side with the bull. You should side with the *torero*," the Know-It-All began, and then he kept going after that. He explained that *torero* meant bullfighter while *matador* meant killer. All of them in the ring were bullfighters, he said, but the one who appeared last, the one with the red cape, was the matador. He went on to explain that the fight was not really a fight as the bull would most certainly die—it was instead better to view it as a tragedy. He used other words, too, like *spectacle* and *pageant*, and then he talked about how the idea really was to kill the bull as quickly and expertly as possible. "He should not suffer," he said. "There is actually a time limit on how much he can suffer." He pointed at the clock.

For the rest of the bullfight, the Know-It-All continued to talk and inform, only stopping here or there to stand up or clap or wave a hand-kerchief in the air. By the third round I was used to his comments, and I was used to the bull's blood—the actual ring seemed far and distant from where we sat, making the bull seem as small as a mouse and the *toreros* as tiny as toy soldiers. The only difficulty I had was with the idea that I was supposed to side with the matadors. They seemed too arro-gant to me, too pleased with themselves, particularly when they turned their back on the bleeding, panting bull and looked up at the audience, their ballerina posture so stiff, so regal.

The whole time I'd stare at the bull, at the blood that ran in a wet patch down its back, dark spatter marks appearing beneath his shadow on the sand. It seemed impossible not to like the sufferer better—partic-ularly after having watched that same bull run like mad, sprint from one side of the ring to the other, charging one cape and then another; sword after sword had been stuck through his back, yet he kept running, kept moving. He never backed off. He didn't stop charging at the capes or suddenly lie down or hide himself in some remote part of the ring. It was as if his entire lifetime was that twenty-minute round, and nothing had happened before and nothing would happen after—perhaps in his little nugget of a mind those minutes were experienced as years; good years were when he chased a *banderillero* off, made him hide like a child behind a wooden barrier or nervously sprint over the ring's wall; good years were grabbing the cape with his horns and throwing it on the ground, stomping on it. But in any case, despite the good years, the swords still came, one after another through his back, and he could still run around energetically with certain cuts, while others dug deeper, slowed him down, made the sand spit up less under his hoofs.

I thought about all of this while I watched and watched. Perhaps it was the whiskey that made me think like this, perhaps it was the sun, but it saddened me a little, made me feel tired. I looked sideways at my father, thought of how if I were a normal daughter and he were a normal father, I could put my head on his shoulder. Instead, I looked back down at the ring. They were in the process of cutting off the bull's ear. You could see the vigorous back and forth motion of an attendant sawing at it with what looked like a simple jackknife, and then the crowd across from us, the Spanish side of the ring, had their white handkerchiefs in hand (the Know-It-All identified this as approval of the audience, of "the chorus"). The matador went around the ring holding that ear, his trophy. He had killed his bull quickly without much blood, and when he hit the bull with his sword the bull went down fast right on his side—he didn't stumble or anything, he wasn't like a dog who had been hit by a car. He just fell.

That particular matador was the star of the fight that day, but what I personally found to be the highlight happened at the beginning of the next round, after they swept up the bloody sand from the previous bull, after they reprinted the white circles that the bull's hoofs had smudged. The trumpets played. Then a big fat brown bull came out and went around and around, insane—from the second he was unleashed, he could not stop running and kicking sand and charging at the barriers where the *banderilleros* hid. When the *picador* on the horse stuck him with what looked like a spear, he practically tried to drive a hole through the horse's side, and then when another *banderillero* tried to sidetrack him, tried to lead him away with his own fuchsia cape, the bull ran through the cape so quick he fell down on his stomach and then got up on all fours ready to attack someone else. He even chased another guy over the ring's wall and then tried to vault himself over the wall, too; perhaps he envisioned himself running through the aisles, jabbing each audience member with his horns.

In any case, the entire ring became suddenly taken with this bull, with his anger and his fighting and the way he just started blindly ramming his head into the wall. People across the ring started to stand up, to clap, and then white handkerchiefs slowly started to spring up, although within our section no one had a white hanky—as tourists we didn't know any better. Only the Know-It-All did, and he held his handkerchief high, our single representative waving and waving at the Spanish handkerchiefs; and, slowly but surely, starting with the Spanish side, every single person in that ring, the sheiks, and the Japanese in front of us, and the Indians and the Africans behind us, and the Know-It-All beside us, and the Spanish, who hooted and shouted in a giant arc across from us, all of us screamed and screamed until the call was made and that bull was taken back with only one single bleeding wound in his back. He was saved. No matador fought him that afternoon. Yet even when he was no longer in that sandy ring, after he strutted away, the entire audience was still on their feet, still whistling and yelling, and what I felt right then, what we all felt, was a tingling, tight feeling, an overwhelming awe, not just for that bull but for the will to live.

After the bullfight, we went to a bar close by called El Rincón de Jerez. It was a somewhat well-known bar that Celia had told me about before. They had the ritual of turning out the lights every night at eleven o'clock and then candles were lit as people sang a prayer in the direction of a plastic figurine, La Virgen del Rocío. The ceremony, I was told, was taken very seriously, although many tourists as well as the Spanish themselves often dropped by for that eleven o'clock moment to witness the weirdness, to see the room go dark and the flames flicker.

The Virgin hung on the wall on the far end of the bar in a long flowing white dress, her head very small, very serene, with two rosy circles on her cheeks. The rest of the bar all around her was filled with photographs, mostly black-and-white, of bullfights. There were close-up shots of matadors' faces, their expressions heated and agitated, and there were the bulls running and turning, occasionally gouging someone in the leg or stomach. My father seemed more interested in the bullfight photographs, in the old posters on the walls, but then he noticed the Virgin figurine and another dark, frameless picture of Jesus on the Cross. I told my father about the ritual, and he got very excited about it, as if he expected an entire performance and not just a five-minute prayer. He apparently still had a high from the bullfight, or maybe it was

from his whiskey, or maybe it was just from the thrill of being in a place
he had never imagined himself to be.

"Let's stay," he said, "let's stay until eleven."

It was eight-thirty at the time, and I didn't know if I'd make it. We
had been in the sun all day long, and I knew we were going to have to
get up and do it all over again tomorrow. Besides, the room was
crowded, stifling, and we had no barstools to sit on—and it seemed a lot
of work right then to stand there and drink with only the blue-and-
white-tiled wall to lean on.

We ended up staying though, as he wanted, and right before ten,
around quarter of, the women from my father's hotel, Doria and Maureen, showed up. They were both wearing white, short-sleeved shirts
with collars, and khaki pants. They looked as if they were planning on
going on safari—all they needed were some hats and a jeep and perhaps a lion to come charging at them. Once my father saw them, he
turned, pivoted so that they could not see him face-to-face. "They're
here," he said.

I paused, considered acting as if I didn't know what he was talking
about, and then I said, "They're *your* friends."

"No," he said, shaking his head. "I don't like that Doria."

"Why?"

"She's a drunk. It's one thing to be a drunk man," he said very seriously without looking me in the eye, "but a drunk woman is a sad, sad
thing." He made a face. "Awful."

I suppose I could've made some nasty remark, but I was too tired by
then, too hungry. We hadn't eaten since the afternoon, and that was
making my head a little light, dizzy. I felt so uncomfortable at that point
that I didn't even care anymore if Maureen came over, if she told my
father about my "uncle" or made some other unpleasant comment. At
that moment, I only wished they would come over in their safari outfits
and chase us out.

"I do like Maureen though," my father said abruptly.

"Why's that?"

He smiled, waited. "She's got a nice pair."

I nodded, looked away. I suppose at that point anyone else would've thought he was very drunk for saying such a thing, but he wasn't. He was a controlled level of drunk; there was a sheen across his face, his coloring was a bit pink, and the five o'clock shadow seemed to have become suddenly more evident—as if alcohol made facial hair grow in faster. Yet the "nice pair" comment seemed to reveal less about his drunkenness and more about how comfortable he was becoming around me, because he normally used to talk like this—something I had forgotten. When I was a kid he was always making inappropriate comments or observations in front of me, and often my mother or someone else would yell at him, hit him on the arm—"Don't tell her that," they'd say, and then he'd wait and whisper whatever it was in my ear. Once he told me my mother had the cutest ass in America, and another time he pointed out some hookers on the street that we were passing in our car and explained to me that their skirts were so short because they came from somewhere "warm, really warm, extra warm." My mother had told him to shut up, and then he kept saying it over and over, looking at me in the rearview mirror, "warm, really warm, extra warm," and I laughed and laughed, even though I didn't get it.

"We didn't see you guys, did you see us?" Doria was suddenly inches from my face, with Maureen smiling behind her. They had weaved through the crowd, but I had not noticed them coming. I had been thinking the whole time about the "nice pair" comment and my father—I had just dug up in my mind another instance in which he once told me as a kid that this homeless person sleeping in a sleeping bag on a bench was not, in fact, a person but "a clever mannequin."

While I thought of this, my father was talking to Doria, but I couldn't hear him. It was busier now as it got closer to eleven o'clock, and you couldn't hear anyone unless they got right in your ear. Maureen was sipping her drink, looking at the back of Doria's head, a red lipstick mark smudged on her glass. After a moment, she smiled at me, awkwardly though, and I knew even before she opened her mouth she was going to say something about the night before.

"Pardon me for last night," she said. "I was so drunk."

I shook my head, told her she seemed fine.

"I act like an idiot when I drink sometimes and . . ." She shrugged, smiled awkwardly. The khaki shirt was a very warm color against her face, but she still looked sunburned to me. She was very neatly put together, her mascara, her lipstick, the slight brush of peachy color on her cheeks. Even her posture contained a certain awareness of herself, a certain worry. She made eye contact with me only occasionally, but mostly she looked behind me at the still wall.

"I upset your friend though, didn't I?"

How she even remembered Borja or his face or how subtly uncomfortable she had made him—through the blur of how drunk she had been—was a mystery to me, but I told her anyway, "No, no. He just wanted to leave there."

She nodded, and I became paranoid that she was envisioning where he wanted to go from there, as if she could see the big pink letters of the hotel sign and then the white bed with its white pillowcases and the dark wooden headboard. I glanced away from her at my father—he and Doria seemed to be having some sort of similar conversation, one in which she was apologizing or explaining something from the night before. I suppose that should have made me curious, but I preferred not to be. I imagined them sitting side by side in the hotel bar with the flat, disinterested look that I saw on couples who sat at the bar at Shooters: both of them talking, their mouths opening and closing, drinks sitting before them like props.

After fifteen minutes or so, Maureen and Doria lost interest in us, or maybe decided to leave us alone—in any case, they moved away from us, and my father said in my ear, "How come you get Maureen and I get Doria?"

I shrugged—I had just bought us two more drinks, and I was holding his because Doria had bought him one, too.

"I wanna trade."

I shook my head, said flatly, "No, she's mine," and then he laughed as if I had said the funniest thing in the world—which gave me an odd sensation right then, perhaps because I was drinking or because I was so tired, but for whatever reason, I suddenly felt very strange in this crowded bar as I waited for everyone in the room to sing to the Virgin figurine, as I heard my father laugh, as the smell of ham mixed with cigar and cigarette smoke drifted all around me.

At eleven o'clock, the lights finally did go out, and each of us held a lit candlestick in our hands. I glanced across the room at Doria and Maureen, noticed the amusement in their faces, as if they were about to see a circus act. You would've thought that people might put their drinks down or extinguish their cigarettes, but that wasn't the case. Only the lights changed, and everyone faced the figurine, including the bartenders and the kitchen help. They had handed us little pamphlets that had on them the words of the prayer we were going to sing. I didn't know what everything on the pamphlet meant, but there were a lot of easy *olé* shouts, and the major line was, *"Dios te salve, Maria,"* God save you, Mary.

During the song, a woman with no shoes came in and knelt; then another person ordered her a beer. Whether she really had shoes or not, I don't know. Whether she was a regular occurrence, I don't know. I just stared down at her, watched a man place a mug of beer down next to her. The rest of the room sang—including the bartenders—and there was something creepy about watching the two of them sing in their stained white shirts, the candlesticks in their hands, bottles and bottles of liquor on shelves behind them, the Cruzcampo beer taps in front of them, the yellowed pig legs dangling nearby on the wall. But perhaps I felt that sensitivity, that oddness, only because of the conversation my father and I had had just before the lights went off, before the smell of lit candles permeated the room.

"So tell me more about this guy," my father had said, "the one you live with."

"Harlan?" I said, as if there were several other possibilities.

"Yeah."

I shrugged. "He's my best friend."

"Yeah, but what's he like?"

I didn't know how to answer that. I didn't know how to explain Harlan's entire personality, or who he was, or even what he was, during the ten minutes we had before eleven o'clock struck, so I just said what I might've hoped would bother my father. I told him that Harlan took care of me a little. I told him how Harlan cleaned up the apartment, how he sponged down the shelves in the refrigerator, replaced the baking soda. I told him how he did my laundry sometimes, not all the time, but occasionally, when things got to be too much. I told him how Harlan left Godiva chocolates in the refrigerator in a tiny gold box. I told him how Harlan vacuumed the carpets religiously on Thursday afternoons, but only after I had woken up, as to not disturb me. I left out the fact that he did all his cleaning stoned, sometimes wearing a pair of sunglasses that had one missing lens.

"He does all that for you?" my father asked, as if that seemed impossible.

I nodded.

He took a sip of his whiskey, swallowed. "And what do you give him?" he asked, perhaps expecting that I myself had an entire list of things. But, of course, I didn't. There was only one single thing I helped Harlan with, a secret thing, something I refused ever to talk about. So I shrugged my shoulders, acted as if I didn't know what my father meant by that question; then I looked away from him at the clock. Praying time was soon to begin.

$$\overline{17}$$

HARLAN ONCE AGAIN

Whenever I talked about Harlan to anyone, I always avoided, tried to circumvent, this other small part of his personality: his sickness. It always seemed to discredit him, make him something that a normal person might find hard to understand, hard to feel for. But sometimes he did get sick, so sick—and when I say sick, I don't mean sniffling and sneezing. There was nothing physical about it except occasionally he threw up. It was never a lot though, never a prolonged series of flulike bouts; it was like what accompanied a migraine or a suddenly dizzied stomach—an amount of nausea that would not put a normal person, not even a child, into such a fit of trembling and rocking. He was always on his knees, his face very close to the toilet, as if he were contemplating putting his face in the water or crawling down into the depths of the toilet itself, rubbing his nose against the grayish white porcelain. He mumbled during these episodes, said things that made no sense, things I could never hold on to, never even retell myself later the next morning.

The fits were always at night, almost always in the bathroom.

The fits had no telltale signs beforehand. And they took hours to be over. Yet they always ended.

Only once did he get sick outside the bathroom, in the kitchen, in our sink. His face that time was very close to the drain. There was something about what he felt, what he feared, that strangely seemed to have to do with water and how water left our apartment—it was as if he planned to go somewhere with the water, become supersmall and ride away, slide down pipes, fall into an underground world that had only water to hear, only the soft splish-splash of dripping droplets.

This strange condition remained nameless for me—although Harlan once told me, "It begins with an *S* and it ends with an *A*." He held his arms out wide to show me how long the word was, how giant and crushing. Then he laughed. He laughed from smoking pot. He laughed at the serious set of my face. "Don't be fuckin' stupid," he said, and hit my shoulder, openhanded and playful, "I don't have it." He stared at me. "I don't."

At the time he told me this, I hadn't yet experienced any of his episodes. We were living in the dorms, in the midst of one of our nightly meetings in the floor lounge. We had only been talking about colds before, about having tonsils out, and then Harlan had veered into mental illness, into his single two-month-long experience in—as he put it—a hospital "for the moody and extrasmart."

Talking about such things was very strange territory for me; I had known no one in my life who had ever been in such a place—in my hometown, kids who had mental problems just beat on one another or set their houses on fire or tormented animals; yet no matter what they did, they never disappeared for a while, never "went away." They just stewed a lot, rocked back and forth on car hoods, threw rocks at invisible targets.

Harlan himself had never told me what exact event led him to being in the hospital. And I never asked. It seemed like an invasion somehow to ask—if he was going to tell me, he was going to tell me, and if he wasn't, he wasn't.

I did know—or thought I knew—that it had something to do with a school bus. I envisioned Harlan freaking out on his school bus, wearing skin-tight pants and a shirt that was pulled off one shoulder, his hair in his face. I had a photograph of him like that from when he was sixteen, when he was going through his "I want to look like the lead singer of INXS" period. The school bus itself I got from his films, which always contained a disturbing school-bus scene. The other kids in these scenes were always evil, the driver always wore dark glasses, and the main character of the film was always having some sort of trauma in his little green seat. What sort of trauma Harlan actually had, whether he was holding himself and rocking (first film), or wearing bright red lipstick talking to a monkey puppet (Godiva Assassin movie) or yelling at the driver to take his "X-ray" sunglasses off (unfinished film)—whether it was any of these episodes or something far worse, I could never know, I could never guess. Besides, I never really liked talking about any of it in the first place—I found the entire topic mildly scary. Not because Harlan seemed like a crazy person to me, but, instead, because he seemed so much more normal than me, as if he were, in fact, on a higher plane.

"If I was really as fucked up as they thought I was," Harlan had told me, "then I would think I was Master of the Universe or I would think I could read your thoughts; I would think that the telephone was talking to me; I would think that there were people following me, people who knew I could hear your thoughts and the telephone's chatter, people who wanted to get me, know my power." He was talking fast, defensive but not agitated, talking the way the kids in my public-speaking class spoke when they had done a lot of research and desperately wanted to prove it.

"People can't tell you you have something as fucked up as schizophrenia and think you won't read up on it, find out about it." He listed off for me some of the symptoms, named them on each finger: auditory hallucinations, paranoia, illogical ideas, incorrect use of language, silly talk, incessant pacing or rocking, talking to inanimate objects, and, last but not least—the symptom that disgusted Harlan the most—lack of hygiene. "Do I lack hygiene?" Harlan asked me with one hand on his hip. "Do I?"

I said no.

"Have you ever seen me *lacking* hygiene?" he continued, making it a joke, laughing a little.

"Well," I said, changing my answer, "not usually." I pointed to his fingernails, told him they were a little gray underneath. They were not really dirty; they were perfectly short and, from what I could see, bitten down, but as a joke I argued with him anyway, told him they weren't kempt. He stared down at his nails, examined them, then told me to go fuck myself. I told him to go scrub himself. Then we laughed—all of this was really just a momentary deviation, a childish break, from all he had really been telling me.

Yet whatever Harlan had read about schizophrenia, or been told, had apparently gone beyond just unkempt fingernails, as, according to Harlan, schizophrenics not only didn't shower or shave—something he did at least twice a day—but also that they wouldn't do household chores or even throw things in the garbage. It was only later when I finally lived with Harlan that it occurred to me why he was so meticulous about cleaning our apartment, so systematic and dedicated—it was as if with each clean dish, with each vacuumed room, he were fighting off his supposed prognosis and its symptoms.

"It's all such bullshit," Harlan had said that night he first told me, and I had nodded. He was so irritated, so passionate about it, that he had dropped the careful career speech we learned in school and he was using his native harsh-sounding Massachusetts accent, which came from his hometown, from some far distant place he normally erased by using more solid-sounding r's. "But I don't have it," he said. "I'm not like that." He put his hand on the wall as he said this, as if he were feeling for something, a special indentation perhaps, or a sudden surge of warmth. "I don't have it," he said again without looking at me, and I said softly, believing him, "I know."

It was only after we moved in together that Harlan's sickness seemed to set in and take shape for me. As a sound: It was distant gagging and then a muffled voice traveling down the long hallway that divided my bed-room from the bathroom; it was the abrupt flush of the toilet; it was the rattle of a toothbrush or a mascara tube or a box of floss falling on the white tile.

Whenever I heard these things, I'd get up, I'd go find him, I'd sit in the bathroom Indian-style on the floor next to him. I never touched his back, his arms, his neck, just his ankle. When he threw up, it rarely lasted long, but afterward he would still keep his head against the toilet seat, as if he were too tired to move, and I would stare past him at the toilet paper roll, at the little white perforated dots in each dangling square sheet.

"Sing to me, Cath," he'd say. "Sing to me."

Sometimes, though, I wouldn't even know at first that he was in the bathroom; I'd be asleep, but then I'd hear his voice down the hallway, soft, barely audible: "Sing to me"—and it would take me right out of my dreams. He probably could've mouthed those words, not even uttered them, and I would've felt them underneath all the images that filled my night. The skies, the trees, whoever's face was in front of me would instantly dissolve, and I'd crawl out from under blankets in a tank top and underwear, not even aware of the cold apartment, of the goose bumps that ran up and down my legs. I'd curl up near him on the bath-room rug, my hand instantaneously on his ankle—as if I were pulling him out of something or, at least, holding on to him so he wouldn't sink deeper, further, away.

"Sing to me, Cath," he'd say.

But I never sang to him—I just hummed. Softly though—as deli-cately as I could. I hummed the way that I imagined if I ever became a mom I would hum away monsters under the bed, lightning in the sky. I hummed my hum close to his face, not touching, but so close that if he were thinking really hard, lost somewhere, he could still hear me, still feel my breath like a warmth, like a small weak wind.

Sometimes we'd stay in the bathroom together all night, a triangular-shaped room that had no bathtub, just a stand-up shower, a sink that was too small to wash your hair in, and a toilet that was so old that you had to pull on a metal chain to make it flush. The bathroom door didn't even shut completely. It was like being in a closet, a brilliant white closet that smelled like Listerine and bubblegum-flavored toothpaste. A closet that was too full of scent, of light, to let you drift or dream.

Within the bathroom I'd sit and sit with him. I'd even sleep a little sometimes, but with all that light I was still awake. I kept a tally on these nights, in the same way I kept a written tally of my tips for each month. He averaged only two fits a months. Although in the month of December, he had six. When I left for Madrid, we had lived together a full year and he had had a total of twenty-seven fits, but I didn't write "fits"— instead I called them "episodes."

These episodes never necessarily coincided with any enormous emotional event either. He could get ignored by the love of his life. He could get hung up on. He could be slapped in the middle of a winter street, in the middle of a crying fit. And he was fine.

He could work all day and night in the editing lab for a film that he giggled about, danced about, sweated in his socks about, and then the following week in class, all the nose-pierced boys would sit with one leg up on their chair, their chin on their knees, and trash his film. It lacked feeling. Lacked a mental picture. Lacked consistent characters. There was no clarity in terms of time. Certain shots seemed unwarranted, extra, like "he was in love with his own visions." But he didn't care. He could go to Godiva and sit there after being basted in comments, in jealousies, and listen to old women bicker over the hazelnut cream vs. the apricot sorbet sponge, and he'd just stand there behind the gleaming glass case, one hand on his hip. "Do you want a taste?" he'd say. "Can I give you a taste?"

In all of these instances, Harlan was normal—well behaved when he had to be, a yelling maniac when it was time.

His sickness came from somewhere else, from a different doorway. Often it seemed it came from the toilet itself, like some sweeping force that crawled through the pipes, pushed the fuzzy pink toilet seat up, and then it entered, loud and noisy, through the bathroom door, which was impossible to shut. That's how he explained it to me once—right after I came home from work and found him wrestling with the bathroom door, trying to slam it shut from the hallway. I heard him whimpering, growling at the door, before I even got in, before I pulled him away and pushed him against the wall, told him to stop. "Please," I said, "just stop it."

Once I told my mother about all of this, but I said in a casual way, as it were a completely normal occurrence that was, oddly, starting to bother me.

"He's having panic attacks," my mother told me in her doctorly voice after she sat silent for a minute, touching her ear. "How often does it happen?"

I shrugged. "Only every once in a while."

It didn't happen with the frequency she seemed to be imagining. It had only happened, at the time, about five or six times. It was something that existed in the background of our lives; it was almost imaginary since his attacks came deep in the night. In the morning or afternoon, we didn't mention it. Even in our glances at the kitchen table over bowls of Frosted Flakes, it did not exist. It was erased from us, gone. It's weight, its severity, didn't even keep us from getting stupid and snappy with each other in our day-to-day mood swings. It was simply a dream to us, one we shared and avoided in daylight.

"It's only happened a few times," I told my mother.

She kept staring at me; she wanted to know the exact number.

I pretended to count on my fingers. "Like four times."

My mother kept touching the rim of her coffee cup, making half circles. "Does his mother know?" she asked, which was a typical response. Anything that happened in anyone's life seemed to be something that she thought could be handled only by the mother.

"I don't know if she knows."

"Maybe you should call her?" She posed this idea as a question, even though what it really was, from the way her eyebrows were raised, was a statement, a command. It was as if she thought that such an idea should've occurred to me long ago. Somehow that pissed me off, made me suspect she was saying that I was failing him.

I yelled, "I'm not going to go tell his mom on him, OK!" and then I stared at her all fiery, as if I were trying to say with very set of my face: I am not failing him.

Failing him to me meant exactly what she wanted me to do, to snitch—or it meant not waking up for him when he called out to me, not humming in his ear. If every night of every day he needed me to go in that cold bathroom and shiver with him, then I would. It seemed the least I could do, seeing that in many other ways I gave him nothing. I was rarely ever home. I was rarely nice to his boyfriends. I suppose I entertained him late at night with my bar stories and my negativity, but that didn't seem to equal the care and thought he gave or the compliments or the sudden shrieks of laughter he let loose after I said something that I had no idea had any wit, any meaning, to it.

But my mother didn't understand this, she didn't understand that telling on him was, in my mind, not just betraying him, but also refusing to do the one thing I felt I alone had the power to give him. All my mother saw was my defensiveness, my sudden anger, and it seemed to leave her unsure of what to say. In her approximating gaze, I felt she somehow thought that I was actually a part of his illness, as if the two of us sat around in the bathroom in our underwear taking turns vomiting, and then held each other, shaking and shaking, fearful of all the things, real and imagined, that rumbled around inside of us.

So my mother and I just sat there quietly, and it was clear in that silence that she had no intention of intervening further. We just watched the snow fall down outside in big heavy clumps that looked delicate and beautiful only when they hit the window in front of us. But then those snowflakes melted. They dripped down the glass.

Out of the quiet, after the refrigerator near us began to hum, my mother said, in a voice that was very careful, full of thought, "It has always seemed very strange to me that the people who are the most alive, the most vibrant and funny, have the most . . ." She paused, put her hand to her chest as if she preferred to use a gesture rather than say the actual word: *pain.*

Perhaps she was remembering the time when Harlan was taking the picture of us on the front steps. He kept telling my mother and me to put our heads closer together, louder and louder until he started yelling, *"Closer,"* and then because my mother looked so startled by his yelling, he let out a loud gigglish shriek that made one of our neighbors open a window and tell him to "shut his fuckin' hole."

That only made him laugh louder. "Lady," he said, "my hole's been shut all day and all night. I don't know what you're talking about!" Then he looked at my mother, covered his mouth as if he had momentarily forgotten she was even there.

I stared at my mother while she thought of this, or whatever else Harlan brought to mind, watched the slight expressions and movements on her face. She was watching the snowfall. She seemed to be concentrating on a particular tree in our yard that wasn't holding up too well in the snow—its branches were weighted down by all its icy whiteness and hung lower than usual, almost leaning on one another. I watched the way her eyes moved back and forth ever so slightly, not up and down with the snow. Then I noticed the soft, small wrinkle at the corner of my mother's lip—saw it deepen, and within that subtle facial tick I knew she was not thinking about Harlan, she was thinking about my father. It was as if my father and all the feeling she had for him existed, hid itself, in that one soft line that extended diagonally from her nose to her mouth, a line that once surfaced only with smiles, with frowns, but now it was imprinted like a permanent record on my mother's still, pale face.

Against the snow outside, against the mild coldness of our house, I thought I knew in particular what my mother was thinking about—as she had recently told me one specific story about my father. It involved snow and freezing temperatures and a car that had no heat. The story was about my father's father, my grandfather, and how he died.

The story started, in the way she originally delivered it to me, with my own father lying on the couch. He was seventeen; it was ten o'clock; he was watching TV. He was alone in the house when his father pulled into the driveway. The driveway itself was big, circular, and the headlights shone into the dark house. They continued to shine and shine, and my father ignored it, watched TV. He was apparently dreading the moment the headlights went off; that would be the moment when his father would slam the car door and then rumble his way through the house where he would, like a magnet, gravitate toward my father, sitting in his blue jeans and white T-shirt, barefoot and sleepy. What sort of beatings my father endured when he was young were often hard to picture, as they were always described to me in such flat, lifeless language as "he was hit," "he was thrown," "he was punched." Without specific body parts mentioned, without specific rooms to envision, those actions seemed as calm as walking and talking and breathing. So I could never entirely understand what exactly my father feared sitting on that couch, perhaps rubbing his feet together with the same friction-filled intensity that he had when I first saw him again on that Holiday Inn lounge chair. All I do believe, as my mother has presented it this way, is that in his fear, in his waiting, he was not thinking about much else. He was not taking into consideration the current temperature, which was somewhere in the teens; or that the heater in the car did not work and his father refused to fix it; or the fact that his father always drank until he passed out.

Needless to say, my grandfather froze to death that night—and in the morning when my father woke up in the gray coldness of his empty house, he still didn't go outside to the car. The headlights were no longer on, but through the window there was still the eerie sight of exhaust, like a puff of guilt hovering then dissolving.

My grandmother and my Auntie Joy, who was only twelve at the time, were the ones who finally came home, finally discovered my grandfather. In the car the dial on the heater had apparently been turned all the way up, as if my grandfather had forgotten the heater was broken, or perhaps he just hoped at the coldest moment it might magically turn on.

From that day forward, it was always believed by my aunt and grandmother that my father purposely didn't save his father. To them, it was obvious in the fact that he didn't go out to the car that morning; instead, he made some toast and just sat there with it. It lurked within his decision not to go away with his sister and mother that weekend— they had gone to an aunt's or some such place, and he had insisted on staying home. He had a plan, they believed, an intent, but they were not angry with him, according to my mother. The episode simply changed their understanding of him. He became someone that they couldn't look at directly in the eye for too long as they might find something inside his stare, a certain sensitivity, a certain anger—one that was not just his, but their own.

All of this my mother told me on a summer afternoon when I was seventeen, sitting on a hot, black blanket in a state park. As she spoke, I picked up blades of grass, shredded them bit by bit, as if they were the pieces of information my mother was handing me, secret documents that no one could know about. It was a story that my mother must've wanted to tell me for years and years, but she controlled herself, kept it for later. This was the way she worked. She siphoned off pieces of my father, stories and details, so I could come to know, slowly, the more important fragments reserved for when I was older—in hopes that with more age, with more maturity, I would eventually understand. Or as she said, "Eventually see."

I suppose all of those stories sat there inside of her, perhaps secretly connected to that little deepened wrinkle at the corner of her mouth. They lingered and they arose and they were at that table where we had originally been talking, fighting actually, about Harlan. Yet in the few minutes I saw her thinking about my father and the few minutes I spent thinking about what she was thinking, Harlan and his "problem" had fallen away, drifted. It was smaller now, not so severe.

In my mother's mind, though, Harlan seemed to have resurfaced;

perhaps she saw that day on the front steps, heard his laughing at the neighbor. Maybe she heard him, as he took the photograph, say, "Closer. Can't you hear me? *Closer!* " In any case, a brief smile came across her lips, and then she said, "He is so sweet though, so funny."

I nodded, said distantly, "Yeah."

$$\overline{18}$$

Monday's Tour

Monday morning my father was not waiting for me outside of the hotel the way he had been the day before; instead, he was still in his room primping in the bathroom mirror. How he was even up was a surprise to me; he was still unaccustomed to the time change, a difference of six hours. His watch, still set on Eastern Time, sat ticking and ticking in front of me on his nightstand, curled up in the black-and-white Holiday Inn ashtray. I picked it up, held in my hands until he came out of the bathroom, a purple vent brush in his hand.

"What are we gonna do today?" he asked me, as if that somehow affected his hair, perhaps how much hairspray he put into it.

"I don't know. What do you want to do?"

"That bomb," he said, "the one you told me about before, we could go look at where it happened." He wasn't looking at me but at the mirror, and he wasn't even looking at me in the mirror. It was as if all the ease we had developed the day before at church, at the bullfight, was gone again. He was different, I was different, everything around us felt different—the sunlight in the window was brighter, the stripes on the wallpaper seemed spaced more widely apart, the skin on the back of my neck was suddenly bumpy, flaky, itching.

"We're going to the museum today," I said flatly, "and then . . . we'll see some other stuff."

"I want to see that bomb."

"There's nothing to see," I raised my voice a little, annoyed—somewhere inside myself I always had a strange sensitivity to what people could gawk at and what they couldn't. "It's just a torn-up sidewalk and some construction." I put his watch down on the bed. "You didn't come all the way to Spain to see a hole in the ground, did you?"

He didn't answer. He just put on his shoes, carefully buckling the straps. The air conditioner behind him changed speeds, got softer, made the room feel suddenly awkward, yet that discomfort had nothing to do with my raising my voice, or with the bomb itself—it was simply that I had somehow underhandedly asked him the question: Why are you even here?

"Whatever you want," he said in the voice of someone who can feel a fight coming on and doesn't want it. "You want to go to the museum, we'll go to the goddamn museum. You're the boss." He stood up, gave me a wry smile. "You're the *capitán*." He took a step forward as he said this, as if he might kiss me on the top of my head, but then he grabbed his watch lying next to me and placed it with great care on his wrist.

El Prado, the major museum in Madrid, was closed on Mondays, so I took him to the modern art museum, Centro de Arte Reina Sofía. I had gone before with Isabel, and it had been more crowded then—it had been on a Saturday, late evening but still daylight, and they were having some sort of festival outside of the museum. The benches had all been covered with brown paper and they had crayons and paints for kids to use to draw things on the benches or on the bare cement. The names Julia and Javi and César were written in bright red paint next to blue hearts, green pyramids, flowers with giant petals. And then there were bongo players, lots of bongo players, the kind who played in such uni-son that it made your heart feel like it was beating faster and faster.

But on Monday morning with my father, there was none of that—not a bit of color; just a solid gray cement square out front, a few tourists on the stairs holding guidebooks and maps. My father seemed surprisingly pleased with the museum though, with its glass elevator and high dome-shaped ceiling. Within each numbered room, each *sala*, the walls were bright white with startling fluorescent lights.

"It's like a hospital in here," he said, and I nodded.

We looked at Picasso first, at *Guernica*, their national treasure, which was guarded behind bulletproof glass; then we looked at the other paintings and drawings of his, ones that featured twisted, pained horse heads and other weird-shaped items that, upon further inspection, had human teeth and eyes. I showed him Dalí too, showed him headless women's bodies with tigers charging at them, limp-looking telephones, a bowl with Hitler's head—small and dainty—floating in it, and then Dalí's own version of scary twisted faces.

After looking at a few more rooms of art, my father was eager to go—all those strange faces seemed to make him uneasy, made him want a drink. I didn't take him to a café though; I dragged him up through the south section of El Parque Retiro, which was only a short distance from the museum. He tried to get me to stop in the McDonald's on the way "just to sit for a bit" (they served beer at McDonald's), but I said no. I had written a list of things we had to do at scheduled times. The top of the list said: Monday's Tour, and the second item on the list was the park—I wanted to show him this famous statue they had of the devil.

When we got there, stood in front of it, the statue itself didn't really look like the American version of a devil, no pitchfork, no beard; instead, he was an angel with giant wings that were bigger than the rest of his body. His back was hunched over, and his face was not exactly evil; it was cowering and pained, the face of worry, of confusion, the very expression of sickness.

"It's the only statue in Europe," I said, "the only one of the devil." Esteban had told me that.

"Does that mean Madrid's evil?" my father asked me—which was exactly what I had said to Esteban, but my father delivered it as a joke.

I told him no and then I explained—as Esteban had—that Madrid, in terms of elevation, was the highest capital city in Europe, closest to the sky, closest to the sun, closest to God.

My father nodded at that, squinting up at the statue, and then we walked out of the park, up Paseo del Prado, and stopped at a monument that had a burning flame; it had been built in the the name of all the Spanish who had died for their country. It was not as giant as American memorials often can be, and the little tiny torch, the flame, was somehow affecting. It made me feel suddenly sad, morbid, as if the whole world were as delicate as those flames, as extinguishable.

We were supposed to go to Palacio Real next, that was number three on my list; but I ended up changing my mind and guiding us toward Puerta del Sol, toward the actual spot my father had wanted to see: where the bomb exploded. It was just a touch outside of Puerta del Sol, closer to a metro station called Callao—we had to walk down a narrow cobblestone street that was filled with tiny shops, shops that sold lots of shoes, lots of purses; shops with beige underwear taped to the windows; shops that sold tablecloths and napkins and handkerchiefs, all embroidered, all fancy, their prices written in black Magic Marker on square tags.

The bombing had been two weeks before, and the area where it had happened now simply looked like a regular, nonintimidating construction site. Some of the windows in the neighboring store, Fnac, were blown out on the bottom two floors, but it was open for business; certain doors were just closed off. A thick plastic netting—like a fence—was draped everywhere, and giant planks the size of regular household doors were doubled up and set on their sides, sealing the area off. A slow-moving line of pedestrians passed by the planks, and those tall enough peeked over as if they half expected to see the parked car in which the bomb had exploded—or perhaps just pieces of it, a charred steering wheel or a badly deformed license plate. There was even one little boy who sat perched on his father's shoulders, his lips pressed

tightly together, his expression confused, as if he were looking at a
scrambled message on a blackboard. He said, *"No hay nada, Papá.
Nada."*

My father and I walked behind the little boy and his father, moving
slowly, sluggishly in the heat. There were two lines of people, both single
file, all looking at the same thing, but moving in opposing directions. You
couldn't really see anything though, just a heap of gray cement tiles,
yellow tubing that was thrown haphazardly like pickup sticks on the
ground. And then there was netting mixed with long blurring sheets of
clear plastic. Nothing melted and blackened, nothing to evoke the
potential powers of that devilish statue we had just seen. There was just
the sun's brightness and the mild auditory hallucination that glass was
crunching beneath our feet when, of course, it wasn't—it was just our
shoes against pebbles and concrete.

"Who did that anyway?" my father asked me as we were walking
toward Palacio Real. "You never said who did it."

I nodded a little, said, "ETA," and my father gave me the same blank
expression that I originally gave Celia and Isabel when they first mentioned that three-lettered name to me. The morning the bomb had gone
off, the two of them sat me down in our yellow living room, a coffeepot
in front of us, and talked to me very purposely as if they were introducing me to something, initiating me into a type of vulnerability that they
already understood. They spoke in the same simplistic terms that someone might describe to a wide-eyed child, which, in that moment, at that
time, I was the equivalent of, as I had never been anywhere near a
bombing before.

The name ETA, Isabel told me, stood for three words, and the people
who called themselves ETA were *terroristas.* *"¿Entiendes la palabra terroristas?"* Celia asked me. Do you understand the word *terrorists?* I said,
"Sí." They were quiet for a minute after that—we just sat there in our
nightgowns, all of which happened to be varying shades of lavender.
The two of them were smoking cigarettes, and the smoke moved in
slight ghostly bodies throughout the room.

After a minute, Isabel continued to explain that ETA consisted of a certain section of people and that these people were from a certain section of Spain. *"El País Vasco,"* she said, making the shape of Spain in the air with her hand, showing me with her fingers two inches apart where that northern Basque region was. She said that ETA wanted that area to be separate from Spain, its own. *"Independiente,"* Celia added.

"But they won't let them be?" my father asked, after I repeated to him all of what Celia and Isabel told me.

"No," I said. "Not everyone up there wants to be separate. Only a few do."

"And so they keep putting bombs here?"

"Yeah," I said, nodding, and explained how Puerta del Sol was not just the center of Madrid, but also the dead center, the heart, of Spain. For some reason, after that, I started giving him an entire geographical lesson on Spain as we walked down calle Mayor past a religious shop that had a priest's robe on a mannequin. I told him how Spain had different provinces in the same way that there were different states at home, but there weren't as many, and the differences between those regions were more dramatic than, say, the differences between Texas and Massachusetts. More than just a different climate and a different temperament, the provinces had very particular dishes and dances and music that were their own—even their own language.

"You mean dialect," my father said.

"No, language," I told him matter-of-factly. "It's not Spanish." Even if Spanish was your native language, I explained to him, you couldn't speak those other languages or understand them. There were even some in those areas, older people, who refused to use Spanish, spoke only their regional language, no other. There was a certain local pride, a mini-nationalism, that they all had for the smaller section of Spain from which they hailed.

The first person I had actually met in Spain, Raúl, the stalking store owner, had identified within three sentences that he came from Valencia. Even my roommates had very quickly told me they were from Asturias, from Gijón, as if I would readily understand what that was, what it meant. What province and city any Spanish people came from seemed instrumental in knowing them, their identity—it was almost synonymous with learning their name. Borja, for example, was originally from Sevilla—hence we had to meet in a Sevillana bar. Carlos, my boss, was from Barcelona—a giant photograph of Barcelona's skyline perched above his desk. Esteban himself was from Madrid, born and bred, and, as a consequence, he considered himself an expert on the Madrilenian lifestyle, on its never-ending night. He also couldn't pass certain sites in his speeding car without quizzing me as to what they were. In particular, there was a building next to the post office, Banco de las Américas, that had *fantasmas*, ghosts, and every time we passed it I had to admit that I knew this, or he would tell me again and again. Even the elevation of Madrid he knew in exact kilometers.

"My God," I'd say, "you're obsessed."

But if Esteban or any Spanish person was obsessed with anything—it was making you know, making you see, what their world was. But it wasn't a boring level of instruction as they were great storytellers, great historians, and they told you things about themselves, about their country, with a calmness, a sense of pacing. There was even this one time that a strange old man sat down next to me—I was reading on a bench—and he started telling me stories in a low, low voice. He had a cane, a cane that he moved when he sat down, a cane he fidgeted with as he spoke. He didn't acknowledge me entirely, didn't ask me my name, he just looked straight ahead and spoke. He told me in a strange roundabout way about Franco, about what Spain had been like with him there—he told me about the curfews Franco enforced on the entire country, how people couldn't be out after ten. That's why *Madrileños* stay out so late, he told me; then he went on to tell me what his house had looked like as a kid, he told me about the bathroom sink. Then he went back to Franco, talked about *los años de hambre*, the years of hunger. He pointed at a sandwich shop, Rodilla, across the street, and said, "Some of us were so hungry, we ate cats."

"*Todos los gatos en las calles,*" all the cats in the street, he said, and made a popping sound, as if all of those cats had not been eaten but had instead dissolved mysteriously, leaving only their collars behind.

I actually told my father the story about the cats as we approached the palace, as we walked around its gardens and spotted a small gray cat nuzzling his face against the wrought-iron fence. The entire garden was filled with cats. If you stared long enough at the trees and the sloping lawn, you could spot at least twenty of them rolling on their backs or sleeping on a rock or simply sitting there wide-eyed and watching. "Hey, Mr. Fluffy," my father called out to one of them, and it came over, let my father pet it. I watched him pet the cat with his free hand; in his other hand, he had a can of beer. He had gotten it out of a vending machine in the street—claiming it was too hot, the sun was too bright, he needed a drink. "We would never eat you, Mr. Fluffy, never," my father said. The cat was purring. "That's right, me and Catherine *love* Mr. Fluffy." He tilted his beer can toward me, as if he might offer me some. "Right?"

I nodded.

"Right?" He said louder.

"That's right, Dad," I said flatly. "I love Mr. Fluffy."

My father smiled slightly at that—it was the first time since he arrived that I had called him Dad.

La Latina is beauty to me. La Latina is calm. La Latina is my favorite section of Madrid. Because it's old, a simple kind of old, free of the looming grandiosity of Palacio Real; it's a neighborhood that has nothing but bars and restaurants, apartments and churches. There are no major museums, no stampedes of people pushing you—only delicate-looking buildings that appear to be drawn on the sky in front of you, and narrow cobblestone streets where only one car can pass.

La Latina was number four on my list of things for us to do, not because I rated it number four, but because it was a good final stop, particularly after walking through the many rooms of Palacio Real, after seeing a dizzying number of crystal chandeliers and velvet curtains, after staring up at too many ceilings that had floating angels on them, after walking through a never-ending stream of gold and brightness and silver. La Latina was an oasis after that, a place to rest, to sit. A place to finally have a drink.

We went to a *taberna,* a tavern, on calle Cava Baja, sat at a long bar that was made of very dark wood. There were not a lot of people around; it was early, only six. On the wall across from us they had tapas and wines by the glass listed on a chalkboard. I chose a glass of Ribera del Duero because that was what Esteban drank. My father had a Johnny Walker Red. I ordered some tapas, too: *croquetas* and *gambas al ajillo* and *pulpo a la gallego,* and two small tart creations that had tomato sauce and capers and ham. While we ate we didn't talk much—I had already shown and told him enough about Spain for the day, and now it seemed we had to return to something about ourselves, something of our own.

"Have you talked to Auntie Joy lately?" I asked abruptly, after a long pause, after we had just ordered our second round. My aunt seemed like a safe subject. She still talked to my mother and me; she still talked to him.

"Joy," he said, squinting, as if he had to remember who she was, "No, I haven't seen her in a few months. Not since Christmas."

I nodded. I imagined them sitting together Indian-style next to a heavily tinseled Christmas tree, gold bulbs hanging, pine needles all over the wooden floor. I knew my Aunt Joy visited him, but not frequently, only three or four times a year. She thought he was insane. She didn't say insane though; she was not the type to use such language about her own family. She told me once and only once that he was becoming strange and that he said things that didn't make sense. I was on her back porch when she said this. I was sixteen. We were eating chocolate cake that had powdered sugar on it.

How she started to tell me, I can't remember. I remember it was the end of spring and sunny out. She had a birdbath in her yard that was very white and delicate-looking against her green lawn. I stared at the birdbath instead of her once she started talking about my father, but I don't know what she said at first. I was looking at the birdbath, thinking about its width and size, thinking about how many birds could fit inside of it. I wondered if the water was cold, if it was dirty. Then I wondered why my aunt even had a birdbath. She didn't like birds. She said they were noisy and full of shit.

I listened to her talk about my father only when she got to the insanity part. She was talking about how when she had visited him he had had all the shades pulled and kept looking out the window. He asked her if she saw anyone outside when she came in, and she said no. He asked if a black Lincoln was still outside the apartment building. She said she hadn't noticed.

"He was so fidgety," she told me. "He kept touching everything: coasters and pens and scraps of paper, and he even moved the TV over a little, as if he thought there were something behind it, some sort of camera or tape recorder or a person hiding . . ." She shook her head and then she paused, as if she was deciding whether or not to tell me the rest. She pursed her lips and then she put on some Chapstick, which she always kept in her coat pocket. She took her time with the Chapstick, stared into the cap as if it had inside of it some of the information she was about to give me.

Then she said, "So he took out a piece of paper—it was actually the back of an electric bill—and he wrote in very clear, calm letters: 'There are people following me.' " She sighed after that and then she said, "So I asked him who was following him, and he motioned for me not to speak. He gave me the pen and the electric bill to write on, put his fingers to his lips. And then I had to write out, 'Who is following you?' It was as if he couldn't hear the question unless I wrote it down, and then he took the electric bill back and wrote: 'Federal spies.' "

She went on to tell me how he claimed he could hear the people, the spies, in the hallway talking to one another, pacing, waiting for him to come out. At the time, I had only a year before read a letter in which he told my mother he had a neighbor who was singing so loudly, so miserably, that it was driving him crazy. The woman's name was DeDe; I would forever remember that name. As I looked out at my aunt's birdbath, I pictured the name DeDe as if it were written in red cursive against the white porcelain. I wondered if my father had ever really heard DeDe, if she was really there.

At the time, I did not yet know the story of how my father "let" my grandfather die—that I was told when I was seventeen. That was strangely the way things worked when a parent left you. Different sources told you different stories; often they matched, but sometimes they conflicted, and you had to sort out for yourself who was lying and who wasn't. Some days you believed one thing, some days another. Yet each time you were told a story, one you believed, it was as if you were learning something new about yourself, as if the episode directly involved you, perhaps was secretly all about you. Then you took every detail—every tidbit of information—and stored it, shelved it, according to time and theme, along with all the real memories you had. But the stories you were told often became more real, more alive, than the ones you actually remembered. You almost felt that you had actually been present for them. For me, it was as if, in fact, I had been hidden behind that TV my aunt said my father needed to look behind; I was in the black Lincoln; I was listening outside the door; I was pacing with the spies, whispering angrily, "What the hell is he doing now?"

"For all you know, Catherine," my aunt had told me, "he thinks he's protecting you by not talking to you. He thinks if he communicates with you, sends one single note your way, something will happen to you. He believes this stuff," she said, and shook her head. "I saw it in his eyes. He really believes."

But that theory of hers made no sense. He still sent me birthday cards—I had gotten my sixteenth-birthday card only a month before our birdbath conversation; if he were so paranoid and nervous, he wouldn't have sent it at all. In my mind, that spy story halfheartedly became something stagy my aunt had created, something that she concocted to make me feel I had an answer concerning who my father was and why he left.

"He wasn't all there," was how she put it, yet the simplicity of such a claim didn't entirely work, not in my memory, not in the present—my father was too conversational, too casual in the way he stood and sat, too observant. Earlier that same morning when we were in the glass elevator of the art museum, he had even noticed that I had a small burn on my finger—he stared at it, asked me how I got it, did it still hurt?

He was normal from what I could see—outside of the drinking—particularly so on that late afternoon as we sat in La Latina. His hands weren't even shaking the way they sometimes did. He was just sitting there telling me how, when he had told my Auntie Joy that he was coming to visit me, she had told him in a telephone conversation not to come, that it would be a big mistake.

"Then why did you come?" I heard myself say. I asked the question calmly, resolutely, as if it did not affect me. Then I added, because he didn't answer right away, "I mean, what made you decide to in the first place?"

"Your mother," he said softly, looking not at my face but somewhere else, at my shoulder perhaps. "She asked me to come."

I waited a minute. "Did she pay for the trip?" He didn't answer at first, so I asked again, louder, "Did she?"

"Yes," he said.

I added, "You mean Gerry paid."

"I'm not very good with money," he said quickly, with the air of someone who was about to go on a big rant, but he didn't. "I'm as bad as she is, but I don't buy blouses or couches or hats,"—he looked at me a minute—"or leopard dresses."

"Then what do you buy?"

"It's not that I buy anything. I just have a hard time." He looked at me, annoyed. "I don't make a lot, ya know? Do you know that?" He waited. "And I still pay for things from living with you and your mother. Still I do." I knew he paid the mortgage for our house, but that had been years and years ago.

"I don't have a lot," he added rather softly.

He kept staring at me while I thought about that, drank my wine—he didn't look angry, didn't look sad. He just had the brand of seriousness I had been waiting to see come out of him. I knew it was in there somewhere, but through the alcohol and his ha-ha-ha humor, it was like looking through a piece of smoked glass, you could see the shape of things, but not their intensity, their color.

"Your mom says you don't like Gerry?" he said abruptly, after a few minutes.

"No," I said matter-of-factly. "I don't like Gerry." I glanced at a guy next to us who was going through his pesetas on the bar, counting them, placing all the heavy coins on a ceramic dish. I watched the man put the money in piles, make small stacks of 100 pesetas. My father kept touching a spot on the bar, a certain darker circle in the wood, and there was something in that slow, dull moment, something in the sound of the change on the dish, the look of a candle that was lit behind a half-full whiskey bottle, that made me want to leave.

Within a half hour we did leave—our great excuse for separating being that I had to get up in the morning, go to work. It was still a little early to turn in, only eight o'clock, and I felt a little guilty for wanting to leave him—so much so that I accompanied him all the way to his hotel. We sat side by side in the cab, silent, our knees almost touching.

"But *why* don't you like Gerry?" my father asked a bit softly after we had been in the cab a while. We were on a side street, a row of brick buildings all around us.

"Because I just hate him," I said.

My father shook his head, as if I were being irrational, dramatic—as if my disgust for Gerry were really a secret disgust for him. He stared out the window some more. The brick buildings were still there, but they weren't doing anything of much interest—no lights were turning off and on, no people coming in and out, but he stared and stared.

"But why hate Gerry?" he asked after a long pause.

"I don't hate him, hate him," I said. "I talk to him when I have to. I tell him when I call home when my last day of classes are. I tell him if it's very cold in Boston." I gave a strained smile. "I talk to him about how windy it is."

For the six and a half years before I left for college, I had seen Gerry every day in my living room; I went to restaurants with him; I saw him open presents at Christmas. He gave me rides; he bought medicine when I was sick. He did all the things a father was supposed to do, although there was always something odd and strained about it, as if he was doing things he knew he had to do, things that were expected of him. But, honestly, neither of us ever liked the other, and it didn't have to do with what everyone else always thought it did, that Gerry had replaced my father. That simply wasn't true. Gerry certainly wasn't the one who kept my father away—my father controlled that. If my father had ever wanted to come back, all he had to do was walk right through the door. The locks had never been changed. The furniture was different furniture, but it was all arranged in the same layout as when he left. His pictures were still on the walls; my mother still glanced at them when she breezed down that hallway. It was all the same. Gerry's presence in our house had not altered any of that.

To answer my father's question, though, Why hate Gerry? I said flatly, "Well, for one, he's always nasty about Harlan. He doesn't like Harlan, even though he's never even seen him."

This was the one instance that my father didn't say, when referring to Harlan, "The gay guy?" Even with the slight buzz of four whiskeys, he seemed to know better without any further explanation. I went on to tell him how Gerry had come to my apartment once—and only once—to visit me with my mom, and how he had needed to make a phone call but refused to use my phone because Harlan used it; Gerry apparently thought he might "catch" something.

"He's a fuckin' moron," I said loudly—which made the taxicab driver glance at me in the rearview mirror, as if he were shocked I could say anything, in any language, with such vehemence.

Of course, in my story to my father, I left out that I had actually kicked Gerry out of my apartment, told him to get the fuck out. My anger had had nothing to do with Harlan being hurt, though; as Harlan was not home at the time. It was simply the fact that the night before Harlan had had one of his late-night attacks and then, hearing Gerry say, "The phone's probably got something on it," made me go nuts, as if Gerry weren't just talking about Harlan's gayness, but also about his mental instability, and after staying up all night, after holding on to Harlan's foot, after humming until the humming hurt, after all of that, any crappy comment about Harlan—no matter how ignorant or stupid—seemed to have some validity. It was as if in that moment standing in my hallway Gerry—with his corduroy shirt and his Santa Claus mustache, and his thick fat hands—had gained some sort of secret intelligence.

So I screamed at him, "Get the fuck out of here. GET OUT!" and then my mother pushed him down the long, dark hallway to the door. She did not say good-bye; she didn't say she'd call me; she just pushed him out and shut the door delicately, as though it might break.

"And that's why you don't like him?" my father asked after I gave him the abridged version, the one in which Harlan and the night before were not mentioned.

"I can't stand him."

"OK."

"He makes me sick."

"OK, got it."

"He's a piece of shit."

"All right, Catherine," he said, a little too loud, a little too agitated. "Please, that's enough."

$$\overline{19}$$

WHY HATE GERRY?

If anyone were to ask me, not just my father, why I didn't like Gerry, my most popular answer, most simple, was that he was homophobic. This answer was very attractive, very noble; it referred to a population of people to which I didn't belong—and it made the most sense: My best friend was gay, so, of course, I would have such sensitivities. Yet the truth was, I couldn't stand Gerry for another very particular reason, and homophobia was merely the easiest to mention.

To Gerry's credit, though, I suppose it is rather important to mention that he did love my mother—"so much, almost too much," as my Auntie Joy once put it. He had no children of his own, no ex-wives, no ex-girlfriends he spoke much of, yet he was fifty, a full-grown man who had gone his entire life on his own. Then by some miracle, he found my mother, and he seemed forever grateful for that miracle, and he expressed it in numerous gifts. He bought her pearls and took her on weekend excursions and smiled at her from across the room, as if she, indeed, were the brilliant center of his universe—and people saw that in him, liked him for it, for being able to love someone so obviously, so freely. But I always saw his unending, jubilant desire for my mother to be simply a buildup of all the things he refused to feel for other people. It was as if he took all his feeling, all his love, and foisted it on my mother, let her empty him, and then he walked around, as he always had before, disliking anyone else who didn't resemble himself.

He did not like black people, he did not like Hispanic people. He used the N-word quite frequently, usually coupled with an adjective like dumb, stupid, or crazy. He hated Puerto Ricans the most, though, and anyone who spoke Spanish was, in his mind, a Puerto Rican, or, as he cleverly liked to abbreviate it, a PR. The fact that I was going to go work at a PR agency in Madrid often amused him, made him smile a little, on the verge of a sneer; and more than once he had asked my mother why I wanted to go to Spain in the first place, what was with my sudden interest in "spics"?

None of these reasons, however, had anything to do with why I hated Gerry—I had hated Gerry ever since I was thirteen, long before I had had any personal involvement with a gay person or a black person or a Spanish-speaking person. My world at that time was, in fact, as white and dull as Gerry himself.

I started hating Gerry on a gray April day. I started hating him sitting at the kitchen table. I started hating him with a schoolbook wide open in front of me.

It was Sunday morning, and I had just come home from sleeping over at a friend's house. My mother kept asking if I wanted something to eat, had I had breakfast? Did I want some toast? How about orange juice? I kept telling her I had already eaten at my friend's house. Each time I said this, she nodded distantly and it occurred to me in the set of her face, in the fact that she was suddenly so eager to serve me, that something was wrong. She had the look that I would later recognize, from my own long nights awake with Harlan, as the look of someone who was not just tired or disoriented but literally afraid, somewhere inside herself, of all the emotion that had taken place the night before.

Gerry arrived shortly after I came home. He had slept somewhere else, where exactly was never made clear, but in any case he was very angry with my mother, so much so that when he came through the front door he looked as if he were ready to burst into tears at the sight of her.

Over the phone all night long, they had apparently been fighting about some letters Gerry had "discovered"—he kept using the word *discovered* as they argued about it in front of me. The "discovered" letters were in the trunk of my mother's car, and they were, of course, from my father. I pictured the letters as a big heaping stack, tied together with a fragile pink bow, Gerry leafing through them as he sat in the front seat of her car, pausing only to look at the house, at the beige aluminum siding, at the white door, at the little baby world he once believed only my mother and he shared. But with each letter he read, he saw a house that was not his but my father's, a house that contained my father's presence in the picture frames on the walls, in the heaping lace of my mother's wedding dress, which she still kept in their closet, and in the Coca-Cola bumper sticker on my bedroom door. My father was everywhere in there, and he was big, he was giant; he was someone who could push Gerry and his big curly mustache aside with one easy wave, with one easy "Dearest Doll"—that was the salutation my father used in each of the letters, "Dearest Doll," and Gerry, in all of his arguing anger, kept repeating it, as if were some hideous evil chant he couldn't get out of his head.

So Gerry hated my father, and he hated those "Dearest Doll" letters, and he hated the idea that my mother wrote my father letters in return. Those letters and their "discovery" were like physical proof of my parents' constant connection. It was no longer just a sinking feeling he sometimes got; it was now a real live thing, one that made him feel gypped and cheated as he stormed through that front door ready to scream and scream.

Initially that screaming was probably intended only for my mother, but then he must've seen me in the background at the kitchen table, and in that moment I must've become worse than the house we lived in, worse than the letters he repeatedly read, as I was a sitting and breathing vision of my father and mother, not just a piece of paper with words written on it.

They continued arguing for a while upstairs, away from me; my mother didn't like to argue in front of me—she seemed to think it would put me into a trance or something, make me fall back to the summer night when my father hit her with the brick. But in any case, after their argument had ended, about an hour later, Gerry came downstairs to find me. When I saw him, I already felt like a target; I had caught him eyeing me when he first walked in the door, as if in his mind he had drawn a circle around my head and then within it marked an X.

"What are you reading, Catherine?" he asked. I didn't answer him. His voice was creepy and soft. He was still wearing his brown leather jacket with a rip in the side that revealed black shiny fabric. "Tell me what you're reading?" he said again, sitting down and pulling his chair very close to me and the social studies book I had open in front of me. I had been trying to do my homework, answer all the odd-numbered "Questions for Discussion," but their argument sidetracked me, kept me looking up at the ceiling, listening for footsteps.

"Or were you not reading anything?" Gerry said abruptly, after he had been quiet a minute. "Were you just listening to something?"

At first I thought he was referring to the fact that I had been eavesdropping, but then once my mother came out of the bathroom and headed back toward me, he started to say what he wanted to say, what he was leading up to. "Did you know . . . " he said. "I bet you didn't know that your father . . ." He paused, looked at me with that deadness in his eyes that you would never use with a thirteen-year-old, only with an adult you very much want to weaken. "Your father used to hear voices."

This was way before my aunt had said anything to me, way before anyone would ever have the nerve to say such a thing.

My mother came into the kitchen right after that—she didn't have to hear what he was saying to know something was wrong. All she had to do was notice the way that my lips were pressed together tightly, as if I were holding words inside of myself while he sat in a chair very close to me, so close I could see all the pores in his face, with the white hairs coming out of them, a world of bristle, a world of roughness, settling and growing on his face.

"What are you saying to her?" my mother asked in a calm, tired voice.

"I'm telling her about the voices." he said matter-of-factly, enjoying himself a little, so much so you would have thought he was drunk with the way he was suddenly making such a happy game of it all.

"What voices?"

"The voices in James's head."

"Gerry!"

"Your father's name is James," he said, ignoring my mother. "I guess you might not know that, seeing that he never talks to you, but that's his name."

"Cut it out!" my mother screamed, and she came farther into the kitchen so that she was standing above us.

"I'm *not* trying to be mean," he said, and stood up alongside my mother. "I'm just telling her so that if she hears voices she'll know where they come from." He shrugged. "James heard voices; she hears voices."

One quick minute passed, and then my mother smacked Gerry in the face—it was so unexpected, so sudden, that I flinched along with him.

"She does not hear voices!" she yelled as he backed away from her so that she couldn't smack him again, or perhaps so that he couldn't smack her back.

He stood there for a minute, his posture rigid, and then he said in a very calm, authoritative voice, "Have you *ever* seen her, have you ever watched her just sit there? I'm talking with nothing else around, not a TV, not a book, nothing. She's just staring off!" He looked up at the ceiling momentarily, mimicking me. "Her eyes are all over the place. For hours. And no one's talking to her, and she's not talking to anyone, but she just *sits* there, she just *sits*. What *do* you think she's doing?"

He paused. My mother stayed quiet.

"There's got to be something going on in her head," he said, and he cocked his head a little to the side, pointed at his forehead, made that particular circling gesture that's reserved for only one word: crazy.

My mother touched the handle of the refrigerator, perhaps to anchor herself. The gesture was calm, natural, and then everything in her seemed to squeeze up tight. She screamed, "Get the FUCK out of here! Get the fuck, fuck, fuck out of here! Get out. Go where you were last night!"

He didn't move.

My mother clenched her fists, made a growling sound that came from somewhere deep down inside of her, far away from the three of us, and it seemed to echo against the kitchen walls, against the morning grayness outside. It was only after that that Gerry backed away, his face as red as if fire had just been blasted at him. He did not look at me. His gaze stayed with my mother, and it was only in her shaking hands, in the audible rasp of her breathing, that he seemed to feel a quiet remorse— one that he clearly didn't know what to do with.

After Gerry left, shutting the door gently, my mother and I stayed in the kitchen. We were silent. A few minutes later my mother poured herself a glass of orange juice, and I watched her fill the tall narrow glass, listened to the lapping sound of the juice as it came out of the carton. She held the glass, her hands trembling, and then put it down, as if she were afraid she would drop it. Then she sat down, cleared her throat.

"Your father didn't hear voices," she said and waited. "Do you hear me?"

I didn't say anything. I was doing this death stare thing that I had learned in dance class. Whenever you did a pirouette they told you to stare dead in front of you at one given point—it was supposed to help you keep your balance, keep your head from rolling all over the place. I did the same stare now at the kitchen table, not in the direction of my mother; instead, I fixated on a photograph in my social studies book of a canoe. I wanted to get in that canoe, lie down on my stomach, and sail out of that kitchen away from my mother.

I was so angry with her, more so than I had ever been before. I was angry that we lived with Gerry, angry that we had no money. Those two things went hand in hand; I was certain of it. And the money that my mother needed Gerry for was all around us. It was in the orange juice glass, which was made of a kind of crystal, a kind that had flecks of sparkly things in it; it was in her robe, which was shiny and teal, the kind you couldn't wash in the washing machine; it was in the phone, which was not ringing and ringing as it once had, bill collectors' voices no longer on the other end, their strange, inhuman voices that sounded like computers, voices that asked for my mother by her entire name, including her middle initial, and then left 800 numbers for her to call them about her "account."

With Gerry those voices were gone, silenced; but wouldn't it have been just as easy not to answer the phone, to take it off the hook? Wouldn't it have been easier to get the kind of robe that you could wash, or the juice glasses without the special flecks? Did we really need that? Did we really need Gerry? It seemed an unfair trade-off.

My mother wasn't looking at me while I thought about all of this—she was off in her own world. She touched the wall, looked down at her arm, dabbed at her perfectly dry face with the checked dishrag that was on the stove. Then she cleared her throat—this meant she was going to say something, but she didn't right away. She paused, looking around the kitchen, at our Gerry kitchen, with its waffle maker and coffee grinder and food processor. All gleaming and silver.

"All your father ever said—it wasn't about voices." She touched the glass of orange juice, its lip, as if checking for a chip. "He used to try to stop drinking though—that's true. And it was really hard because . . . because for people who drink a lot"—she looked at me—"people like your dad, for them, they are so used to what the drinking does, that without it, everything gets mixed up."

What my mother was saying didn't entirely make sense to me. I continued staring away from her as if I were disinterested—but I was listening, heard every word, enough so that the conversation would return to me years later when I sat on that porch with my aunt.

"But there's a difference," my mother said, "a difference between people who are always mixed up and those who are only for a little while mixed up. And your dad was only for a while like that. Whenever he tried to stop drinking."

"How many times did he try to stop?"

"A few," she said, nodding her head up and down, as if this were something to feel good about, something to be proud of. "And your dad, he's really thoughtful, and I think that makes it all the harder for him." I didn't know exactly what she meant by that, but then she started telling me how my father told her once that when he was alone in a room he felt as if he weren't really alone in the room. "He said he could think forever about things." My mother nodded again after she told me this. "He told me that when he was young, when we were first dating. He said it because he would get quiet a lot, and I didn't know why; I would get fidgety, think he didn't like me. But that wasn't it, he said; that wasn't it." She took a sip of orange juice and her hand remained wrapped around the glass. She took another sip. "I asked him in a letter if he missed us."

I looked up, but not directly at her, to the left of her face.

"And he wrote back, said that whole story again. It wasn't like he was answering my question, but he was." She was rambling a little, talking too fast. "And he said in another letter that when he's in the car alone, when it's silent or when there's music, he can talk to anyone he wants right there in his head." She waited, as if she thought I might say something, make an insightful thirteen-year-old comment. There was the distant muffled sound of our neighbor yelling at his dog. "Hey, get over here. *Get* over here!"

"He never ever said he heard voices," my mother continued. "Gerry just thinks that; he thinks that's what it means to be mixed up." She shook her head. "Just because you think of things or remember things doesn't mean you hear voices." She stared at me. "Do you know that?"

I nodded, my eyes returning to the photograph of the canoe. After a pause, I said, "Will Gerry be back?"

"Yes."

"Will he . . ." I didn't know how to word it right. "Will he stay?"

"Yes."

"You want him to come back?"

"Yes."

Each time she said yes, she said it like she was in a court of law, speaking into a microphone.

"Why?" I said, a sudden flush, a heat, on my face. "Why do you want him here?"

"Because . . ." Her lower lip started to quiver. "Because, honey, you have to understand . . . we need him."

20

THE MONEY IN THE ENVELOPE

On Tuesday morning I got a phone call at work from Esteban. Initially when the secretary told me a man was on the phone for me, I thought it was my father. I wasn't supposed to see him until six, but I had given him my number at work in case he needed me—I told him just to say my name into the phone and they would understand, come get me. But then, once I answered the phone, I heard, *"Hola, Guapa."* Esteban's voice was so happy, so nonchalant, that I didn't recognize him at first.

I said stiffly, *"¿Sí?"*

"It's me. *Soy yo*. Esteban."

"How did *you* get the number here?" I asked. "Did I give it to you?"

"I have all your numbers," he said smugly. "I am your angel."

"Oh, yeah?" I said and wrote on the paper on which I was doodling: angel = pimp.

"I want to see you," he said. "I want to talk."

"About Borja?" I glanced at the doorway as I said this, as if I thought the secretary were listening, hiding behind the white wall, the navy tip of her shoe just slightly visible. But she wasn't there; it was just Esteban and me and a whole lot of paranoia.

"I want to talk to talk," he said, "but I do have something for you from Borja."

"What is it?"

"I'll give it to you when I see you tonight." He started talking about where we could go, but I interrupted him, told him I already had plans. He seemed momentarily taken aback by that, as if it seemed impossible that I would ever have plans of my own. After a pause, he decided we should meet for lunch. He wanted to meet in Chueca, a neighborhood that was very close to where I worked. It was also the designated gay area of Madrid, and often when I spoke to Isabel about going out with Esteban, she made a quizzical face when I mentioned places that weren't in Chueca—she seemed to think that all gay Madrileños were practically quarantined there.

"I'll meet you at Romanesco," Esteban said first, and then changed it to a place called El Jardinero. I hastily took down the address, told him I had a lot of work to do, that I'd see him soon. Two hours later, I sat across from him at a table that wobbled. Near where we sat, plastic flowers hung on invisible strings above the bar, and the air-conditioning made them sway. The walls were pink, and there were scattered ladybugs painted everywhere—our red tablecloth and black napkins matched the ladybugs.

"How do you say ladybug?" I asked Esteban when I sat first down.

"*Mariquita,*" he said, smiling as if the question were cute. He was still standing after getting out of his seat to kiss me, and now he was pouring wine in our glasses with his free hand behind his back like a waiter.

We talked for a long time about nothing. I didn't tell him my father was visiting me—that seemed something he didn't need to know. I just talked about Celia and Isabel, about work, about how hot it was getting now that it was July. He talked about his plane ride, about how much cooler the weather was in Caracas.

It seemed we had to drink more wine to say anything specific, anything that related to Borja. I didn't know if he had talked to him or not.

I didn't know if he knew that I had stayed with Borja at the hotel or if he knew what happened with that woman Maureen being so obnoxious to him. With each gesture Esteban made, with the way he touched his glass, smiled or didn't smile, I tried to guess all that he knew and thought. But it wasn't working.

After the waiter came over four times, we finally ordered our food, and I went to the bathroom. When I came back to my seat, we had a new bottle of wine, and there was an envelope in between my silverware. It was not a business envelope, or a greeting card envelope, but an envelope that matched fancy stationery.

"A love letter from the waiter?"

"It's from Borja."

"I don't want it," I said quickly, so quickly that it felt like I was about to lose control of my face. "I'm not seeing him again. I don't want to see him."

"We know that." He paused, stared at the table, touched the edge of the tablecloth, moved his fingers back forth as if he were wiping up dust. "If you don't like him, or don't feel comfortable, then you don't have to do it." He smiled a strained smile. "You choose what you want to do."

"I don't want it." I moved the envelope over so that it covered my knife.

"It's for you," he said, as if I was being childish or falsely noble. "It's not just money," he said. "It's a little freedom for you while you're here. To travel, to see things. Don't you want that?"

The waiter came over right then, put our spinach salads down in front of us. There was a plastic ladybug, the size of a button, on the plate, a garnish.

Esteban stared down at his salad, moved the ladybug with his fork. "You will only be twenty once," he said, without looking up at me. "You will only be twenty in the month of July this one time, and then it doesn't come back again."

I thought about my father momentarily, I thought about the bullfight we had been to, the way that the whiskey and Coke had felt between my knees in the hot, hot sun—I would never live through a moment like that again, never have that same sort of excitement mixed with anxiety and awe as I sat and stared at a bleeding bull.

"I believe young people don't even think about that," Esteban was saying. "You don't ever think about what you can't have over again. But you should." He pointed at me. "You really should."

I nodded. I believed him then, I did. But then he ruined it by getting too dramatic.

He said, "And then someday you'll die."

"OK." My voice was a little sharp. "That's a little much, don't you think?"

"You *are* going to die."

I shook my head. "I know that I'm going to die. I'm not stupid. But that has nothing to do with the envelope in front of me."

"It has everything to do with that envelope," he said, his voice getting so loud that another table of men glanced over at us. "If you had a few days to live, you would do everything you wanted in those few days." He pointed at the envelope. "What's in there lets you do what you want."

"You're quite the philosopher today."

He said, "I am, I am," and took a sip of wine. He seemed suddenly content with himself, as if he already knew that I would take the money, that I would spend it. Maybe I was mad at him for that, I don't know, but I brought an end to his smiling by asking, "And how's Juan?"

His face instantaneously lost whatever glow it had. He moved forward in his seat, had his hands on the arms of the wooden chair. "He's fine."

I suppose I knew all along that way far back, lurking behind the discussion of death, sat Juan. He seemed firmly perched, somewhere in the back of Esteban's mind, as if on a throne—all of Esteban's visions and thoughts governed by him. I didn't imagine Juan to be a particularly bossy type though, not an angry ruler. I pictured him as a frail boy with light-colored eyes. I pictured him sitting on a dock overlooking a series of boats, with Esteban sitting Indian-style next to him. They both wore sunglasses and matching thin rings. They did not touch.

"And how's Harlan?" Esteban asked me, bringing me out of my seaside vision and back to our ladybug table.

"He's fine," I said, and then frowned. His question seemed somehow to parallel the two, Harlan and Juan, as if he somehow knew that Harlan himself was not entirely well either. Of course, I had not told Esteban anything about that; I knew better. I kept that hidden. Even from myself. Within those first few weeks in Madrid, I felt no worry about Harlan, even when his letters got a little testy, a little angry—if anything, they made me feel better; he was being regular, normal, releasing the things inside of him.

Only the conversation that I had had with him on the metro station pay phone concerned me. He had seemed so upbeat, too upbeat, and, as always, I was so wrapped up in myself and my problems that I didn't question his behavior until later, after I sat in the train, listening to the three-bells signal that sounded at every stop. I had begun worrying about him only then, but by that point my activity with Borja, with my father, had sectioned it off, stifled it.

I thought about all of this as Esteban and I quietly sat across from each other, picking at the last pieces of spinach on our plates. Behind us there was a waiter polishing silverware and putting the pieces in separate straw baskets—the forks and knives and spoons jangled as he separated them, and the noise of it all made me tense, edgy, as if the waiter were in fact angry, and on the verge of throwing the whole pile onto the floor.

"How is Borja?" I asked after a long pause, after Esteban and I had sat there for too long not speaking. "Is he OK?"

Esteban just stared at me, his elbows on the table, his hands folded. The tension that I sensed from the waiter, I realized then, wasn't from the waiter; it was emanating from Esteban like a wave of heat. He took a sip of wine, swallowed it slowly, and then he said, "Borja's gay. He's not in love with you."

"I didn't ask you if he was in love with me. I asked you if he was OK."

"Of course, he's fine. He went out with you once, Catherine. You act like you think you cast spells on people or something." He shook his head. "You shouldn't give yourself so much importance."

"Fuck you," I said. "I was just asking if he was OK."

"He's a grown man, for God's sake!"

Again the people at the other table looked at us. We drank our wine as they glanced at us, but we didn't look at each other. The waiter came shortly after that, and Esteban asked for *la cuenta*, the check. When we left I took the envelope, looked up at him as if I were doing him a favor, and then put it in my bag. Then he walked me back to work. We were silent, just walking, our feet clapping down against cobble and cement. When we got in front of my office building, I couldn't think of anything to say. So I asked him how to say ladybug again.

"Mariquita," he said rather stiffly. "Do you want me to write it down for you?"

"No."

We stood there for a few minutes more. A woman who was humming passed by holding two grocery bags, a baguette of bread sticking out of one of them. She said *Buenos días* to us, in that soft, high-pitched voice older Spanish women have, and then I watched her move slowly down the hot sidewalk in her orange dress.

Esteban turned to me once she was farther away, his shoes making a scratchy sound on the cement. "You will call me next," he said. "I will not call you."

I nodded, said OK, as if what he had just said meant nothing to me. Then we waited a moment, kissed each other good-bye.

After lunch I did nothing for an hour or so—I just doodled and felt tense and kept glancing at my new envelope. I would've left early if I could've, but I had to talk to Kansas Katy, and she was not in her office until nine; it wasn't nine in her time zone until it was four P.M. in Madrid. The week before Carlos had told me that Lysol would not pay for an additional person, a companion to come with her to Spain, and I dreaded telling her this. For a whole week after he told me, I purposely left the office before four so that I wouldn't have to tell her. I had actually grown to like Kansas Katy very much—she was the only American I talked to on a regular basis during that first month away, and her voice, her slight country twang, comforted me. Within the first two weeks, I had often felt homesick and didn't know I was homesick—I just thought I was tired or headachy or moody. Often I tried to blame it on the new time zone or on jet lag or on my immune system, but all it really was, it seemed, was my mind's inability to expect things, to maintain regularity, to know what was to come. But Kansas Katy had established a certain schedule for me—I knew every few days that she would call, and at the end of each phone call she gave me the exact day that she would call again. Then once she called, she always acted like a fairy godmother, constantly repeating how brave it was, how wonderful that a young woman like myself would travel so far alone.

"You'll never be the same," she said once. "Never again."

Somehow, though, through all that awe she felt for what I was doing, I knew she would not come by herself. I knew that once I said they wouldn't pay for a companion, whether it be her father or her cousin or a newfound beau, she would falter, and all that excitement and enthusiasm she felt for the trip would turn into a depressing form of regret, the kind that comes when you are afraid of what you want.

Later that day when I finally talked to her she was very friendly, upbeat. She asked me what was going on with Felipe, and I told her, "Nothing, not yet." Then, as quickly as I could, I told her that her mystery companion could not come, at least not courtesy of Lysol. She didn't say anything at first, so I started rambling, talking about how if she wanted to come with someone else it really wouldn't cost that much to pay for an additional ticket. But then I stopped myself; I thought in admitting it didn't cost that much for an extra person to come, she would feel cheapened somehow—as if she wasn't worth much to Lysol.

"Yeah, but"—she said after a long silence—"the truth is, no matter what, I'm probably . . . well, I know . . . I'm just not going to come." She waited a second or two. "But I bet you knew that all along, didn't you?" Her voice wasn't nasty, wasn't accusatory; it was the voice of someone who was admitting something, the voice of someone who was a little disappointed with herself—and that disappointment was drifting across wire, across an ocean, to a person she didn't even know.

I said, as nicely as I could, "Why won't you come though? I don't understand. If you want to come, come. Nothing can hurt you here; there's nothing *that* different."

She didn't answer, and then I felt suddenly upset, emotional—although all that feeling seemed to have to do with the conversation I had had with Esteban, and the money in the envelope, more than anything else. Every woman I knew, it seemed, had to depend on someone else to give them things, had to have someone else accompany them through their lives—they couldn't just be on their own. And that bothered me, fired me up, made me want to yell at Kansas Katy, but if I did yell at her I wouldn't be yelling just at her, I'd be yelling at every single dreamy-eyed girl I had ever worked with; every single nervous, lip-biting girl; every single fast-talking, I'll-kick-your-ass girl; every single one who wouldn't, who couldn't, do any of the things they did without some guy behind them, calling them, touching them, checking in on them. I could not stand that kind of crap, which perhaps was irrational, but in my mind it was a weakness—what was so goddamn impossible about doing things on your own?

But, of course, I didn't say any of this to Kansas Katy. I certainly didn't scream at her; we were just silent, and in that silence I kept ruminating about what made me not want to depend on other people—on men—and I knew my mother would say it had something to with Gerry, with how much I hated her need for him, but, more realistically, she knew and I knew, it had everything to do with my father. Yet that was the terrible thing about my mother or my Auntie Joy or anyone else trying to analyze me and psychoanalyze me—they were always so quick to point out the things that were bound to be wrong with me, yet they never bothered to consider what was good about my father leaving me when I was so young: It taught me to live without men. It taught me not to depend on them—and although that was perhaps negative in the eye of a psychologist, it was, at that moment, on that phone, in that office, what set me apart, what made me different, what elevated me into a larger, less limited world. A world in which I would didn't *have* to depend on people like Gerry or Borja or whoever else showed up—I could if I wanted to, but I didn't *have* to.

Needless to say, though, amongst all this thought, my conversation with Kansas Katy didn't end so hot. I didn't know how to explain all those things I felt; I didn't know how to make her see what I saw; and, of course, I didn't really know her either. So we sat in a three-minute silence, and then she said that she would call me back the following week on Wednesday with her final decision, even though we both knew she had already made it.

I said, "OK, all right."

"Will you miss me when I don't call anymore?"

I shrugged, as if she were standing before me, and then said, "Probably."

"Well, maybe it'll take me longer to make my decision," she said. "Maybe it will take a real long time. Maybe I'll have to keep calling and calling; you'll have to keep describing things."

"Yeah?"

"I'll have to keep thinking and thinking, keep weighing the pros and the cons, keep trying to decide if Spain could be a nice place, a pretty place."

I smiled and let out my breath in a way that let her know, let her hear that I was smiling. I said, "You should do that. That's what you should do. Yeah. . . ."

I met my father after work in Puerta del Sol at a bar called El Taurino— on our way walking toward the bomb site the day before he had pointed out the bar, stared at it, because it had giant bull heads on the wall, about six of them, their fur still shiny and thick-looking, their horns pointed straight out. I knew he would remember it, would be able to find his way, so we decided to meet there. I had no idea he was going to bring Maureen.

Maureen was of course one of the women we had met by the pool earlier that week, the one who I had seen with Borja, the one who my father claimed had a "nice pair." The two of them showed up an hour late. He claimed they had gotten lost, but the real deterrent lurked in his eyes, in the way his arms swung when he walked in, and even in his lips—his lips got more and more chapped the longer in the day he drank.

Maureen, on the other hand, had a simple happy glow, a drunken one. She said, "Hello, miss," when she first sat down. Her hair was down, and she looked younger, fresher that way. She also had on a lot of jewelry—all gold, but a brassy kind of gold, the kind that doesn't look so flattering against fair skin. She *was* pretty though. She had the small, small face I often associate with Englishwomen, the high cheekbones, the angularity. Her mouth was a little thin though, and when she wore dark lipstick as she had the night I saw her with Borja, her lips became even more dramatically small, like the mouth of a child.

"Invited me along," she said, and pointed at my father. "Is that OK?"

I nodded, said, "Sure," and then looked at my father. "You're late though."

"I got los'," he said. He had the map the hotel gave him in his hand, and he tried to show me where they had come from, but all he really did was make a big spiral shape over the middle of the map. The level of drunkenness he had now attained was how I had originally pictured him to be when I stood in the elevator of the Holiday Inn. Yet he hadn't been like this with me for the past two days; he had been controlled, reasonably regular. He had actually seemed to me quite systematic about what he drank and how much he let himself drink within given hourly intervals. It appeared to be the only reason he even wore a watch. Even *what* he drank seemed to be governed by time. For instance, he drank beer exclusively in the beginning of the day and then, after what seemed to be exactly four hours, he drank whiskey and only whiskey. The only exception was the first day he arrived, when he was drinking whiskey in the morning, but I suppose he had been confused about his rules then— he was in between time zones.

"Are you guys ready to go?" I asked my father, while Maureen was up from the table putting on her lipstick in front of a mirror that was delicately placed between two bull heads. My father shrugged, said yeah, but in his face I could see that he didn't know where we were supposed to go. I could've taken him to a museum or a café or the post office, and he wouldn't have known the difference. I said, "We are going to go shopping now," in a voice that suggested I knew his confusion.

"Shopping," he said, "and then a nightclub."

I nodded. We were going out later that evening with Isabel. She was taking us to a nightclub as she had promised long before my father arrived. That was one of the great things about Madrid, she claimed, you could take your father out to a nightclub and it wasn't strange or outlandish the way it might be somewhere else. And the whole reason we were even shopping was to find my father something to wear to the club—he claimed he had nothing to wear, nothing good enough.

"You just sit," I told him when we finally got to a clothes store, one that was around the corner from the café. I pointed at the couch that was in front of the dressing rooms. "We'll find you something."

"I don't like the couch," he said as he sat down. "And it smells weird in here, like popcorn. Ask them if they're making popcorn." He paused for one solid moment. "Hey, how do you say 'popcorn'?"

I ignored him, and so did Maureen—we were flipping through hangers of dress shirts and black pants. She had a good eye; she picked out pants, draped them over the rack, fingered the lining, the pockets, the buttons on the waist. She seemed to know just the right size, too, as if she had already seen his waist, measured it.

"I don't know if I can buy my clothes in a popcorn store," my father was saying. "I don't know if a popcorn store's the place for me."

I said, "Shut up, OK," a little too sharply, actually, to the point that later when he went into the dressing room, there was a silent awkwardness between Maureen and me. I asked her after a few minutes where Doria was, and she smiled as if I had just said something devious. She said, "Oh, she's off somewhere," and made this flippant gesture that seemed to suggest they were not good friends, they didn't even like each other, they were just on vacation together.

"And where's *your* friend," she said, "your *tío*?" *Tío* can mean either uncle or guy.

"He's off somewhere, too," I said.

She nodded. We were quiet for a moment again.

Then she pointed at my father's dressing room and said, "He doesn't really know you at all." She pronounced at all "a tall." "That must be hard," she added, but she didn't say it in a genuinely sensitive way, more like a dull observation.

My father came out of the dressing room shortly afterward—I hadn't responded to Maureen's comment. The three of us just eased over toward the register without speaking. My father had picked out one shirt and one pair of pants, and the total came to 16,000 pesetas, which was about 100 bucks. My father took out his wallet, fiddled with the compartments—the same compartments which I had watched him go through at every single bar and tourist attraction we had been to thus far. I never paid. I only assisted him with counting the money, told him what the different-sized coins and pastel bills were worth. But in front of this cash register, my father had no money in that wallet of his, just small change; yet he was too drunk, too slow, to admit it.

So I paid. It was quick, reflexive—all I had to do was reach in my bag, find my envelope of money, put down four bills of 5,000 pesetas. I had not counted how much money was in the envelope and I wasn't going to. It seemed safer not to know its entire value—I would just spend it bit by bit, I had already decided, until the bulk of the envelope thinned out and was gone.

"Girl's got money," Maureen said as we walked out of the store, a smirk on her face, as if that was one additional thing my father didn't know about me. He nodded anyway, thanked me—he was suddenly serious, behaving as if he were tired. I told him he should go back to his room, get some sleep—we weren't going out with Isabel for another four hours. He said OK, somewhat obediently, and kissed me—as if we were Spanish all of a sudden—on each cheek. Meanwhile, Maureen went out into the street to hail a cab.

"So what's the deal with her?" I asked while she was away from us, and he shrugged, acted as if he didn't know what I was talking about. "I just had a few drinks with her. That's all." He was lightly swinging the bag of clothes he had in his hand. "I need something to do," he said. "Something else to think about. It can't be just me and you all time." He paused, waited a careful second or two. "Right?"

I nodded. "Right." Then we stood there a minute, watched Maureen hail a cab with two fingers in the air.

THE GIRL BEATEN UP

Later on Tuesday, right before Isabel and I were about to leave to pick up my father, my mother called. Celia was the one who answered—she was packing, going back to Gijón that night, and she had the phone right next to her in case her boyfriend Francisco called. I was talking to her from the doorway when the phone rang, and once she heard the pseudo French and Spanish mix of my mother's voice, she smiled wide.

"*Una francesa,* " she said, handing me the phone and then touching the crown of my hair as if I were an eight-year-old child.

"Yeah, Ma?" I said into the phone.

"Whatcha doin'?"

"Standing."

"Oh," she said. "Very nice. And . . . where's you know who?" This sort of phrasing meant that Gerry was lurking somewhere in the house or in the yard, perhaps leaning right up against her, hugging her from behind with his eyes squeezed shut.

"Who do you mean?" I said. "Do you mean *Dad*?" I said "Dad" loudly, so loud that if Gerry were near the phone, he would hear me and would start fidgeting, start rubbing his elbows in slow methodical circles.

"*Dad,*" I said, "is at the hotel. We're going out later."

"Are you guys getting along OK?"

"Mostly."

"Mostly?"

"Yeah, mostly."

"You . . . haven't fought at all?"

"You mean has he hit me in the head with anything?" I smiled at Celia as I said this. She smiled back—she had no idea what I was saying.

"He would never hit you," my mother said. Her voice was matter-of-fact. "He is the one person who would never hit you."

"What do you mean, the *one* person?"

She ignored me. "You're getting along OK?"

"Yes."

"Well, if you are about to go out . . ." She paused. "I'll call you later. I'll call you maybe when he's gone. But you can call me . . . if anything gets hard. Don't let it get hard without me? OK?"

I didn't say anything. I was standing with my back to the wall, my posture stiff straight, one arm up along the wall, my fingers on the low arch of the doorway. As a kid I used to stand in this same posture-conscious pose while I watched my mother make dinner at the stove.

I'd stand behind her, and she'd say over her shoulder, "You getting taller back there?"

"Yup."

"Real tall?"

"Yup."

"Supersize tall?"

"Yup."

"Killer tall?"

"Yup."

But my mother couldn't see me in my pose now, she couldn't see the dress I was wearing, the one that Monica had once said I looked like a million pesetas in; she couldn't see the superhigh shoes, couldn't see my

eyes that were wet from too much eye makeup; she couldn't see my
father's face with its faltering eye contact; she couldn't hear Esteban's
voice or Borja's or Harlan's. In many ways she didn't know anything
about me, yet I loved her more than anyone else in this world, had loved
her the longest, but I often kept her the most distant—as if she were a
living, moving memory, a vision, a perfection that could not end.

"You'll call me later?" she said again. "Right?"

I told her yeah, and then she must have heard my stretch in my
breath.

"Are you doing that thing against the wall?"

"Yup."

"Well, don't hurt yourself, for Christ's sake," she said. "You sound
like you're hurting yourself."

There was a pause after that, and then she told me she loved me, and
I waited, touched the doorway with my fingertips. Then I said it back.

If I had known that Monica was going to meet us later that night, I probably would've had some sort of nervous fit. It had been enough already
that day dealing with Esteban and Kansas Katy and my father and Maureen and my mother. I did *not* need Monica. I didn't need her smile or
her laugh or her flashy swear-filled English right then. Even the fact that
Isabel was soon meeting my father was uncomfortable, worrisome—I
called him three times before Isabel and I left, before my mother called,
to make sure he was dressed and shaved and reasonably sober. I also told
him Maureen couldn't come.

"Don't worry," he said. "I don't want to bring her. She's kind of
mean, ya know."

Just in case she did show up, though, in the cab on the way to my
father's hotel I told Isabel what little I knew about Maureen, but I delivered
everything in a ha-ha sort of way, and I left out key elements of the day,
like the fact that my father was drunk and that I had paid for his clothes.

"*¿Dijiste algo a tu madre?*" Did you tell your mother, Isabel asked
me, referring to Maureen, and I said no. She smiled at that, as if that

made me a protective person, a decent one. That smile actually stayed on her face right up until she met my father. She seemed to have this entertaining vision of his being this playboy father—one who never called or wrote letters when I first arrived, but now while he was visiting was picking up English chicks on the side. That vision faded quite quickly, though, once she met him, once she sat across from him in the ritzy bar we went to before the nightclub. He was wearing his new outfit, all black, and in the dim lighting he looked fine, but you could still see how tired he was in his eyes—they were a little red, watery. The bar itself was in a restaurant I had been to with Esteban, one that used to be a theater, and the ceiling was so high it was dizzying. A giant mirror the size of a wall was on one side of us; on the other, a room full of people, hidden only slightly behind gauzy curtains, ate at giant round tables.

During the half hour we were there, my father had three Johnny Walker Reds and Isabel and I each had one whiskey with Fanta Limón. Because we were sitting right at the bar, my father only had to casually push his glass forward to get it filled up again—you could've almost not noticed. But Isabel herself was, in my mind, the epitome of watchfulness—she was only one year older than Celia, but she sometimes seemed years and years older; she was more observant of people, more readily aware of what was wrong with them. About Monica she had once said, "I like her very much. She is a good girl," *una chica buena* were her exact words, "but she is very uncomfortable being a good girl, so she tries and tries to be a bad one." That judgment I thought about quite often; it seemed to be one of the smartest, single-sentence evaluations I had ever heard—it even momentarily came to mind when Isabel finally remembered to tell me in the cab, on the way to the club, that she had told Monica we were going out with my father, and Monica had said she might meet us. What feeling that information inspired as I sat wedged between my father and Isabel is hard to pinpoint, as I halfheartedly decided to believe, just to relieve myself, that Monica would definitely not come. She did not like me, and there was nothing feasibly fun about hanging out with my father and me.

She wouldn't come. She couldn't come. There was no reason.

But then Monica was standing there, at the bar of the nightclub—a place called Arabia—when we first walked in. She was wearing a light gray crocheted dress with black underwear beneath it. The holes in the knit weren't so big that it was incredibly revealing, but it was revealing enough that people glanced at her and then glanced again. How I even recognized her so quickly was strange—it was as if I possessed some sort of radar for her, as if she changed temperatures where she stood or emanated a certain energy, a color. I hadn't seen her since that night at Esteban's, five weeks before, and now with my father talking in my ear, telling me he was going to go to the bathroom for "a sec," that night with her and Paco and Dan seemed entirely distant, like something I had dreamed.

Once she came over, I stood somewhat behind Isabel, as if I thought she wouldn't see me or address me if I just kept my distance. But then Isabel pulled me by the hand toward them. Monica eyed me but did not kiss me hello as she had done with Isabel. She just said, "Catherine, hello," and asked me in English if I had seen Esteban since he came back from Venezuela. I said no.

"And where's your father?" she asked in Spanish so that Isabel could understand.

"En los servicios," I said, just as my father came back from the bathroom, stood at my side. I introduced them, and Monica reached out to shake his hand; he paused, confused—the same way that I often did when Spanish people chose to be American and shake my hand as opposed to being Spanish and kissing my cheek. As she shook his hand, she smiled at him rather warmly. Then she looked at me momentarily, nodding as if she knew everything about my father and me, as if it had all been written out for her, like a confession, once I had slapped her.

"You're the owner of Coca-Cola?" she said to my father, and smiled with the confidence of someone who can be ambiguously mean and funny all at the same time. If she was being mean, though, she was being mean to me, not to him; and if she was being funny, it was for his sake, not mine—she was the type, from what I had seen before, who worked extra hard to entertain men, give them a fine time.

"I never ever said he was the owner of Coca-Cola," I said sharply, mildly annoyed, and Isabel just looked at me, her lip twitching into a wary smile. She didn't understand our English, but she could still read facial expressions, see Spanish words in the set of my lips, in the way I kept rubbing one of my shoulders as if I needed its softness.

"Oh, no, I'm not the owner," my father said. "I did create the formula though." He smiled at Monica, and she smiled back.

"Must've been a lot of work," she said, but he couldn't hear her over the music. "Must've been a lot of work," she said again.

"It was." He nodded matter-of-factly. "It was a lot of work." He touched my shoulder. "Wasn't it?"

I looked at his hand. His joke made me feel he was allying himself with Monica, or maybe it was the fact that he seemed refueled with alcohol all of a sudden, as if he had gone into the bathroom and drunk something he had his pocket, something he poured into a travel-size shampoo bottle or a mini-mouthwash.

Perhaps Monica actually recognized that as she offered to buy us a drink. She looked at Isabel, looked at me, after we didn't answer right away. She offered again, *"¿Una copa?"*

Both Isabel and I still hesitated, and then we decided to go upstairs to the second floor for a drink. At the top of the stairs a woman was dancing on something elevated, but she wasn't a belly dancer—she looked almost like a flapper. She wore a hat with sequins and a dress that was tight on her stomach.

Despite the name Arabia, the first floor had looked like any other nightclub: dark maroon walls, a dusty-looking chandelier in the entrance, and a giant room only for dancing, a bar full of candles on each end; only the second floor looked Arabic with the small, round backless stools you could sit on, little tables that were coppery-looking and metal, like oversized drum symbols made into tabletops. The entire warehouse room smelled of sweetness, of honey-traced hookah smoke mixed with lit candles and incense. We sat on a couch that was low on the ground, a couch full of red embroidered pillows. The music playing sounded Arabic but had Spanish words, and it was too loud, so loud we couldn't talk, so we just drank, my father always finishing first. He went to the bar twice while we sat calmly with our first drinks; each time he asked me if we wanted anything, and then he went alone to the bar. He knew how to say whiskey in Spanish because it was the same as in English, and then the Spanish numbers appeared on the cash register, clear and easy for him to read.

While he was at the bar the second time, I watched him stand there and wait to order, one elbow on the bar, the other hand on the back of his neck. A couple sat in the space between our couch and the bar. They were arguing. The girl seemed young, only seventeen or eighteen. She had a shirt that had black fur trim, and she kept touching it. Their argument didn't attract much attention; it was the dull kind you commonly see across a room, the kind that might have to do with a missing lighter or a rude friend or a misunderstood drink order.

The only reason I even noticed them was because of her fur collar, which seemed unpleasantly warm for July, and also because she had been pointing and I had thought for a moment that she was pointing at me, but it turned out she was just pointing as she spoke. Her mouth opened and closed against the music, against the rush of what sounded heavy and loud, taxing to talk under, and the guy I saw only from the side. He was big-backed and husky, with a goatee and a hawkish nose. I watched her face as he responded to her—I saw her touch her bracelet, her forehead, then look away from him.

I took a sip of my drink, glanced at my father at the bar, and then at Isabel, who had gotten up and was talking to someone on the other side of the room, her hands on her hips. Monica was still next to me; she was gazing at the dance floor in the direction of the flapper-type dancer. I looked at the dancer, too, watched her hands go up in the air, and then I looked back at the arguing couple. And the girl was no longer in her seat. She was against the mirrored wall, and her boyfriend had one hand firmly around her neck. The music dulled what was happening, made it all seem dreamy. No one, from what I could see, had noticed or cared. He kept shaking her, one hand on her throat, the other on the top of her head, across her forehead, as if he were holding her in place. Then she said something back to him, and he started to push her harder against the wall, but it looked like slow motion, unreal against the music, and somehow, watching this, I had risen out of my seat, half believing—although I could not hear it or see it—that the mirror was cracking behind her head.

Someone came over to the two of them right then, an older short man who wasn't entirely capable of restraining the boyfriend—and the girl continued to get slammed against the mirror, her hands not fighting him but instead flat against the wall, as if she were trying to soften each backward blow by pushing all of her weight backward, too.

Monica had stood up and was next to me, and I touched her arm as if to orient myself, to make sure the shape next to me was human. My father emerged in my sight right then. He was halfway over to our couch with his drink in his hand, and he stopped to look at the rush of men who finally came over to the couple, pulled the boyfriend completely off of her. They dragged him out of the club, and amongst a small circle of people she leaned against the wall, as if it were her only safety, her only form of balance.

Then, dramatically enough, they brought out a stretcher—it could not have come from an ambulance, as it was too soon for an ambulance to have arrived—and the men who attended the stretcher were doormen, walkie-talkies in their back pockets. It was as if they kept a number of stretchers in the club, perhaps in a special closet somewhere along with brooms and mops, cocktail napkins and Windex.

Meanwhile, people were still dancing. The music was theirs, the whiskey was theirs. They were in a separate world, a separate life, one where everything was stretcherless and blind. Bartenders kept making drinks, one song turned into another song, certain dancers had their hands in the air.

The only real difference was that I had gotten to my feet and I was staring at the mirror where the girl had been. There was no blood, no shattered lines across the glass, no gruesome signs of anything. The white stretcher had been the worst of it.

And then my father, who was near us—but not too near—was afraid to come over. He stood against a low wrought-iron railing as if he were watching the flapper-looking girl or the dancers, but he wasn't—he knew, even from a distance, sensed how glassy my eyes got, how shaky my hands were, even though he wasn't close enough to see such a thing. But I felt he could see it, as if a special circle had just been drawn right around me, a circle that marked my weakness, a weakness I had had in schoolyards as a kid when I watched girls get shoved too hard, heard their knees smack against cement, imagined the bruises forming like blue-petaled flowers beneath their pants. It was a weakness I carried with me in Shooters, too; perhaps it settled itself on my tray, made the drinks spill a little as I heard men talk around my silent drink-delivering presence, heard them say a certain woman they knew had "sugar tits" or "blow-job breath" or a "useless, flat ass." This same woman could be in the room, could've just left their side, or she could be elsewhere, a nameless bare body, but those comments still had the same power, still would go and go, run loose, and spiral up above my head.

And those comments came from all sorts, not just bearded, big-bellied men with hillbilly clothes—it was men in suits and men in soft-looking granddaddy sweaters; men who said "thank you" and tipped well; men who were drunk and men who weren't; men who played pool and men who just stood, jiggling change in their pockets, leaning against the green walls; men who seemed to fill the room, lurk in every corner, populate the universe.

"Your hands are shaking," Monica said in my ear.

I said, "So?"

"They are, they're shaking." She waited, stared at me. "Do you want to go downstairs?"

Before I could answer, she pulled me by the arm, and I walked toward the stairs with her, weaved through people whose arms and cigarettes seemed constantly in the way, and then we got down to the brightly lit foyer. She led me outside, past a sliding glass door, to a bar that was outside. There were trees and potted plants everywhere; the bar was made out of yellow brick.

"Do you want ice?" she said, once we stopped walking and were in a solid space of our own. "Ice will make your hands stop shaking. If you hold something cold."

That made absolutely no sense to me, but before I could say yes or no, she went over to the bar. I stared at her back while she stood and waited. Her hair was shorter than it had been last time I saw her, and I could see her dress's black tag against the top of her bare back. She looked very different to me right then: without her face visible—her perpetually mocking, smirking face—she was just a sweep of reddish brown hair, long arms, a crocheted dress, heels that were so high they seemed to make her permanently aware of her posture, even her neck seemed stiff. She had temporarily lost that entire aura of mocking superiority, even when she turned, when I saw her face; her red vampy lipstick was still intact, overdrawn around her lips, but her expression was calm somehow, delicate-looking.

"Toma," she said when she came back over with a rocks glass full of ice. She put a cube in my palms. "Together," she said, putting both my hands together and holding them like that as if she thought that without her assistance I might open my hands, drop the cube. We stayed like this; I watched the water drip out of my hands onto the gray cement. Even when the entire ice cube had melted, Monica still had not said anything else. She just put another cube in my hand, started the procedure over again. She was taking care of me and in such a soft, motherly way—in the same way, perhaps, as someone who wasn't her mother once took care of her. She didn't say a word either, just stared off at the few people who were standing in clusters on the fake cobblestone patio. It was a hot night, yet the smell of rain in the air seemed to emanate from all the plants and skinny trees. Otherwise, it was just hot and dry and dark out.

Monica stayed quiet, I stayed quiet, my hands froze. Not once did she ask me a single question as to why my hands were shaking, or whether she should get my father or did I see how hard that girl got hit? Wasn't it crazy? Didn't it happen so close to us? What do you think they were even fighting about? Do you think she'll keep seeing him? Keep getting hit? Those were questions that Isabel or Celia might've posed to me, but Monica seemed to me that night, in her distant silence, to have traces of other things inside of her, darker things, things that made her hands more therapeutic than the ice—the ice that seemed at the moment just an excuse, a less-than-awkward reason to hold hands.

"Do you want to leave?" Monica asked after about ten or fifteen minutes. "I can give you a ride home."

"I have to get my father."

"I know," she said. "I can go get him."

I waited. "Isabel's going to think it's weird of me. To leave now."

"So?"

"So I don't want to look weird."

She shook her head, looked away from me. "If something bothers you, it bothers you." We weren't holding hands anymore; the ice was all melted, and I had my numb hands at my sides. "I'm tired anyway," she said. "I'll tell her I'm tired and that you're . . . that you're mad at your father. She already knows that."

"I'm not mad at my father."

"I'll go tell Isabel," she said, ignoring my reply, "and then I'll get your father and then we can go. You stay out here." She pointed at an orange plastic chair in the corner, motioned for me to sit.

In Monica's car my father seemed to have regained the drunkenness from earlier in the day in the clothes store. His fourth or fifth whiskey seemed to be his magic number, bringing out a certain all-consuming blur, one that kept his speech not just slurred but irritating to listen to. When he came out of the club with Monica, I knew he was wasted from the way he waved at me childishly once he stood a few feet in front of me.

In Monica's car, I sat in the front and my father sat in the back. I shouldn't say he sat though, he really reclined, leaned his head down on the leather seat next to him, his hand on the back of my seat as if to keep him from sliding forward when the car came to a stop.

"Smells like cologne back here."

"I spilled some perfume," Monica said.

"Smells like cologne," he said again, as if she hadn't answered him. "Smells like a lot of cologne. A big barrel of cologne."

"You don't like it?" she said, and smiled at me sideways.

"Smells like cologne."

"Guess what kind?"

He made this deep, inhaling sound. "Nausea cologne. It's a special nausea blend."

"He's going to throw up," she said to me matter-of-factly, and rolled down the windows.

The sudden blast of wind hit my face; it reminded me of riding in Esteban's car.

"Careful on the bumps," my father said. "I don't like the bumps." I could hear his hand moving against the gray vinyl of my seat, as if he were smoothing something out or patting me on the back. As we drove and drove, I didn't paying much attention to where we were going—I was just looking out the window, staring at the bars we passed; the store windows; the people on the sidewalks, walking in clumps; a group of teenagers in front of a neon-blue bar, drinking beer out of a cup that was the size of a giant popcorn container.

We were near my neighborhood, heading to my apartment.

"We have to drop him off," I said abruptly.

Monica looked in the rearview mirror, then glanced at me. What she saw I don't know—I refused to turn around. "He's going to get sick," she said. "You can't leave him." She was about to take a left onto a street near my apartment; there was the tick, tick, tick of the blinker, the green arrow aglow. "And Isabel isn't coming back all night. I know she's not. She's with these guys who will be out all night, all morning. And Celia's in Gijón, right?"

I didn't answer.

My father was silent in the back, as if he wanted to pretend he was unconscious. I knew he was awake, though; I could hear his hand still moving along the back of my seat.

"You can't leave him," Monica said. "You can't let him get sick alone."

Those words reminded me of Harlan all of a sudden, like a sudden sickening wave. Perhaps I was a little drunk, too, as I felt on the brink of tears right then. I thought about how I had left Harlan, left him all alone. I left him in our dark, smoky apartment, stoned and sick. And now I was with my father, silent and distant toward him, as if he were an irritating drunken acquaintance and not a person who once took care of me when I myself felt ill.

Against the movement of Monica's car, against passing street lamps and wind, I remembered, slowly, loosely, feeling very nauseous once when I was in an amusement park with my father. I had been five at the time, and I had gotten the same queasy, uncontrollable feeling my father currently had—but I, of course, hadn't drunk too much, I had eaten too much: popcorn and licorice and ice cream and pizza and some sort of drink that was so red it turned the top of my lip red. Then I got on rides, or really my father let me get on rides, that spun and spun while he watched on, drinking beer from a plastic cup.

When I started to feel sick, he brought me to the big aqua door that was the entrance to the women's restroom, and I told him that he had to come in, I couldn't go alone. I had to argue with him a little, whine. Then he did come in, but he held on to my hand, gripped it hard, as if he believed the women inside would take me away from him once they saw us. We went into the handicapped stall. The floor was cement, unpainted, and it was wet.

Getting sick I didn't really remember; it had been entirely traumatic to me. One of the worst things that ever happened in my life, I later claimed. And what I hated the most, even at the age of five, was the awareness as I left that bathroom that everyone knew I had been sick. There was a line of women, a sudden busy surge. They had listened and they had known and then they looked at me with their terry-cloth visors and their bright blue pants and their giggling children pressed against their legs, and I felt not just embarrassed, but entirely awful—as if I had done something that was unacceptable and wrong.

My father had carried me out of the bathroom, out of the park, through the parking lot. He was not a very strong man, and I was not that small for five, and when we got to the car he was sweating in the early summer heat. In the car, he had me lie down in the backseat, similar to how he was now positioned in Monica's car, except I was smaller and his backseat was bigger and it didn't smell like perfume, it smelled like dirt-stained floor mats and melted plastic and heat.

We did not drive right away. We just stayed out there in the parking lot with all the doors of his silver-blue Buick open. He sat with the driver's seat pushed forward, on the floor of the car. I asked him why people threw up, and he told me it was because there was something bad inside of them that had to get out.

I said, "Something bad?"

He amended his answer: There were "bad guys" who needed to get out—that was the terminology my mother used for germs, "bad guys."

"And if you don't get sick, the bad guys will just sit in your stomach," he told me, and touched my cotton shirt, made a circle with his finger. "You have to get rid of them or the bad guys will take over your stomach. They'll start opening bars and casinos."

I nodded, as if I took this very seriously, and then I laughed—I knew what bars were, and I knew what casinos were from watching the TV show *Vega$*.

"I don't want that," I said, smiling, and he said matter-of-factly, "No, no, you don't." Then we had sat there until the car cooled down, until whatever discomfort I felt—and he felt—drifted.

Once Monica parked out front of my apartment, I led my father by the hand through my building, down a hallway, and into the bathroom. I pulled one of my towels off the rack, folded it in a perfect square, and left it on the corner of the pink sink. I set my toothbrush on top of the towel, first diagonally, then vertically—I was like a nurse setting instruments on a table. My father just stood there stiffly, watching me, and then he sat down on the corner of the bidet, facing the toilet. I stood above him in my three-inch heels, arms folded.

"Do you want a robe?"

He shook his head, said no. He had the slight yellowish look to his face that tan people get when they are sick. His forehead was shiny, his back, from the look of his shirt, was sweaty. He didn't smell like his cologne anymore, or Monica's spilled perfume; he smelled like whiskey, and it was strong, so strong that if you passed him on a subway or in a grocery store aisle, it would hit you as hard as a sudden temperature change, make you veer sharply away.

He touched the doorknob to the bathroom, gestured for me to go outside. I could hear Monica's high heels against the apartment's hardwood floors—she had come in with us—and now she was pacing in the hallway.

"Do you want me to wait outside the door?"

"No," he said. He touched the slight scruff on his neck. "Go talk ta your friend, go play some music." He smiled a sickly smile, one that made his lips look terribly thin and chapped. "I'm OK," he said. "I'm jus' fine."

While my father was in the bathroom, I sat across from Monica on the couch. I put the radio on very low, so low that no matter how fast the songs were, it sounded sad. Every once in a while, beneath the music, there was the sound of the toilet, a loud flush. In the walls, there was also the occasional hissing gurgle of hot water running through pipes to apartments upstairs or perhaps to the sink where my father splashed a bit of water on his face. The flushing was what bothered me though. It seemed, sitting there, that all my life, no matter where I went, that sound would have some pained connotation—it incited a heat, a slight burn, as if it were the very sound, the very roar, of illness.

I thought of Harlan right then. I thought of brightness and fluorescent bathroom light. I thought of his words, "Sing to me, Cath. Sing to me."

The low music was against those thoughts, and I started to cry a little—but my worry for Harlan hadn't brought it out; my father being sick hadn't entirely done it either. It wasn't even the two of them, placed back to back. It was, instead, just a slow, heaping feeling I had, one that made everything seem not just unmanageable, but dizzying, as if I were still on some amusement park ride, the Tilt-A-Whirl perhaps, and everything that was happening kept spinning and spinning.

I sat on the couch feeling like this, my bare feet tucked under me, a tasseled pillow on my lap. Monica was directly across from me, not looking at me, and while I cried, I made sure to do so softly, without breathing differently. I just occasionally touched my face, wiped a tear away, but I did so casually as if she wouldn't notice that I was upset if I just kept my expression relaxed.

"You were supposed to go to Gijón," Monica said after a while, after the third or fourth flush. "Isabel said this weekend you were going to go." She pointed in the direction of the bathroom. "But now no."

"No."

"And Celia's there now?"

"Yeah."

She was playing with a shoelace she had found hanging off the side of a bookshelf. She wrapped it around her finger, let it unravel, then she momentarily stared at the shoelace as if fascinated by its yarnlike fabric. Meanwhile, I stared up at the clock on the wall opposite us—it was almost two o'clock in the morning, but it felt much later, as if morning birds would start to chirp at any moment.

"How long is your father staying?" Monica asked.

"He's been here four days, and he'll be here four more. He leaves Sunday morning."

"Eight days," she said. "That's a long time."

"Yeah." I smiled a bit, embarrassed. Most people could successfully spend eight days with their father.

"Maybe you should take a break," she said. "Maybe . . . you should go to Gijón for a day."

"I can't do that."

"Only a day. What is a day?" She was still looking down at the shoelace, not me. "He will be sick all day tomorrow anyway."

"I can't."

There was the sound of cars beeping outside, of boys with high-pitched voices talking to each other from different sides of the street.

"Maybe he needs a break from you," she said. "Maybe he won't drink so much, get so sick, if you give him a break."

My father came out of the bathroom right then. He had the lavender towel I had given him slung neatly over his shoulder. He was still fully dressed, except for his shoes. He had taken off his shoes and socks, and I knew without looking that they were in the bathroom flung haphazardly in different directions. "Is this where I sleep?" he asked, pointing at my bedroom door, and I nodded, said yeah. He was close enough in the wide doorway to see that I had been crying. He stared at me only one moment longer than he would've if he hadn't noticed, but in that passing stare, I felt the validity of what Monica had just said, I felt the intensity of this entire visit, not just for me, but for him.

"Do you need anything?" I asked as he walked away, my voice soft.

"No, I just have to lie down," he said, turning toward me, but looking at the wall. "I have to rest."

Monica looked at me as he said this, and then after he went in my bedroom, she took the Madrid–Gijón train schedule off the fridge. She must've noticed it while I was in the bathroom with my father, while she somberly paced around the apartment.

Most trains took six to eight hours to get to Gijón; there were four direct trains a day.

"You should just take the eight o'clock train in the morning," Monica said matter-of-factly, as if we had already had a discussion or come to some agreement about my leaving. "I'll take you to the station. Tomorrow," she said. "I'll drop your father at his hotel and take you to the station."

I nodded. I was so tired right then that if she had told me to go to Barcelona for the day or to the park up the street, I would've nodded halfheartedly, too.

"It's just for a day or so," she said to reassure me.

"It's not too awful to leave him?"

"No," she said, and I stared at her as if I thought she might change her mind. "No," she said again.

I nodded.

I woke my father up at five-thirty in the morning. I was packing a bag on the floor while he slept on the bed. He was still fully dressed, the lavender hand towel from the night before still on his shoulder. He hadn't even gotten under the sheets. He must've just slept motionless, his legs straight out like open scissors, his hands alongside of him. When I knew for sure he could hear me, when his eyes fluttered open, I said, "I'm taking the eight o'clock train."

"To work?"

"To Gijón."

"What's that?"

"To where Celia is, where she comes from." I was folding a dress. "I'm only going a day, though. Is a day OK?"

He didn't say anything. He had his hand over his head, as if he were blocking light out, but the shades were still pulled, and only a dull gray light filled the room. At first I thought he might've had his hand on his head because he had a headache, but then it seemed from the way his fingers casually groped his hair that he was checking the positioning of his toupee, which was still perfectly in place.

"You can rest while I'm gone," I said, and put a small perfume bottle I never used into my suitcase. On my bureau, a postcard from Harlan was next to a letter from Felipe, still in its envelope. I considered whether or not my father might've read them. The postcard, I was almost sure, I had taped to the wall with Harlan's other postcards, and Felipe's letter had been in my nightstand.

"Monica stayed over," I said after a minute, after I put the letter and postcard away. "And she's going to give us a ride." My father nodded with his eyes shut, and I could not tell if it was because he was upset or because his head hurt.

"Is it OK that I go?" I asked in the tone that a regular daughter might use with a regular father, one that asked for permission, approval.

He said, "Yeah, I think that's best." Then he sat up. His feet were bare, the pants I had bought for him wrinkled, the shirt unbuttoned only at the sleeves. "And if you don't want to come back before I leave," he said, "you don't have to." He did not say this meanly; he said it tenderly. He said it as he rubbed the scruff that had already set in on his face and neck.

"I'll come back," I said, not looking directly at him, and he nodded, still touching his face and frowning as if he doubted me, as if he thought I was doing to him what he had once done to me.

22

TRADERS

Monica and I dropped my father off first before we went to the train station. He sat in the backseat, his eyes covered by his hand, as if the morning sun were too bright for him, as if it were burning something inside of him. When we got to the Holiday Inn, to the small sign with its green cursive glamour, my father got out, said good-bye to Monica without using her name—I was sure he couldn't remember it—then he waved at me, and I waved back at him. I considered kissing him good-bye on the cheek, but his facial scruff looked as if it might hurt me, might leave a tingling burn.

Afterward Monica and I were silent in the car—neither one of us had slept well. She had slept in Celia's almost child-size twin bed, and I had slept practically sitting up on the couch. I could've gone and slept in Isabel's room, but I didn't know when she was coming home and I didn't want to talk to her when she did. I was a little mad at her. She hadn't come out of Arabia to say good-bye to me when we left, even though she'd known there was something wrong with my father and me. Monica had told me it was because some guy Isabel had an all-consuming crush on was with her, a guy named Sergio, whom I had heard of before. I knew that he spoke French and had the bluest of eyes, but still . . . I thought she should've come out; I thought she should've said something.

I was actually thinking about this, wondering if there was really any validity to my hurt feelings when Monica asked me about Esteban. She wanted to know when I had seen him last. I didn't lie to her as I had the night before. I told her how we had gone to lunch. We were driving down Castellana as she asked me about this, and it reminded me of the numerous times Esteban and I had driven up and down that same street— he seemed to prefer that street, migrate toward it. He could drive fast on Castellana, speed and speed—everything was a straight direct line, no rotaries, no turns. Just wind.

"Do you know what Esteban does?" I asked Monica.

"What do you mean?"

"For a living?"

"He doesn't work."

I waited. Then I said, delivering it almost as a joke, "I think he's a pimp."

"What's a pimp?" she said pronouncing it peemp, not pimp.

"You don't know what a pimp is?"

"No."

"How can you know English so perfectly and not know what a pimp is?"

She didn't say anything.

"*Pimp* is an important word."

"What's a *peemp*?"

"It's a guy who sells women. It's a prostitute's boss, sort of. He gets a percentage or a special amount or, I don't know, I don't know what a pimp gets. I've never met a pimp before, not a real one."

"So you think Esteban is a *peemp*?" she said. She was smiling, not looking at me but out the windshield, and there was something in that smile that made me feel as if Esteban were a notorious pimp and I was complete moron for even asking.

"So is he one?" I asked.

She shook her head. "You like to make things more exciting than they really are, don't you?" She glanced at me. "You have that problem; nothing is as simple as it is. I have a friend like you, and he thinks that walking across the street isn't walking across the street, it's saving his life. Everything is do or die." She paused, checking the English expression, "That's what you guys say, 'do or die,' right?"

"Yeah."

"Do you know who that friend is? The one who acts like that?"

Before I could ask, she said, "Esteban . . . and," she added after a pause, "I think, I think," her voice got louder, more agitated, "I think he thinks that if he helps you out, then he can save that boyfriend of his a thousand kilometers away. I think he thinks that. He's not a *peemp*, he's not a peemp at all." She glanced at me. She had no makeup on, just sunglasses. On the bottom of her chin, there was a scar that I normally wouldn't have noticed. It was short but had definitely involved stitches—it brought to mind the vision of her as a kid falling off monkey bars and landing face first on cement.

"I know about that guy though," she said, and smiled. She was talking about Borja. "I know all about him." She waited, as if she thought I might say something, but I didn't. I just sat there. "Esteban thinks he's helping you," she said. "But he's not helping you just to help you. He's a trader." She glanced at me again. "A trader with God."

I frowned, looked at her sideways.

"And he thinks if he is good to you—he likes you, I'm not saying he doesn't like you, because he does—but he thinks if he fixes, helps you." She looked at me. "He thinks there's something wrong with you. I told him about your frigidity problem—"

"WHAT?"

"Yes," she said matter-of-factly, "you are frigid."

"Oh, *really?*"

"Well, what about Paco?"

She was talking about that guy we had gotten into a fight about in Esteban's bathroom, but at this early-morning moment, I could hardly even remember who or what Paco was, he was just an unappealing blur. "I am *not* frigid," I said. "I just find many men repelling. There's a difference."

"Well, I told him anyway," she said, shaking her head. "I told Esteban all about it, and like I said, he's a *trader*."

"A drug trader?" I thought maybe she was translating things wrong.

"No, he's a trader. The way I just explained it to you."

"A trader with God?"

"Yes," she said, "and so he found you someone who would take care of you without . . . That guy has his own frigidity problem or, I don't know, something close to it." She curled her lip up as she said this, as if such a condition was as repugnant as having insects crawl all over her. "He has very little power right now," she said, and I didn't initially know whether she was referring to Borja or Esteban or Juan, or maybe even God, but then it was clear that she was talking about Esteban once she added, "He cannot do anything else to help Juan."

We were quiet after that, and the word *Juan* seemed to be drifting around the car, even the way her voice had dropped a little when she said his name lingered. Even though neither of us had ever met him, she had said his name with such familiarity, as if he were a friend of ours, as if he talked with us all the time, as if we had a clear mental picture of how he held a coffee cup, or stared off, or casually touched the edge of a tabletop.

I said, "So wait . . . you're trying to say that Esteban thinks in setting me up with Borja that he's going to cure his boy of leukemia."

"Leukemia?" she said, and glanced at me, the lines on her forehead deepening. She waited a minute, as if she were debating telling me something—which temporarily made me think that Juan had some other disease, something Esteban didn't want to mention, something far worse—but then Monica shook her head, as if she had made a silent decision to herself, and then she returned to the central idea, the idea that Esteban was trying to cure Juan with Borja and me. "No, don't be stupid," she said. "He doesn't *think* that. He doesn't *know* he thinks that, but *I* think that's what he thinks. Why else would he pay so much attention to you?

"People do that," Monica continued. "They act like they like people, like they are being good, but they aren't really being good, they're just trying to get something. They're traders." Whether she made up that term or translated it from something in Spanish, I didn't know, but I kept thinking of that concept as we drove down Paseo del Prado, past the museum and the park and the devil statue somewhere off in the distance.

"Do you want me to go into the station with you?" Monica asked.

"I can figure it out."

"It's big."

"I can see that."

As we approached, the train station looked in the distance like a space station from the outside, with its giant gray shell of a roof—and the closer we got, the more it looked like a giant circus tent made out of metal.

"I'll go in with you," Monica insisted. "You'll get lost. You'll miss your train."

I said, shrugging, "If you want . . . " and then I thought about how she herself was being entirely too nice to me. She had called Celia's house for me, talked to her mother, told her I was coming. She had called the train station despite the schedule—she insisted on checking the times. "This is Spain," she said, "You have to check everything or they'll fuck you."

I almost had her call Carlos for me, had her tell him I wasn't coming to work, that I was sick. But that seemed sort of childish, so I called him myself and he was fine with it, almost pleased. He said, *"Bueno, bueno. No pasa nada."* And then in English, "I'm very busy anyway."

Meanwhile, as I dealt with Carlos, Monica was in the kitchen making coffee for my father and me—I could hear the clink of spoons and plates, the opening and closing of the metal lid on the coffeepot, yet I did not question at the time why she was being so nice. I was too tired. I just liked it and wanted it to be that way.

"Why are you being so nice to me?" I asked Monica later, after we had bought my train ticket and we were sitting in a café in the station. I had had in total three cups of Spanish coffee that morning, which meant that despite my tiredness, I had become suddenly aggressive, jumpy. If I had started grinding my teeth or trying to race people across the station, it would've seemed strange or unusual.

"What do you mean, be nice to you?" she said, and lifted her sunglasses, which were very yellow, very Gucci, off her face. It was bright in the station, almost like a greenhouse even though the windows weren't that big; it was the fact that they were so high up near the domed ceiling, that the light came pouring in, flooding a whole suitcase-carrying world with sun and heat.

"Are you trading?" I said. "Are you trying to get something by being nice to me?"

"There's nothing to get from being nice to you."

"In trading it doesn't matter. You can be nice to a bug."

"Maybe I'm being nice to you for Esteban," she said, and in her face, in the way her lips tightened and her eyes got more intense, I felt a certain overwhelming concern emanate from her; it was as if she believed Esteban was in great danger, and you could see that danger particularly in her eyes; it was not that her eyes changed shape or even that they developed a sudden flicker of glassiness—there was none of that—it was simply her gaze, it contained more power, more light, as if she could move objects on the table with the intensity of what she felt and feared.

It made me a bit uncomfortable to be able to read all of this on her face. It was as if everything had become suddenly dramatic, and I was so sick of that, so sick of it from the night before. I picked up her Gucci glasses, put them on. I looked around the station at all the palm trees and the dark green vines that wound around the wide tree trunks. The center of the station was filled with trees and ferns and other odd-looking plants that had brown designs on the leaves. Even the table at which we sat was supposed to look as if it were made from bamboo, as if we were in Africa or Bora Bora or anywhere, really, that wasn't Madrid. There were even birds chirping overhead, although they weren't real birds—it was a just soundtrack of some kind—yet if you closed your eyes beneath a pair of sunglasses, if your caffeinated heartbeat suddenly slowed, it almost seemed as though you were already somewhere else, as if you had already begun your trip.

$$\overline{23}$$

GETTING TO FELIPE

Unlike Madrid, Gijón is the type of place where, once you arrived, you knew nothing bad could happen to you. You could feel it in the car ride parallel to the boardwalk, where the waves crashed against rocks, came up over the railing, sprinkled the cement tiles of the boardwalk. There was wind, too, the kind you could never find in July in Madrid—I could see the wind in the people walking along the beach, in their hair moving across their faces, in the way their shirts billowed.

Celia had picked me up with her mother at the train station. It took them a while to find me, and while I waited I sat in the bright sunlit train station with no sense of panic about when or how they would find me. It was as if I could've just stayed there for a day or two, staring. When they found me, waving at me, I noticed Celia's mother first—she looked like a girlfriend of Celia's, not her mom. She had on a green dress that was long and linen, strapless. Her shoulders were tan, her makeup careful around her eyes, a golden yellow eye shadow on her lids. She was wearing a shade of coral lipstick that looked bright against her skin, against the dress, against the bright sun outside. She kissed me on each cheek once she met me and then she squeezed my hand momentarily, said, *"¡Qué chica tan guapa! ¡Qué chica!"*

I smiled a little—I was so tired that my face actually felt sore as if pressure had been applied to my eyes, my cheeks, the delicate bones along my jawline. But it still felt nice for her to compliment me—as we left the train station, I walked closer to her than I normally would've. That was the secret intelligence of older Spanish women: They knew the minds of girls just a little bit better than anyone else. They knew to smile at you once they met you; they knew to touch your arm; they knew to tell you something nice about yourself—something *physically* nice about yourself. It was the quickest and perhaps most powerful way to instill a comfort between the two of you—it erased any worry, any potential cattiness; it was a calm, subtle ease.

"¿Te gusta España?" Celia's mother asked me, touching my arm. Do you like Spain?

"Me encanta España," I said, which literally meant: It enchants me—although in practice it had a less dramatic meaning: I like it so much. Celia's mother liked that response—it was as if I had just expressed warmth toward her and not for the country in which she lived. In the car, she glanced at me occasionally in the rearview mirror as I looked out the window in the backseat. I was a little paranoid that she thought there was something strange about me, but she told me she thought I had an ethereal face. Celia's mother, I had forgotten, was a painter, and Isabel had mentioned once that their mother was always staring at people, trying to picture them as other things. I recognized the word *etérea* in Spanish only because it was close enough to English, *ethereal,* and as Celia's mother said it, she had made the gesture of a halo around her head.

I smiled at her again, said, *"Gracias,"* and then we drove and drove.

Out the window, I watched the boardwalk unfold around us with its palm trees and giant numbered signs that said: LA PLAYA DE SAN LORENZO. Above the boardwalk's benches there were awnings that blocked out the sun, let people read their newspapers without squinting. A man was painting a bench, and I watched while we were stopped at a light as a seagull came over and he gently swatted it away. Even the street lamps had some sort of calm to them: They had no rust and were white, their tops a bright silver.

"We are almost home," Celia told me once we passed the boardwalk, turned down a street away from it. For the rest of the ride we were quiet, or maybe it seemed so because I was in such a daze. I was so tired—the coffee I drank at the train station had kept me from slipping into a sleep that actually mattered. I had energy only to stare out the window, to worry in a soft way that wasn't that uncomfortable.

I didn't know what Monica had told Celia on the phone—about my coming and leaving my father. I heard only part of the conversation, during which Monica told her I was coming, and there were a lot of *sís* and *nos* on her end, which I suppose answered specific questions. But Celia hadn't asked me anything about my father since they picked me up; she had only smiled at me, touched my shoulder once, and it occurred to me only as we pulled into their driveway that that was perhaps why her mother had been so eager to tell me how nice I looked, how angelic—it was as if she were trying to tell me: You have done nothing wrong.

Once we finally got into their house, they let me sleep. The bed I slept in was a twin bed, hard, and the room itself felt cold, as if it were in the cellar and not upstairs on the second floor. The pillows on the bed were smaller and thinner than regular ones, and they smelled strange, like tea leaves or mint mixed with something sweet. Nevertheless, I slept and slept, and when I dreamed I did not have images of anything. It was comfortable and black.

When I woke up from my nap, Felipe was downstairs sitting in the darkened kitchen waiting for me. When Celia first woke me up, told me he was waiting, it seemed too soon, like a sudden invasion. She said, *"El está, él está. Tu amor."* She was sitting on the edge of my bed, her hair no longer loose the way it had been at the train station—now it was held up in a complicated twist that probably had taken the whole two hours I had been sleeping for her, or her mother, to create. With all her hair swept off her face like that, her nose looked like a kid's nose, so small and fragile.

"Francisco's on his way," she told me. "But Felipe . . . he's already here." Then she smiled a smile that was very steady, soft. It was as if in her mind she were presenting me with a gift.

"*¿Estás lista?*"—Are you ready?—she asked me.

I nodded even though I could have slept for another two hours. I told her I was going to go to the bathroom and then I would come out, meet Felipe.

"He's been waiting for an hour."

I nodded but didn't smile. His insistence, his dedication to meeting me, made me feel as if he had already put together who I was. Sitting in the silence of the empty house, all there was for him to listen to were the sounds of things overhead, the creaking of floorboards, of a door opening and shutting, then nothing—just a distant dog barking, constant and nagging. Amongst all these sounds, he probably waited for voices, particularly the sound of mine, a voice he already thought he knew—he heard it saying things to him, heard it talking in its American way, a broken, self-conscious Spanish. My voice, its pitch, probably sounded like a version of Celia's slightly raspy voice, since she was the one who told him about me and the little things I said.

Downstairs, amongst the unsteady barking outside, the barely audible tick of the grandfather clock, he already knew what color I would be wearing, the cut of my collar, the way my neck would look against it; he knew the way I'd sit across from him, the look of my hands on the table, the way my palms would feel if he were to reach out and touch them. All the details, descriptions, and stories Celia had given him only strengthened his visions, gave him a smaller, clearer window through which to imagine. I became beauty, perfection, the miraculous thing he had been long awaiting, and not just in that kitchen, but during dispassionate kisses on doorsteps, against the clatter of parties and talking and music, amongst dreariness and happiness, amongst car rides and wind, amongst everything and anything, I had always been there—unformed though, not entirely physical. Until now.

After Celia went downstairs to tell him I would be coming down, I took an extra, extra long time in the bathroom. In the mirror, I made a thorough investigation of my face. My skin was blotchy, a little sun-burned from walking around so much the past few days with my father. I put on a bit of powder, some lip gloss. I brushed my teeth. I looked at myself from the side. I put my hair up in a ponytail with an elastic I had around my wrist, then took it back down, reparted my hair, and sat down on the corner of the tub. I looked at a shampoo bottle and read in Spanish what it did for you. I learned a new word, *emolientes*, emollients.

Twenty minutes later, I came down, my slippers slapping loudly on the marble staircase. They were in the living room. They were having coffee. My cup was on the tray, waiting for me. The tray was flowered, the cup white, my saucer blue. I concentrated on these items when I first walked into the room, as if the sight of them might tranquilize me, make me feel all right. I did, of course, look at Felipe but it was a quick darting look as if we were across a room in a bar and I was trying to avoid his glance, keep him from coming over. He had brown hair, parted to the side. It had a slight messiness to it, a waviness that I liked—most Spanish boys I'd met had untouchable stiff-looking hair that looked drawn on. His lips were nice, too; they were fuller than mine, a deeper shade, and his eyes were easy and calm, boyish. When he kissed me on each cheek, his hands on my shoulders were extra warm, as if he had just held them in front of a radia-tor or perhaps before the rising steam of his coffee cup.

He asked me if I was tired. I said no.

He asked me if I was hungry. I said no.

He asked me if I missed the United States. I said no.

He asked if I wanted to go out later, to a bar. I said *sí*.

Celia's boyfriend, Francisco, came in shortly after that, and I kissed him on each cheek. He was much taller than me, and he had a crew cut. He held his coffee in both hands when Celia gave it to him. His hands seemed too big to be Spanish hands—they looked German or Russian. He had wide nails and long fingers—the hands of someone who could throw things or fix things with ease. I don't know why I was paying so much attention to his hands. I suppose it made me less nervous, kept me from looking at Felipe's hands, kept me from staring awkwardly down at my own.

Francisco started telling us a story about getting his car fixed. Celia interrupted him, put her hand on my knee, and explained that he had just gotten his car fixed that day, that was why he was a little late. I nodded. Francisco smiled momentarily, and then kept talking. He was the type of storyteller who mimicked other people's voices—he didn't use tags like he said or she said to differentiate who was speaking, he just changed the pitch of his voice—he showed stupidity and anger and nervousness through a combination of his face, his voice and the way he moved his hands. I suppose I only noticed this because he wasn't speaking in my language, and sometimes he spoke so fast, used so many swears, that I lost pieces of it, but then because he was so animated, I still figured things out. If he looked at me, I still nodded and if Felipe laughed, I laughed, and if Celia let out a gasp, I did, too.

"*Catherine, entiendes todo, ¿no?*" Francisco asked me at the end of his story. He was touching my shoulder.

I said, "*Sí, sí.* I understand everything."

He looked at Felipe, told him I was really Spanish and not American. He said I was a Spanish princess. Then he leaned over and started touching Celia's chin. "*Como Celia.*"

They started making out after that. They were both on the flowered couch and Felipe was all the way to the left, sitting in front of me. I was in a chair. Felipe and I drank our coffee. It was now cold and I hadn't put any sugar in it so it tasted worse. I sipped though; I smiled. I looked at different objects in the room as if I had to memorize them.

"Do you like the beach?" Felipe asked me abruptly, in very careful English.

I said yes.

"OK, OK," he said.

That was as far as our conversation went.

In the late afternoon I went for a walk on the beach with Felipe, but before that we had driven around a while with Celia and Francisco, Felipe and me in the backseat; and then we walked together, the four of us, through a park that was full of roaming loose peacocks. They were all over the cement benches or appearing behind greenish yellow bushes, their heads the size of a child's fist, their necks moving unsteadily, bobbing along while their entire plume dragged behind them.

"Do you like royal turkeys?" Felipe asked me in English—royal turkeys was the literal translation for peacocks, *pavos reales.*

"Yes," I said with a smile, "I love royal turkeys."

This was our odd way of communicating, a mix of Spanish and English, which was sometimes a bit incorrect, but it kept us equal, on par with each other.

We walked by ourselves on the beach, only after Celia asked if I was OK, *cómoda*—comfortable—and I said *sí.* Our walk was right as the seven o'clock sun started to lose its glare, but it was not some cheesy romance book moment; there were lots of kids still on the beach splashing one another and growling and throwing small rocks and shells at one another while their parents called out their names from beach blankets: Aná, Manuel, Barbara, Hector, Ramón. Even a little blond-haired Borja crossed our path, his mother shouting his name from nearby, and then she screamed, *"¡Comportáte!"* Behave.

During all of this, Felipe asked abruptly in Spanish, "Do you like children?"

I shook my head, answered honestly, "No."

He smiled, seemed to think that that was funny. "You are still young," he said.

I shook my head. "I am still smart."

As we walked, he occasionally bumped into me. I was on the side by the water and he had to stumble around sand castles and plastic pails to stay alongside of me. I had on a long black skirt, and he had his pants rolled up a little. We were both getting a little wet, but the water was warm, and the splashing children seemed to keep their distance.

"Do you like Spain?" he asked after a minute, again abrupt—as if he had thought of the question, then wasn't sure about it but then decided to ask it anyway.

I gave my standard response. *"Sí, sí. Me encanta España."*

He smiled happily at this, smiled with the same brightness that Celia's mother had expressed, the same brightness that all of the Spanish seemed suddenly to take on once I said I liked Spain. They smiled so openly, so intensely. It was as if I had just said in code that I liked them, adored them, wanted to live with them, be with them forever.

Such a response I didn't entirely understand, as I didn't necessarily get upset if one of Celia or Isabel's friends told me they had visited the United States and didn't like it. Celia once said, "I suppose the United States is just so big, it's so giant that it must be hard." She frowned. "It must be hard to feel like all of it is yours."

I thought about her saying that sometimes. I even thought about it a bit while I walked on the beach with Felipe, while we talked our strange mix of Spanish and English, while the water that he explained "went on to France" washed across my feet. The children's voices were low then, distant against the sound of waves and wind. One of the beach umbrellas we were passing had Coca-Cola written all over it—it looked like one of the umbrellas that went over a café table, but now it was tilted on its side and two teenage boys who were chewing gum sat under it on the bare sand.

"But even if you like it here," Felipe said, and paused, "do you miss home?" He had started the question in English and ended it in Spanish.

I shook my head no—this was the third time he asked me if missed home. He had asked me at Celia's house, then he had alluded to it again when we were walking amongst the peacocks. "Why do you keep asking me that?" I said.

He cocked his head toward me, as if he were looking at my face, but he wasn't, he was looking past me at the distant line where the ocean met the sky. "You just seem very serious," he said, shrugging. "Like you miss something."

I nodded. *"Soy seria, "*—I am serious. Then I added, as if it were a joke, *"Muy, muy seria."*

He smiled at that, and we kept walking, and then he said softly in English, a minute or two later, "Catherine is serious."

———————

Later that night—after I went home and changed, after Celia made me try on four different dresses, including one of hers and one of her mother's—we went out with Felipe and Francisco to a bar called Casa de Catalina. Catalina is the Spanish equivalent for the name Catherine. "It's your house," Felipe had said when we first walked in. He pointed at the lettering on the door. "This is Catherine's house," he said again, and touched my back—I had on a thin dress, and I could feel his hand, the shape of it. Against the loud music of the bar, he had to lean in when he spoke to me, and in the dim lighting, his face, the scent of his cologne, the way a certain dimple formed in the corner of his mouth—all of it was marked with a certain unavoidable feeling. It sent certain small-winded fantasies through me, certain visions.

On the beach walking next to him I had not felt like this—it was not entirely easy for me to feel attracted to someone, never simple. He had said earlier that day while we sat on a beach bench waiting for Celia and Francisco, "Sometimes it is very hard to talk to people you don't know at all—he pronounced "at all" the way Maureen did, "a tall." "It is hard because you have an entire pool of things about you"—I smiled at the word *pool*—"and I have an entire pool of things about me, and you do not know which ones to pick, the deeper ones or the . . . the . . . other ones. *¿Entiendes lo que digo?"* Do you understand what I am saying?

I nodded, said, *"Sí,"* then smiled.

I was starting to like how oddly we talked to each other, and I was starting to like just walking around and being seen with him. As we first walked through Casa de Catalina together, a lot of his guy friends thought I was his newfound girlfriend, and they whispered in his ear, hit him in the back, pretended to ring his neck. He didn't quite make eye contact with them; he just smiled.

He was also the star of his small group of friends because he was the only who could pour the *sidra* quite right—*sidra* is a light-green cider that has a natural frothiness to it, particularly when you pour it from a certain angle into a glass. In my Spanish books in high school they always showed the especially skilled waiters who could pour the bottle of *sidra* behind their backs, with the wine-size bottle in one hand way up high and the glass way down low. There was an art of some kind to it, and Felipe could pour from the highest, blindest angle. "I was once a waiter," he told me in English, and one of his friends who also spoke English said, "But Catherine, do you really like men who wait?"

In addition to all of this, we also had the great fortune of meeting a girl in that bar, one who inspired in me a hideous cattiness. Her name was Silvia. From the moment I entered the room, sat in the wooden chair at the long table next to her, she stared at me in a way that I had never noticed a grown-up woman do. As a thirteen-year-old waiting in a line at an ice cream parlor, I might've seen another strange thirteen-year-old looking at me this way, but not since. It was the look of someone who immediately did not like me, and would never grow to like me, simply because of the way I looked. In appearance she herself looked quite sweet—once she let go of certain menacing facial expressions. She was short and petite, with a matching petite face. Her lips were full of shine, her eyes carefully done up, her smile flashy and white.

When Celia introduced me to her, we did this weird motion in which we pretended to kiss cheeks, but it was more like I was kissing air, or perhaps her big hoop earrings. I don't think she knew at first glance that I was an American, but within moments it was made clear by my accent, by the r's that didn't always roll off my tongue as perfectly as I wanted them to. After that, she disliked me with more ease, as if my foreignness made it all the more OK.

"¿Por qué estás aquí?" she asked me once I sat down next to her. Why are you here?

I took *here* to mean Spain. I said, "I have an internship through my university." Then my Spanish started to make me stammer a little. I had to pause before I could add, *"En Madrid tengo una practica con una empresa."*

"She only works a few days," Celia added, "and then she gets to do whatever she wants." She was smiling as she said this, as if I lived the dreamiest of lifestyles.

Silvia did not smile. She said, "You go to a university?" and cocked her head to the side, as if this were perhaps a lie.

I said, *"Sí, Boston University."*

"You mean you don't go to Harvard or Yale?"

At first I didn't understand what she was saying because she pronounced Harvard without the H and Yale "Yall." Then, when I did understand her, I just shrugged.

She raised her eyebrows. "You don't know why you don't go there?" She stared at me as if she were waiting for me to admit that I wasn't smart enough to get into such schools. I shrugged again and looked at Celia, who wasn't paying attention to the conversation; she was watching Francisco try to pour a glass of *sidra* with the same elegance as his cousin. Meanwhile Felipe had just come and stood behind my chair. Over the music and the chatter he couldn't hear Silvia and me talk, but he seemed to notice in the way she looked around the room, sitting across from me, that something was wrong. He asked me about it a half hour later—when we were no longer sitting with her, but were on the other side of the narrow, thin room.

"Spanish women," he said to me in English, "they envy."

I shrugged. "But she's very pretty. What does she envy?"

He smiled at me as if I had said something very sweet. "They envy."

For the remainder of the night, I kept catching Silvia looking at me, not all the time, but often enough. At first I pretended not to notice, but pretending just allowed her to stare longer, and within that long stare I came to see what she envied—within the soft, simple set of my face she saw someone on vacation. She saw someone in a long white dress that looked more expensive than it was, like something I might've picked up one leisurely day when I did nothing but collect shopping bags in my arms while men smiled at me, opened doors for me, told me I was *preciosa.*

The more I drank, the more aware I became of her. Amongst her stares, amongst her glares, I became a little obnoxious, a little more self-confident. I smiled back at her, not a mean smile, but the type a child often gives, a smile of someone who is innocent and knows nothing and is happy. When she came over to ask someone for *fuego*, a light for her cigarette, I paid her three compliments. I told her I liked her sandals and her handbag and her lip gloss. I was purposely annoying her with kindness, and Felipe recognized that. He said in my ear, "There is something mean about Catherine Kelly."

He was entertained by the two of us though, and his shyness was slowly leaving him. Perhaps it was because he was drunk or because it was near midnight and the room had gotten a bit dimmer; in any case, he started to help me irritate Silvia. He became the enamored boyfriend who kissed my hand, rubbed my shoulder, touched the tips of my hair. Then he'd say, with his lips almost closed, "Is she looking?"

And along with his playful forthrightness came my own. I touched him back. Something I may not have done without Silvia. She was our excuse, our magical reason, to fall gigglishly into each other's arms. I even caught Celia's glance at one point, and she smiled a big wide smile that made her lips take up half of her face. She was very, very pleased—in that way that some people get when they think they have intuited something, when they believe for a moment or two that they have paranormal powers.

Meanwhile, Silvia sat in a corner still watching me periodically. I could feel her gaze without looking, but I tried to ignore her, forget her. In a corner, away from her, Felipe and I kissed and kissed so long, so deep, that in my mind we were not in that bar, but instead back in Celia's living room, back to the moment we first saw each other, and I was kissing him without hearing his voice, without letting him hear my own.

Whenever we stopped, took a rest, Felipe moved his shoulders awkwardly, took a sip of his drink—he didn't exactly look at me but at the wooden wall behind me. It was as if he didn't know how to act, as if he were eleven, and that pleased me. I liked to know that I could put someone out of sorts.

It was only when we had become a bit tired, when we no longer wanted to drink or stand in that smoke-filled room, that I caught my last glance of Silvia. I had just said good-bye to Celia and Francisco. Felipe was going to give me a ride to her parents' house. I suppose it looked as if we were leaving together, were about to fall under some crisp white summer sheets all alone. Standing near the doorway with Felipe, I looked up and saw Silvia—she was not looking at us, but in the set of her face I knew she had been. She was looking at a picture on the wall, the kind where you can see your own reflection if you stare distantly enough. The picture was an old 1930s ad for Coca-Cola, a blond woman smiling. I stared and stared at her, felt Felipe's hand on my shoulder, and it was then that I felt a certain sympathy, a certain sadness, for Silvia, as if she weren't some unpleasant stranger, but instead a black-haired Spanish version of myself.

I sat with Felipe for about two hours outside Celia's house. We sat on her front steps, listening to the sound of music far off, slight guitar notes coming out of an open window. We talked mostly, without touching, as if we were suddenly afraid of each other now that we were out of the bar and alone.

At one point while I was laughing at something, he touched my face with the back of his hand—something I normally did not permit. Kissing on the lips was one thing, but, touching my face another. To some, this may not make sense; the lips are, after all, part of the face, but in my mind, the face was separate from the body, a higher entity. It wasn't just a physical piece of you, it was your very identity—and to let just anyone come along, press his fingertips against that, was worse than being naïve, it seemed downright stupid.

But Felipe was different. He was allowed. He touched my face delicately, hesitantly—and it felt good and careful and slow. I didn't look at him as he did so; I looked ahead of me, although I leaned into him. I could smell his skin and the fabric softener of his shirt. "Are you happy you came?" he asked.

I listened to the music in the distance, paused, and then said, *"Por supuesto."* Of course.

After Felipe left, I called my father. I used the phone in Celia's kitchen. It was dark, only the light above the sink was on, and as I dialed I had to position myself at an angle so that I could see all my calling card numbers.

I wasn't sure my father would be in his room, but then he answered, said, "Hola, who's this?"

"Me."

"Oh, hi."

He was drunk. There were two ways to tell he was drunk: either from his slurred speech or simply in the way he spaced out words, the way he breathed. I could hear the TV in the background. It was on loud, and a newscaster's voice was talking; then there was a sound similar to roaring race cars.

"What are ya doing?" I asked with the voice of someone who is talking to a child.

"Watching TV."

"You didn't go out?"

"I was at the pool earlier. I'm really tan now," he said. "So tan."

"Oh, yeah?"

"I am olive."

This, I presumed, meant olive-skinned. I said, "Great." Then, I paused. "And where's Maureen?" I halfheartedly wanted him to say he had been going out with her, that she had become his new tour guide.

"She left," he said, "the two of them, Maureen and Doreen, checked out." The other one's name was Doria, not Doreen, but I didn't say so. "I've been by the pool," he said, as if he hadn't told me that before.

"You sound tired," I said, "Do you want me to let you go?"

"No." He waited. "Are you having fun where you are?"

I said yeah—pronouncing it as if I were questioning it, as if I wasn't sure. Only five minutes before, Felipe asked me to stay another day in Gijón, but I hadn't really given him an answer. He knew that my father was still in Madrid—although he had said absolutely nothing about it all day. He seemed to know not to. I was sure Celia had informed him that my father and I were having difficulties. What kind of difficulties she described were probably more generic than the real thing—I had told her nothing, and I trusted that Monica had told her very little, too. She probably just told him how my parents were divorced or how my father hadn't called me in the first few weeks that I had arrived. To her, those things were a major oddity. And that was probably an oddity to Felipe, too, which was perhaps why he put up with how quiet I often became that day—he may have even found my quietness endearing and fragile, full of "seriousness."

"What's it like, where you are?" my father asked me abruptly, after we were silent a bit.

I told him Gijón was a beach town, just like Rye Beach, where he lived, except it was sort of a city, too—there were shops and restaurants and theaters that didn't get boarded up in the winter. "They have Coca-Cola here, also," I told him. "Lots of Coca-Cola." It was everywhere, worse than Madrid: on umbrellas and hanging off grocery store signs, on the walls of buildings, on the sides of paper cups that rolled haphazardly out of trash cans, on the backs of white plastic chairs.

"You can stay longer, you know," my father said, interrupting me while I was talking, rambling on about the Coca-Cola signs. Then he added, "Take as much as you can." Whether he meant I should take as much as I could of him, or that I should take advantage of my time in Gijón, I couldn't tell. I told him that I was thinking of staying a little longer. I suppose maybe he knew that somehow, knew that was why I was calling. "But I'll call you tomorrow," I told him, "and I'll let you know when I'm coming back."

"Take as much as you can."

We were quiet after that, just the race car noises on the television in his room. Their revving engines didn't have their usual angry sound though; they were instead dull and draining. I had to hang up right then. I said quickly, "OK. All right. I'll talk to you later, OK?"

"OK," he said, and I nodded and put the phone down, let it click.

I spent the next day at the beach with Felipe; then during siesta, we drove back to his parents' house for lunch. I met his little brother in the front yard. He introduced himself as Juan Carlos, which seemed a rather regal name for such a small child wearing a red-and-white-striped shirt. When introduced, he leaned over like a grown gentleman and kissed me on each cheek. He had the kind of eyelashes that were so thick, so black, that he looked from a distance as if he were wearing eyeliner, and his hair was a shade that did not match his eyelashes or his black eyebrows; it was a dark sandy blond.

"You are the American," he said to me in Spanish.

I said *sí.*

"I do not trust Americans," he said slowly, with an air about him as if in his mind we were suddenly in a movie and he was a Spanish corporal. "You will have to pass a few tests before we can have you in our house."

Felipe told him to shut up and stop acting weird. *"No estás en una película hoy."* You are not in a movie today.

Once we got past his brother and went in the house, we separated—I took a shower and changed out of my beach clothes in one bathroom while Felipe did the same in another. It felt a little bit awkward getting ready in his house. I didn't want to come out with my hair wet and dripping, but I didn't want to be a beauty queen primping and blow-drying my hair while they waited. I opted not to wash my hair, just tie it up, but then I seemed to be ready too soon. Felipe was taking a shower in the other bathroom, and I didn't want to be alone in the kitchen with his mother. I had already met her when we first came in. She was short and small-boned, and she seemed to walk with careful guarded steps. Her hair was shoulder-length and black, with some lighter streaks, and she pulled it behind her ears over and over as she spoke. She exuded a strange distant warmth toward me—the type my mother's friends often gave me when we stumbled upon them in a mall or a grocery store. It was a passing warmth, I suppose, a warmth that she knew didn't have to last.

To avoid being alone with her, I waited an extra while in the bathroom, sat on the edge of the tub. Juan Carlos was outside the door. I could hear his footsteps, even his breathing, which was very audible in the still silence of the house. After a while he started softly knocking, or really patting, on the door. He kept saying in a low voice: *¿Qué haces?* What are you doing?

"Mi dedo puede verte." My finger can see you. *"Tiene una cámara,"* he added after a minute. It has a camera. "Why are you hiding in the bathroom?" Juan Carlos asked me after he had put his finger camera away from the bottom of the door.

"I'm not hiding," I told him. "I'll be out in a minute."

"You don't have to worry," he told me. *"La policía se ha ido"*—the police have left. I opened the door. "My mother told them you weren't here." He was standing with his hands on his knees, his eyes looking up at me so that he made me feel outlandishly tall. He walked with me down the hall to the kitchen, the floor making a creaking sound with each step we took. "My mother told the police you were gone," he said. *"Mi madre miente muy bien."* My mother lies very well.

"¿Que dices?"—What are you saying—his mother asked, hearing him.

"Que mientes bien." That you lie well. He looked at me. *"Ella miente mucho, casi siempre."* She lies all time, almost always.

"I lie," she said in Spanish, looking at me, "when I say I have a nice son who behaves." She touched Juan Carlos on the chin, made him squeal. "I have a nice son who doesn't shut up." She shook her head, smiled at him, as he waved his finger camera at her; then she looked up at me, asked me if I liked something, but I didn't know what the something was. I knew she was referring to whatever she was making for lunch, and I knew that it was fish from the smell that emanated throughout the house, along with the sound of oil spattering on the stove. I said, *"Sí, sí,"* as if I readily recognized the name of the fish, as if it were my favorite.

Felipe came into the kitchen only a few minutes later, after I had sat down in a wooden chair, ankles crossed. His hair was wet and he had on a gray T-shirt, his face more tan than before. He touched my arm, sat down next to me. He smelled like soap and toothpaste and then a little bit of cologne, a kind of cologne that was an older man's type, perhaps his father's.

His father was actually supposed to come home from work for lunch, but his mother told us he had called while we were showering and said

he couldn't come. This didn't seem to surprise Felipe or annoy him, but
Juan Carlos, as we ate, put his finger in the middle of his father's empty
salad bowl and said, looking at me, *"Mi padre no es un padre muy bueno."*
My father is not a very good father.

I thought Felipe would get mad, or at least his mother, but the two of
them just nodded and continued eating their salads. "And why is that?"
Felipe's mother asked, casually. She looked at me, smiled as if she
wanted me to see it was all something not to be taken seriously. "What
has your father done to you?"

"He is not here," he said. "He is not here to protect us from the
American spy." He pointed at me. "She wants to blow up the house." He
was smiling as he spoke, as if everything to him was a big imaginary
joke. "But I will be the one to stop her."

We continued eating. I smiled. Felipe smiled. His mother took a sip
of water.

"The bomb is in the bathroom," Juan Carlos continued, "hidden in
the wall."

"Do you like the fish?" Felipe's mother asked me.

I had just taken my first bite. I said, *"Sí, sí."*

"She has never had a fish before," Juan Carlos said without looking
up from his plate. "They don't have fish in the United States."

"They only have monsters," he added after a dramatic pause. "Sea
monsters."

"Yes," I said in Spanish, laughing a little. "We do have a lot of
monsters."

Felipe nudged me, told me his brother had been reading a lot about
Cristóbal Colón—Christopher Columbus. Felipe stared at Juan Carlos as
he said this, and you could see in his eyes that he greatly appreciated his
brother, as if Juan Carlos was always and forever the entertaining life
force of Felipe's day. Felipe's mother, on the other hand, seemed a little
more weary—in her sideways glances as Juan Carlos started going on
about Cristóbal Colón, about sea monsters and other types of ancient
traveler worries, she seemed to be both proud and preoccupied, as if she
thought his mind possessed too much, as if it were overflowing.

"Somos los descubridores," Juan Carlos kept saying. We are the discoverers. He repeated that three times, as if he thought I did not know, or perhaps I had forgotten, that the Spanish were the ones who discovered America. Then he added pointing at me, *"Te descubrimos."* We discovered you.

I nodded, said, *"Sí, Juan Carlos. Ya lo sé."*

His mother put her fork down. "Did he tell you his name is Juan Carlos?" She shook her head at him, and he looked down at his plate, his fingers gripping the edge of the table. Apparently his name was only Juan. I had heard her call him Juan, and I thought that was short for Juan Carlos, or that maybe Carlos was his middle name. I wasn't sure, but they explained to me that Juan Carlos was, in fact, the name of the king of Spain and that Felipe's brother had suddenly started calling himself that, even writing Juan Carlos on his papers at school.

"If Felipe is the prince, I am the king," Juan Carlos said rather matter-of-factly. The Spanish prince's name was Felipe, something Celia sometimes teased me about when she spoke of Felipe.

"Neither one of you is a prince *or* a king," Felipe's mother told Juan Carlos as she got up from the table. "You are just two normal boys."

Juan Carlos nodded at this, not seriously though, playfully, and then once his mother was on the other side of the room, he whispered across the table to Felipe and me, *"Dos chicos normales y una espía americana."* Two normal boys and an American spy.

We took Juan Carlos with us for a drive after that—just to give their mother a small afternoon break. We drove down to the older section of Gijón called Santa Catalina—which in English means Saint Catherine.

"You are not like Santa Catalina. You are no saint," Juan Carlos told me from the backseat. He had one of those annoying bottles of bubbles with him, and he was blowing them in the car. Some trailed out of the car and popped in the wind, while others floated forward onto my shoulder and forehead. "You are not a saint at all," he kept saying, with the plastic bubble wand in his hand. "You are something else." Then he added,

with great enthusiasm, *"Una chica muy mala."* Which could be translated to mean I was a bad girl or an evil girl, depending on the context.

"Yes, yes," I said calmly. "I know."

The whole time Felipe said nothing—he just listened to us. He never
scolded Juan Carlos, never told him to sit back in his seat or keep his
voice down, or to keep the perfumy-tasting bubbles from exploding on
his lips. It was as if instead he was watching me out of the corner of his
eye, observing me, administering some sort of test. I remembered his
asking me if I liked children on the beach and how he had smiled when I
said no. To some people how good you can be to a child, particularly a
difficult one, means how good you are in general. It felt like that then in
the car, and it felt like that as we walked around; I was undergoing a test,
it seemed: How good can you be to the weird boy? And the test went on
and on as Juan Carlos insisted on holding my hand only after he had spit
into his own; as he pretended one of the holes in the sidewalk was, in
fact, a mine; as he screamed when I put my foot near the mine, as he
insisted in a fast, muffled Spanish I couldn't entirely understand that the
camera shop we passed was not a camera shop but a microfilm shop full
of *información secreta*.

His spy obsession, of course, evoked in some small distant way my
aunt's story about my father's fear of spies. It actually seemed, as I listened to Juan Carlos happily chatter on and on, that perhaps such paranoia and its heart-thumping thrill were rooted in all of us, universally, as
kids—it came from childish fantasies and our old ability to believe in
those fantasies; it came from the clarity in which we once used to envision all the wonderful things and the fearful things, to the extent that
they came alive, burst through cement, crawled up sewer pipes, touched
your lips, your face, your throat.

Juan Carlos's imagination only calmed down later when we stopped
walking—when we sat down in the grass of a field that was behind a
church. The field was on such a high elevation, it towered over the
ocean, made it seem distant and scary. Sitting in the grass, Juan Carlos
stared up at the clouds and informed us that the clouds were not moving
but the earth was. I nodded. Felipe had his head on my lap and his arm

stretched up touching my shoulder. Juan Carlos did not seem in the least bit uncomfortable about this. He put his head on the other side of my lap so that his head and Felipe's head were touching. He asked us what we saw in the clouds, what the shapes made. I gave him a bland answer, told him I saw rabbits. Felipe said he saw a mountain. Then Juan Carlos told us after a thoughtful pause what he saw, *un culo de un mono*, a monkey's ass. Then he laughed, gestured for me to lower my head closer to the two of theirs. He whispered: "We are sitting under a monkey's ass."

After we dropped Juan Carlos off, Felipe and I went to a café, and I told him that I was leaving the following morning. I think he had half expected me to stay all week; he frowned a little and then asked me at what time the train left. I said, "*Siete.*"

"Who will pick you up in Madrid?"

"A friend of a friend," I said, purposely answering in English so that I didn't have to identify the gender and raise any foolish worries.

I had called Monica earlier in the morning to tell her I was coming back a day later than I had expected—she had offered when she dropped me off at the train station to pick me up when I returned. When I spoke to her on the phone, though, she was a little distant toward me. She told me that she couldn't come but that Esteban had already said he would. I would be arriving at three in the afternoon, which I knew was a little early for Esteban—he didn't like to start "participating in the world" until after siesta. I suppose I could've told her to forget it, that I'd take the metro or a cab home—I wasn't some lost child who couldn't get home on my own—but at the same time I rather liked the idea of seeing Esteban. There was always a part of me that tremendously missed anyone I fought with.

"Did you like my brother?" Felipe asked abruptly while I was staring off, thinking about seeing Esteban.

"Of course," I said. "How couldn't I?"

He nodded at that, sipped his beer, which was in a giant German mug, and looked past me at the sidewalk. "I thought you did," he said, smiling only slightly and looking down at his beer, touching the handle of the mug with one finger. In some quiet, purposely controlled way, I could tell he was very pleased. It seemed for the same reason that he had smiled so brightly when I first told him *me encanta España*; he was equally impressed by the fact that I liked his brother—as they were extensions of himself, parts of him, which talking and walking and hanging around at the beach would never, ever get us to. There were parts of people, very hidden parts, that could only be revealed by the people they chose to care about, the people they felt were theirs. This I only understood from Harlan—as he was not a part of my family, not innately connected to me, but it made me feel very separate from certain people when they didn't like him. During the time when I was so taken with Lenny, the one moment I truly felt unsure about him was when he told me in passing, in front of an open refrigerator, that he thought Harlan was the typical fag: listening to ABBA and dancing around and acting as if he were deeper and more messed up than everyone else.

I disliked Lenny right then—as strongly as I would've if he had said something insulting about my mother or my father or the set of my nose.

And for Felipe, Juan Carlos seemed to have that same power, the same weight, and so for the rest of the evening, I brought up his brother a lot, I mimicked the things he said. Felipe nodded each time, smiled, and somewhere in his face I could tell I was becoming a bit giant in Felipe's eyes—I could feel it—so much so that when he told me he would soon come to visit me in Madrid, I believed him and didn't think, as I normally would, that he might be lying.

$$\overline{24}$$

GETTING AWAY FROM FELIPE

The following morning at six, Felipe showed up to take me to the train station. He was in his small, steel, blue-gray car, sitting out front, waiting for me while I wrote a thank-you note to Celia and her parents. He did not beep or rev the engine or come to the door and knock. He just sat there with his hands flat on his knees, waiting for me, his eyes closed as if he thought in just being there, so close to where I was, I would feel him, know he was there, not even have to pull the kitchen curtains back and peek.

"You cheated, didn't you? You looked," he said when I first got in the car, and without his having to tell me what he was talking about, I knew, saw it the morning ruddiness of his face, saw it in the way the pillowcase had left a small grid on his cheek.

"I was writing a thank-you note," I said, which I knew had nothing to do with cheating or looking, but it seemed a fine response. I had learned from my mother that if you gave an answer that had nothing to do with a question, the person often didn't ask you the question again.

Felipe wanted first to take me to a café, a nice one, in the center of town, but I told him no, that we should just go directly to the train station, have coffee there. I was feeling very tense about getting back to Madrid, getting back to my father. In my mind, the stakes suddenly felt high, as if I were very close to missing the train and if I didn't make it on this particular train back, something would happen to my father, something hideous and awful. He might hit his head by the pool or tumble down some stairs or get beaten up, or he would spend the whole day in his bed, all curled up with his head under the pillow, his watch in his palm ticking and ticking.

So we sat in the train station, in a café that was not that impressive or swank. There was just a bar with one angry-looking man behind it and two high school cafeteria–style tables that had wheels on the bottom and stains from days past on their sticky blue surfaces. Felipe did not sit across from me but right next to me, his knee touching mine.

"You will be sad once your father leaves, won't you?" he said abruptly. This was the first time he had asked me about my father since I arrived.

I shrugged—I had not gotten that far in my mind as to what it would be like once I got back. I stayed as much in the present as I could; I stayed with our walks and the ocean and Juan Carlos and the taste of *sidra* and the smell of Felipe's shirts and the strangeness of his attention and gaze.

After hesitating a long while, I told Felipe yes, I would be sad about my father leaving. It seemed any kind of separation always left me a little bizarre behaving, off-kilter. I thought about all of this while Felipe touched my shoulder, my arm, my fingers, and I felt a little irritated by him. I suppose if you are used to so much affection it is nice, but when it is new and foreign, and you are pensive, it feels like an invasion—it felt as if he were trying to rub my thoughts away, and I didn't want that. I wanted them to stay. I wanted to carry them with me on train, sort them out, put them in piles the way back home I often put my tip money in piles, sitting Indian-style on the floor in my bedroom. I'd divide everything up according to denomination, face all the bills to create a strategic chart once the total was clear and sure. I wanted to handle my thoughts that way, too, add things up, make calculating numerical plans.

Before I got on the train, Felipe said, "So should I come on Sunday?"

My father was leaving Sunday morning, and it was now Friday. It would mean I would go exactly two days without Felipe, and then he would be there again. I said, "If you want to, yeah." I did not say it in the warmest way, it was more like I was confused, like I was experiencing mental static. I don't know if he sensed this or not, but I knew as I stood there—the train in front of us, dramatically long and red, the engine hissing lightly as if it were, in fact, powered by old-fashioned steam—that he was looking for a type of response that came out of a black-and-white movie, one in which I touched the grid the pillowcase left near his eyebrow and told him I needed him to come, he had to.

But those were words that I did not know how to say in Spanish or English—not even in a bashful, shy-eyed combination of the two. I just wanted to sit in my seat and look out the window at the passing hills and mountains and the black velvet bulls in the distance. I did not want to stand on that platform any longer, or catch a glimpse of other people's pants legs and suitcases near the electric glass doors that opened and closed. The air smelled too harsh, like chemicals or furnace soot, and I had the sense that if we waited too long we would be covered in a film, a grayness that would darken our faces and blacken our fingernails.

So I left rather abruptly, but first I kissed him good-bye, and I suppose that kiss was as good as telling him all the things I could not say because he seemed very happy when we finished, as if I had just told him to stay and stay with me, always.

He was still smiling, his girlish lips broad and wide, when I looked at him through the window, even though he could not see me through the glare. He stood there for ten more minutes until the train left, and then he waved, somehow certain that I could see. From a distance, his legs looked very thin and long, as if they took up more than three-quarters of his height; on his feet, he wore red flip-flops, but in the sunlight they appeared lighter, a hot pink. When the train started to move, to edge away, Felipe's wave and scarlet lips fell quickly out of sight. I put my chair back, looked out the window at the passing piles of metal and green tubing of a construction site, and I felt the world of Madrid, as well as other worlds, returning.

The week before I left Boston, Harlan and I got into a huge fight—not a fistfight, so to speak, but the sort of fight that contained such force, such anger, that I revisited it on occasion—particularly on that morning that I traveled the vast hilly space between Gijón and Madrid; against the thin morning fog, against the brown grazing horses, against the big black bulls, which seemed small and fragile in the distance, I was again there in my kitchen yelling at Harlan.

The fight originally started over Lenny. He had come to the apartment looking for me—he apparently knew I was leaving. How he knew, I never found out. I didn't tell him, certainly; I hadn't even laid eyes on him since the night he resurfaced in Shooters and upset me so. That had been in March, and the afternoon he came to my apartment was at the end of May.

During those two and a half months, I had decided to leave for the summer, take the trip to Spain. My teacher had originally presented the idea to me in February, right around my birthday, and I had told her no, I couldn't afford it—and then that same day I went home and put together a money chart, forecasted the next six months, and found that if I really wanted to go, if I just took out one extra loan, I would just barely make it. Weeks passed and as I lost my temper more and more at Shooters—yelling at customers when they tipped me badly, flipping them off, throwing their quarters back at them—it started to seem as though I couldn't afford not to go.

My mother told me to go. Harlan told me to go. The girls at work said, "Why the fuck *wouldn't* you go?"

But that transition in which I switched from being worried and money-conscious to being desperate and eager to leave coincided with not just a growing desire to do something else, to be something else, but also two other events: (1) Lenny made his long-awaited appearance at Shooters, and (2) Harlan had another "episode," one that seemed so dramatic in its length and severity that I worried he was, in fact, physically falling apart.

That night I had stayed up until morning, the whole time I hovered over him in our bright, bright bathroom, looking at the clumps of gray dust that had settled around the toilet. I noticed a smeared lipstick mark on the wall, a cobweb around the pipes under the sink, a layer of grime on the metal toilet paper holder. All the while I held on to Harlan's foot, I waited for the shivering and shaking to end. Then, when he seemed better, I took him into his room, but I didn't leave him, I slept on the floor next to him—his mattress and box spring, which were on the floor, put him only inches above me. I fell asleep watching him, fell asleep noticing how his hands curled up beneath his chin when he slept.

Everything was fine after that night, though—and during such hiatuses I always tried to believe things would stay that way; this was one of the few instances in which I still demonstrated a belief in God. I prayed that God would see Harlan, see the way that his eyelids pulsed when he slept, see his long blond eyelashes, see the ringlets of hair on his pillow. He was just like a little girl. I thought God should see that. And it seemed He did, because during the months of April and May, Harlan had no further problems, and we lived as though that was always the case—until the afternoon Lenny showed up looking for me.

I walked through our front door with a pizza box in my hand, my keys in my mouth. Harlan was in the kitchen; he had no lights on, but it was still bright outside, and even though the kitchen had no windows, there was still the sense of daylight being present, the sound of birds on a telephone wire still in my head.

"The Lemming was here looking for you," Harlan said, once I set the pizza down and took the keys out of my mouth. He was smoking a cigarette, and it gave him an older, rougher appearance, even though he held it vertically, daintily, next to his face.

I tossed my keys from one hand to the other; I was trying to decide if Harlan was stoned and making a mean joke. Sometimes when he was stoned or bored, he said things that purposely upset me. "The Lemming as in Lenny? Lenny was here?" Then I smiled bitterly to show I wasn't stupid—I wasn't going to play his dumb joke.

He nodded with the cigarette still long and vertical, like a miniature baton. "I told him you were at work."

There was something about the way he said that, the way he blinked only once as he spoke, which made me unsure. "What do you mean?"

"I told him you were at Shooters." His voice was rising, getting bitchy.

"He *was* here?" I said, trying to sound as if I still didn't believe him.

"He was at the door, Catherine. He wasn't even buzzing. He came right to the door."

In the set of Harlan's face, in the meanness he possessed, he was clearly telling the truth. "You knew I was coming back," I said, exasperated. "Why didn't you tell him to wait?"

He inhaled his cigarette, the tip went fiery, and then he just stared at me as if he were trying to memorize my face. "Why are you going to Spain?" he asked.

"Why did you tell him I was at work?"

"Why are you going to Spain?"

I shook my head as if his question was something I didn't hear. "Why did you tell him I wasn't coming home?"

"Is it so that he'll come after you?"

"What?"

"OK," he said, and held out his free hand. "Did you decide to go to Spain because (A) You wanted a break from Shooters; (B) You needed an exciting experience; (C) You wanted to get away from . . ."—he extended his arms as if he were referring to the entire room, including himself— "Or (D) Because you wanted to attract that moron's attention."

"I don't know *what* you're talking about," I said, letting my voice get deeper, like a growl. "I am leaving because I have to." I felt the heat rising in my face and my chin start to tremble, so I waited, I breathed, and I said calmly, "I need an internship to graduate."

He cocked his head. "It's not to get him to come and find you, to profess his undying love for you."

"How would he even fuckin' know I was leaving?" I threw my keys down on the table, made Harlan flinch.

"I don't know, maybe you sent him a message in a bottle," he said. "In a beer bottle maybe, and then you rolled it from your bar to his bar. Right down the fuckin' street." He stared at me as if he were reading me, looking right through me. He said, "It's not like you haven't imagined such a thing. That he would come, that he would know. Right?"

I screamed, "Fuck you!" and then, as I knew I would, I started to cry—but not over Lenny, over Harlan, over the fact that he was taunting me. He knew as much as I knew that every night before I went to bed, amongst the layers and layers of things I worried about, amongst the mental stacks of money, against the envisioned plane ride with its blue-and-white seats, amongst the words and words of Spanish, amongst all of this, I still dreamed of Lenny, and within those dreams he knew I was leaving, he could feel it, and he came. He cried. And in all of these fantasies, every single one, I refused him—sometimes nicely, sometimes with a cold deadliness.

"If you are leaving because of that *fuck*," Harlan started screaming, "you need to say so right now!" Then he stared at me with the intensity of someone who might get up and slap me. "You need to say so." His eyes went glassy. "It's shitty to make me think it's because of me."

There was a silence after that, a certainty that I tried to cover up by screaming at him, "I just want to go, OK, I just want to go!" My voice had the sudden desperation of someone who was pulling on something, yanking. Harlan just stared at me, his gaze intense, and then he put out his cigarette, which he wasn't even smoking anymore, and shifted his weight in his seat so that he wasn't looking at me but instead at our 1960s–style stove.

I sat down across from him, arms folded. I glanced at him angrily. "It's not about you, and it's not about Lenny." I waited. "It's because I don't feel good, Harlan. I don't know *why*. I just need a break."

He nodded distantly, as if he felt sorry all of a sudden. "Tricyclically speaking," he said, "probably you do."

"Need a break?"

He nodded, and then we sat in a thoughtful silence, as if we were both thinking about what I needed a break from. It wasn't as if I had lived through some traumatic event, no one had died, I hadn't lost a limb or gotten suddenly sick. I was just living a regular life, one with work, one with sleep.

"Can you just do me one thing though," he asked, "while you're in Spain?"

I waited, as if I had to decide. Then I said, still angry, "What?"

He leaned his elbows on the table, on top of the pizza box. "Could you only talk to normal boys, ones that aren't weak?"

I shook my head, frowned. Harlan seemed to envision Spain as a country that contained mainly men, noble-faced men with thin legs and matador stances, and perhaps a handful of women, all elderly, dressed in black and holding fans.

"What do you mean weak?" I said.

"Like me." He pointed at himself. "Like Lenny."

"You're not weak."

Harlan didn't answer that. He talked about Lenny instead. He said, "If he comes to this front door and he hasn't come,"—he looked at his watch—"for, oh, let's see, practically *years*. Then he's weak, Catherine. He's not worth your time; he's not worth your mental energy." He was touching the picture of the pepperoni on the pizza box, his finger going around and around it. "You pick men who aren't as smart as you, who aren't as sensitive as you." The only two men he was referring to were Lenny and Rick. "You pick people you have no chance with."

"So do you."

"Yeah," he said, and smiled a little. "Me and you deserve each other."

I nodded distantly—as if there were something very sad about that, about the fact that we meant so much to each other, yet we couldn't make the other entirely happy, there was a missing part of us. An emptiness.

Harlan's finger was still going around and around the pepperoni. I shooed his hand away, started to open the pizza box. I said softly, almost in a whisper, "Come on, let's eat."

It was two days after my fight with Harlan that Lenny resurfaced at Shooters for the second time. He came around six, which was a slow time of day in the summer. The room seemed as empty as it did when we were closed; the only differences were the monotonous Top 40 music playing overhead, and the sun, which came through the warehouse windows casting a dull light on the wooden floor. The other waitresses and I were all crowded around the bar playing Hangman when Lenny arrived. Because we were all in a cluster, all five of us, he stood near the doorway as if he hoped I would see him and come to him.

The girl who handed the pool balls out at the front desk could just as well have announced in the same repetitive voice she always used with the overhead microphone, "Catherine Kelly. Catherine Kelly, you're ex-boyfriend is now here," because everyone noticed him as if he was a giant reflective piece of light and not just a skinny boy standing against a green wall. Before I started to walk over to him, my tray in hand, my friend, Robby, said, "Tear him up, girl."

I nodded, walked stiffly toward Lenny—although my footsteps, against my will, still bounced to the music. He was wearing jeans and an orange T-shirt that was too bright. His hair was shorter, neater, and he didn't look as cute to me anymore. He said, "I came by your house."

I nodded to let him know Harlan had told me. I said, "Yup."

"Were you there?"

"No," I said matter-of-factly. "I was at the Pizza Peddler."

He nodded at this, as if it were all starting to come together for him. We just stood there after that. I was glad I had my tray; it gave me something to do with my hands. "I wanted to come by," he said, then stopped, started again. "I wanted to come by and talk to you, but . . ." He was looking down at my tray, which I held in front of me, not at my side. He seemed to be staring directly at the pile of cocktail napkins, at their calm whiteness. "I know I acted like a jerk," he said. "Like an idiot."

I nodded.

He pressed his lips together, looked past me at the floor, his gaze going back and forth a little, as if he were watching a mouse scramble around on the carpet. "I don't have explanation," he said finally, a little flatly, and then he corrected himself. "I don't have *an* explanation." His eyes met mine. "I don't know why I stopped talking to you. Nothing happened, nothing. I just . . ." He shrugged, then stared at me as if waiting for a response.

I didn't really feel like being mean to him right then—it would've actually taken great physical energy to do so. He looked too shifty, too afraid of me. Yet I also had no desire to help him out or redeem him either. I felt he deserved to be mildly tortured. So I said, "Look, I don't want to yell at you or anything. There was a time . . ." I looked at him sideways, curled my lip up. "But you shouldn't ignore people like that. It's crappy, and it's easier for you. And just because it's easier for you doesn't make it OK. It's selfish," I said. "It's shitty."

He nodded, looking down, as if I were his mom scolding him. Right then I thought of his mom who left him, but I shoved it aside. I was still quietly angry with him, and I still maintained—despite my own crap—that nothing that ever happened to you gave you the right, the excuse, to act selfish and awful. Still, I couldn't be overly upset with him either. He seemed very young standing before me, very unsure of what was happening around him.

I was nice to him after that, offered him a drink, but he said no. He asked if we could talk sometime when I wasn't at work, catch up.

"I don't have time," I told him. "I'm leaving in a few days."

He nodded at this, and I realized in that nod that he already knew where I was going and that that was exactly why he had the nerve to come. I didn't dislike him for this, though. I found it mildly endearing. I was just as Harlan had said I was, forever taken with the weak, with people so challenged by their emotions and sensitivities that the simple act of talking to someone took mental practice and sudden spurts of nerve.

When Lenny was on his way out, he said, "I've missed you, you know," but he didn't look at me, he looked behind me, following perhaps the shape of another waitress walking behind me. I guess I was supposed to say I missed him, too, but at that moment I knew, strangely, that I didn't really miss him. I had missed only his comfort.

I knew that even more so, though, on that train from Gijón, looking out the window, the sun's glare on the window. All the obsessing I had ever done over Lenny was not about him, as I had merely been with him for three months. Only the fantasy he provoked had lasted longer. His sensitivity, custom-made for me, I positioned in a supreme place in my mind so that no customer at Shooters, no stranger on the street, no mystery Spaniard, could ever compare. He was the ease with which I could say anything—including all the things I never told him; he was someone who existed invisibly next to my pillows, someone who could read through the touch of a finger what I felt. He was like one of Juan Carlos's fantasies, a childlike dream—a ghostly entity who did not, and couldn't ever, exist.

Only on trains did I ever have these sudden obvious revelations. It's something about movement, about the steady shapes of grass and telephone wire and parked trucks all passing with such swiftness that it makes all feeling, all weight, seem as though it can be left behind, abandoned.

I thought about Shooters after that. It seem a place that could not exist simultaneously while I rode past black bulls that stood in the distance amongst white and brown spotted cows, amongst horses with thin, fragile-looking legs. Shooters was a dream right then. And it seemed that when I went back to Boston, it couldn't actually be there anymore. It would be demolished perhaps, just a grassy space littered with beer bottles, a single brass fixture from its walls lying against wet dirt. Or maybe it would be turned back into a roller-skating rink, or a flashy nightclub. Or a darkly lit supermarket.

In any case, Shooters did not exist for me anymore; it couldn't—not after spending a whole week with my father, not after sitting in a bullring, not after riding around in Esteban's Porsche or being with Felipe on the beach, not after looking at that water that went to France, not after listening to Juan Carlos talk about explosives, not after meeting and sleeping with Borja. Not after all that. It was as if Spain had, in fact, become for me, as Harlan had envisioned it, a world full of men—and those men were somehow impeding my swift return to that green, fake, fern land of Lenny and Rick and the rest, the land of stripteases on pool tables, of bare feet against green felt, the land of shots—tequila, Jaeger, Kamikazes—all burning and burning, right down my throat.

On the last night I worked, Rick had even asked me, "So, what are you going to do when you come back? You're going to go, fuck around, and then what?"

It was the end of the night, and I was trying to count all my money. I just shrugged, and then he asked me again, and I said, "I have no idea." I was moving my lips unnecessarily with each pile of bills I stacked, and I didn't look up at him. I was always cold like this to Rick—as if he were not my boss or someone I had ever touched, just a pest.

"You're gonna come back here, right?"

"Probably."

He stretched his legs onto a neighboring chair, put his arms behind his head. We were in the office. I was sitting at a desk, and he was sitting at a desk; we were on opposite sides of the room. He had a drink on his desk, already half gone, in a plastic soda cup. Out of the corner of my eye, as I recounted my piles of money, I could see him tapping a pen against his front tooth—he tapped and tapped, then the pen hit him in the face, made him flinch.

I laughed.

"You are going to miss me," he said, staring down at the pen as if he were trying to figure out how it had just hit him in the face. "You know why?"

I didn't answer. I just put the money from my cash out on his desk. He counted it quickly, within seconds it seemed, and then, "Do you know why?" he asked even louder and more obnoxiously. Whether he was drunk or suffering from the high he usually got when the night was over and he didn't have to do anything anymore, I couldn't tell. His hair, which was usually gelled back in little stiff lines, was coming undone, cowlicks forming. He got up from the desk, squatted near the big green safe. "Do you wanna know why you're gonna to miss me?"

I shook my head, yawned, and watched him put his key in the safe and turn the dial.

"Stop trying to memorize the combination!" he screamed at me, joking, of course. "The numbers are not for you, Catherine. The numbers are secret." He said under his breath after that, "Secret, secret, secret," hissing the s's as if he were a cartoon character and not himself.

"You will miss me, though," he said, not looking at me but instead at the inside of the safe, "because I take care of you." He did not deliver this as a joke, but in a very serious voice, as if he actually believed it and could only bring himself to tell me so after he had taunted me for a few minutes.

"You take care of me?" I said, pronouncing each word carefully, as if I hadn't heard correctly.

"That's right," he said, and started naming instances when he had taken care of me, which included the night that I had flipped out after Lenny showed up, the night the guy asked me if I got fucked too hard and I just left. I had not gone back that night, and even though Rick called to find out "what the fuck The Farmer had done" to me, I didn't pick up. I simply showed up the next day of work as if it were nothing, my eyes not even worried or glassy.

The owner had wanted me fired, but Rick had talked him out of it, told him I worked hard. There were other times besides that, though— the customers themselves often wanted me fired. I had thrown a quarter at a girl once, smacked a guy for putting a piece of my hair in his mouth. Another time I spilled red wine on a woman's sleeve and when she yelled at me I told her to go fuck herself.

But Rick was being a little dramatic in his account of how many times he had taken care of me—he was making it sound as if every night I attacked people, physically or verbally, "like an angry dog."

I shrugged. "People upset me, OK?"

"That doesn't matter," he said. "I don't care what people do to you. It's that I take care of you; that's the point." We were silent for a minute. He closed the safe and it made a hollow sound, as if there were nothing in it. "And if the people bother you so much," he began, "why do you suppose, why do you guess, you stay here?"

"Because I have to pay for school."

He rolled his eyes at this. Often at night after work he gave me trouble if I complained about how much money I made, particularly if I donned the emotional desperation of someone "who has to pay for school."

"Then go to a community college," he'd tell me. "BU is like a million fuckin' dollars."

But what he didn't understand, what a lot of people didn't understand, was that was the very reason I refused to quit or transfer or do whatever a normal-minded person would do when she couldn't afford something. It was like when I was a kid and I would go shopping with my mother, and the bags and bags of things would fill up in our hands, and even though we had no business owning those things, they still made us feel as if we did. There was nothing wrong; we were OK. We were doing what other people did—and we deserved it. That's the way I felt about BU: I deserved it. I was smart, I was hardworking, and there were a bunch of other jerks that got to go to that school, why not me? The very idea of going to a different school that cost less actually angered me. It made me feel that, despite my will, I was only allowed to do certain things in this world, all predetermined by where I came from and what my parents could or couldn't give me.

"Fuck that," I would say to Rick or to Harlan or to my mother.

And the more I worked at Shooters, the more tired and irritable I got, the more BU represented in my mind; it became everything I ever wanted, the doorway to it all, and I clung to that school, fought to stay there. Sometimes it actually seemed to me, as irrational as it was, that the bad tips and the cheap feels and the "Did somebody fuck you too hard" comments were all tests to see if I could stand it, if I could really hold on to BU—and the people who did these things, drunk and slurring, were like special agents, hell-bent on ruining me.

"But your school has nothing to do with why you work here," Rick was saying to me. He put his gold pen ridiculously behind his ear and posed his face regally to the side, took a sip of his drink. "It's all about me." He was acting a jokey sort of arrogant, which was full of smiles and abrupt glances as he filled out some paperwork—it was a type of false arrogance that was supposed to reveal something beneath it, something that couldn't be said seriously. It was as if he believed that we had some special, secret rapport, one that went beyond our bickering and meanness, one that perhaps made him feel better about himself, made him feel noble.

But to me Rick, with his jiggling keys and arrogant grin, was no saint of mine; instead he was the very representation of something a bit more useful and large: money. I did not think of this sitting in front of him in the brightly lit office though—only later, in retrospect, on that Spanish train as I thought of Shooters and its potential nonexistence. Through memory, through physical distance, I saw like a repetitive set of pictures that every conversation Rick and I had ever had was while we were counting money, or holding money, or arranging money in stacks. Even that night I slept with him, we had been counting money first, subtracting and adding amounts on a calculator.

"I take care of you," Rick had said again in the office that night in this purposely Mafioso way, as if he were some grandiose pimp. I had nodded and said sarcastically, "That's what I like about you," and then we went downstairs and the party began, and the girls who were younger than me, the skinny one and the redhead, took off layer after layer, and the *Hasta la Vista* cake sat near me, and the shots went around and around, and when everything in my vision felt uneven, as if the room were on a permanent drunken slant, I left, and all the girls hugged me in the stairwell. They said they'd see me soon. "You'll be back," they said, "You will." I smiled at them as if such certainty were comforting, and then in the cab, I shut my eyes, listened to the lulling wind from the driver's open window, felt my hands shake.

$$\overline{25}$$

IMPROVEMENT

At the train station, Esteban was waiting for me, leaning against a stanchion. He was reading a tabloid magazine, *Hola*, with his sunglasses on, his hair wet-looking and gelled. I don't know how we even found each other; I felt lost amongst all the palm trees and plants, the big greenhouse glass ceiling letting the sunshine blast right into the room—it was like having your eyes dilated and then walking outside into summer, into the whiteness of heat. But I found Esteban, or rather he found me, waving at me, calling my name while I stood in front of a turnstile looking lost and uncertain.

"We have to leave here quickly," he said after he kissed me on each cheek. His face next to mine smelled like a mixture of his musky-scented cologne and the aloe vera gel he "hydrated" his hands with. He took my bag off my shoulder and then pulled on my hand like a child. "Come on, hurry," he said, pulling on my hand a little harder. "This place is about to explode."

"What are *you* talking about?" I said toddling after him.

He didn't answer; he just kept weaving through the crowd of travelers who were walking around aimlessly or staring up at the wall to read the train schedule or calmly standing next to the information desk, or the kiosk, or the café. The two of us in our high-speed weaving were making the same thonking noise with our sandals, a thonking noise that seemed to make my adrenaline go up, make my palm sweat against his palm.

"What do you mean 'explode'?" I asked about three times, getting louder and louder.

Esteban turned around, said, "Shhh," and then I saw the slight smile on his face, which maybe I wouldn't have seen if he hadn't been wearing those sunglasses—the sunglasses seemed to give him the ridiculous illusion that I couldn't see the expression on his face.

I let go of his hand. "You're such a fuckin' ass! I've been on that train for eight hours. Eight." I put up my hands, showed him eight fingers. "I don't need to be running around through this train station like an idiot."

"Listen," he said, pushing his sunglasses up so that I could see his eyes, his eyes which were both bloodshot and amused. "*Hola* says Atoche,"—the train station—"is going to blow up by the end of this year." He waved the rolled-up magazine in my face. *"At any moment,"* he added dramatically. "It's a target."

He was worse than Juan Carlos.

I said, "Whatever, where's the car?"

He turned one way, then another, then he put his finger to his lips as if in deep thought; finally we walked in the direction we had been walking in.

"Are you still angry?" Esteban asked me later when we were in the car—whether he was talking about the race through the train station or Borja, I could not tell. But I said no, shook my head, and smiled a small smile.

"How was your trip, anyway?" Esteban asked.

"Nice."

He smiled at this, as if this were a unique and exciting response to the question.

"I met a boy there."

"Oh?" he said, as if this were a sudden surprise, but it wasn't. I had already told him long ago that Felipe was sending me letters. I remembered telling him in a bar that had mint green walls and dark lighting and tall candles that dripped in a mess on the table between us.

"And I also made an exciting decision on the train," I told him, making a triumphant gesture with my hands.

"You're going to move to Spain and marry?"

"No."

"You want to see Borja again?"

I gave him a look, one that was a mixture of discomfort and annoyance.

"You are going to, you are going to"—he snapped his fingers—"you are going to love me forever."

I didn't respond to that—I said, "I'm not going back to Shooters."

He shook his head. "Shooters?"

"The bar I work in. I'm going to leave."

"Ahhh." He nodded. "And how does it feel? How does it feel to do something you actually always wanted to do in the first place?" His voice was a little sarcastic, as if he thought my decision wasn't really a decision but a thing I couldn't avoid.

"It feels nice," I said. "Extra nice," which was true—it felt in that very odd way as if I had thrown something I hated out a high, high window and it would forever be descending farther and farther away from me.

Esteban put his hand on my knee. I was not alarmed. I said, "*Why* do you have your hand on my knee?"

"Because I want you to feel nice," he said. "Extra nice." He raised his eyebrows as he said this—he was joking, amusing himself. He had his sunglasses on again, and they were dark and tinted blue. I couldn't see his eyes when I looked at him; I only saw the way the wind from the moving car made his shirt open and close revealing a certain amount of chest hair that he would've been embarrassed about. I thought of saying something about the hair, the patch of "bedroom carpet" as he called it, but instead I just laughed, nudged his hand off my knee, and told him, "You're so gross, OK?"

He put his hand back on my knee a few seconds later, and then I waited thirty seconds before abruptly pushing it away. We kept doing this the whole ride—it was like some stupid childish way for us to try to make up.

"Do you want to see the statue of the woman with the ripped-off arm?" Esteban asked me. We were on Paseo del Prado, right near the glamorous post office, and in the center of the rotary there was the Estatua de la Cibeles, which was the statue that had been accidentally broken by a few unruly drunks after the Spanish won a World Cup game. I had heard about it, saw the footage on the news of the excited fans jumping around and splashing in the statue's fountain, but I hadn't realized how close it was to my work; I had for some reason associated the statue with the soccer stadium, and had thought it was somewhere else in Madrid, farther north.

"I've passed this before," I said. "It looks OK to me." The statue wasn't just of the woman—she was on a chariot carried by lions, and her arm seemed a smaller detail, not as important as the big wheels of the chariot or the lions and their own prancing paws.

"Cibeles is the mother of all gods," Esteban explained after we had completely passed by her. "The mother of love," he added with a bit of false drama.

I nodded.

"But she doesn't really need an arm," he said as he put his hand on my knee. I smacked it away. Then we drove and drove, playing the game some more, until we got to my street and parked.

We were quiet for a minute sitting in front of my little pink apartment building. It had been a day or two since I had been there, and in our silence I thought about what it would feel like if, years later, I returned to Madrid and sought out this building. I imagined it would be a very uncomfortable feeling, like a sudden wave of grief, as the people I now knew might not be here anymore, and my father himself would not be in some hotel up the street, but probably somewhere else, some-where way far off.

Esteban lit a cigarette. He smoked cigarettes only when he was drinking or about to talk about something serious. "So," he said, "why didn't you ever say your father was here?"

I shrugged, didn't look at him. "Because I didn't feel like it."

He ashed his cigarette out the window. "Why do you do that?" he said, and paused as if he were trying to put the idea together completely. "Why do you never tell everything? Why do you tell parts of things, and then later tell everything?"

"Because I need time," I said. "I need to warm up. Make myself trust you." I shrugged, stared off, considered what I just admitted. It seemed my only way of telling anyone anything—including my mother or Har-lan—was to first tell them just a little, a surface amount of information, and then I'd wait to see how they reacted; if it was all right, if it seemed OK, I let my trust go further, I told more, I let the actual story I was telling get deeper, more specific, until what I had unraveled was a whole different thing.

"I would've known," Esteban was saying, "if you had told me your father was here, I would've known why you were acting like such an *ass* at lunch the other day."

"I wasn't acting like an *ass*."

"Yes, you were." He paused. "And you need to let people know why you're being an ass, if you're going to be an ass." He was yelling at me a little, not quite, but sort of. He was looking out the windshield as he spoke to me, as if he were still concentrating on the road, still driving. He took a drag of his cigarette. I had in my hands the small bottle of aloe vera he kept on the console—I twisted the cap open, twisted it closed.

"Did you spend any of the money yet?" he asked.

"I bought my ticket to Gijón with it."

"And you had a good time," he said. "So you spent the money well." I was not looking at him when he said this; I was looking up the street at a passing car, but in his voice I felt something odd. I felt like Borja and whatever money was in that envelope had nothing to do with each other right then. I developed this sudden certainty—which I would later doubt—that Esteban had given me that money, that it was his. And whether it was out of charity or "trading," I did not know, but they seemed at that moment the same exact thing.

After a long still pause, Esteban said, "You should go see your father, no?" His cigarette was burning and burning, held close to his face.

I nodded, said yeah, then softly opened the car door.

"Can I call you later in the week?" he asked.

I said yeah.

"Can we drink a lot?" he asked, and before I could answer, he added, "Monica will come. And we will sit together and you two can slap each other." He smiled.

I got out of the car, held my bag over my shoulder. "And you won't try to sell me anymore?"

"No," he said. "Pimps like me . . ." He waited so that I could infer that he had spoken to Monica; then he smiled as if the accusation was the most wonderful, glamorous thing he had ever heard. "Pimps like me," he began again, his voice haughty, "only like nice girls. Friendly girls. Girls," he pointed at me, "who don't slap."

I had already made the decision on the train that I would not run right over to the Holiday Inn to see my father. Instead I would wait, I would take a shower and sit on my couch and settle in, wait for night to come. I tried to call him, let him know I was back, once I got back to the apartment, but he wasn't in his room. Or at least he wasn't answering. I left a message in Spanish that they should tell him in English that I was coming to see him at nine.

"¿A las nueve?"

"Sí, a las nueve," I said, and then I became paranoid from the strange doubt that seemed to linger in the hotel operator's voice. Perhaps my father wasn't there anymore, perhaps he had left. I asked if my father still had his room, and the guy seemed to think I was very stupid. He switched into English and asked me why I would leave a message for someone if I didn't think he was there. "You are only able to leave messages for people who are actually in the hotel, and Mr. Kelly is still in the hotel." Then he concluded, "I am leaving him your message."

After I got off the phone, I went through my mail, which was all laid out in a fan shape on my bed, along with a note from Isabel. She was gone to a place I didn't recognize—a place I later learned was in France. She was with the guy she had stayed with in the nightclub, Sergio. She spelled his name in big letters so that I would remember who he was and she made the O in his name a heart. She also wrote that she hoped I was OK and that she was glad I went to Gijón.

As I read this, I took out of my pocket another note I had, one that Felipe had given me at the train station. I had read it just as the train pulled into Madrid, and I suppose, in retrospect, the note was partially why I was so quick to fall for Esteban's little bombing prank. The note itself was not from Felipe, though; it was from Juan Carlos. It began: *La policía ha venido*. The police have come. Then it said, in Spanish:

> *They were asking questions. They wanted to know about the briefcase. I didn't tell them about the money. I didn't tell them about the microfilm. The microfilm is in a toothpaste box under my bed. No one should be suspicious except my mother.*
> *I told the police you definitely weren't going to Madrid. I told them I knew nothing about your plan to blow up Palacio Real. I said you just left without saying anything and broke my brother's heart.*

Felipe's handwriting appeared only beneath the broken-heart part; he wrote: *No es verdad*—That's not true. And below that: *Nos vemos muy pronto*—We will see each other soon.

Amongst the rest of my mail, I found what looked like a Hallmark card from my mother and a postcard with a cartoon mouse eating a cheese dinner with a knife and fork at a table that was really a spool of thread. It said underneath it: Don't lose your cool, don't lose your spool. You don't want to do that, babe.

In the smallest handwriting possible, Harlan wrote on the other side that he was sorry he had acted like such an idiot when I called him about my father. He said he knew it meant big things, dark things, to have my father with me for an hour, never mind an entire week. As I read this, I wished I had read the postcard before I left for Gijón—Harlan's judgment meant a lot to me. He had a way of making me feel less guilty or more guilty, depending on the instance. He had even written on the postcard at the very bottom: Just because he's there doesn't mean you have to spend every second with him. Take breaks and remember: He's the one who took a long, long break from you.

On the last night that I was in Boston, Harlan made me feel far less awkward for leaving him—it was the day before he crushed the mouse with his slipper, only a few days after Lenny had stopped by and Harlan had gotten so angry with me. I had been out late, doing last-minute, panicked errands, and when I came home, I found a box from Victoria's Secret on my bed. It was a gift from Harlan, a bra and underwear set. A note across the top said: So you can match and be nonretarded!

He had bought me the underwear because I had come home from my going-away party at Shooters the night before, drunk, slurring, and rambling. I told Harlan about the stripping girls and their mismatched underwear, and I concluded with great drunken intelligence that if their underwear as well as my own underwear matched, we wouldn't be such "fuckin' retards."

"If we could just match," I explained, waving my finger in front of his face, "we would be fine young women. Very fine. Extra fine. So fine." I nodded. "Yup."

So Harlan had apparently bought me what I needed to convert, and I sat there on my bed looking at the underwear, at its pinkness and lace. I envisioned Harlan going through the drawers and drawers of bras and panties, while salesclerks watched him from a distance, snickering perhaps—probably believing the underwear was for his own narrow hips and small-size chest. As I thought of this, the rest of the apartment was quiet. Harlan's bedroom door was shut, the light on. I remember looking down the hallway at his door, a sickening feeling going right through me. It was as if there was something in there, waiting for me, that I would never forget seeing. But when I went down the hallway and into his room, I found nothing but the rumpled lion sheets on his bed, the still-blank TV set, and the wavy blue lines that flashed on his stereo.

He came home a few minutes after I went in his room, called out to me before he was fully in the apartment, "Have you finished packing yet?"

He had just come back from the Store 24, and I knew before he unveiled his purchase that it was a pint of ice cream. He ate one practically every night. "I want you to be out of here by six," Harlan said. He had on this light-blue Rasta hat, which he wore out only when he was stoned.

"So did you get stoned," I asked, "before or after you went to Victoria's Secret?"

"I got stoned *in* Victoria's Secret." He made the gesture of putting a joint to his lips while he flipped through an invisible rack. Then he smiled, said, "Actually, I want you out of here by five."

I watched him take the ice cream out of the plastic bag, open the container with great difficulty, and then search the silverware drawer for a spoon without looking, just feeling with his hands.

"I want you out of here by four." He was going to keep doing this all night, until he had announced all of the possible number combinations on the clock. "Here," he gave me a spoon. "You are going to have some, too. I got you your favorite, Chunky Monkey." That was not my favorite—it was his.

"I don't want any," I said. "I want to feel thin, ultrathin, when I come off that plane."

He looked at me, shook his head as he always did when I got weird about food. He said, "There are actually special compounds in this, special Chunky Monkey compounds." He put his hand up to his head, wiggled his fingers. "It loosens things in the brain, increases serotonin levels." Harlan knew all of the brain chemicals and their functions. "It makes the skinny girl realize she actually is skinny. Here . . ." He handed me a bowl. "Try some."

We ate the ice cream in his room, not in the dark, depressing kitchen. Outside, through his open window, we could hear the muffled sounds of people passing by, their footsteps louder than their voices. We lived in the South End and often late at night on the old brownstone stoops, our multicultural neighbors sat outside and drank 40s and happily insulted one another. Sometimes Harlan and I would listen, copy the entertaining things they said and fall into a gasping, weeping laughter.

"Do you wanna know who I want to listen to?" Harlan said in a voice that was so casual I knew I was going to be taunted. He went over to his stereo, touched the pink elephant above it, and then the music came on. The kind I hated. ABBA.

We ended up talking for an hour or so, the annoying *Best of ABBA* CD on repeat. We talked about what he would do with my mail, my bills. I left him a checkbook. He promised to water my plants, even though I had none. He also said he wouldn't go in the bathroom while I was gone. He would wait until I came back. It was delivered as a joke, but it bothered me.

"Yeah, but are you really going to be OK?"

"I'm going to be great," he said without any sarcasm in his voice. He waited until I looked at him. "Really."

I don't know if I believed him. I don't know how you can believe anyone when they say that. I remember staring at his fingernails, at the way that the little half moons seemed whiter than mine, bigger. Outside there was the rumble of beer cans, of someone actually kicking a can— lightly though, as if that person was alone and very bored and walking slowly.

ABBA's "Chiquitita" was playing. The words to any ABBA songs were always so clear, so fully enunciated, that they had a way of amusing Harlan more than any other music he played. Whenever he found me on the floor of my bedroom, making money piles with my tips, he played the song, "Money, Money, Money"—he especially liked the part that went: "Money, money, money, must be sunny in a rich man's world." There were certain parts of that song that were so high pitched, so fast, that it would ruin my ability to count, and I would yell at him;

then the hideous "Dancing Queen," only seventeen, would come on and
I would be subjected, if he was in the mood, to watching him twirl up
and down the hallway.

"Chiquitita," however, was not one of the songs he normally used to
torture me, as it was a bit serious even though it had fast, polkalike
music going on like a big whirling mess in the background. Against the
tinkering of the can outside, in our own sudden silence, Harlan started
singing the words, loudly, obnoxiously, and so stupidly that a week later
in Madrid I'd hear the song in a grocery store and it would make me
laugh in the fruit aisle amongst the bright whiteness and the slight scent
of rotting melon. It was the way that Harlan moved his hands that made
it funny, the way he fluttered his fingertips, the way he smiled as if he
was entranced by something, singing the words:

> *Chiquitita, you and I cry*
> *But the sun is still in the sky and shining above you*
> *Let me hear you sing once more*
> *Like you did before . . .*

Then from outside in the darkness, somewhere on a stoop—while Harlan was still singing—a voice shouted, "Turn that shit off or I'll give
you a *chiquitita*! I'll crush your head in with a lead bat! A banana bat,
motherfucker!"

Harlan and I had looked at each other, less than alarmed, and then we
laughed and laughed, our shoulders shaking, our faces inches from the
carpet.

$$26$$

RAÚL AND HIS MARS BAR

After I read Harlan's postcard, I took a shower and went up the street to buy a bottle of whiskey for my father—I thought that would be nice somehow, make him happy. On the way back I passed Raúl's store and found him standing in the doorway with one hand leaning against the closed door, the other holding a Mars Bar in his flat open hand. He apparently saw me leave and, for whatever reason, knew I would be coming back—or perhaps he just hoped I would. I stood on the corner only a few feet away from him. The sun had a glare that made me squint.

"*¿Te gustaría un Mars Bar?*" he asked, but he said it softly and from a distance, as if he still remembered my yelling at him three weeks before. In the quality of his voice I almost thought I scared him, upset him, as if yelling at him was something he believed long ago had to do with him as a person and not the suffocating way he had sat so close on the steps next to me.

I asked him, "*¿Porqué quieres que tenga un Mars Bar?*" Why do you want me to have a Mars Bar?

He shrugged. *"Es un regalo."* It's a present.

I nodded and then didn't move away from him on the sidewalk, didn't move toward him. Just stood there. Above us was the sound of quibbling pigeons; a whole horde of them sat perched on some rooftop nearby, invisible.

"OK," I said, and pointed at the Mars Bar. "OK."

It took a minute for Raúl to properly ingest that I had finally accepted. He took a step forward and opened the store door for me, then he smiled a nervous smile, as if he had always known I would sooner or later say yes, yet he had never envisioned what would come afterward.

Once inside, the first thing I noticed was the Coca-Cola sign that was actually painted directly on one of the store's walls, covering its entire windowless width. The store itself was just a giant room, one filled with the smell of pipe smoke mixed with the sweetness of oranges and pineapple. There were no aisles; all the food was stacked along the four walls and it made the room brighter, as most of the packaging for Spanish food was in reds and yellows and greens. The colors and pyramids of cans actually seemed to make a giant design on the wall, all skillfully put together against the drab, checkered floor.

"Hola," said a guy who was squatting on the floor, going through yellow packages of spaghetti. He had thick-framed eyeglasses, and his shirt had palm trees on it. Whether he worked there or was a cheerful customer I could not tell; but he made me feel at ease. I said *"Hola"* back to him, and then I followed Raúl into the back of the store.

The back room wasn't a dark room—I probably wouldn't have gone in if it had been—instead, it was rather bright; there was a section of blue stained glass that covered a window, and it brought a blue light into the yellow pale-walled room. The entire store looked as if it had once been a single-room apartment, the back area sectioned off by double doors. A sink was in the corner, but it was more a bathroom sink than a kitchen sink, and a hot plate sat near it on a white nightstand. Along the walls was a series of high dressers, all made of different-colored wood, all with different kinds of knobs and handles. A circular table sat in the corner of the room, near the stained-glass window.

"*Siéntate,*" Raúl said after he put a small, embroidered pillow down on one of the table's chairs. Flamenco music was playing on the radio so softly that it made the singer's voice sound as if he were in pain but trying to keep quiet about it.

Raúl put my Mars Bar on a plate that was as big as a dinner plate—it had hand-painted blue flowers with big wide petals all along the rim, a yellow circle in the center. Raúl cut the Mars Bar in pieces as if it were a log of cheese, and then then he gave me some napkins, the kind that come in a silver dispenser and had the words, *Gracias por su visita*— Thank you for your visit—written on the front.

"*¿Te gusta España?*" he asked me. Do you like Spain?

I nodded, gave him my standard answer: *Me encanta España.*

He smiled and nodded back at me, as if he had already guessed this. "But do you miss home?" he asked.

That was perhaps the fifteenth time someone had asked me that. I said, "*A veces.*" Sometimes. He nodded again, this time in a very serious way, as if this were somehow something he had hoped to find true about me. A woman came into the store right then, the bell on the door rang, but it was a single bell, a very small brass one, and it let out more of a tinkle rather than a loud ringing. I thought Raúl would get up, but he didn't. He didn't even turn to look, and the guy with the eyeglasses in the main room said, "*Hola,*" and the woman said, "*Buenas,*" and then everything but the music was quiet.

Raúl asked me where else I had been in Spain. I told him only Gijón, and he seemed to think that was the least interesting, most bizarre place to have gone. He told me before I left I had to go everywhere in Spain. "*Todos los sitios,*" he said, "*Todos.*" He started telling me specifically where I needed to go. I had to go to the South, to Sevilla and Granada and Cordoba; I had to go to the North to Bilbao and San Sebastián; I had to go to places right outside of Madrid like Toledo and Ávila and Segovia; I had to go to Salamanca, too; but most importantly, he said, "*Tienes que ir a Valencia.*" He shook his head up and down, stared right in my eyes.

"You are from Valencia," I said matter-of-factly, and he answered with great zest, "*¡Por supuesto, muñeca!*" Of course, doll.

Then he stood up, packed a silver kettle with coffee. He set it on a hot plate and stood across the room, one hand on his hip, telling me things about Valencia. He said it was on the coast, on the water, and you could eat paella and sit on a terrace and drink a very light white wine and feel the breeze, which wasn't as salty or fishy as other seaside breezes. He told me about rice paddies, then orange trees. He said the peels of their oranges were of a different texture, of a higher quality. "They're so sweet, so juicy," he said, "You have to eat them with a knife and fork."

Then there was the Holy Grail—you could find it in Valencia and only Valencia. He didn't say Holy Grail though, he said it in Spanish, and when I didn't understand he said in very timid way, Oly Grail.

I said, "*¿Qué?*"

"Oly Grail."

"*¿Cómo?*"

"Oly Grail." Then he wrote it down on a piece of paper with the H intact, and I said, "Oh, *sí, sí*."

"You can see it," he said. "You can go there." He talked about the bullring in Valencia, too, made a shape with both his hands to show how much smaller it was compared to the one in Madrid. There was also a cathedral, he said, that was so beautiful and ornate that it made you believe in God. "Even if you don't like God for some reason," he said. "You see the cathedral, and he's yours all over again."

I nodded, eating my Mars Bar, stirring the milk in my coffee with a spoon that was so small it looked like one of those foolish souvenir spoons, a collector's spoon—and if it had just said "Valencia" across it, it would've been perfect and right.

We sipped our coffees, and I looked up at the clock above the register in the other room. It was getting late, and I was meeting my father at nine. I had the feeling that I had to tell Raúl I had to leave soon or otherwise he would keep me in his back room eating Mars Bars and drinking coffee, smiling at me, watching the way I stared up at a picture he had on the wall of a woman who had very light eyes and dark hair that was parted in a crooked way to the side.

"That is my mother," Raúl said, and I smiled. I told him she was very pretty, and he said *sí*. He told me that if I could meet her, he would let me, but he couldn't. I didn't know if this meant she was dead or just far away, but I didn't ask—instead I just gave him the nicest, warmest look I could give him with my eyes. When he spoke of her, he used the present tense. He told me how her favorite phrase was *"Esto es una mierda."* This is shit.

We went on like this—talking about his mother, his father, and Valencia—until I finished my Mars Bar and my coffee. Then he seemed ready to let me go. He walked me to the front door and told me to come back again. I said I would. He asked how long I was staying until, and I said I had five more weeks, until the end of August.

"Do you look forward to going back?"

"Sí y no," I said, shrugging. "I like it here; it makes me feel different."

He nodded, said *sí*. "When you leave it will be hard," he said, motioning to his eyes. "You will cry. You will cry because you have met so many people, and you don't know when you will see them again. It's just like leaving home, but it's the opposite, because you don't know when you will come back to them. At least when you leave home, you know you can come back.

"But that is also the good thing about leaving home," he said after a minute. "It teaches you how to keep people with you." He pointed at his forehead. *"Te da un otro tipo de vista."* It gives you another type of sight. "People can't be with you all of the time," he said, shaking his head. "Not right next to you, but they can still be with you."

From the way he had spoken of his mother, I couldn't tell if he was talking about people who have died or people who live far away, but I smiled anyway—as if it were something I had always wanted to hear.

Across from us in the sun, a boy was sitting on the front steps of my building, drinking what looked like chocolate milk out of a baby's bottle. I watched the boy as if he was of great interest to me, but what I was really thinking about was how I had been avoiding Raúl for so long, as if he had some sinister plan for me when, in fact, all he had wanted was to sit me down, to tell me about his mother and his father and where he came from. The Mars Bar was simply what he used to get me there and standing next to him on that sidewalk, it seemed perfectly logical that you used what you had—a candy bar, an envelope of money, a little brother—to get people to see who you were.

$$\overline{27}$$

IN DARKNESS

After I left Raúl, I went home and changed my outfit three times. I became the way I had been the first day I met my father—obsessed with looking right. I even called him when I realized I was running so late; it was already ten. "Everything all right?" he asked me and I said, "Everything all right with you?" He said yes, and then I promised to be there soon.

I took the subway to his hotel, which was perhaps my first mistake. I should've gotten a cab. My second mistake was the shortcut I decided to use: Across from the metro station, Avenida de Americas, there was a set of stairs that led down into the basement floor of a shopping plaza, and beneath that, an underground garage that led—once you got up the stairs—to the same street as the hotel. I suppose if I had thought about it for one second longer I would've realized that it was almost ten o'clock at night and I was about to head through an empty under-ground parking lot that had no light. There was just darkness—and that darkness carried anything you might imagine in between the two staircases that were about fifty feet away. Unfortunately, I was not imagining much.

There was one car that looked to be white, but could've been tan, sitting by itself in the corner, and a shop window that was lit with one dull, hazy pink bulb. The shop was a cheap shop, one that had dresses for only 1,000 pesetas, dresses that you knew even before you tried them on wouldn't fit right, wouldn't fall evenly across your chest and waist. I stopped with the bottle of whiskey in my hand, feeling lightly calm, casual, not the least bit worried.

I did not hear anything in the garage until I started to move away from the window, toward the staircase that I could see only dimly. A streetlight from outside, as well as the hum of traffic, guided me there. I had taken this shortcut many times during the past few days when I was visiting my father, but it was usually filled with cars, with at least one or two passing people who had bags in one hand and jangling keys in another.

The footsteps seemed, at first, not to be footsteps. They seemed like something inside of me, like my heartbeat, my pulse. Then I thought momentarily that it was footsteps above me, on the street, but that didn't make sense no matter how hard I wanted it to—it was simply the hollow echoing sound of someone in a narrow space, his shoes making a slight scratching sound against the pavement. I started to walk faster. Running seemed out of the question, too obvious; I was afraid of making a fool out of myself. There was just someone walking behind me, that's all. Someone who could've just come into the parking lot—although that seemed unlikely, and upon further thought was impossible, seeing that the footsteps came from a different direction.

Then the thought occurred to me that perhaps he had been somewhere all along, watching me. Crouched.

I started to run. His footsteps, behind me, started to run. I still thought I could make it, though. I could get to the staircase, to the top where I knew, just above us, there were people drinking at tables, traffic rumbling, light.

Before I fell, his hand came down on my bare shoulder. It hurt, felt literally as if he had cut my skin with something. There was never any question that the person chasing me was a he. I did not have to turn to see that, to see his face, swollen and pink as if he had been crying, and his hair, which was wet-looking, as if he had just put his head under a sink in a restroom somewhere. He must've let the water run and run, drip all down his shoulders and back, as his shirt had water splotches all over it, too.

What color his shirt was, however, is unavailable in my memory. Did he have a mustache, blue eyes or brown? Again, unavailable. His pants, though, I remember—they were dressy and pleated, the zipper down.

After he pushed me, after I fell, the whiskey bottle smashed, and I sat with my face inches from black tar thinking of the glass, of what all the triangular pieces might do if someone pressed them against my skin. I had fallen forward on my hands, so I crawled like that; the cement and its sharp pebbles felt like nothing against my palms. Once I got up on my feet, he pushed me again. He was like some schoolboy who kept waiting for his opponent to get back up on his feet, circling a little while he waited. I wanted to get up, to spring up and run, but it felt as if my mind could not push me there. It was almost the same feeling of watching a movie and wanting the girl to get up, get up, but she just pants, she trembles.

I couldn't do anything right then—the sudden smash of the whiskey bottle breaking seemed to have taken all of the energy out of me; it was like hearing the sound of gun shots or a sudden explosion. You're just left breathing hard. Sudden movements become slow, drawn out, soundless.

I did keep getting up though, but in a slow, dulled way, as if I were dizzy. The fourth time or the fifth time that he pushed me, he didn't push me on the ground, he pushed me near the wall against the staircase—I was actually only a few feet from being able to climb up, up, up out of that garage. But that climb seemed at that moment entirely unmanageable—my imagination, its fearful side, had already taken over, and we were no longer two staircases below the street, but twenty. I suppose it was easier that way, though, to concentrate my imagination on the stairs, on the giant size of each step, on the railing that might be slippery and wet, rather than think of what was more hideous, more of a mind spin: What was he going to do with me?

Within those blurred moments of being pushed and getting up and then being pushed back down, that's perhaps all that paralyzed me—it wasn't the actual action going on, the tug of war we were playing with my balance; it was, instead, what was impending: my face smashed against the cement, a tooth falling out, my skirt pulled up from behind, a very slow, very long slash made along my leg with a knife.

What he decided to do with me, instead, though, was very different: He made me watch him jerk off. He sat down across from me, I was near the wall of the stairs, and he spread his legs wide, leaned back and rested one hand behind him while the other moved back and forth along some invisible line that I could see only when he stopped, when he rested a moment. As odd as this may sound, there was actually something calming, almost soothing, about watching him touch himself—because it meant, or so I believed, that he had no intention of touching me.

The whole time, with each stroke, he stared at me, looking right at my face, my chin trembling, my lips trembling—and I looked back at him, tried not to blink. It seemed to be my job right then to watch. If I just sat there, if I just listened, if I just let myself hear his unsteady breath go up and down, everything could be OK—he'd leave me alone, blur back into the recesses of the garage.

When he was finally done, his hand was wet and he took his time staring at it. He had on a gold watch that was thin, like a woman's. He touched the band of the watch momentarily, then traced the shaped of his hand with one finger. After a minute or two, he looked up at me, smiled a smile that was closed, self-conscious, as if inside his mouth he had no teeth. "*¿Te gustó?*" he asked. Did you like it?

I didn't answer. I knew not to say a single word in Spanish—if he heard my accent, if he knew I was foreign, I was sure it would make it harder for him to leave me. I'd become a more special victim, one he should stay longer with, perhaps pet with his wet hand. Unfortunately, though, that's exactly what he ended up doing, despite my obedient silence. He leaned over, sat up on all fours, and then he put his hand, which was still a little wet, on my arm, one of his fingertips moving in circles like a soft spider. That's when I started to cry, and I cried so hysterically that it seemed hard not just to breathe, but to get air, to find air, to make it pass through me and move around inside of me, give me the power to stand. So I just sat there with him, crying, yet not just crying because he was touching me, but because he was infecting me—and not merely with his fingers and their filmy wetness—but with his sickness. It would be forever in me, forever moving inside of me, forever a feeling I'd have in a garage or any desolate place. In any kind of darkness, he would be there. Following.

He finally left after what seemed like an hour, after squatting a while, staring at me—then he went up those scary Alice in Wonderland stairs. Whether or not he ever ended up zipping his pants before he left, I don't know. I wouldn't look at him anymore. I only heard his footsteps go up the stairs, but I didn't so much as glance at his pant legs. I was certain that if I watched him leave, he wouldn't really go; he'd come back. Only after I sat there for what could've been a half hour but seemed like five minutes did I know for sure he was gone. Yet it had become in that mysterious space of time very frightening to leave that garage—it seemed getting up and going out into somewhere new, like that wide-open street above, offered the possibility of more trouble, while staying there in that still garage, I felt, was keeping myself hidden and safe, keeping myself my own.

How exactly I made my way to the Holiday Inn from that point is sketchy. I know that I walked up those fearful stairs and into a coolness, a slight airiness, as if that garage had been a suffocating box I just burst out of. Across the street in a café, there was music playing, an American song, Sonny and Cher, "I Got You, Babe."

The street was filled with people who seemed to be walking too slowly, taking their time, enjoying the rushing breeze of car traffic while the African street vendors screamed above everything, *"Barato. Todo es muy, muy barato."*

Night kept things easy though, kept my face hidden. I looked down at the sidewalk as I walked. I didn't want people looking at me, seeing what had just happened to me. They might even stop me, touch my arm, ask me if I was going to be OK.

In the Holiday Inn elevator I kept my head positioned down, I did not want the mirrors in there, didn't want to see myself in my splotchy-faced, shaken state. Instead I looked down at the mint-green carpeting, at a pencil that was lying diagonally, inches from my foot where my big toe, I noticed, was bleeding a little—from a fall, from the glass, from something long before, I couldn't tell. But I kept my gaze away from my toe and stared at the pencil. It was a number two; I saw the number, and I suppose as I glided up those flights to my father I held on to the number two as if saying it over and over in my mind was a pleasant diversion.

When I got to my father's room, at first I knocked very softly on the door—almost so that he wouldn't hear—so then I could knock harder, pound. But he was there waiting for me—he opened the door right away. I don't remember his expression or the way he stood, except that he was wearing a white T-shirt, which made him look extra tan, and he was barefoot. Initially, he didn't seem to notice that there was anything wrong with me—not at first, but then I stormed in and stood in the space between the bed and the bureau, right in front of the full-length mirror. I told him in a very sharp, simplistic way what had just happened in the garage—I used the words "fucked-up guy followed me" and "jerked off."

"Jesus!" my father said, and then he came closer to me, as if he were about to touch me, and I backed away. His actual touch, the vision of his hugging me, repelled me, made me feel suddenly violent.

"And you've just been sitting up here," I said, pointing at a red-and-yellow J&B bottle behind him. "You've been doing nothing!"

I really believed at that moment that my father should've known that something had been happening to me; he should've had some sense of heat overcome him or a tingling or an itch—and then he should've stormed out of that hotel room, should have detected where I was in the garage, what section. He should've come.

"You should've fuckin' known!" I said, and he just stood there. He didn't nod or flinch or tell me I was making no sense. His shoulders were straight, his posture stiff. He had one hand behind his neck, rubbing the neckline of his T-shirt as if some invisible tag itched.

I said, "I really fuckin' hate you sometimes," but I didn't scream this. I said it calmly, as if it were something that both he and I always knew, and only now, among the severity of what I had just gone through, I could finally say it with calm, indifferent force. I said it again: "I hate you."

He had a drink on the bureau in a clear plastic cup. He reached for it quickly, as if within it there was a response or an elixir or a feeling. He said, without much emotion, "I know you do."

The room was somewhat dark, lit only by the bathroom light and a small lamp. His hair, I noticed, looked from the side somewhat stiff and overly combed, as if he had spent hours preparing for my arrival. But against his drinking, against the sound of the ice that moved in his cup, I only felt a certain rising within me, a kind of pain, one that I could never feel through the cut on my toe, the scrapes on my knee—it came from somewhere else, somewhere distant, somewhere in which I held and felt everything.

"You fucking left me!" I yelled. It was a shriek, something people in other rooms could definitely hear—people passing in the hallway would stop dead, but I didn't care. There was just the dim room, the heat in my face which felt like fire—as if my breath were literally warmer. "I was eight," I said, "and you fuckin' left me. You didn't call, you didn't write, you didn't do shit!"

I was crying, crying so hard that what I felt had nothing do with the guy himself in the garage, but with the overwhelming feeling that came with him, with the fact that he existed—as he had mutated in my mind, and he was no longer just a pervert: He was darkness; he was evil.

I repeated probably five more times that my father had left, all in different ways, all with different swears, and then I added again, "I was eight."

"You are twenty," he said after a moment, his voice so soft it was as if he were talking to his cup of whiskey, not me.

I said, "What?"

"You are twenty."

"Exactly, you come back now. Which is a little late."

"That's not what I'm talking about." His voice was rising now, as if it were his turn to yell. "You are twenty," he said for the third time, and pointed at me accusingly, as if I were denying my age. "I left when you were eight. You don't see the difference in that?" I shook my head. "You have had twelve years of your own. To be your own!"

"What the *fuck* are you doing here?" I screamed back at him. "Why *are* you here?"

He didn't answer me at first, just blinked.

I swallowed, wiped my runny nose with the back of my hand, and then said in a steadier voice, "Why did you come to see me now when you could've just driven down the fuckin' street at any other moment of your life. Why come now when you have to come so far, visit me in . . ." I put my hands up, gestured at the room as if it were the embodiment of Spain with its pale blue walls and its green rug and its lacy white comforter. "Why bother?" I shouted. "Are you dying? Did you almost get hit by a bus? What was it?"

"Because she said I should," he said, with the slow enunciation of someone who is being incredibly careful. The unidentified "she" was, of course, my mother. "She said that with you here, you might be able to understand it better, what it felt like to leave, because you're so far . . . so far from what's yours." He stood up, paced.

I moved away from him a little, put my hand on the door frame to the bathroom.

He kept pacing, and then he stopped said, "What's it like to be here, Cath? What's it like to live in Spain?"

"Besides tonight . . . " I said. "Besides tonight, it feels good, like the best thing I've ever done."

"No, it doesn't," he said flatly. "Sometimes it's fine, sometimes you feel good, but then you see something from back home or someone writes you or there's a song you hear or something just feels wrong. It feels wrong here, even if you love it; it feels wrong here sometimes, doesn't it?"

"Being in a foreign country is not like leaving a daughter. It is not the same fuckin' thing."

"But it is; you think you have it all down. You think you can live like this, live here, away, but can you really? Can you not think about before?"

He started spilling into other things after that—talking about hearing the name *Catherine* in a grocery store or in a mall, or reading it somewhere, even when it belonged to someone else on the cover of a magazine.

"That's your own—"

"Even the door squeaking; the door *squeaks*. Squeaky," he said, pointing at me. "It squeaks . . . or crayons, crayons bother me, you never played with crayons, never liked crayons, but there they are. I don't like to look at crayons. Or Magic Markers. Or construction paper."

"Your own fault," I said. "Your own shit."

"I know that," he said. "I know that. But I am just telling you anyway so you know it and I know you know it, because your mother says you *don't* know it. She says you underestimate everything and everyone, and she goes on and on about it and then she tells me that if I come here, if I visit, that in this place, in a foreign world . . ." He made quotations with his fingers to show my mother's exact wording, and repeated, " 'in a foreign world' you could understand, understand what my foreign world has been like without you."

There was a pause, just the hum of the air-conditioner.

"You cannot ever leave anything or anyone you ever had. It stays." He sipped his whiskey. "I did not leave you. I only protected you."

"Oh, please," I said. "From *what*?"

"From me. From growing up *with* me. That is the only goddamn thing I can protect you from. I can't protect you from other people and what they do. I can't keep people from hitting a girl in a nightclub. I can't fix that day I hit your mother. I can't keep you from hanging around with older men in foreign countries and saying they're your *uncle*." I should've flinched right then, but I didn't—it was as if I already knew he knew. "I can't protect you from all that," he said. "I'm not all powerful. I'm not God!"

There was quiet, still the air-conditioner hummed.

"And even God," he said, controlling his voice, "can't stop bad things." He picked up the bottle of whiskey as he said this, poured me a glass. But he put it on the bureau in a spot that I would have to reach over to grab. "You see this." He pointed at the cup. "I can pour it for you. I can put it in front of you. But if you reach for it, you reached for it."

I picked up the glass, took a sip, stared at him.

He was standing against one wall, where the closet hangers seemed inches from his head, his whiskey on the bureau. I stood near the bathroom, my drink in my hand and then on the TV set. The whiskey tasted awful and hot, and I kept drinking it.

"That whiskey is yours," he said. "Don't you *ever* blame me for it." He waited as if he thought I was going to say something and then kept talking. "You didn't come to Spain because I told you to. You didn't live in Boston because I wanted you to. The places you have gone, the people who you know, are yours. You chose them."

"I know that."

"You don't act like you know that."

"But I do," I said. "I do." I was speaking softly, not quite looking at him but at the bare hangers near him. He was rubbing his lips together, turning his plastic cup in his hands. He looked older to me then, tired, and in that silence, in the way the ice in his glass jiggled slightly, I saw how small he was, how powerless, how incapable he was of even looking at me.

All my life, I was always told—always encouraged to believe—that any bad thing, any hurt or anger a guy inflicted, had to do with my father and what he did to me and what I couldn't quite stomach. Yet in that hotel room, staring at him, I had the slow, odd inclination that it might be the opposite: He was the one who fell victim to all the things other people, other men, did to me. When I was with Lenny, in love and thrilled, my father was someone I could imagine as a comforting presence, a person who was not bad, merely tortured and self-involved like the rest of us; yet after a late-night attack in a garage, after such terror, he was the epitome of all that negativity the natural world brought forth: He was loneliness, he was isolation, he was insanity and violence, he was death.

He said, "You can't blame me anymore."

"I don't," I said. "I don't blame anyone for anything."

"No, you should blame someone." He stared at me. "Anything you don't like about you. It's yours. You made it. You let it happen." He seemed to be talking more about himself then. He seemed to be talking about his own father and his own drinking and whatever it was inside of him he could not, and would not, get under control. He had the same anger, the same irritation, that I had had long ago talking to Esteban about Monica, telling him that she didn't have a right to be an asshole just because of her parents, or whatever it was that made her that way, and he had screamed back at me, "Well, she certainly has had help!"

I would remember that line forever. I remembered it in the hotel room with my father, remembered while we stood inches away from each other, remembered it as he poured himself more whiskey and I put mine down. It seemed the two of us were on the same par then, the same as Lenny and Monica and whoever else had the ridiculous excuse that something was controlling them, something that went beyond their own minds and hearts and shaky hands, something so powerful it was godly. And throughout our whole lives, the whole retarded gang of us would sit around and struggle with that excuse because we knew it wasn't true, and we got mad at other people for saying it was true, but then we ourselves secretly liked our excuse, treasured it—especially when it was used to pardon us.

"And I didn't come here for you to forgive me," my father said after a pause. "If that's what you think, you are thinking the wrong thing." He put his glass to his mouth but didn't drink it, just smelled it. "I know even if you said so, you wouldn't really mean it."

"Then *why* are you here?"

"To see you, to talk to you." He took a real sip of his drink. "To find out what I missed." We were quiet for a minute, and then I nodded as if I were accepting that answer, giving it approval. "But if you want me to give an apology," he said softly, almost in a whisper, "then I'll give you one: I'm sorry, I'm sorry for every screwed-up thing I've ever done. Every single one." Then he added, looking straight at me, "And I'm sorry that man tried to hurt you tonight."

———

When I was eight, I picked the first real fight I ever had with my father. We were in the car. It was raining and late. We had just seen *Sleeping Beauty*, and my mind was filled with the energy-zapping images of pastel fairies struggling against a devil-horned witch. In the movie, the Walt Disney version, those two forces fight over the fate of Princess Aurora—the evil witch prophesying that Aurora will prick her finger on a spinning wheel's spindle and die, or as they say in fairy tales, "fall deep asleep." To avert this fate, the king hides her far away in the woods with the fairies, and he burns all the spinning wheels in the kingdom. I always remember that particular scene the most—outside of the prince fighting the dragon—the scene where all the spinning wheels are piled in a monstrous stack, set on fire, and then you see from a distance how high the flames burn, even higher than the castle.

"Would you do that for me?" I asked my father in the car. "What the king did for Aurora? Would you burn all those spinning wheels?"

"Of course," he said, but he didn't look at me when he said it, and we were at a red light. The rain was light, only speckles on the windshield. "But did you see that it didn't matter?" he said after the light changed. "She still fell asleep." His voice was very serious then, as if he were tired or upset about something else. "I can't save you from everything. Some things will just happen."

I waited, shook my head. "So you're saying you wouldn't burn the spinning wheels?"

"No, I would, but one could still be somewhere."

"So," I said accusingly, "you would only try to burn some?"

"No, there could be too many," he said. "Too many to deal with. Or they could be hidden somewhere, in someone's basement or backyard. I couldn't get all of them."

"So you don't care," I said. "You wouldn't try to do a good job."

He was getting aggravated with me. "That's not what I said. I said I would try, but I could fail."

"You don't care," I told him, and then because I was crabby, and his voice was annoyed, and we were still far from home, I started to cry. It was that light dull kind of crying that children use when they are tired and upset and they know that it will soon pass. My father didn't say anything as I sniffled. He kept driving, kept moving the steering wheel slightly. He looked sullen, though, as if he suddenly recognized that I equated—like all children—protection with love.

"It's going to be fine," he said finally, "just fine," and in his voice, in how I remember it, in how low it sounded against the raindrops, I sensed something, a certain vulnerability—not just to spinning wheels and witches, but to all things, all darkness.

28

WHAT THE *GITANA* COULDN'T PREDICT

I slept in my father's hotel room that Friday night, and in the morning we woke up together on opposite sides of the room. I slept in the bed and he slept in a chair that was in front of the television. After we finished fighting, we spent the night watching a late-night game show, *Gente Con Chispa*—People with Spark—and in the morning the television was still on, its volume turned low. On the pillow next me was a box of dominoes. My father had given them to me while I watched a contestant feel for a rubber ball in a tank full of earthworms. "A present," he had said softly, and placed them a distance away from me on the bed. The dominoes were off-white, ivory-looking, like something one of the African vendors on the street might've sold him. I stared at the dominoes when I first woke up, traced my finger over the creases in the packaging, over the accented ó in DOMINÓ. As I did this, I glanced at my father in the chair—he was looking groggily out the window—and I thought of the time when I was kid, when I had refused to believe that God played dominoes, and I wondered if that was why he bought them for me, if it was supposed to mean something.

For the rest of the morning, we were silent and awkward in the hotel room. Once we were out in the hotel café, in the brilliance of day, we were somehow better, new and improved, as if screaming at each other was all we ever needed. We arrived in the café around eight o'clock, and the waiters in the hotel seemed happy to see us, as if we were the nicest, most attractive guests in the hotel. We sat outside, at a table that was too big, big enough for eight. It was very bright out, and the blue umbrella above us was cocked the wrong way, it didn't block the sun. When I ordered my *huevos revueltos,* the waiter noticed how bad I was squinting and he and a squad of four others adjusted the umbrella. When it was perfect, our original waiter went around the umbrella and fixed all the tassels so that they hung nicely, untangled.

My father just sat there, sipping his orange juice, his hands trembling.

"Do you think you should order something?" I said, pointing at his hands.

"No." He looked at his watch. "I'll wait a half hour."

I nodded and our waiter came back over bringing us newspapers: for my father, *USA Today* and for me, *El País.* We read our papers and drank our coffee like an old couple who were long used to each other.

The entire morning went like this: very calm, uneventful. We ate our breakfasts and a half hour passed. My father got a beer, I got another *café con leche.* We stared off. In the sky, I remember, there was a big long streak near a cloud, and it felt to me, as I looked up at it, that nothing unhappy could happen right then. No car bombs could go off. No planes could crash. Bulls, in all rings across Spain, fought hard, ran fast, earned swarms of waving white handkerchiefs. None of us that morning could get hurt.

I remember that feeling with such clarity. I suppose I only felt it, only retained the memory of that odd, short-lived sensation because of what happened next.

A *gitana* came up to the table. She had been weaving through the tables, talking to most people for only a short period. The waiters, of course, saw her, but they didn't do anything; they never did in most other restaurants either—I don't know if it was out of respect for them

Christina Fitzpatrick

or some superstitious fear, but they never kicked the begging *gitanas* out of the *terrazas*. They let them move around the tables, graze their flowered shirts against your bare arm, smile at you. Their eyes were always a very light green or hazel, the type of eyes that are striking against such olive skin, both awesome and scary at the same time.

"*Guapa,*" the *gitana* said to me, "Give me your hand." I had one hand on my lap, the other open-palmed, lifeless-looking, next to my coffee cup. I don't know if she thought I had purposely set it there on the table like that, preparing for her arrival, but that wasn't the case. I never liked fortunetellers, even when I was kid I didn't really like them in stories—whether they were benevolent fairies or long-nailed witches.

"I can tell you your fortune," the *gitana* was saying in Spanish. "I can tell you all."

I tried to ignore her. There was a bright yellow building far off, a Mexican nightclub, and I stared at the red lettering along one of its walls: ARRIBA. There was a picture of a cactus on the side of the building and it had sharp-looking black needles. I kept my eyes fixed on the nightclub. My father—already used to seeing the *gitanas* by this point— kept his face in the newspaper. He took a sip of beer without looking up.

"*Guapa. Guapa por favor,*" the *gitana* kept saying, and my father messed things up by looking at her, amused. He said, "What's this one asking you this time?"

I said, between closed lips, "Don't look at her."

He looked right at her anyway. "She's got gold teeth in the back."

"Stop it," I said. "Don't look at her."

The *gitana* kept standing there because she seemed to think we were discussing getting our palms read. She said, "*Guapa,* I can tell you all about the *caballeros* you know. I can tell you who will fall in love with you."

I shook my head, said, "No, no."

"I can tell you who will stay and who won't."

I said again sharply, "*Te dijé que no.*"

She held my gaze for a moment, a moment that felt oddly dramatic—as if she could see in my face an entire list of people I would be separated from, their names in one column, the dates of their departures in another.

I actually felt oddly in danger with her standing over our table—as if she were something that had dropped out of the sky, something hell-bent on altering things. It was as if she were on the verge of telling me all that would ever happen to me, as if my entire world would soon be unraveled. All those choices my father had insisted I had, I wouldn't have. They would already be checked off, filled in, closed. And I had no business knowing—on that bright, sun-filled morning, with the radio on in the background, a woman's voice, uplifting and sensuous—that my father was never ever going to be what I mildly imagined he might become. He wasn't going to meet me in Boston on certain fall after-noons, yellow leaves falling one by one on a car hood, us sitting in a café, laughing. He wasn't actually ever going to visit me in Boston. Never come in my apartment and comment on the stuffed animals Harlan kept in his room, all in a circle around an open children's book. He wasn't going to come to my graduation. He wasn't going to send a congratula-tions card. On my twenty-second birthday he wasn't even going to send a birthday card (on my twenty-third, though, he would send two).

What my father was going to become was only this: a mild, distant presence. One that I could control through my feelings, through how I thought of him, not through the mysterious, somewhat careless things he often did.

The *gitana* did not tell me that though—thankfully—as she also did not tell me who else would leave me. She didn't whisper those names in my ear. She probably would've even been able to say them, if she did indeed know them—she surely wouldn't have had problems with the soft English sound of the H in Harlan.

Harlan would leave me, leave this entire world, three years after I visited Spain, a year after we graduated from college. The year I started to write all of this down.

It would happen in a shed, with a rope, in his mother's backyard.

It would happen in June.

It would happen in the afternoon.

It would happen in a way that I never saw but can always envision: He is shirtless and barefoot. There is a chair next to him, a lawn chair—it's green and white. The shed light is on, the bulb bare. The doors to the shed are like a barn's, red and white, and if I were to walk through those doors, in my mind, in my vision, he would hang rather high, his toes not merely small precious inches from the floor. His waist, the brown hair around his belly button, would be eye level, and I could put my finger in one of his belt loops, I could put my face against his stomach. I could feel warmth coming through his skin. I could feel pulsing.

I'd find out about Harlan through a soft pink envelope, through blue ink on paper. There would be no soft, feminine voice, no *gitana*, to tell me. The letter would be from his mom, and her penmanship, if I looked at it from a distance, would form a body on the page, like a giant L. It said:

> *Dear Catherine,*
>
> *Harlan hanged himself last month.*
> *He had been very sick for a while, very sad.*
> *It came for him quickly.*
> *It wouldn't leave him.*
> *He isn't suffering though. Not now.*
> *I'm sorry to have waited so long to tell you.*
> *I'm also sorry to have to tell you in this way, but it is very*
> *hard for me on the phone. Writing it down is much easier. It's*
> *like putting together a list. This way I also don't actually have*
> *to pronounce the words, don't have to hear myself saying it.*
> *He spoke of you often.*
>
> *—His mom*

When I opened that letter, I opened the envelope very carefully, as if I already knew that it was something I would keep all of my life—hidden away in a tea tin full of mice-filled postcards, all with my name, my address in Spain, written in curly extravagant cursive. I opened that letter sitting on my bed. There were papers and books spread on the bed, and I didn't have the capacity to move them, not even to shove them off onto the floor. I just sat up, very stiff, and the light that came through my curtains got dimmer and dimmer until I could not see the letter, only feel it, the thin glossy paper stuck to my fingertips.

I didn't cry. What I felt inside of me felt like nothing incredibly irregular. I was in a room. I was sitting on my bed. I had something in my hand. I temporarily couldn't even remember what Harlan looked like or sounded like. It was as if my mind had already decided for me: You must wait.

I later wrote Harlan's mother back though, asked if I could have a few things, including any of the letters I had written to him—I thought that way I could remember more vividly, with more clarity, that summer during which I was so far away from him, yet so close, much closer to him in some ways than when I slept in a nearby room, in a place where I could hear him breathing, snoring, whispering—saying, "Hey, girlie, you up?"

But unfortunately Harlan's mother never could find those letters, and so my summer in Madrid became one of the many things that I had to rehearse over and over, just to find, just to feel, what we once were. It was my own weird way of grieving, as I had no funeral to go to, no wake, no place to go and physically see him. So I had to deal with him in that other cavernous place: my mind.

29

8,578,346 MEN

On my father's last night in Madrid, we went to Plaza Mayor—which was between La Latina and Puerta del Sol, meaning in between the very old neighborhood and the very touristy. It had shops that sold souvenir spoons and charging ceramic bulls and Don Quixote T-shirts, and there were stands outside on the cobblestones that sold odd objects: pencil drawings of movie stars; hand-carved Virgin Marys; rosary beads, all different colors, all different lengths, hung, as if they were diamond necklaces, against blue satin. There were, of course, cafés and bars amongst these stands and shops, all with different-colored tables, different-colored umbrellas, Coca-Cola emblems on some, Bacardi and Cruzcampo on others. But even with those umbrellas, Plaza Mayor was only a comfortable, enjoyable place to sit at night—as during those July days it was very hot, and the waiters were very hot, and the tourists weaving around you were hot, and there was an overwhelming feeling during those afternoons that you may never make it through: You might fall to the ground, hit your head, bleed. Getting back up, waking up, wouldn't be so easy, not unless some water got sprinkled on you or unless a little giggling Spaniard—perhaps Juan Carlos himself—blew bubbles onto your face.

Only at nighttime did the air get cooler in Plaza Mayor; the sky became a place you could actually look at, and you could sit and whoever sat across from you comforted you—as it was a place you did not want to be alone.

My father and I drank sangria that night. The waiter had insisted we have it. He also insisted we have five plates of *tapas* that we didn't really want either, but we had agreed, or I had agreed, because of the way the waiter talked to me. He spoke in carefully enunciated Spanish, even though I could tell from the way he nodded when my father spoke that he knew English perfectly, and then he told me I had a wonderful accent, like a true *Madrileña*, and the whole while that he took our order, he kept fidgeting with his glasses, pressing the section at the bridge of his nose and then the side, and then at one point touching his ear. He seemed mildly sweet to me; I probably would've ordered anything he suggested—and when I explained this to my father, about all of the food we were soon getting, he said, "Well, he's a top seller, isn't he?"

"I like him."

"He's a little bit old for you, don't you think?"

I nodded and purposely stared off—we did not at any point ever talk about my "uncle," or anything else Maureen might have told him. I did, however, tell him about Gijón and Felipe; he seemed to like hearing about Felipe's brother the most, though, as if he were the trip's reigning highlight.

"But you'll have to add more to your collection," my father said abruptly, after we were quiet a minute and I gave him a suspicious look. The word *collection* was the term that Harlan used for all the boys who had "rung his bell." My father must've read the word on the back of one of Harlan's mouse postcards, understood its secret meaning. Often Harlan made the comment that "he had added yet another to his collection," as if all the boys he adored were old coins that he threw haphazardly into a trunk. In terms of my own collection, Harlan always said I had a meager selection, a selection that was worthless compared to his.

"In a glance, Squeaks," my father said, "how many will be in your collection?"

"How many men?" I said.

He nodded, took a sip of his sangria. Our waiter came over right then, put down five plates of the most expensive cheese and ham and chorizo that one could ever order. "How many?" my father said again, and I knew once more it was his small attempt to play that game we once played at the Blue Lagoon.

I didn't answer at first; I just shrugged indifferently and watched him eat a peach from the sangria pitcher. He was wearing the shirt and the pants that I had bought him and the sandals he'd had from before. He looked quite nice, quite tan, and his hair even looked natural that night. I had told him earlier that he looked nice, and he had smiled, looking somewhat embarrassed.

"*¿Todo les gusta?*" the waiter asked me before leaving the table. I said *sí* and then he smiled, patted my shoulder.

"How many in the collection?" my father said.

"I don't know. Five or six."

"That is incorrect." He was using his game-show-host voice.

"Maybe ten."

He leaned forward and said, "That is again incorrect."

A few yards away, there was a guitarist, a young woman in an off-the-shoulder halter top, who was playing a song across the plaza. People were clapping for her in the distance, and someone who had a clear American accent shouted, a little drunkenly, "*Olé.*"

My father looked behind him as if scanning the area for the disruptive, drunk American, and then he said, "In a glance"—he motioned at the entire plaza filled with people—"how many in the collection?" Then he corrected himself, "How many *men?*"

"Women don't count?"

"Not right this second, no. They're too easy." He waited. "In a glance, how many?"

The repeated wording "in a glance" was my cue to use a grandiose number like I did when I was kid, when I sat at the bar next to him, pretending to know with autistic speed the number of pebbles in fish tanks or ice cubes in a bin.

I decided to be nice, play along—I said with the certainty of a machine, "8,578,346 men."

The drunk American in the distance screamed, "*Olé*, baby. Oh-fuckin'-LAY!"

"See," my father said, as if that shout was from his lovely assistant, "You answered it right. You answered the final question."

"So what do I win?"

He put his hands up, gestured toward the entire umbrella-filled plaza. "You win everything," he said, and then added more softly, "you win it all."

My father was leaving very early the following morning, and we had decided without exchanging words that I would say good-bye to him that night. From Plaza Mayor we walked to Palacio Real, sat outside on a cement bench. We had leftovers from our sangria in little plastic cups and in the nighttime, with a bit of wine, the palace was a different building; it was more glamorous, more powerful, too tall.

Where we were sitting, there were big round lamps that gave off a soft moonlit effect, and there was the actual moon, which was only a slight sickle shape above the palace. A couple in their sixties were on the bench next to us. I watched the man take a mint out of his shirt pocket. He unwrapped it and placed it in his wife's mouth. She took out a silver compact, put on lipstick, and then she kissed him on the cheek, left a big red mark on his face. *"Esta noche es preciosa,"* the man said to me, catching my glance and gesturing up at the sky, and I nodded.

"What?" my father asked, wanting to know what the man said.

"Tonight is precious," I explained, and then I told him how the word *precious* in Spanish, *precioso,* did not mean entirely the same thing as it did in English. It didn't have so much to do with value or importance, but instead beauty. A city in Spanish can be precious, or a building, or a view.

We looked up at the edge of Palacio Real, at its walls, which looked gray in the night; small sculpture images of kings were lined up on the roof.

"Will you miss Madrid when you leave?" my father asked, and I answered yes with certainty—as if the city were not just a place to me, but a heat-pounding feeling, an electricity. I thought of the hot dry air, the pink sidewalks, the car exhaust that smelled strangely sweet. It seemed Raúl was right when he had told me that traveling, in moving around and seeing, you were training yourself to hold on to things, to see them without being with them—training yourself for the internal art of missing and losing and grieving.

Even at that moment, while my father and I sat side by side, I was preparing for him to leave. I knew it was only minutes away, and it seemed I had to hold on to everything right then, remember with photographic accuracy the couple next to us, as well as the lamplight, the moon.

We said good-bye to each other later though. In front of my doorstep. He walked me home that night. I didn't ask him to, he just casually said he planned to. He said so while we were eating in Plaza Mayor. Amongst the buzz of all those people in that square, I had nodded, knowing that the gesture was not a gesture, but an act of precaution after what had happened the night before.

When we got to the front of my building, we stood at my doorstep side by side, our shoulders practically touching, looking out at the street, at parked cars, at Raúl's storefront, at a sign that said, LARIOS GIN.

"Well, this is it," my father said.

I kept staring at the Larios Gin sign—it was bright yellow, and it flashed in digital numbers the time in military hours and the temperature in Celsius.

"I should go now," he said after a minute, after I hadn't said anything. The time was 23:58.

The temperature: 28 degrees.

I said, "Yup."

We hailed a cab, I talked to the driver, the passenger door was opened.

I kissed my father good-bye a little awkwardly, Spanish-style, on each cheek. He kept his hands on my shoulders when we were done. He left them there for a whole minute as if he needed balance. Then he got inside the cab, closed the door. The door shut with a slight squeak. Through the half-open window, my father waved to me—it was the kind of wave that seemed somewhat painful. I nodded, I gave the same wave back.

I stayed on the steps after he left, didn't go directly inside. I could see the top of Palacio Real, its brass cross, from my doorway. From the distance, you could tell where the lamps might be, but it wasn't a bright stadium light, just a vague shadowy light. I thought of the old couple we had seen on the bench minutes before; I thought of the kiss mark the woman had left on her husband's cheek. If I were a painter, I could've painted it right then. Even the palace itself, its big looming walls, its grayish whiteness, its dizzying number of windows, all of it stood practically right in front of me, overshadowing all the parked cars that lined my street.

My father's departure only two minutes before had set these details in my head, ingrained them there. Yet there was nothing new or mysterious about this—as his absence had already altered my memory years ago, converting everything I saw and felt into image, sound, color. And those things reverberated in my mind, gave people's voices a certain memorable melody, gave colors an unforgettable brilliance, gave buildings an indestructible shape, a permanency.

Every person I ever knew became reachable, every place I ever came across I could revisit. Nothing could be lost.

The art of missing had given me that. The art of missing had power.

I was not unique in this way though. Anyone who had missed out had it. It came slowly but surely, torturously, taking hold of the mind, reigning over it, reformulating what was important and what wasn't. For me, in particular, it came when my father left me as a kid; it came like a giant white blast. It came and devoured hours and hours of my time, making me wish for things, making me want. But then it evolved and became like some odd-shaped gift my father wrapped up and handed me, as from the moment he was out of my sight, anything I later stumbled upon, anything I loved—whether it be a palace, a person, or a city—turned into a precious vision, one that I could forever revisit, find comfort in, adore.

The morning after my father left Madrid, I called Harlan. It was nine o'clock in Madrid, three in the morning in Boston. I told him about my father's visit, but in a very brief way. I said, "Everything went OK."

He didn't say anything after that; he was silent, as if he didn't believe me or was giving me a chance to say something else, but then after the silence went too long, he said, "You can tell me the real story later." There was another pause after that. He was eating ice cream; I could tell from the way he enunciated words.

"So," he said, "do you wish I was there?"

"Yeah." I was sitting in the living room, using the big red 1950s phone. I switched ears, as if the phone were hurting me. "Do you wish I was home?"

He paused, as if he had to ponder, and then he said, "Sometimes I go in your room."

"You better not be going through my shit." I was joking, but I made my voice sharp. "Don't touch my things."

"Too late."

"*Don't* touch my things."

"I touch all of your things," he said with ice cream in his mouth. "I touch them and touch them and touch them. I just can't stop." He was laughing.

He got quiet for a minute after that—I could hear his ice cream spoon tapping against something: perhaps the wall or the phone or his front tooth. Then he said, "I don't really touch anything in your room. I just stand in there."

"What for?" I asked. I had my chin on the back of the couch, and it felt hot from the sun coming in the window. I was looking outside at the building across the street, squinting.

"If I stand in your room," Harlan said, "I can feel you a little bit."

I smiled. "Let's not get freaky, OK?"

"I'm not. If I miss you, I go in your room and it fixes it. You are in there."

"That doesn't make any sense," I said, looking down at the braided yellow-and-white fabric of the couch. "Maybe if I had been beaten to death in there, maybe then I would still be there. Catherine, the angry ghost."

"No, no, no," he said in the voice of an old grandmother. "You can be alive and happy somewhere far, far away, and I can still feel you in that room."

"You're being weird."

"Highly perceptive," he said, "just highly perceptive." I could tell he had gotten up from the sound of his voice. He stretched, made a loud groaning noise in my ear. "So where's that boy of yours, Bobo?"

"Felipe?"

"Right, Bobo."

"He's coming in a few hours."

"Well, aren't you a busy bee. First the drug dealer and then Daddy and now him." He paused. "You won't stop writing me, will you?"

"No."

"You won't forget?"

"No."

"You won't stop?"

"No, Harlan."

"You sure?" he asked, and then before I could answer: "Are you sure you're sure?"

"I'll write you," I said. "I won't stop." And then I added, after a silence, "Not ever."

EPILOGUE

AUGUST

Madrid is a city that everyone must leave in August. The streets empty, small stores close, restaurants take *vacaciones* for weeks. Only the people who absolutely cannot leave stay, and only uninformed tourists come to visit. It is not a ghost town exactly, but there is an odd feeling at night, a ghostliness, as if all the beautiful buildings are awake with their own special visitors.

Originally, I was supposed to stay in Madrid and work the entire month. That was what I arranged with Carlos long before I arrived. He himself was going to be on vacation, but I was supposed to sit at his desk, answer the phone. I decided that such a fate was impossible only on the weekend my father left. Once he was gone, it seemed all my real work was over, completed, and the advice Esteban had given a few days earlier still lingered in my head.

His advice: You are twenty. This is summer. Do all that you can.

Whether or not it was the thrill of following that advice, or something else, my last days in Carlos's office didn't feel sad. In retrospect, it seemed as though I had only been in that big mint-green room for a handful of days—as everything that really mattered happened all around it, clouding my memory, making it difficult later to recall minor details, like what floor the office was on, what the secretary's name was.

Despite all my distractions, I still got a nice write-up from Carlos— he actually wrote in my evaluation: "She has served us well" which sounded humorous to me, as if I had done military service, instead of simply talking on the telephone with one single American female who he himself would never see.

Kansas Katy was not coming—there was no change to her decision.

"I might come later," she assured me the last time I spoke to her. "For one of my honeymoons."

She had once said that she planned on marrying in her lifetime at least five men, and with each one she would take a separate trip to some far-off locale.

"For any of your honeymoons," I said, "you shouldn't come to Madrid. There are smaller, more romantic places to go to in Spain."

By that point, during that particular conversation, it was mid-August, and I had already begun traveling around with Felipe a bit. I had left Kansas Katy my home number in case she ever wanted to call, and then she did call, while I was sitting in my nightgown on the living-room couch, Felipe next to me. Silent race cars were going in circles on the TV screen. While I talked on the phone, Felipe kept touching the strap of my nightgown with one finger, pulling it off the shoulder and then back on.

"But where have you guys been lately that I would recognize," she asked, "that I would know of?"

I paused for a while, went through a mental list of places. I could have told her about the castle in Segovia that Walt Disney had copied or about a famous cathedral in Barcelona that looked as if it were made of dripping candle wax, but instead I chose the Alhambra, as it was the most clear to describe and the most famous, one of the Wonders of the World.

I explained to her that the Alhambra was a palace in the south of Spain, in Grenada, and it was not easy to reach. Once you were in the city, you had to climb up a steep hill to get there, walk through a wooded area that had so many trees it felt almost cool against the mean, mean heat.

The palace itself was an Arabian palace, not Spanish, with different rooms and chambers that did not connect; you had to walk through gardens to get to one place from the next, gardens that had dribbling water fountains and green bushes and flowers that came in yellow and red. Inside there were no chandeliers like at Palacio Real, barely any furniture at all. Just walls. And those walls were so beautiful, so delicately constructed with etchings and designs that they literally looked like lace.

I told Kansas Katy all of this in the most careful detail I could, but later, after I hung up, I realized, as always, that I forgot one thing, one important thing. I forgot to tell her how it *felt*.

I should've told her about this inscription on the palace's walls, one that said over and over in Arabic: Allah is the only conqueror. It was the sort of grandiose sentence my father would have liked, and I thought about that as I walked with Felipe hand in hand through garden after garden, amongst the heat and the sun and the constant sight of flower petals, and it *felt* to me right then that I was walking in Allah's garden, walking right through his world.

Felipe said to me once, "But after you leave here, you will forget all of this."

"No, I don't think so," I said.

We were in a hotel room at the time—it was afternoon—and we were lying on separate twin beds. The man who ran the hotel wouldn't give us a double bed, *una cama de matrimonia,* literally a bed of marriage—because he claimed such beds were for married people and only married people, not traveling children.

So we rested on twin beds, feeling sleepy from the sun, sleepy from a whole day of searching for a hotel room.

"Catherine's just on vacation," Felipe said, half mumbling, with his eyes shut. "Spain is *just* a vacation."

I told him to shut up.

"I am a vacation," he added.

My eyes were originally shut, too, but I looked over at him, saw that he had his left hand extended out toward me. It was in midair in the space between our beds, palm up, wavering a little. He had his hand out so that I would touch it, and then he could squeeze my hand, pull me right out of my twin bed into his. But that hadn't yet happened, and the man who ran the hotel hadn't yet started pounding on the door, hadn't started saying that he wanted our passports, needed our passports, demanded to see them.

It was right before then. Very quiet. Just Felipe's hand outstretched next to me.

I said, "None of this is just a vacation to me . . . especially not you."

He didn't say anything. He still had his hand out.

I added, after a minute, "You wait, you'll see," and right before I touched his hand, he whispered, *"A ver,"* which is similar to saying, "Yes, we will."

I was also thrown a party in August, one that Celia and Isabel arranged. They had it in our apartment in the early evening on a day when everyone was still in town. A lot of people who initially came and stayed for an hour I didn't know; they were friends of friends, ones who kissed my cheeks, told me I spoke Spanish wonderfully, and then left their phone numbers on a sheet of paper Celia passed around. I was supposed to keep the paper so that if I ever returned—which I was fully expected to—I would have a wide world of friends, not just five or six.

Everyone was chatty at the party, everyone happy. All of us were on the verge of a trip. Celia and Francisco were going to Alicante, Isabel was meeting Sergio in the Canary Islands, Felipe and I were going to San Sebastián. I still had a whole week before I was leaving Spain, a whole week before I saw my mother and Harlan, a whole week before they picked me up at the airport, standing side by side in white T-shirts.

"Where are all the naked girls?" I heard someone shout in English at one point during my party, and I knew right then that Esteban had arrived. He was wearing a purple shirt and was standing in the doorway. He had his hand on his hip, as if indignant at the fact that there were no girls taking off their underwear. He was, of course, referring to that party I had long ago at Shooters. Yet this party and that party seemed not just months apart but years. There was nothing similar. Even the way we drank was different. We had whiskey and wine, not shots, and the intention of drinking was to sip a little in between conversation topics, not simply to drain the glass.

"Will the strippers come later?" Esteban asked after he found himself a drink.

"They'll be here in an hour," I said, "with the hookers."

Esteban liked that. He raised his eyebrows as if we both had some special secret together. I touched his wrist, then his hand, led him down the hall toward where Celia and Isabel and Felipe were. I was very pleased he had come; I had seen him only two or three times in the past month, and I knew he was going to Caracas again. I could see it in his face. I could see it in the way it took a second or two longer for a complete smile to emerge, for his lips to turn up entirely.

In the living room, I introduced Esteban to everyone, watched him kiss Celia and Isabel on each cheek. He touched Felipe's arm, smiled at him, and I watched, feeling strange, as if two separate sides of myself had joined.

Monica arrived later than Esteban, so much later that I almost thought she wouldn't show up. It was only when people had started to leave that she came in through the door without knocking, wearing the same red dress that she had worn when I first met Esteban. It was dressed down though, with sandals, not high heels, and when she first walked in, her shoes made a slight thonking noise, which reminded me of the sound Harlan's slippers made against kitchen tile.

Shortly after Monica arrived, Felipe's brother, Juan Carlos, called. I talked to him for a bit, promised him his brother would be home soon. He claimed that he hadn't seen Felipe since I had arrived, that I had stolen him. Then in the voice of a character in a war movie, he told me that you couldn't trust Americans. From that point he launched off into a spy fantasy again. He asked me if I still needed the microfilm under his bed. Had I blown up more buildings? I told him no, that I wasn't that kind of a spy. I was a good spy, a friendly spy. Then he repeated what he had said earlier: You can't trust Americans.

Esteban must have overheard some of the conversation; he asked me once I got off the phone, "And what will the spy do once she goes back home?"

I took the question seriously. I said, "Get a new job and go to school."

"But what will the *spy* do?" he asked, and I knew he wanted a jokey, stupid answer, so I said in the slow language of someone trying to concoct a good response, "The spy will . . . um . . . submit special information, special maps." I smiled, thought some more. "Explain where your vulnerabilities are."

Esteban lifted his glass of whiskey, poured an additional splash of Coca-Cola into it, and said, *"¿Sabes lo que son, no?"* You know what they are, don't you?

Originally we were talking in English, but then Celia and Isabel seemed to be listening, and so we slipped into Spanish. They were on the couch next to us. Monica and Felipe were listening, too, sitting in wooden chairs on opposite ends of me. The conversation from here forward somehow became a mix of English and Spanish; certain sentences even contained both.

I said, "Well, what do you guys want the spy to do?"

"Fall in love," Celia said.

"Fight evil," Isabel said.

I looked at Felipe. "Never forget," he said, "who is the only one." He laughed as he said it as if it were a joke, and then Esteban pointed at Monica; it was her turn.

"I want her to have intrigue," she said with her glass to her lips and then she added, *"Y sexo."* And sex.

I nodded, said *vale*, OK, and then I asked Esteban what he wanted from the spy. "After all," I said, "I *owe* you." I was referring in my own casual way to the small amount of money, and freedom, he had given me that month.

Esteban smiled, bit the corner of his lip. He said, "The perfect spy, the most valuable of spies, does one thing and one thing only." He gave me a smooth smile and motioned at the entire room. "You have to show them," he said, "show them who we are."

Acknowledgments

AT HOME . . .

I thank my family and friends for calling me and writing me and visiting me while I was working on this book in Madrid. I thank my Auntie Jo for sending a printer and some sheets. I thank my mother for always being a sporty character on the phone. I thank my nephew Joseph Pratt for being my secret fiancé. I thank my brother and his wife Joanne, my sister and her boyfriend Patrick as well as Jessica Powers, Tara Steketee, Paul Schaeffer, Elizabeth Lane, Michelle Sanchez, Won-Jeong Han, Kenny Switzer, Marty Rambousek, and Francine Bravo for being supportive and sensitive and funny.

Special thanks also go to my two closest friends in Madrid: Jennifer Funke and Denise DaGragnano. Even as I write this, I miss them terribly.

I thank my agent, Wendy Weil, and her entire office staff (especially Emily Forland) for their encouraging comments when this book was still in draft form. It has been a happy fate having worked for Wendy as an intern and now having her as my illustrious agent.

I thank my editor, Alison Callahan. Her personal attention and confident enthusiasm for this novel have been invaluable. She offers what every writer wants from an editor: the guidance in understanding what needs to be improved and the creative freedom to decide how. I also thank my first editor, Trena Keating, for discovering my work. She scored me this book deal and without the motivation and excitement it offered, I could not have written what I have.

And lastly, I owe a heartfelt thanks to my home itself: the Brave City of New York.

EN MADRID . . .

Me gustaría dar gracias a Celia, Aná, Aranxa y Carlota—mis primeras amigas en España. Nuestra amistad fue la puerta entrada para esta novela. El capitúlo en Gijón es para vosotras. (Y Aná, no te enfades. La próxima vez usaré Bilbao, ¿vale?)

Hay otras dos chicas muy, muy importantes que están en la otra catagoría porque ellas son americanas pero deben estar aquí con Madrid: Denise DaGragnano y Jennifer Funke. Me ayudaron más que puedo explicar. Son chicas preciosas. Si nunca hubiera estado en Madrid, nunca las habría conocido. Otra razón más para que mis viajes hayan sido un gran regalo.

Quiero decir gracias a un grupo de hombres españoles en particular, todos se llaman Javier: a Javier Alvarez (¿Es tu apellido? No me acuerdo exactamente pero sabes quien eres), gracias por tus vueltas en tu Porsche por las calles de Madrid. Fueron muy útiles. Gracias a Javier Curtichs por mi introducción a relaciones públicas. Gracias a Javier de EleMadrid (gracias a todo EleMadrid, pero Javier especialmente porque él es mi favorito). Gracias a Javier Conte también: Todos los Lunes y Martes el era mi amigo especial.

Gracias a la más sabia mujer en el mundo: Alicia (Pilar) de Arriba Alcalde.

Y últimamente gracias a la ciudad y la gente de Madrid. Espero que esta novela sea tranducida al español y ojalá que uds. puedan ver que su mundo era, y es, una de mis inspiraciones más podorosas.